Dead Blossoms:

The Third Geisha

a novel

by

Richard Monaco

This Book is Dedicated to the Memory of my Father and Mother

For my Daughter, as Always....

To Jodi

With Special Thanks to
Professor Leverett Butts of Georgia
For his Unselfish Help

Additional Appreciation For help with Japanese Background and
History:

Jason Yamada
Taki Sakai
K. Sunoda

plus

Too many books and movies to mention

"If a bird won't sing, kill it."
Haiku attributed to Oda Nobunaga (1534-1582)
Warlord

PROLOGUE

Late Spring 1552
Off the coast of Japan

The high-tiered, square-sailed, awkward Portuguese trading ship tilted wildly, almost parallel to the sea as a massive wave high as a hill peaked over and dropped the vessel, awash, while the remaining sails flapped and shredded.

It rolled, helpless, in mist and mad water as the terrific typhoon slammed, howled, hissed and raged. No seaman used to the Atlantic's hurricanes was ever prepared for this level of fury. Few ships could ride it out. They were tumbled and heaved and cracked and shattered and lifted and dropped by winds that could exceed 140 mph.

Two seamen, a black man and a white were clinging to the uptilted windward side as the top-heavy ship heeled and broached-to. Their baggy Portuguese outfits were plastered to them. The white man's long hair whipped in the intolerable wind that sucked away all sound and even breath. He was a powerful, medium-sized Scotsman, Colin MacGileray by name, whose outsized, thick, chapped, iron-hard hands clutched the railing like steel hooks. The Zulu, uMubaya, was a tall black man with the thick legs and powerful torso characteristic of his people. He happened to be a prince who'd seen a ship for the first time at the place that eventually became known as Cape Town. On impulse, he boarded and was signed on. He made a mark on a parchment sheet and understood that to these strange people it was like a drop of blood to seal an oath. It amused him because it was needless since they had the word of royalty.

At sea the prince discovered he had a totally unsuspected ability: he could learn languages and their strange talk (Spanish, Portuguese, Italian) made sense to him with amazing ease, endearing him to the crew; he often found himself translator in disputes or story-telling. Colin had promised to teach him the highland Gaelic

He was never seasick anymore. The sea amazed him: the blue brilliance, the vastness, the calms and sudden violence, the mists that could shut you in what seemed an infinite silence as if the world had melted and left you a floating spirit. The size and mystery absorbed him.

1

Let my younger brother enjoy the king's plumes and the women, he'd once articulated, contemplating the slow easy swells of the Pacific while on watch. *I will see what can be seen and take brides where I find them....*Maybe because of the one he couldn't have. The tall, beautiful captive who'd freed herself and left. The taste was bitter. Lingeringly bitter.

Now, this was the lion's leap: the moment without choices, where he might simply end, as the next gust blew loose a sail tatter that flopped and vanished into the rain and mist like some huge-winged ghost.

Colin and uMubaya were clinging near the rear castle as a thin-bearded Italian gentleman in low boots, tights and a ruffled shirt with his cape flapping around him, a big sack roped around his shoulders, came crawling on deck, clutching his way towards the rail near them.

Colin recalled how the quiet fellow was generally reading, writing or drawing pictures. He was tall with dark, delicate features and seemed to look not just at what was before him but at something that was not.

The artist, Colin thought. *This is no time for art....*

Colin was an outlaw and rebel in his country from a mountain clan that never bent an inch to the English, he'd gone to sea with vague hopes of making a fortune in the far places of the earth....

The ship clumsily tilted down the reverse side of the several-stories-high wave in another long, sickening roll.

The Italian clung to the rail he'd just been slammed into by the reverse tip. His face was pale, sick and desperate as they now ploughed down...down towards the deep trough in a seemingly endless drop....

"I think this vessel with not endure long!" the Zulu shouted in Spanish, close to his companion's ear.

"No day to swim!" Colin shouted back.

The Black man laughed.

"I cannot swim!" he yelled.

I now am wishing, he thought, *I stayed home and maybe wed pretty Ulele...put the rim around my head....*The circlet of fiber and dried tendons woven through a married man's hair like a coronet.

"No day to learn, my friend!" responded the Scot.

The wind was so intense it was blowing the tops off the waves. The ship now seemed to pause (at the bottom) and vibrate (Colin thought) like a trembling sheep. As they rapidly went up the front of the next ocean mountain they were on the high side of the craft, again. The storm seemed to inhale, hold, then explode out it's immeasurable breath so that one mast cracked, up high, and spars and lines came whipping and crashing across the deck – as did the overdressed Italian, caught by gust and water, rolling down the steepening tilt towards certain death as the lee side began to submerge.

Without hesitation the Zulu released his hold and part ran, part rolled downslope, got one hand on a rope and grabbed the doomed man's wrist with the other. They were brought up short just over the rail as it went under.

What difference will it make? Colin asked himself, skidding and sliding down the deck, noticing other sailors clinging on in desperate clumps. *Why not die in company?*

He reached them, grabbed the rope and uMubaya who then got both hands on the Italian. They were in the sea but until the ship actually foundered they'd survive; except the rope snapped and they were instantly gone into the seething fury. Colin cried out a Celtic death-prayer and surrendered himself.

But a spar had come along with the rope and as the ship reeled away and down the following wave, (already all but vanished in blowing mist and seething rain) the three of them managed to hang on and loop themselves together....

Now, over the strange, sound-sucking drone of the typhoon there was another dull, deep sound, a rumbling, resonant krooom...krooom...Colin knew it was land, very close.

God keep us if it be rocky shore, he thought. *God keep us, anyway*....

It wasn't: they came in on softness, as if, the Italian numbly thought, a soft cloudiness had embraced them and rolled them high, dry and spent onto what he knew was a beach; by then it was dark and as the storm veered away from the coast and the wind and rain died the exhausted men slept.

Maybe this is a magic place, thought as he passed out, sinking through violent waves and the air's mad contortions as the mist of his dreams blended with memory...then nothing....

The Zulu sat up first, squinted and blinked at the most beautiful, shimmering white beach he'd ever seen. The morning sky was bright, cloudless, the sea, beyond the gentle breakers, a softly shattering blue.

3

Behind them, left and right along the easy curving shoreline was a wall of intensely blue-green pines, twisted by the constant winds.

We live, he said to himself. *Maybe there truly are spirits to protect as well as hurt, thought hurt seems much favored, overall....*

He stood up, coughed and spat a few times. The waves crashed crisply. The rising sun (about nine o'clock) was in his face so he shielded his eyes and scanned the empty sea. The others were stirring.

"Christ's bloody hands, it's hot," said the Scot in his own tongue, then in their common Spanish: "Where are we landed?"

The Italian was rubbing his face and yawning. He noticed his clothes were
dry, stiff and stained with salt. The heavy bag he'd clutched and roped to himself was on the sand beside him.

"Ah," he replied. "*Alma redemptoris*...the angels have preserved us."

"I agree," said the Zulu prince. "But, who knows, for good or ill."

"Maybe known to God alone," the tall Italian said. "I am Lorenzo Gentile of Padua."

"I am uMubaya, son of King waMiswati."

"I care little for kings. I care a shit only where we have been cast," declared Colin, "like Jonah, the cursed Jew. Or can this be the Cathay whence we were bound, land of the yellow men?"

"Jonah's fate was harder," put in Gentile. "But, I can say, the captain of the Santo Pedro believed we were off the barbarian coast of the land named Neeho or Ni-hon or some such."

uMubaya stood over them, back to the sun, taking in the vibrant shock of dense, sunbright pines.

"I saw this on the map," he told them. "A large island land, vague in form with few things marked upon it."

"Like the honor of the English," muttered the Scot.

"Few have ever been here," Gentile added. "A place, so say the brave Jesuits who were cast up, as were we, of rare beauty, violence and mystery."

"An island," muttered Colin. "I pray they have ships."

"Maps are a great wonder," said the thoughtful Zulu. "I mean to learn to make them." Shrugged. "All things seem more and more a mystery."

4

The sun shimmered all around them. The trees wavered in heat blurs. He couldn't see a foot inland. In the distance there were hazy hints of great mountains.

PART I

One

Outside Edo, Japan
Three months later

The midsummer sky was a cloudless, bright shimmer of purity. The sun was just spraying light through the tops of the ornamental pines that enclosed the rock garden surrounding the little inn. A low stone wall enclosed the garden.

Jiro Takezo lay sleeping, in spatters of sunlight, among the dense, rich flowerbushes, part of his slightly frayed, blue and black cotton kimono pulled over his face and partly pillowing his head. His *katana* (long sword) was under his left arm, the black lacquered wooden sheath gleaming. His *shogo* (short sword) was still in his sash belt. His soft snores blended with the drone of the bees working the morning glories and chrysanthemums.

Above the thread of stream that tinkled and purled softly among the rocks a camellia tree had just dribbled down a few blossoms onto the cushiony grasses. A bird trilled. A few streets away a child's voice was calling someone....

Two samurai moved easy and quiet as shadows on the resilient, rich earth. They both wore the colors of their clan, yellow and black silk clothes, baggy pantaloons fitted tight to the calves by bindings down to the straw, split-toe sandals; on top were long, vest-like overshirts with extended, pointed shoulders. They were impeccably groomed; hair shaved well above the forehead and then tied in a modest topknot. One was stocky with a round face and a clean scar across his nose and cheek; the other slightly taller and bony with high cheekbones and a hooked nose.

By the time they stood over the recumbent man, the hushed morning's drowsy near-silence was broken by a slight ping: the only part of him that had moved was his left thumb, bumping up the swordhilt a fraction to ease the draw. A familiar sound.

"Excuse us, Sir Jiro," the bony man said, carefully. "We come in the name of Lord Izu."

Takezo grunted, yawned. He could partly see them through the slit where the fabric parted - though it still hid most of his face.

"Why do you keep your face covered?" asked the scarred man, who was in his twenties, with a vaguely distainful attitude, clearly unimpressed by this slovenly samurai sleeping it off in public. To not uncover could be taken as a kind of insult. "Why do you lie here like a drunken peasant?"

"I cover my face so as not to see yours," Takezo replied, stretching and
yawning again. "Too early in the day."

"Insulting," said the man whose older companion touched his arm, suggesting restraint. To minimize violence in a warrior society required a little care.

"Lord Izu needs your help," the bony man, a captain, went on.

"Maybe help drinking sake," said round-face.

"Be still, Yoshi," said his senior.

"Insulting to lie there, face covered, Captain Mori."

"If I see your head, young Yoshi, I may not be able to resist cutting it off."

Yoshi part-drew his sword but the older man stepped in front of him. They noted the one on the ground didn't stir an inch. Behind him another Camilla dropped softly. The slight sound reminded Takezo of a poem he admired. Couldn't remember it. Someone had come out of the back of the inn and could be heard drawing water from the well.

"Fool," hissed Captain Mori. "You would be defeated. We are here to serve our lord, not fight."

"Don't worry, I won't kill him. I need my rest," said the tall man on the ground. "What does Izu want?"

The sun was slightly higher and cast long shadows of the trees and men over the rocks and dense flowers. The bees hummed on. The woman at the well was singing a folk tune in a high, lilting voice.

"All know you are a sake keg," said the still furious Yoshi. "Maybe you can't stand up."

Captain Mori shoved him, this time and whisper-shouted:
Be still, fool!"

Takezo was amused.

"It is possible," he noted. "Bring water to pour over my head and send for tea. Then we talk."

"You take us for servants?" Yoshi wondered.

"We can go inside and have tea," Mori suggested.

Inside, thought Takezo, moving his head. It hurt. Last night was coming fully back to him. *I began inside....*

7

He remembered Miou's expression, eyes slit in fury holding the golden comb up in his face as he backed towards the doorway, then was in the doorway, the half-moon rising behind him, lighting the garden in subtle silver, the red and yellow lanterns inside enhancing her glowing beauty. Faint, cherry-scented incense smoldered in a silver bowl near the futon. Her fine nose was slightly curved, long, rich hair tied behind, two ribbons of unbraided hair framing her face, eyebrows drawn high on her forehead, real ones shaved. She was styled like a noblewoman as befit a high caste courtesan.

'See this? See this?' she cried. 'False gold! You are mere talk. You won't work for a clan so you're poor. A man your age. Get out! You promise. You drink. What are you worth? Find another to lie to, sheep-face!'

As she'd hurled the jewelry point-blank at his face he automatically caught it. He'd bought the piece from one of his regular informers who swore it had been pawned by a noblewoman. He'd backed a step through doorway.

'Hear me, Miou,' he began.

'Your words are wind in dried leaves. What do they say? Go!'

She'd slammed the wood and paper door shut an inch from his long, fine nose. As he'd been only a little drunk he went and improved on that with a vague idea of trying to find the salesman – without result. He'd stumbled back as the moon was going down above the inn roof. He thought he'd called her name a few times. Maybe he had. Maybe he'd talked to a bush….

"You can go inside," he told them. "Get to know her."

Then he unveiled his face and sat up, holding the side of his long head. The mellow, golden spray of sunbeams in his eyes really hurt. He winced. A man over 40 but looking much younger, with light skin and almost golden eyes like an introspective tiger. The light, exalting the red and white blossoms of the camellias and the stunning richness of the day was a shimmer and blur he kept blinking to clear. The bees flicked and droned….He had a feeling something like just before a poem found words.

Could we but live, he thought, *without our duty to time, life would move left and right but never forward…or maybe time won't go forward if life is still…what a strange brain I woke up with today, with fools in front of me and Miou sweet as vinegar….I'll try not to kill anyone before breakfast….*

8

"Yoshi," commanded Mori, "go in and get someone to bring out water and tea."

"Maybe a little sake," added Takezo.

Yoshi just looked at him.

"For breakfast?" he asked.

Takezo shrugged.

"Time goes only left and right, today," he said.

He sat there, tall, fine-featured and handsome as the famous Noh theater actor, Seki, with his slightly arched, long nose and perfect lips to contrast his usual disarray of dress and careless manner.

"Left and right," repeated Yoshi. "You are always drunk?"

"Or, I am always sober. Who can tell which, if time cannot go forward?"

Without standing he drew his short sword in a glittering blur and held it up near the round-featured man's face. That face lost complexion for a moment because there was a single bee impaled on the blade's tip.

Yoshi went across towards the inn and onto the porch. Mori bowed.

"*Sensei*," he said, meaning master.

"Ha, ha," was the response. "Who can master his heart?"

"Who knows? Must we try, Takezo-san?"

"Ha," grunted the other. "Keep it from falling in love." He stood up, blinking but without a significant wobble, sword at his side. "What does Izu want of me?"

Yoshi was now coming back, followed by a serving girl with a tray and a bucket of water. Another woman was standing in the open doorway, just a silhouette in the shadow beyond the polished wood porch. Her form was obscure but not her voice:

"No drunkards on this property!" she called out.

"He may be sober," laughed Yoshi, with scorn. "No one can tell."

"Hmn," Takezo said, looking at the bee impaled on the tip of his sword, "if time went sideways this insect would still live."

"Always talk," she called over. "Better to listen to the wind."

Flicked the bee away. Sheathed the weapon. Took the bucket from the young woman and poured it over his head, soaking his shoulder-length hair and upper body. Grunted. Drank a little and spat. He didn't turn to look at Miou in the doorway. Didn't have to.

"Well?" he pointedly asked Mori.

9

"I do not know the lord's mind," Mori said. "He asks you please come with us."

"Why are you still here?" Miou wondered. "No more to drink here."

"Pay no attention," he murmured.

"You like women's insults?" wondered Yoshi.

"You talk to her, then," he suggested. "See how you fare." To Mori: "I'll join you." Walked a few steps and stood in the hot sun, squinting at her outline in the doorway. "I will replace it," he called over to her.

"That's nothing. That's why you're stupid. The trinket is nothing."

"Then what?" He opened his arms, symbolically helpless.

She banged the sliding door shut and was gone.

"No woman dares insult me so," said Yoshi.

"Yes," said Takezo, starting for the gate, brooding, then shrugging. "I'm sure you are feared by women."

"Even by whores," Yoshi remarked.

Takezo looked at him; let it hang.

As they reached the road the yellowish dust was bright and puffed up around their feet as they headed down towards the central section of Edo.

"I know a bathhouse on the way," the *ronin* said.

"Yes," said Captain Mori, conciliatory, "but it would be a kindness to not leave our lord waiting in uncertainty, Takezo-san."

"I'll smell a little longer, captain."

"Most gracious of you, Takezo-san."

They all paused as they passed an open space which stood just inside a gated checkpoint between a long, low log and brick jail and a canal where poled long boats were carrying people and goods to and from the suburbs.

In the unenclosed yard three samurai in red and white were standing around a man in a loincloth who was staked down, outstretched, on a low mound of sand. One held an unsheathed sword.

"Blade test," said Yoshi, with a certain relish, taking a few steps closer.

Condemned criminals often were used for testing the edge of a new blade. Crucified men were commonly slashed to shreds in outlying execution grounds.

Takezo looked, dully at the scene, remembering the story of a famous outlaw who, as they tied him to a pole, said to the samurai executioner: "If I'd known you were going to test your precious sword on me, you dogshit, I'd have swallowed a few rocks to chip the edge."

The bright sun glittered as the blade went up. The target twisted his face away and stared blankly across the dusty space towards the three watchers. Takezo thought how the entire world for each person existed only because he or she looked, heard, felt, even imagined it...and the entire world was now coming to an end, right there...he unconsciously said a kind of prayer for the man.

Whatever's left that a sword can't cut, he said to himself, *will not be in the world...*The world was always ending with every death of everything alive, he didn't quite put into mental words. *Time rolls over us like a stone....*

The bright blade came down, the samurai shouting a *kiai* to amplify his power as he struck and the dense, sharp, slightly curved, perfect steel edge sliced completely through the belly into the sand that protected it from nicking.

The man's expression, maybe 100 feet away, didn't appear to change as his body separated into two parts - gouts of blood and intestines spilling out, soaking into the sand and dust. The eyes kept staring, head twisted to the side. Takezo, troubled, headachy, turned away in disgust as the swordsman was wiping the blade and studying it and Yoshi said, with a curt nod of approval:

"Good cut."

Walking on, the *ronin* remembered how he used to sit alone and examine a good sword, feeling the weight, admiring the mirrored length, the subtle wavy patterns near the super-tempered edge produced by heating and cooling, the fine lines that resulted from the endless folding of the red-hot steel...all the secrets, art and magic that went into creating a matchless weapon.

They like to say it mirrors the soul of the user, he thought, with a slight snort. *Souls like mine with plenty of blood to reflect...or this Yoshi, maybe, without a thought in his head that wasn't put there by somebody else....*

"Izu's castle is much changed," commented Takezo as they turned off the street into a stable. The hostler was watering several horses in the muddy, dung-reeking yard. Steam rose from the standing pools as the sun's angle increased. "Smells more like Hideo's place."

Hideo was a rival lord whose wife, Issa, once had Takezo temporarily declared an outlaw after he protected a peasant boy accused of killing and robbing wounded samurai. The insanely bloody civil wars were then at their full fury, the country in chaos, and Hideo looked like he might take control of Edo, still a castle town, and the surrounding area at the time. Eventually he submitted to the dominant lord Nobunaga. Takezo defended his actions by killing a few of Hideo's best samurai in a series of duels. Issa held a grudge, it had been said, like a jug holds water and kept the stopper tight. Takezo, the *ronin* was a borderline social outcast, anyway, worked for lords, merchants, local *ippuki* police, even commoners. He was independent, had ninja skills and was a natural detective.

"Were you ever in service?" Mori wondered as they entered the barn.

"Don't like so many rules," he grunted in reply.

Inside was a sweet, strong odor of horses, hay and grain. Streaks, threads and slashes of sunlight worked through warped, uneven boards into the dim coolness.

Is this an ambush? He asked himself. Doubted it.

"Think you can always do what you want?" Mori asked.

"Depends on what I want."

He was thinking about Miou. She always told him he should join a clan where his sword would gain him a good living.

She's annoying, he said to himself. *She weakens me....*Smiled at himself, knowing she pleased him well and that he often needed her prodding. They crossed stray shafts of golden light, passing empty stalls heading into the surprisingly deep interior. Kept remembering her touch and scent, delicate mouth open in easy surrender...discovering the surprise lush wetness as his softly questing fingers worked between her sleek, sweet legs....Grunted and cut the memory short.

12

They stopped at the far wall and were facing a stocky man in full lacquered wood and steel-link armor with a closed, silver mask of a face snarling in demonic fury. His helmet, displaying a quarter moon and star of worked gold, proclaimed high rank. He sat on a low, backless stool, hands on thighs, just behind the fine spray of light.

Both retainers knelt, then sat back on their heels in the musty straw. The leader seemed relaxed and completely confident, Takezo noted. He also noted this wasn't Izu. He knew Izu. The samurai wore his colors but they might not even be his men. That was curious.

Takezo just bowed since he didn't have to kneel. Oh, he knew he really should have knelt but, lacking so many things, his pride, some said, was his gold. And he was a miser with it. Without the power of a great clan at his back respect was life and death to him.

"My lord, Mask," he said, quietly, "what do you ask of me?"

"Insolence," softly hissed Yoshi.

"Your views are not needed," said the shadow-blurred lord. His metal-muffled voice had a kind of purr in it.

"He requests insolence, my lord?" the *ronin* asked and noted the man on the stool seemed amused. Yoshi prostrated himself, face down. This delighted Takezo as being the price of a secure place in life. "If I have any left I'll share it with him."

Face in the stink...secure until you offend or fail, he pointed out to himself. *Or just die, as all do, in any case....*

He blinked and winced slightly as a fanning of sunlight touched his cheekbone and eye. He moved his head slightly but the bright patch was too wide. He resisted moving further out of stoic pride. None of them would have shifted even though he, again, was free to. He wanted to maintain his manners.

"I have met Lord Izu," he said, to move things along.

"This is not a masquerade. He is a good friend. He needs your assistance, Sir Jiro."

"You compliment me, my lord...."

The brightness hurt and he had to close his right eye - which annoyed him.

"Are you comfortable?" the man asked. A slight, amused jibe.

Well, whoever he was he had a sense of humor which the *ronin* appreciated.

13

He opened his eye again and refused to wince. His hangover headache wasn't helping, either. At least his mind was off Miou, for the moment.

"Quite, my lord," he lied.

"You are a samurai, after all," said the seated man.

I should have knelt and then I'd be better off...he's letting me know it....

"I kill well," he agreed. "But no man orders me to do it."

Irrepressible Yoshi, back on his knees, growled low in his throat.

"You are not being asked to kill, Sir Jiro," said the armored lord. He hadn't stirred since the conversation began. "It is not killing that makes a knight."

"True, lord. There is rape, theft, pillage. War, greed, revenge. The torment of peasants for sport." He knew he was doing it again. He always did. He blamed the headache and Miou. "Maybe *sir* is an insult."

This was too many for Yoshi who sprang to his feet and drew his sword.

"Intolerable insolence!" he cried.

Captain Mori jumped up to intervene despite his own cold fury. Takezo had an unconnected, abstract idea that the light beam was like a shaft of love or intelligence cutting into the darkness of life; too bright to be comfortable. He'd closed the tortured eye, again.

Why can I not control my tongue, he was thinking, *or my heart?*

"Hold!" said Mori, watching his lord who hadn't budged.

"Intolerable!" repeated the roundish man and struck at the tall, aquiline-featured warrior who hadn't moved. That should have been warning enough. That and the bee.

The stroke that might have cleaved the head off a bull flash-ripped down through the sunbeams, the *ronin* leaned back a few inches and felt the air whipcrack as it missed his nose and his body seemed to flow sidewise as if jerked by an invisible string so that he was instantly behind his attacker whom he seemed to dance with, spun, tilted, disarmed and hurled, staggering, maybe thirty feet back across the length of the barn; then he just stood there, holding Yoshi's sword and looking at the still unstirred lord.

"Your views are your views, Sir Jiro," the lord said, as if nothing had happened. "There is some truth in them. There are many, like me, who work to bring order to our land. Izu is another."

14

"I apologize, sir," said the tall *ronin*, nodding a martial bow of respect for the older man's tolerant poise. "I am often unruly. How may I serve?"

Am I so corrupted by my work, he wondered, *that I assume all men lie?*

Captain Mori had gone back and stood near Yoshi who was on his feet, again. The lord tilted his head, slightly.

"Something troubles you," he said – almost a question.

"Of no importance. But you are most observant, sir. A matter of the heart."

The man nodded and laughed, softly. Then went still, again.

"I know your reputation," he said. "And your poetry. You have a wide understanding and I think you will be able to communicate well with the strangers from the ship." A slight pause to confirm that Takezo knew what he was talking about – further credit to his intelligence and tact. The *ronin* nodded. "Lord Izu took in the first three of them found."

"Yes."

"A difficulty has arisen."

Takezo now stood in shadow while stray shifting sunbeams penetrating the big, cool space softly illuminated the seated lord, the light diffused by the clouds of dust motes and fine straw stirred by the brief struggle. He thrust the sword he'd taken into a bale of hay.

Who is this lord? Takezo asked himself, staring at the snarling facemask and dully gleaming red lacquer armor.

"The three foreigners," the masked man was saying, "were found on the beach. They were fortunate to come in where the slope is so gentle." He shrugged. His tone told the *ronin* he regretted their good fortune. "Izu sheltered them. Fishermen found their strange ship and towed it to shore. It is said more foreigners were alive on board."

"Interesting. Where is this craft?"

The other may have shrugged, almost imperceptibly.

"Not known. Perhaps the seamen found a way to sail on."

Why don't I believe this? Takezo thought. *The poking finger....*It would poke at his mind when something didn't fit, was missing or subtly false.

"One man is black as moonless darkness and comes from some savage land. Another is pale as milk with hair the color of dull coals. The

15

last is less pale and a scholar in his country. His wisdom interests Izu who has offered him a temporary place in the clan."

"Ah. And the 'difficulty' you mentioned, lord?"

He thought he heard Yoshi mutter something in the background.

"The pale one with eyes the color of the sky," was the reply.

"He is the difficulty?"

"One. There is a second: Lord Hideo's daughter."

"Ah."

"You understand?"

"The clever one more beautiful than stars reflected in still water," said Takezo.

"The one who speaks her mind so freely."

Admirable, brave and dangerous, he mentally commented.

"They ran away together," the lord said, neutrally.

Takezo appreciated romance. He also appreciated the fact that the shame of this rested with Izu, in the end.

"And Izu wishes me to find them? Others could do as well."

"Not to find her. Unnecessary. To find *him.*"

"If he looks as you say, sir...." Takezo began but the seated man gestured. "How can he conceal himself? So Osan has been found?"

The other hesitated.

"Yes," he said.

"And....?" Takezo pressed.

A softened sunbeam now lit half the man's helmet and scowling, demonic mask.

"We will direct you where to begin your search, he said. "You will be well-paid." Held out a small, gold tablet, then lobbed it to Takezo. It glittered through the bright lines. "Take this. Authority from Lord Nobunaga. Most will respect it."

So he's in it, thought Takezo. *Interesting....*

He'd seen him once in Kyoto, recalled the heavy-featured, stolid face, the thick mustache.

At this point Nobunaga was the most powerful and maybe ruthless lord in a country of ruthless lords. He'd imposed a shaky peace on most of the madly warring clans that had kept the nation in bloody turmoil for so long. His clear objective was to take Kyoto and set up a strong *shogunate* central government.

"You are leaving things out," he said.

16

"You will learn what you need to know," came through the face mask, as if the metal mouth spoke. "No reason to overburden yourself at the beginning of a journey."

He just sat there, hands on thighs, like a warrior in a painting, the demon-frowning mask half in shadow.

Or an actor, Takezo thought.

Two

Two days before

At gray dawn light rain was blowing up the beach from where the surf crumped and softly boomed, invisible behind a wall of warm, whitish mist. The inn stood on a rocky rise above the coastline, surrounded by wind-twisted scrub pines and brush at the end of a seaside village maybe 60 miles from Edo on the seacoast side of the great bay.

Colin woke up and lay there on the *futon*, a rolled-up blanket under his head. He couldn't deal with the wooden Japanese pillow.

He listened to the wind and pitter of rain on the treated paper windows. Heard uMubaya's low snoring from the pallet across the room. Osan's samurai bodyguard, Nori, was sleeping sitting up, sword under his armpit, leaning on the wall of her adjoining room. He was stocky and generally looked meditative and serious.

They'd been lying low there for less than a week. When uMubaya went out or when they'd traveled he wore a priest's outfit with a huge, beehive-like wicker helmet that completely hid his head – Osan's idea. His sleeves were long enough to conceal his hands. Colin wore a cowl-like hood and she'd dyed dark and styled his straight reddish hair and used makeup on his face that passed casual scrutiny.

That evening, as the fog was just gathering and the sky was still clear, Nori and uMubaya walked on the beach, the Zulu just wearing a hood in the moonlit dimness. They sat down near the softly breaking surf in sight of the warmly-lit inn where Osan and Colin were having tea in private. The half-moon was well up in the east over the ocean and silvered the edge of a long line of oncoming clouds. The air was mildly cool and soothing. uMubaya remembered the rocky coast of his father's kingdom where there were stretches of beach and constant winds. Very dangerous waters, a Swazi fisherman had once told him.

He was telling Nori something about his home country when, suddenly, red torchlight tossed shadows around them. The black man

17

assumed it was Colin but the samurai instantly was crouched, hand on sword hilt.

A thin, medium-sized fighting man with a pointed chin and wide, bony shoulders came out of the night behind the fluttering light with a young woman, who kept her head down-tilted, as was custom. She was a commoner by dress and manner, slim with long limbs.

"Wondering who was out here," the new man said. "We are going back to the party."

"Fine with us," said Nori.

uMubaya put his hood up but it was too late.

"Interesting," the stranger commented, at the same time studying Nori. "I know you. I used to serve Hideo." The flame shadows hollowed out his deep-set eyes above cheekbones that looked like ax cuts. "Is this a demon?" Indicating the African whose eyes just showed in the shadow of his hood.

"A foreigner," said Nori, frowning. "Under the protection of my lord."

"In any case, a wonder." His head jerked towards the woman. "She and I were contemplating the moonrise." Smiled. "You must come to the party. Up here at the inn. You are my guests."

"Thank you. Where did you come from?" Nori asked.

"From the north. I am guarding a merchant and his baggage. No more service for me. I like the pay and don't have to bow to the soft wretch. Come." Started walking up from the beach.

"My friend here is weary," said Nori. "It-"

"I won't hear of it. Come. We must meet your friend who is not a demon."

"He -" Nori knew they'd have to go or try to kill the man and risk commotion. And he'd come from the north and would know nothing about their situation.

"It would be insulting to refuse," the wide-shouldered man said, walking on.

They followed him. The slim, graceful woman reminded uMubaya a little of Osan. He thought of his betrothed Ulele – not without regret at times – but the most attractive woman he'd ever seen was the northern one from the burning hot lands on what he now knew they called the equator where the sun could kill the unprotected; the Masai captive princess, a slender, long-limbed beauty with a proud, long back; high-cheek bones and distant, almost insolent eyes. He'd instantly wanted her. Her name was Mer'ce.

After they found her alone, wandering on the beach in Zulu land she was brought to the King's ikhanda. Instead of forcing her to marry or just mate with him, uMubaya spent time with her, learned some of her speech, courted her....She'd treated him with royal disdain and declared she had no wish to mate into a nation of fat people and mentioned that in her land a boy must kill a lion with a spear by the time he was 13 or else he could not become a *maron,* a warrior. Had he done that? He hadn't, of course – but argued that he could probably defeat their best fighters. This produced much amused scorn. Annoyed, he took her alone with him into the bush to find a lion. She told him he'd be eaten and how could his big, clumsy Zulu spear penetrate? The innuendo was clear. After a few days they came on a pride and he'd fought a hunting female. Mer'ce went up a tree to watch and mockingly encourage him. The lioness in defense of her hidden offspring charged. In a near-miracle he killed the beast as he fell, bleeding and semi-conscious, under it....

She left and he never forgot her. Because there'd been one moment, before she went, which left him with a hollow ache and a feeling he would long for her forever...he was young enough to be sure it would be forever....

Nori and uMubaya had gone to the party with the bony samurai, drank with the men and prostitutes there and, later, semi-staggered back to their room. They'd been offered women by the host but both refused – though uMubaya had been pretty tempted.

Colin was uncomfortable thinking about how he'd tried to have Osan while they were gone. She'd tilted her beautiful head aside and neither said yes nor no. She'd let him hold her but no more. He'd automatically caressed and tried to press her to open into surrender. Overwhelmed by wanting, body and soul, he almost gasped saying he was dying with desire. His massive hands were gentle but implacable.

She used only words to resist which might have been all that stopped him.

'When you adulterate gold,' she'd told him, 'do you not cheapen it?'

He didn't follow.

'Love you," he said. "Me...love you."

19

'You cannot force a flower to bloom by squeezing the bud. You can kill it, Co-rin, or leave it to itself.'

'Bloom?'

She picked a flower and bud from the vase on the floor table and showed him what she meant with pantomime and words; then held him, gently.

'You not love me.'

'You tell me what I feel?' she wondered, smiling, slightly.

She'd gone to sleep on a futon under the window. He'd lain down on one across the long room and stared at the shadows from the single lamp in the middle of the floor, moving like slow, dark wings, he'd imagined. Music and voices from the party were faint. He'd dozed and half-woke when Nori and the Zulu stumbled in.

What could I offer such a woman? He asked himself, lying there, much later, staring at the faint glow of the window as the wet dawn subtly intensified as one of the two men snored like, he thought, like a sick hound. He remembered his homeland: dark wooded glens, mist spilling slowly among raw, dark-rock mountains, tiny, almost steely-bright blue, yellow and white wildflowers growing in harsh places on spiky bushes....*She is lovely and gentle...* Tried to find the poetry. What could he offer, hillman turned seafarer? *We have to leave here...I should bring her back to her family...I think she came only to show them she could...her mother, anyway...there's a bitch-wolf....*

With a slight groan he rolled and levered himself to his knees, then upright. His head ached a little from drinking too much high-proof *sochu.* Nearest thing and a poor second, he felt, to the malt brew back home.

He went quietly out the door and headed, barefoot, down the corridor that led to the sea side of the long inn. There was a latrine maybe 50 yards away but he figured to urinate among the rocks and pines and drink some well water – then back to bed - the others wouldn't stir for awhile yet.

He stood on the porch, weaving slightly and watched the dull, sourceless gray glow incrementally increase. He felt blurry.

"I love you, Osan," he murmured, in Gaelic, out into the foggy wetness. "Yet...it's true...what can I offer, here, in this land where...."

He stepped down among the rocks and trudged a few steps. He had vague notions of finding a ship and having the captain marry them.

20

They might let them wed just to save face, he considered.

Fog softly flowed as if the dark, wet bushes coldly smoked. He practically tripped over what he took for a sleeping woman. He tried to focus, thinking she shouldn't be sleeping in the rain. The upper third of her body was under a bush and her clothes were parted, showing a long-limbed, beautiful, naked body.

His stomach clenched, his heart pounded and he dropped to his knees. There was enough light now to show color. The color was red and it hit him like a fist of ice and steel.

"By St. Stephen's balls!" he cried. He touched her kimono and his hands came back bloodstained. "Oh, sweet God! No...Sweet God, no!"

Because he knew the kimono and the combs he'd been watching move in the soft lantern light earlier that evening, the graceful limbs and hands.

He gagged out a cry in a kind of mad sickness and pulled her out of the shrubbery and then keened in highland agony because her head wasn't there.

He didn't hear himself - there was now a commotion inside and, suddenly, a round face under a peasant's straw hat was peering between the pines that lined the road that dead-ended here.

He stood up, stained bloody across his pale silks.

"Murder!" cried the face. "Murder!"

Colin just stood there in the slowly gathering leaden light, not looking up as Nori and uMubaya came outside and stumbled towards him.

Later Colin had only broken, blotted impressions of Nori trying to kill him as the Zulu rode his back down into the sand...blurs...outcries....

Three

Takezo walked over the bridge on the road to Hideo's stronghold. It was slightly downhill on the far side of the river and the noon sun impacted the dust into quivering, blurry heat-shapes. The sky was so bright blue it hurt.

This was not so massive a place as the one on the south side of the bay miles from the growing city with complex mazes and blocking walls before you reached the actual main structure. Edo had been a fishing village and had expanded quite a bit but nothing like what was soon to come when it would be the unofficial capital and eventually, renamed Tokyo, the biggest city in Japan and, in population, the world.

He knew where they'd be keeping the body until tomorrow's burial ceremony. With half the troops, not to mention Izu's men and peasant recruits, out scouring the countryside for Colin and the other two it was a good time to investigate. The missing head had maddened the clan. A disgrace, in itself. Izu was in trouble.

He passed the gate where tradespeople and others were going in and out and went to the door he knew accessed the cellar, the coolest place in the huge building. At the portal a small, hunchbacked man with a severe limp responded to his pounding, opened the wood and metal door and stood blinking into the day's dazzle. He was bald with an uneven scraggle of beard.

"Hm," he grunted. "Are you delivering the buns? Where's Oku?"

"*Hm.* Are you the keeper of the gate to hell?"

"Looks like me does he?" Liked that. Chuckled. "No doubt you'll be knocking on that gate soon enough." In the brightness the sloppy clothes fooled the gatekeeper until he saw the swords at the other's belt. No commoner carried *katana* and *shogo*. "Who let a samurai bum like you through the gate? Did you steal those swords? You'll find hell in a minute, in that case."

"You talk a lot, bent man. Show me to the body of the lord's murdered girl."

"You order me, you vagabond? I am, Momoichi, master of the cellars."

"I have authority, *Sir* Momo."

"Authority. From the king of the devils?"

"Interesting. Very likely."

"Get away from here and go beg your supper, *samurai*."

Takezo sighed. He didn't need this. A number of peasants and castle folk were starting to gather amused. He reached into his pouch for the Nobunaga's talisman but the fellow was already stepping back and shutting the inward opening door.

The *ronin* shoved it and knocked the little man down. He heard him scuttling and cursing in the dimness as he stepped inside, trying to focus past the bright wedge of sunlight spilling in around him. Something flashed the light near his head and his body barely ducked back with that uncanny, instant awareness that comes to those who, somehow, have "opened their spirit." He needed it because this was as close as he'd come to death in a long time: the wicked weapon (a kind of long-handled scythe) hooked at his skull, slit his left ear and creased his neck.

Dog dung! His mind said. The deadly little man came quickly and unevenly out after him. *Clear why they don't need a guard here....*

There was a spiked ball and chain that attached to the base of the scythe handle. He began to spin the ball before him in humming, looping, figure-eight arcs. The idea was to hit an opponent or catch his sword arm – except Takezo hadn't drawn yet.

"I apologize," he said, "for my rudeness."

"Too late!"

One of the female watchers yelled, to general laughter:

"Chase him old Momo!"

"He looks like a hungry dog caught by the butcher," another said.

Momo whirled the ball over his head. The *ronin* drew but, because he didn't want to fight or attract more attention, hesitated, pointing the blade level out front so the ball whipped the chain around his wrist, binding it to the handle and the surprisingly strong, bent man started pulling him into range of the scythe.

"Aaah," grunted Momo, with satisfaction.

"He's dead," someone else commented from the sidelines.

"Foolish to pull me where I wish to go," said Takezo, angry now.

And he charged the man which made the chain slack and no more than an annoying decoration. At the same time he drew his short sword with his left hand and blocked the vicious scythe-chop, then slammed Momo on the side of his skull with the flat of his long sword. The hard, round head rang like a block of sounding wood farmers use to signal.

He untangled himself while Momo groaned and rolled over in the sunbright cloud of dust they'd raised.

"So many bad tempers," Takezo said.

Old Momo, touching his head and not saying much above a mutter, led the way down a ramp into the dark coolness under the castle, holding a torch that flapped their shadows around them.

"You should have circled when I rushed you," the tall swordsman commented, thinking over the fight. He'd used the scythe and chain but never liked it because once you were committed there were few options. Touched his cut ear. Not much blood.

"I should have hit you the first time," the limping man said, bitterly.

"A point."

They'd come to a big, cool chamber where the light showed a single wooden coffin that looked like a barrel, tied with thick cloth across the top like a birthday present, used to bear the body to the graveyard.

"During the fighting days," Momo said. Touched his head. "Arr...you dog."

"I might have split your skull."

"During the fighting days, this place was full of high-and-mighty dead men."

"Is this the woman?"

"Woman? A body. Arr...." Touched his head, again. "Important men were saved for a proper burial. They kept better down here"

"Did they appreciate the honor?" Takezo asked, drawing his short sword and freeing the coffin top. The light now showed a small shrine that had been set up on a table a few feet away.

"Ha. The rest went into a hole where they fell or were left to feed the birds."

"Better to be important and saved for worms." He lifted off the cover. "Bring the torch here."

"What do you hope to see? She has no head."

The body was folded, neatly. It was soft and slightly swollen, now. Spices had been poured in to mask the scent.

No head but hands, thought Takezo, studying the strange ring on her thumb where it was still too-large, though the fingers were somewhat swollen. He lifted the hand and noted it seemed to be gold. *Odd....Why? She's not Chinese...who wears rings?* Sometimes people might take up a Chinese style but generally it was very rare. He was puzzled. *It was put on her...who put it there? Why?*

It was thick with a blood-red, dull, flat stone in an elaborate setting. He twisted it off, easily, and stowed it in his belt pouch.

Her mother looks a little Korean, he decided. *But I never noticed a ring on her....*

"What are you doing? Stealing from the dead?"

"Who said this was the lady Osan?"

24

"Mmm." The hunchback's round face was half-lit by the shifting flamelight as the samurai's wide set, penetrating eyes watched him from his own shadows.

"There's no head," Takezo emphasized.

"That's clear. Makes a problem for the ceremony."

"Who washed and dressed her?"

"Her mother. The lady Issa. And some others. Anyway, she goes in the earth soon enough."

"Ah."

"A mother ought to know her child, head or not. Better put that back or you'll have no head yourself."

Did Issa put this on her for some strange sentiment? That lady seems as tender-natured as a sea-snake....The girl had a rebellious nature but why wear something that doesn't fit?

He took the torch and peered back in at the body. Someone had pinned a silken cloth over the neck creating an eerie impression. On impulse he adjusted the pale kimono where it had fallen over one shoulder. Had to lift and free it so that much of her naked body was exposed. This close the nasty pungency of decay overcame the stinging, almost choking spices.

In the shifting shadows he noticed something strange: pressed the softening flesh between her thigh and public hair to better expose a tattoo, very small, of what looked like a lily.

That must have hurt, he thought, covering her and setting back the round lid. *A ring, a tattoo...did she live among foreigners or with savage men of the north? Hideo's daughter?*

They waded through the torchlight and shadow, up the long ramp back to daylight. The little man leaned, unevenly, along.

"I'll return it, soon enough, maybe," the *ronin* said.

"I'll say nothing, though my skull is sore. As you say, it could have been worse."

"I'm looking for the man they say killed her. If you hear anything interesting concerning this business, leave word for me at Haru's tavern or the Pine and Crane, and you may be rewarded."

"I know Haru's."

Takezo went out into the brightness and heavy heat. The last few days had been hotter than he could remember. Bad time to be an unburied corpse. Salting might be better, he considered. He went to the first front

25

gate, past workers, merchants and samurai. Everybody was drooping a little. Moving slowly, he stopped by the sentry post and asked to see the Lady Issa.

The burly, short guard was unimpressed.

"So this is how to dress, fellow," the guard inquired, "coming to Lord Hideo's court?"

"Am I too formal?" he wondered, reaching out the golden tablet.

"Hah." The guard squinted at it. "What's this?"

"Can you read? Are your eyes sore?"

The sun was hot pressure on the back of his head. He needed a hat.

"Insolence," said the guard.

The *ronin* sighed.

"No one approves of me," he said. "Saddening."

"I see it is a pass. Pass then. Take your bad manners, too."

He entered the castle proper where the next sentry stood, holding a halberd-like weapon. Behind him light poured into the hall from high, narrow windows. The air was much cooler.

This one wanted to know if he had an appointment. He was graceful and friendly-looking.

"Tell her I have something that belonged to her late daughter," Takezo said.

"Give it to me, then," said the guard, but Takezo shook his head. "Do you expect money?"

"I expect to see Issa," Takezo said.

"*Lady* Issa."

"So must she be, whether I say so or not. Unless she's otherwise."

This man wasn't irritated. His eyes showed amusement.

"Are you a samurai or did you steal those swords?"

"I won the *katana* in a duel with a spearman."

The sentry smiled, faintly.

"I'll submit your humble request to the Lady," he said.

A 12 year-old with a short sword at his belt led Takezo to an anteroom. He'd slipped off his *tabi* at the main door and left them with a row of other footgear. Used a footbowl to wash his feet.

The room had a low, sliding door and a woman knelt-walked in with tea. She kept glancing sidelong at him, as most women did. He sat in a loose lotus position, stretched and looked at her soft delicate feet as she made the graceful serving movements.

"Thank you," he said.

"Yes, sir," she responded. "Are you...." Broke off, bowing her head.

He knew what was coming. Was used to it.

"No," he said. "I am not Seki."

"Ah. Yet you resemble him. I thought you might be in disguise."

"Actors are always in disguise."

He liked her face and was automatically flirting. But that brought back the image of Miou tossing the cursed comb in his face.

I'll make Yazu swallow it whole, the *ronin* said to himself, *that wretched thief....*

As the girl was hunkering back out the low door, he said:

"Bring sake."

"Yes, sir," she responded, bowing out and shutting the little panel.

Suppose I live a long life, he pondered. *What will I do with it? Strange, how each woman is much the same yet where they are different, in the smallest ways, is a whole new dish to taste...the mystery is, why they endure men at all...there must be something in nature to blind them....*He liked that idea. Smiled.

While he was employed staring at the wave and half-moon pattern on the floor matting and asking unanswerable questions, the door opened, again.

"Come on," he said. "I'll entertain you, sweet beauty."

"Gracious of you, Sir Jiro," said a man's voice, followed by the harsh, bony, handsome face and goatish body of the clan chamberlain, Reiko. "You flatter me." He chuckled.

"Chamberlain, I'm dazzled."

The wiry man bowed and sat on his heels across the low table. The girl came in with a tray of cups and three jugs of wine. That was unusual: normally, as you drank one they would go fetch another. Takezo nodded back, stiffly as ever.

Reiko's droop-lidded, not-quite-impolite stare was on him.

"How generous," the *ronin* said, indicating the three jugs.

"Why tire this girl with creeping in and out? We respect your great capacities, Sir Jiro."

"Ah," Takezo said, taking one of the jugs before the girl could pour and took a long, long swallow; unseemly, even in a low tavern. Impulse, again. And it was good. Highest quality, cool castle sake.

It annoyed him that Reiko seemed pleased. This chamberlain was known to be as devious as his lord, Hideo, was straightforward. While the master showed temper, the vassal showed very little, of anything.

Supposed to be a good swordsman and master of the spear, Takezo recalled. *Hard to read his weaknesses....*

"Where is the lady?" he asked, taking another deep swallow, as the girl, delicately, poured a cup for Reiko who ignored it and, instead, took a jug himself and sipped, motioning the girl to withdraw.

"Most unfortunate. You should have sent word ahead for an appointment. She is occupied. I have come in her place, Sir Jiro. You may open your heart to me."

"You don't need to call me 'sir.' And, don't you mean open my belly, Chamberlain?" They both laughed, a little. "I'll open my heart to you after the demons in hell," Takezo concluded.

Reiko seemed to like that, too. Nodded and smiled.

"You are as rude as they say," he observed.

Takezo felt pointlessly pleased with himself. He liked irritating authority. Could already feel the alcohol blending with his mind and lifting his spirits into a kind of jocular anger. Very, very good sake. Hint of cherries. He lifted the jug again, as did the other man. They drank for awhile.

"Well," said the chamberlain, "what might you want with the Lady Issa? You say you have something that belonged to her unfortunate child?"

Another swig. Now, there was a slight, bubbling blur in his head. He dimly sensed he was feeling it too fast. His eyes felt softened.

"I want to steal her from her noble husband," he said. Noted that the other's eyes weren't reacting to the insult, itself, but looked he thought, (even through the soothing blurring) sharp and almost worried. "Poor Osan. Such a lovely woman. So gifted." Reiko didn't seem to show pain at this – but that didn't necessarily mean anything. Takezo considered he might have disliked her. It was well-known that men often felt threatened by her mind and competence. "I know your sorrow must be deep, chamberlain."

"Like a hot knife in my heart, Sir Jiro."

"So your heart has been found."

The *ronin* shook the jug. Empty. Didn't want to but reached for the next.

So easy to drink this, he thought. He always had trouble stopping. Unlike many drinkers, he didn't hate himself for it. He tried to recall Genghis Khan's law: *Drinking must be restricted for when a man drinks too much his wits avail him little, his arrows miss the mark and he falls from his pony...something like that, I think...so a man must not drink to....*

"As the Great Khan said," he semi-quoted, closing his eyes, "a man must not drink to excess too many times a month. But who can abstain altogether?"

"Certainly not you, Sir Jiro. May I see what you have?"

"Your real question is: can you take it from me? How much blood is it worth, my lord chamber pot?"

That was extreme. The politician's right hand clenched and stirred, slightly, towards the short sword he'd beside him when he sat. But he smiled, instead.

"Is what worth?" Reiko asked, coldly.

"How much blood for a trinket?"

"We must see, I suppose. Why do you test me, Takezo?"

"Now I'm not sir Jiro anymore, eh?" Shut his eyes again and the room definitely shifted a little. Blinked hard, trying to concentrate. Took another swallow. His lips felt thicker. "We must see, I suppose, too." Laughed. It seemed funny.

Reiko took a sip, from his cup, this time, watching, seeming to almost be timing Takezo's progressing condition.

"We admire your skills," said the chamberlain.

His skills are lost and he falls, the *ronin* went back to the quote.

"From my pony," he said, and laughed, again.

"Eh?"

"That's very funny."

He's tricking me, his mind said. *I'd like to kill him....*Laughed.

He tucked his sword under his belt and stood up. The room tilted, slightly.

"Where is the lady?" he demanded.

"Occupied."

"Bring me my pony, then."

"What use is the ring to you?"

29

"Hm? What ring?"

"Osan's ring. Give it to me, now."

Takezo reeled. Headed for the door. Thought about how he'd have to duck down to get out.

"Who said it was a ring?"

"You did."

"Where's my pony, now?"

"Waiting."

He crouched his way half out the sliding door and then stayed crouched for a few seconds. Shut his eyes but that was no good. Blinked them open.

"Can't trust this room," he said, looking out into the corridor. Noticed feet under robes, passing. Somewhere, far away, the chamberlain was saying:

"Best to rest, Sir Jiro."

So he was Sir Jiro again. That couldn't be good. The impaired spy shook his head like a wet dog and crawled out into the corridor. He decided not to stand, yet.

The serving girl knelt by him.

"I think the wine was strong, sir," she said quietly. "May I assist you?"

Some people had stopped to watch. Takezo grunted and clumped forward on hands and knees. He was aware that Reiko was now standing behind him. He was also aware of men's feet in fine quality *tabi* hose keeping pace with him. Someone snorted a laugh.

Fool, he told himself. *...no restraint...I'm getting older...this kind of life is less interesting...*

The chamberlain's voice, high and far off, was saying:

"We must help this gentleman to a comfortable mat."

"To a dog's bed," someone suggested. Laughter.

The girl knelt along with him, hand on one of his arms.

"If you are a ninja spy," she whispered, "you are the worst one known."

"Mn?" he grunted. "What's this?"

"What humiliation," a second male voice said.

"Shameless," said the one who'd laughed. Laughed again.

"Get away from him, girl," ordered Reiko.

"Trust Miou," the young woman whispered as she bowed away from him.

"She hates me," he reacted.

"She does not, Takezo-san," he thought he heard her say.

*How does she know Miou? S*trong hands now lifted him to his feet. He felt better, letting himself sag in their arms. *A mistake to help me up....*

"Keep his sword safe, for him," chamberlain Reiko recommended.

He was facing the wall where an ancient hanging scroll painting in red, black and gold, depicted an assassination. A lord at formal dinner with his retainers was suddenly being set upon by a samurai in priest's robes. He thought he vaguely recalled the tale. Reminded him of something he'd once done on stage when he was a boy in the acting troupe....

He sagged lower to pull the two men forward, one on each arm, then arched the other way and broke their hold. The movement made the room take a quarter-turn and triggered nausea. Unless they drew weapons he couldn't, not in here. A capital offense, generally, to attack while technically a guest.

He tilted and went at a rapid stagger into the main hall where he saw the blur of the two main doors and sentries – shut one eye and saw one of each.

Better, he thought. *One eye...better than none....* Was that a saying? Should be. Didn't quite chuckle. *Too many people now to attack a guest...even with one eye open....* Had to chuckle that time as he reeled, unpredictably (on purpose) in the general direction of out, seeing lots of bright print outfits all around.

"Help that poor man," cried Reiko from well back.

Someone tried but Takezo spun, half-fell, scrambled up and reeled almost to the big door, a shimmer of bright sun. The serving girl from the room reached for him and managed to get in the way of the next man.

"The lady Issa was occupied," he called out, amused to be thwarting the chamberlain in a childish way since he was a little hazy on whether he really meant to help him or not. "I will come back another time."

Paused and wobbled in the doorway. Looked for the girl but she was gone. He found that, again, curious. Had blurry ideas about her. The sentry was watching him, grinning.

"I'd come again more quietly," he suggested.

31

Another one worth asking a few questions, his uncertain consciousness duly noted, as he went outside, weaving.

Reiko was closer, now.

"Stop him," he commanded. "He has stolen something."

Takezo went out into the shimmering, golden pressure of mid-summer heat. Stood, barefoot and waited, free to fight, now. He'd fought drunk, before. He knew the sake had been spiked but they'd underestimated him. Ninjas, he knew, would have used a drug to put him under or the sleeping smoke he vaguely remembered being taught how to concoct as a boy. Several samurai stood in the doorway just inside the sunglare.

He squinted at their outlines in the stark shadow. Didn't make out Reiko but heard him saying:

"Let him go. Not worth it now."

"Give my regrets to the lady," he told them.

"Come back sober," one called out. "That way we'll never have to see you."

Lots of laughter. Somebody tossed his sandals to him and he slipped them on. Headed away from the castle.

Miou is right, he thought. *I drink like a Mongol....That goat of a chamberlain is playing a game....*

Still a little wobbly, he crossed the short bridge to a curving main street lined with Camilla trees. On the far side, he passed through the gate to the next city ward that at night would be shut and guarded by a district policeman (yoriki). The little city was divided into compartments that could be sealed off whenever a local uprising started. There was good reason for that, from the *buke* (warrior class) point-of-view. Shut one eye and saw a familiar, small, lean, somewhat furtive figure moving between two rows of pushcarts with vegetable and fowl for sale. A dozen goose heads hung over the side. The warrior detective thought he resembled something that lived in a cave and was scurrying back to the safe dimness.

"Yazu!" he called, speeding up after him. Yazu seemed to be limping and Takezo decided someone had probably kicked him. Well, he had another kick or so coming to him as reward for Miou's bad comb. He was married to a fat, mean-spirited woman who gave him little peace. Takezo had planned to look for him later that night where he might be sleeping in the stable behind the Pine and Crane tavern - favorite of both of

32

them. That way, if Yazu didn't go home his wife wouldn't find him drunk in the place, again. Once had been plenty. Takezo had been in a semi-stupor, himself, that night. He remembered the big woman dragging the leathery runt by the hair out the door, amusing and edifying the customers. "Yazu!"

The furtive man twisted around to look, then limped on, more quickly and, before the *ronin* could close the distance, cut from the street across a short board sidewalk, *tabi* slapping, into the crowded confusion of the main marketplace.

"Not my fault, master!" he yelled back. "I was deceived by a villain!"

"You'll soon be beheaded," promised the pursuer, wincing from the jolts as he ran. A moment later a sleek, fat black bull with decorated horns stepped out from between two carts as Takezo, stopping instantly, skidded in a puddle of water and vegetable refuse and bounced off the massive creature.

He snarled, then touched his pulsing head with both hands.

"May 6 devils eat his heart!" he muttered.

I'll find him later....take a rest...no more drinking...see the lady Issa soon enough....

He sat down on the sort of boardwalk and watched the bull saunter on, dropping a few soft "dumplings" in his own memory. A barefoot boy went by, a pole across his shoulders with a half-a-dozen Noh stage painted facemasks dangling on strings. The masks took Takezo back to his teenage days working in the theater. The masks always bothered him because you'd smell your own hot breath and see mainly blurs from the narrow eyeslits. To his fancy, the faces seemed to be gazing around as they twisted slightly on their strings. One beautiful-woman mask looked at him, for a moment, vaguely suggesting Miou - except the long, tilted eyes were just empty shadows.

Miou was a high-ranked *shirabyoshi* – and the joke went that they could wear the *obi* sash belts tied in back like a respectable woman. Plain prostitutes closed it in front for speed in dressing and undressing.

What next? He wondered. *I'm getting nowhere with anything...I've got the stupid ring which endangers me from the clan...got the worthless hair-holder which endangers me from my woman...*Frowned. *If she still is my woman...and what does that mean, anyway? She earns more than I do and I wonder what she wants with me...she should be with* *a wealthy samurai or generous merchant...I thought that comb was a big deal...ha...she doesn't want my gifts, as she pointed out herself...doesn't need them...*

Watched the masks swaying across the street, now facing front, now behind as the boy plodded on into and out of the sunlight. Took him back.

How long now since I was on stage? He squinted one eye. *I liked it, I admit I liked it...most of the time....*

He often used disguises in his work, even when not entirely unnecessary. Maybe, he considered, he wanted to be something else, always.

The sword stuck to me, he concluded.

Four

One day ago

uMubaya had suggested heading to Izu's when they left the inn but Nori explained that Hideo's samurai and, worse, hired ninja stalkers would be covering the ways back to Edo. Without help they'd be taken. Izu would have to die.

"They will attack Izu?" uMubaya had wondered.

"No. he will commit *seppuku*, Nori had explained." The polite word for belly-slitting, *hara-kiri*. "The shame of her death will rest with him. We should go inland. They'll be watching the ways to the city." Jerked his chin at the two of them. Colin was just sitting on a dark rock in the gray rain. "We should escape for the sake of justice," Nori went on. "And for my lady who must be truly avenged."

They could hear the villagers gathering. Someone was beating the wooden alarm gong-wood: bright, musical, muffled by the heavy air. The surf crumpled softly into the unseen beach behind the drizzly mist.

"I won't leave her," said the Scot, in Spanish.

Nori was puzzled and uMubaya translated.

"Then you can die for nothing," said Nori, looking at uMubaya. "We must head for the monastery of *Ichi-wisi*. Otherwise we will never elude the *ninja*. There, we will not have to fear them."

"Ninja?" wondered uMubaya.

"Dangerous men who can vanish in plain sight. Live underwater. Seem to be shadows, silent, until they strike. Masters of all ways of death."

That's interesting," said the African. "Few animals and no men could track me in my land. Save, maybe, the bush people who are closer to animals in nature. I'd like to meet one of these *ninja*."

Nori scowled and shook his head.

"They don't introduce themselves," he said. "They are spies and assassins.The one you meet is already killing you."

There is much to learn here, uMubaya considered. *Many challenges....*

They'd half-dragged the distraught Colin up the foggy beach and away from the village....

The Present

They were now on a road miles inland, the sun bright and hot, crossing down into a perfect little valley, lush, with glittering rice paddies and soft-looking hills all around, a few huts showing. On an overlooking slope there was a stone wall and the top of a temple with a gracefully arched roof showed above the trees.

"What are these monks?" wondered uMubaya.

"Great warriors. Friends of the great *ninja* clans. It is said they taught them many of their skills, in past times."

"But you said these *ninjas* seek us?"

Nori was looking, uneasily, back the way they'd just come to where the road bent out-of-sight into dense foliage. He thought something had moved through one of the uneven patches of brilliant sunlight that broke through the overhanging branches.

"There are many clans," he explained to the African. "The main ones will not serve Nobunaga and his allies. He fears them, if he fears anything. They support the priests."

He turned and went on walking. He felt they were being observed but it might mean nothing. Monastery security, most likely.

Five

Back in Edo

That night, Takezo laid up in the sleeping loft of The Pine and Crane inn which wasn't far from Hideo's. It was a place frequented by poor *ronin*, laborers from the market, gamblers and part-time, unlicensed prostitutes.

Takezo drank moderately and watched the main room below through the spaced boards. He knew the little, limping man would

35

reconnoiter before coming in. In one corner four gamblers in loincloths and open tunics were playing a kind of domino game; a samurai wearing clan colors was drinking from a cup and seemed to be waiting for someone. In the back he heard splashing in the tub room and women's giggles.

Maybe a whore, Takezo considered. *Anyway, he doesn't look so strong....*

His plans for tomorrow were laid. Meanwhile, he kept thinking about Miou. Kept having imaginary conversations with her. Close to falling asleep, he stared up at the boards an arm's reach from his face where the flamelight flickered and shifted shadows. He heard a reedy and familiar voice.

Ah, he thought rolling on his side and watching the furtive fellow insinuate himself inside and squat by a low table. *Yazu....*

"Cheap brew," Yazu called out to the pot-bellied tavern keeper. "That cursed woman. I think she's finally asleep."

The tavern keeper made a covert gesture up towards the loft. Yazu didn't get it; too late anyway as Takezo, with surprising ease, rolled and horizontally vaulted over the loft's two foot fence (as on a child's bed) and dropped, soundlessly in front of the startled thief.

"Don't get up, Yazu," he recommended as the small man scrabbled backwards across the room, sliding on his bony rump. The samurai looked over, incurious, self-absorbed. "No need for politeness."

He noted that he might have under-rated the clan samurai. Up close there was something about him like, he thought, steel under silk.

The gamblers took an interest.

"He looks like a rat in the garbage," one declared, a big, potbellied man with mean, small eyes. His bald head gleamed in the lantern light, leaving his face in shadow.

Yazu had backed into the wall, now talking steadily.

"I swear, good master, I -"

"I see your head before me," Takezo said, "as in a dream or vision. Close to the surf. The waters break softly. The moon sails in a breathless hush. The moonbeams fill your unshutting eyes. Instead of lies there is sand in your silent mouth."

"Pretty poetry," boomed the same bald gambler. "If I'm a judge."

A skinny companion in just a loin cloth, sweaty, with more spaces than teeth, cackled:

"You? You're a good judge of horsedung." Pleased with his wit, he went on. "A good judge of farts, Hachi." Doubled up with delight as the square-headed, proprietor hovered uneasily in the doorway to the next room where his wife was rattling plates and jugs.

"Good master," pleaded the worried but not really afraid Yazu, "I trust in your famous good nature."

"Famous? When you sold me that -"

"Your money is as good as back in your hands, Takezo-san. Your money –"

"Idiot. The money is not the point." More or less what she'd told him. "You humiliated me!"

"I was deceived, sir." He was hoping not be kicked or pummeled. "By a lowlife gambler."

"What's that?" inquired Hachi, the big-bellied poetry enthusiast. "You have the face to insult honest gamblers?"

"Be still," advised Takezo. "Replace this." He dropped the bad comb into the small man's lap.

Pot-belly liked to say he could have been a sumo wrestler. He rolled to his feet and sidled over. He was big and strong, up close, the *ronin* noted. The seated samurai was studying them now, expressionless.

"Be still?" the wrestler inquired.

His three companions were on their feet, now, two holding short knives, the skinny one a *bo* staff.

"I swear, sensei," said Yazu, "I'll satisfy you."

"You'll satisfy a cripple," declared Hachi, the wrestler, weaving slightly from the night's drinking. "When I'm done."

"Are they lovers?" asked the one with the staff.

"Too much noise," said the clan samurai, smiling faintly, however.

"If you fail, Yazu," promised Takezo, "I'll give you to this fat dung-beetle, here."

The bony one liked that. Nodded, vigorously.

"He must know you, Hachi," he chortled. "Dung-beetle."

"No trouble in here," said the proprietor from across the room. His son was peering at the action around the doorframe, just half his face showing. "Settle down."

"You dress like a dirty beggar, samurai," Hachi added on.

37

"My sword is clean, thank you," the *ronin* responded. "Who said I was a *samurai*?"

The seated clan warrior nodded, judiciously, watching.

"Kill them outside," he suggested.

Yazu took the opportunity to scuttle for the door but was blocked by Hachi the wrestler who bent his squinty eyes on him.

"Are you lovers?" Hachi wanted to know.

The pointless jibe fell flat, even with his companions. Takezo sighed. He'd had enough. Being sober made him irritable.

"Stupid nonsense," he said. "Let him pass and go back to your dung."

"Kill them *sensei*, Jiro," Yazu chirped. "Cut off their heads."

"Jiro Takezo?" the skinny staff-wielder said, easing towards the other room where the tavernkeeper stood. The clan samurai took additional interest. Nodded as if to confirm an opinion.

"Coward!" cried bald Hatchi. "Where do you slink to?"

"From harm," said the seated man.

Takezo went, empty-handed, up to Hachi and as the fellow reached to grapple he stepped alongside him like a shadow, spun his unbalanced weight and sent him spinning out the door, much as he'd done with the violent-natured Yoshi in the barn. There was a crash as he tripped and fell cursing in the moonlit yard. He knelt up, holding his head.

Yazu darted out and away as Takezo stepped onto the porch, meditative. The groaning man didn't matter; the others inside; the comb…the dead girl….For a moment there was just the hush of the night, the setting three-quarter moon above the low buildings and soft tree shapes…lanterns like stars, a gleam of lake water where the road bent around the shoreline.

He sighed, deeply. If time didn't go forward but time did…yet there was something that didn't go forward or in any direction. The poet's place. The stillness within and without, utterly untouched by the stain of life, the daily, dull, brutal nonsense of mankind….

Miou. he thought. *Would you were here with me….*

Six

A few hours ago

Miou was naked under a thin robe, reclining among soft pillows. She was on a low, four-poster bed brought from China. The naked man

38

was cross-legged on the floor, wiping a sword down with blacking, covering the silvery sheen completely. Through the open window the sunset was deep and dark as dried blood and the lantern light now gleamed brighter in the room. Behind her was a Chinese scroll painting of Buddha preaching to a black demon with razor cheekbones surrounded by circles of flame and smoke, a wavy-bladed sword in each hand. The room was un-Japanese, in that it was almost cluttered with rare artifacts, paintings, sculpture, pottery and always made her slightly uneasy. It was a rich man's Chinese room, she knew. He was a powerful lord and had spent years in China. And there was more.

"Tanba," she said, using part of his nickname title, Tanba no Kami. "I will not hurt this man."

"Um. You love him."

"Perhaps."

"No reason to kill him. He is, more or less, on our side, for the moment."

He studied the sword. She studied him. She had never been able to read him, clearly. He gave you one level of his plotting maybe two, but there was always more. She was his mistress in a casual way. After all, he had two or three wives and complete families living in separate locations across Japan. Multiple identities. She'd learned that much without really trying because the details were obscure. His power was immense because he controlled a major ninja clan. He was a great threat to Nobunaga.

"What do you want me to do, Tanba?"

He studied the sword, which would be invisible in darkness. He looked like a coiled spring of flowing muscles. She'd been attracted to him from their first meeting when she was still a teenager. He'd seduced her and eventually trained her as a female spy. Trained her in detail: 'use your mouth on it like a baby at the breast; make your mouth deep as a well; lick it like a stick of crystalized honey – men will become addicted to you and you will ride he who thinks he rides you.'

"Do what is necessary to learn what Hideo's captain knows about the plot."

"Sessu?" she said, with contempt.

Sessu would take tea and sake with her; importune; leave haiku; sigh and lament; swear his love. Yes, he was a desirable, generous yet difficult customer.

He shrugged.

39

"You are a talented spy," he said.

"I won't sleep with him. I've slept with enough men, for you."

"Do what is necessary," he shrugged and repeated. "The girl's assassination is a critical matter."

She watched his ax-shaped face, as he worked on the weapon. Read nothing.

"I won't sleep with him."

He looked up.

"You are in love with the drunkard," he told her, amused, perhaps. He always liked the fact that she didn't resort to tears. Not that it would have helped.

"He's...in any case, he will improve."

He laughed, this time.

"Improve a drunkard who thinks he's a *ninja*?" Shook his head. "Not so easy."

"He's a great fighter."

"Perhaps. We've had no reason, yet, to kill him."

"Don't find one, please."

He looked at her. Her eyes were intense, dangerous. He liked that.

"Come here," he said. "I'll accept your petition." Might have sighed, she thought, surprised. "I hope to never hurt him." With emotion, she took in. What seemed real feeling. She was truly slightly baffled.

Seven

Later that night at the Pine and Crane

Takezo thought about going to see her, now. Wake her up. Make love. Except she was there, coming across the moon-tinted yard, holding a lantern that winked part of her face in and out of shadow in time with her steps.

"I knew you'd be in some tavern or other," she opened with, after hesitating as if surprised at having found him.

"I'm not the least drunk," he pointed out.

"Must I applaud?" she wondered.

They stopped a little way from the entrance where the sumo man was half-creeping back into the place, his companions all watching from just inside the door.

"Why are you looking for me?" he asked. "I thought I wasn't worth a frog's fart."

40

"Don't overvalue yourself," she advised. "I want you to come back with me."

"You don't hate me?"

"I'm used to you. And I'm worried. We need to talk." He ran one hand across her back and shoulders, tenderly as they started walking away. "I'm worried about what you're doing."

"Ah. How do you know what I'm doing, woman? I barely know, myself."

"A girl," she told him, "saw you coming from Hideo's stronghold."

He shrugged.

"Many saw me."

"They are your enemies. Why visit them?"

"I'm being paid. For working on a *difficulty*."

"Come home with me. Forgive my sharpness."

He kissed her forehead.

"I prefer a keen blade, Miou," he said. "You are remarkable."

"You can be nice even when you're sober."

"I'll make it up to you."

"Unnecessary."

"No," he said.

At her house he refused sake, much as he wanted a drink. Had tea and sat on the mat with her in the soft flamelight in a cloud of subtle incense and the perfume from the flower garden just without. He clunked a pouch down next to his two swords.

"Keep these," he said. "An advance. 10 gold *ryo*."

"So much?" Weighed it in her hand, then knee-walked and slipped it into a sliding panel with a false bottom where she kept her best jewelry. "How dangerous must it be, my love?"

I do love you, she said to herself. *I cannot help it...you deserve someone...ah, well...what can a woman do? My life is not my own and I can say nothing...they mean him ill....They'll use him and dispose of him like a shattered sword....*

He sighed. He was thinking about Yoshi's attempts to provoke and kill him in the barn. Stared at the dark lacquered wall behind her where their reflections were dim, underwater-like hints. Lord Mask, whoever he really was, didn't want him dead; so, maybe, just tested.

41

"I'm pleased you came to find me," he told her. Something about Yoshi didn't fit, suddenly. "What did you hear around the…" Didn't like saying it. "…where you work?"

"Something is going on," she responded. He sensed she was being careful. "Between the clans. I don't know what. No matter how many *ryo* they give you, I don't think it is worth it."

Suddenly she parted her loose robe and, in a subtle, graceful gesture, it seemed to float away from her and she was close to him, golden, nude, exquisite; her perfume a cloud of sweet excitement.

With an almost formal movement she opened his garment and dropped, graceful as a drooping flower - *Jitsu of love,* he thought - and took his gathering erection into the delicate thrill of her mouth.

"Aaahh," came from him as he both melted and hardened. "Oh…."

A privilege, his mind said as he further melted to his knees, a nearly helpless captive of her sweet suction….

Later, beside her on the futon and silky pillows, inside the gauzy mist of mosquito netting, he felt her heated body gradually cooling as she drifted into a child-like, soft slumber, murmuring vaguely and holding him with a softly fading grip….

He bussed where her eyebrows were shaved away. The drawn-on ones were smeared and asymmetric like a caricature of surprise or maybe curiosity.

Adorable, he thought, kissing her nose which wrinkled at the tender touch.

He was tired but still sober so he had to lie there and let his mind run on: it reached Yoshi.

He was pushing too hard…he wanted an excuse to cut me down…why? We'd never met before? Could he be a ninja? Not strong enough fighter…

He stared out the open window, soothed by her regular breathing where the three-quarter moon was just setting through the distant webbing of pine branches that backed the depthless, nearly all dark buildings.

Unbidden, his thoughts went to childhood as he floated near the borders of dreaming: he was thirteen, winter snow everywhere, bitter wind, dark hills, pines and bare trees under a dead gray sky. He was wrapped in a snow-white, form fitting body suit – winter ninja garb. He'd been trained in a ninja clan from age six to thirteen. At the age of nine he'd been told that when he was an infant his low-ranking *samurai* father had committed suicide after being wounded and defeated in a duel with a man who'd taken away his mother; they said she'd died of a fever not long after. The head of the ninja clan had taken a direct interest in the boy and said he knew his father. Takezo had only blurry memories of this man: he was rarely seen and, they said, never looked the same twice. There was a story some believed that the leader had been raised by wizard-monks and had developed supernatural skills. The boy's first response when he heard about his family was that he'd never kill himself because there might always be a chance to recover whatever was lost and that he'd make sure not to lose fights. His answer had pleased his ninja teachers because they said samurai pride was stupid suicide; the idea was to always survive, do your job and succeed in any way possible. Never waste your training. Die only as last resort. The boy's fighting talent was admired but his discipline was considered lax.

That day, 13 years old, he was supposed to walk 30 miles across that ragged, bitter landscape in a day. An adult would be expected to cover 50 miles. He was to follow a trail, marked by seemingly random blazed trees, chipped stones and so on, to a camp in the hills.

The training was relentless: he'd showed ability throwing weapons and with spear and staff. He was only fair with bow and arrow; a good climber but disliked underwater work, like breathing through a reed or using an air bag with a pipe snorkel for long, submerged swims. He totally hated the *jitsu* for escaping from bonds and manacles by dislocating limbs and in a week he was going to be tested by being tied and left in the snow until he got loose. He knew he probably wouldn't manage it. He imagined himself, freezing, desperate, watched by Osa-Kame, a fellow apprentice who excelled in unarmed combat. He was nearly impossible to hold and Takezo insisted it was because he was part swamp-frog: naturally slimy. The boy had a narrow face, deep-cut cheekbones and long jaw. He was a natural bully. For some reason he hated Takezo and (with two others) had ambushed him one recent night in a vicious fight....

As he'd started cross-country, the blades strapped to his *tabi* chukking as he moved lightly over the icy drifts, he made up his mind to keep going. It didn't matter where. He felt strangled by the clan, the rules, the unrelenting training discipline....

He enjoyed things like the woods in spring and summer, watching sunlight filtering through the massed pine boughs into the cool, sweet-smelling hushed air. Sometimes he imagined the light was writing a message on the misty atmosphere and brownish matting of fallen needles....

After 3 days he'd actually covered maybe 50 miles of freezing mountain forest, living on preserved foods like salted plum and miso. While he certainly would have failed the test, he discovered true endurance and could meditatively catnap while walking and push himself on....

He'd reached a road and sat, above it, on a rock to rest, looking down into a valley where smoke from many small fires rose into the icy, clear, winterbright sky above the next steep hill and suggested brush stroked calligraphy. He idly tried to put meaning, identify written characters in the breeze-twisted, slowly unfolding lines and shapes. The number of fires meant a large town – he had no idea where he might be.

A few minutes later, with the snowy hillside at his back, he'd startled a bundled-up, itinerant actor who thought a ghost spoke from the sunglare and blinding whiteness.

'Where are you going?' young Takezo had asked.

The roly-poly, overdressed man stared around in near-panic.

'Who asks?' he said. 'I am an honest actor and respect all spirits, high and low and -'

Then he'd seen the boy's eyes where the mask-like hood had a rectangular opening, which brought his form out from the dazzling background and seemed convincingly supernatural. The man dropped to his knees on the road's rutted snow.

'Are you praying?' the boy asked, standing up and coming down the short slope.

'Save me!' the man cried, then identified the outfit and actually gained fear. 'I've done nothing! Spare me, Sir ninja! I'm a poor, wandering actor. I have mocked no great persons...who would have me slain? I'm not a bad actor, though some have said one thing yet others have said another so....'

Takezo ended up going to the city with him and apprenticed in their small acting troupe. And, like a true Ninja, he'd vanished like a chameleon (DO YOU MEAN VANISHED FROM THE ACTING TROUPE OR VANISHED IN EACH INSTANCE) ...most assumed he'd died somewhere in the snow and let it go at that...a long time past, now....

44

What would have my life been if I'd stayed on stage? he asked himself, finally closing his eyes. The moon was gone. His breathing was regular. *Probably no better....*He touched her hand and she stirred slightly and snored softly. He went on walking into his past, for awhile....

And then Yoshi was standing over him where he was lying on his back, grinning, holding an oversized sumi-e painting brush, leaning down and writing on his naked body while he tried to get up but couldn't move at all...then he was awake and sitting up in the dark room. He felt someone else there. Listened, tried to see...Miou seemed deeply out...thought there was something near the door, darker than the shadows.

He silently moved from the pallet-like bed, opening the folds of mosquito netting, holding his undrawn sword – his blade would gleam; the assassin's wouldn't. He felt as if his entire body was reaching out and touching into the air like an electric field as when you combed your hair or rubbed silk....

He sensed the unseen *ninja* was suddenly motionless, alert, listening, each aware they'd met at least an equal.

He's hesitating, he thought. *Why? Cannot risk failure? So important to kill me?*

Moved slightly and thought he felt the other withdrawing. A sound would draw a thrown weapon which might miss and hit Miou. He kept himself between her and the door, trying to make out any hinted outline against the faintly luminescent night.

Was that he? I think he's gone....

Knelt back to the futon and reached for her. Gone.

"Miou?" he whispered.

"Did he leave?" Her voice came softly from the back of the room. He hadn't heard her move.

"Yes." He groped carefully around to make sure. "He made no sound. What woke you?"

"You."

He grunted.

"I made no noise either."

"So you say. Of course, you are a *ninja*."

"I was trained. I ran away."

He was by the window, peering carefully, alert for poison, smoke, fire....

"I was told if you leave a clan," she said, voice back by the bed, now, "they find you and kill you."

"I've been dead for years."

"Which clan was it?"

"Who knows."

He thought he saw movement across the garden in the faint, hinted starlight. Relaxed his eyes and looked indirectly. Absently touched his ear where the scythe had cut it. Slightly sore. A line of crusty scab.

"Was it Sandayu clan?"

"I don't remember."

He went back and sat on the mattress beside her.

I know little and yet they want to kill me? Do I know something and not know I know it? He touched her, softly, watching the door and window. *Maybe I'll get enough money to find a new way of life....*

"Did you ever have a child?" he asked her, in a whisper.

"Eh?" She was caressing his chest and stomach. "I don't remember."

He chuckled.

"Memory plays tricks," he said. "It certainly doesn't go in a straight line."

"You say you were an actor. Then you say you were *ninja*."

"All *ninja* are actors."

Her hand went lower.

"Are you playing the part of a priest, now?" Smiled. "I'll pretend I'm a young boy alone in the depths of the temple."

He pressed his cheek to hers. Bit her lip.

"No taste for boys," he murmured, automatically checking his feelings to be sure. "Monjushiri is not my saint. Pretend to be a nun." Bit her lip, again. "Anyway, we are not safe," he pointed out.

"You said he was gone."

She seemed totally confident in him, this time, and it didn't really bother him until later. She dipped her head down except he moved aside and stood up.

"Wait, crazy girl," he cautioned.

Still naked, holding his sword, he felt his way outside, inch-by-inch, into the steady, soft din of summer night-bugs. He crouched and faced into the garden, squinting at rock shapes and blots of bushes and the humped outline of the Camilla tree all blended into darkness.

46

He's watching, I think....

"Coward," he said, in a normal tone. Nothing. He felt no presence. Moved around the side of the building. Circumnavigated. Believed the intruder was gone and went back in without exploring further.

She'd put on the dim lantern and had shuttered the window. He slid the bolt to the door, looking at her lush, incredible lovely body, gleaming softly where she rested on the mat, graceful and open. She'd already wiped off her smeared eyebrows, enlarging her face, in effect.

So beautiful, was his reaction.

All other ideas drained away and there was only promise and magic left; scent and soft sounds and immeasurable smoothness that first his hands, then the rest of him followed as if her flesh were water and he floated into love and dreams....

The night was warm and he half-dozed, mixing concerns, alertness, memories and strange landscapes....

When she woke up the sun had risen and the beams tilted in the wooden latticework that closed like an awning over the wide window, the blinding slashes, raising an odor of hot straw and linen. She knelt up on the futon, pulling a sheet around herself. Her other hand reached just under the edge of the mattress as if to locate something.

"Who are you?" she demanded. "Leave!"

A bearded, stooped older man limped into the sunbeams, wearing a spotless, bright, neat robe and *hamacha* semi-kilt in the style of an entertainer, holding a wooden flute in one hand. His cheeks were puffy and his right eye was covered by a patch. Fat, painted lips and a tilted straw hat completed the unsettling picture.

"May I play for you, beautiful one?" His voice was raspy.

"Who are you?" she asked, fingers of her right hand reaching under the futon where she gripped it as if to rise. He noted this as she called out: "Takezo!"

The man laughed.

"He is sodden with drink, sweet one. No doubt unconscious. Consider me as a suitor. I have skills with my flute that will surprise you."

"Leave! Whose fingers will stop," she said, automatically responding with haiku, "the old, bent reed pipe, cracked by the winter?"

Instead of leaving he began playing. She had a good ear. While he got most of the old tune right, the tones wavered when they should have been steady.

"Do you mean to assassinate me with your music?" she asked.

He stopped and moistened his lips.

"You didn't enjoy it?"

"You do this for a living? I'm surprised you are not thinner."

"Let me play some more."

"I don't deserve it," she said, studying him closely. "Your voice just changed."

"I can sing, too."

"And raise demons? I have heard you sing, Takezo. Though the makeup is skilful. Why do you dress like this? To amuse me? Come back to bed like a man instead of a madman. Did you just empty a sake jug?"

"I am as sober as a sword, as the saying is."

"Fine," she said, lying back and loosing the sheet. "How like you this?"

"So my appearance excites you."

"It's the eye patch. It loosens my virtue."

"A knot rarely tied tight," he commented, picking up a cane and heading back through the sunbeams towards the door to the porch. As he expected the wooden pillow sailed close to his head though he didn't have to duck. "I can never leave you unless you're angry," he went on, sliding open the door.

"Where are you going?" she called after. "If you play they'll beat you. And if you sing they'll kill you."

He liked that.

"I'll deceive my enemies," he called back, going out into the brilliant day, wincing blinks.

"You'll madden them, anyway," she concluded, petulant and concerned. Watchful. Thoughtful.

As he stepped off the porch onto the white-graveled walk he saw something sticking out from under the raised boards. A man's foot and not a pretty one: splayed and bent toes. He went over and found the rest of him lying on his back. He was covered in form-fitting black *ninja* clothes from his ankles to the hood covering his face. The eyes showed, half-closed.

If he's asleep it's the deepest known, he thought. *He must be the one last night but...how? Who did this? Why? Do I have a secret protector?*

He pulled back the hood. Didn't know the face. Checked the body for blood and wounds. Nothing. Odd. Poison? There were even poisons that gave the appearance of death, no breath, no pulse, from which people could be revived. He knew about it from his childhood training. It was a last resort for a trapped ninja. The substance was sometimes used in kidnappings.

Makes no sense, he thought.

The shape of the face reminded him of someone...ran his memories...yes...there it was, the childhood bully, Osa-kame.

Turned the body over and discovered a tiny puncture wound at the base of the skull that might have been made by a pin. That was a death-point and perfectly struck, but by whom? And in the dark of night? He had been unable to even locate the assassin, in the darkness, and someone had struck him dead with a perfectly placed needle-thrust...then shoved the body under there? *I must have a supernatural protector,* he concluded, shaking his head. Smiled, faintly. *At least, I hope it's a protector....She's safe, anyway....*

Glanced at the window. She was in it, looking at him.

"Our friend is under here," he told her. "From last night."

"Our friend."

"He's very unwell. I'll send help."

"What help? The undertaker?"

"He won't keep long in this weather."

"So, you killed him?"

"Someone did. Very strange. Say nothing."

"What would I say? Where are you going?"

"To a funeral. I need to relax."

"Don't let it be yours," she suggested. "I worry. I'll tell someone about the body. Just be careful."

Strong woman, he thought, walking away. *But why did she assume he was dead? I didn't tell her...*

A half an hour later he was digging his cane into the roadway, heading up the hill to the cemetery, sweating in the gathering, mid-morning heat. At least there were big, billowy clouds, intense white against

49

the blue shimmer, their passing shadows a cooling relief. This was the hottest summer he remembered.

The ceremony was in progress. He limped over to where the family stood, semi-enclosed by armed retainers and other mourners. Several Shinto priests were in attendance, in pale robes and stiff, squarish, tasseled caps.

She would have wished a Buddhist ceremony, I suspect, he thought. *Just to annoy them….*

The Buddhists and their *ninja* allies resisted the growing rule of Nobunaga and his vassals. Takezo knew that Osan had spoken out, many times, in favor of "unifying the religions before unifying the clans." "What is accomplished by mere violence," she'd written, "can only be sustained by violence."

They might have doffed her head for those notions, alone, he said to himself. He just didn't accept the idea of the maddened foreign lover decapitating her. He'd know more when he found the foreigner. Better him than Hideo's men who'd probably kill him at once to leave Izu facing suicide or war….

He hobbled up behind the mourners until he stood near Lady Issa, Hideo and their other daughter. Issa was not really beautiful but magnetically sultry, wide-mouthed with fierce, deep, dark eyes. Her husband was almost as tall as Takezo, frank-looking with a well-kept mustache. A cloud shadow was just passing over, dimming and cooling the scene.

Two swordsmen turned and confronted him, scowling.

"Low-born dog," hissed one, "get away from here!"

Seeming to stagger, miss with his cane, he fell near the lord, he said:

"Ai, forgive me."

"Idiot!" shouted one bodyguard.

Everyone there was hot and irritable. The samurai began kicking at the crippled musician who just avoided the blows as if by chance.

"Stop," cried Hideo. "Unseemly fool!"

"Accept my condolences for your dear child, my lord and lady," the cripple cried.

He was on one knee, now, cane gripped in his left hand while he produced the ring and held it up towards Issa.

50

"Is this not your daughter's?" he asked.

Her momentary expression interested him.

"How rude you are. Are you a thief?" she asked him, remote, cool.

He noted she looked at him and not the jewelry.

"No," he replied. "A man gave it to me, my lady."

"My daughter did not wear strange, foreign baubles. What man?" she demanded.

"An unkempt samurai. Tall and good-looking."

"Sounds like the criminal, Takezo," put in Hideo. "Companion of the *machi-yakko.*" (Meaning commoners who straddled both sides of the law, collectively resisting official repression. Rebels who actually had no wish to overthrow anything, just improve what existed.)

"It is not your daughter's?"

"Hand it over, dog," Issa said.

She reached but he closed his hand. Watched her husband watching her, closely.

He's a strong fighter, Takezo thought. *Bad temper, so he can be influenced and led by tricks and lies...he lets her lead...and he listened to his daughter, too....*

Which might explain the mother's subtle hostility to the dead child he felt he'd detected. Possible.

The guards closed in around him and she said:

"Seize him. Take the thing. Then take *him* away and beat him well, as my lord wishes."

The men went for him but her lord interjected:

"Stop. Not at my child's funeral. Anyway, this man is more than he seems. I want no blood shed here."

"My lord," she began.

"Quiet," he told her, then, to the kneeling, seeming musician: "Why keep it if it is not yours?"

"The lady did not say it was hers, my lord."

"Insolent answer," Hideo said. To her: "Is it, woman?"

"I do not recognize it." Her eyes stayed on Takezo's face, cold and curious.

She's worried, he thought. *Not handling him well....*

He bowed himself away past the furious retainers who let him pass with ferocious reluctance. As he started to semi-hobble back to the

51

road, the cloud shadow-just beginning to pass over, he noted Issa turning to whisper to the man beside her who'd been out-of-sight behind a group of mourners. He recognized him, long face and scraggly beard.

Reiko, he thought.

The sudden sunlight illuminated part of her oval face in the shadow of her headdress and the top of his high-shaved head. He knew what that conversation probably meant and so wasn't surprised, a little later, as a couple of their men caught up with him on the road that gently dipped down into the city proper. A beautiful view, all lush bluish-greens, dazzling white and yellow low buildings with touches of red, a few pagodas poking higher, all shimmering in the bright heat. A big cloud shadow was just passing softly and unevenly over part of the bay and city.

The *ronin* felt a poem-stirring, again.

What a beautiful world to look at, he said to himself,

He didn't bother to turn as one said:

"Stop, dog!"

"Always the same insults," he sighed.

He kept limping on. He heard and felt them rushing up close, sheathed swords poised to begin beating him. From the corner of his eye he could see all their shadows stretching out to the side from the still low morning sun, the angles of their weapons and arms. To seem weak was another *no jitsu.*

It was too easy because they expected nothing and were not exceptionally strong swordsmen. He actually could feel that.

As they struck he dropped to one knee and swept his weighted, steel-tipped cane in an arc behind him that cracked both their shins with a satisfying impact as he rolled over backwards and away in virtually the same movement.

One cursed, the other yipped as they went down in the yellow dust. The first drew his sword and forced himself to stand. Takezo was sure he'd fractured at least one bone and took agonizing chunks off the other legs.

He now limped rapidly outside striking distance.

"Samurai beating a poor cripple," Takezo said, deadpan. "Poor *bushi do.*"

"Come here, you stinking pig-dung!" the standing one raged while the other sat and held his broken shin with both hands. "Come here and die!"

"I'll die in good time, brave and skilful warrior." Takezo shook his head. "Now you know what it's like to have an affliction other than your unfortunate face."

And went on as the man tried to hobble, bent-legged, in utterly futile pursuit.

"Insolent..." The man was lost for words. He spat and sputtered, tried to run and fell flat, raising a spume of dust. "I'll find you...you will die...how you will die!"

Eight

At Hideo's

Lorenzo Gentile was wearing the clothes he'd been washed ashore in: a loose green silk brocade shirt with puffy sleeves, white tights, soft pointed low boots. An Italian gentleman sitting at the windowledge of Osan's chamber, half-staring out over the immense bay, blindingly blue under the blinding, nearly cloudless sky.

In the distance, looking north across a narrow fold of the water, he could see
Edo harbor and the shimmering outline of boats, anchored maybe a quarter of a mile offshore in the blurring haze.

He turned back and looked at a gold leaf fan on the near wall with a monochromatic painting of a fierce, armored warrior, standing bent-legged, sword upraised, under a calligraphically graceful pine tree, surrounded by waves of flowers and bamboo, swayed by some soft, unseen breeze....

They are amazing, he thought, *in their violent and sensitive natures...I might adapt this flat style....*

His clothes were too heavy for the heat. He was sweaty and felt slightly dulled. He'd kept the sack roped to him when they'd gone overboard in the storm so he still had pistols, pencils and paper and some clothing – the paper had been ruined.

He had no urge to practice reading Japanese, just then; but he wanted to continue studying an essay written by Osan. His serving woman had given it to him a little furtively. She'd said it was gracefully, yet strongly, composed. He'd been very impressed, as he studied it.

A remarkable mind, he thought. *Remarkable sensibility...would that I might have met her...such an acute nature in this, well, unenlightened land....*

53

"What use are priests and nuns," she'd asked, "who retreat to mountains or don black garments of piety and set themselves apart so that people are ever conscious of them? One whose mind and heart has been transformed by compassion into wisdom and sees through this fabric of dreams confused with memories, memories confused with today so everything we do and see and hear and believe is always somewhat false; such a one ought to stay amidst mankind, almost unseen, and wear away the illusions of the rest of us the way a single drop of pure dye can transform a vat and color 10,000 garments...."

He glanced at the gold-leafed, painted sliding door that showed a moon cut in wavy half by a hard edged cloud above a hushed world of pale-hinted, moonlit mountains and a mysterious river gleaming away into forest darkness....

He sighed, within himself. Wished he could have discussed this with Osan. He'd met her at the same formal function as the romantic Scot except he didn't follow her out into the overcast night when he saw her slip away from the gathering.

Lord Izu had requested he come there to Hideo's city stronghold to study and attempt a "Western" portrait of the dead girl. He considered Izu a good Prince (in the Machiavellian sense) and his balanced and regular features seemed to confirm this.

He'd asked if he were supposed to be a spy. Bland-faced, quiet Izu hadn't quite smiled, looking up from his tea in the warmly-lit reception room, saying:

"Gen-tile-san, could I ask a guest from another land to perform the unworthy work of a base *ninja*?"

He'd taken the point, realizing that these shadowy men were used the way Italian Dukes used assassins: with great respect and subtle contempt.

Nine

On the Road to the Monastery

Colin, uMubaya and Nori the samurai, walked in loose single file. On one side the hill fell away into a lush valley where blue-bright fragments of a wide, shallow river, was intercut by dense trees. Rice fields were visible, further along.

"What a beautiful land," uMubaya commented in his fairly good Japanese, removing his nonsensical headpiece, for awhile.

54

"Do you not miss your home?" Nori wondered. "I cannot imagine living so far from my people."

The Zulu shrugged.

"Much depends on the people," he returned, looking at the deep green, forested hills in the distance and wondering what wildlife might be found there. No lions, he was certain. Smiled faintly.

"What depends?" Nori asked on.

"I have two uncles and several cousins I miss no more than fly-bites," uMubaya told him.

"I see your point, black man."

"And there is so much to know and see." Glanced back at Colin who was brooding along, remote, inward, miserable. "Where are we going, in the end?"

"These fighting monks may assist us. The Yamabushi. They are Buddhist and thus enemies of Nobunaga and Hideo."

"Buddhist? What is that?"

"A religion of peace and inner harmony."

"Yet they are great warriors?"

"Yes. Very skilled.'

"A religion of peace?"

"There is emptiness and tranquility in the center of violence as in the heart of a great storm."

"I saw none in the storm that cast us here."

"It is like meditation: while you strike and defend you are still within."

"Medit....?" An unfamiliar word.

"When you empty your mind of thoughts and actions, peace may enter."

"Where do the thoughts go?"

Nori shook his head.

"Ask the moonlight where it goes at dawn," he said.

uMubaya pondered this and shrugged.

"One of my uncles is said to have an empty mind," he commented. "It seems no advantage."

uMubaya was startled as they came around a bend. Nori had just picked a few red berries from one of the bushes that lined both sides of the road. The Zulu had just followed suit, then looked up and saw two feet hanging in the air above his stooped head. Dirty feet with dark streaks that went suddenly red when a stray lance of sunlight penetrated the overhanging branches.

The man belonging to the feet was stiffly dead, contorted against the dark, leafy, sun-flecked background where he hung, swollen face downtilted, the arms bound lengthwise to a thick branch, nails driven through the palms, too, in incomplete crucifixion, the unbound legs swinging free. A dark bird like a crow was pecking at the distorted face that was now partly lit by another sunbeam. The Zulu noted a flicker of flies around the body.

"A criminal," said Nori, indifferent, picking more red berries. "Always severe punishment for brigands." Shrugged. "Near big towns there are whole fields of these."

"Spoils the view," said uMubaya.

"Is there no punishment in your country?"

"The views are not as good."

For a moment he remembered himself on the way to his near fatal lion hunt with the tall, graceful Mer'ce, passing through what amounted to a Zulu suburb of the main ikhanda: a circle of about 1000 huts, fenced-in, inclosing acres of open land where married men settled with their families. They crossed a high ridge that overlooked the softly rolling hills and fields, clumps of almost olive-green, twisted trees, the little semi-circles of the pale, mushroom-like huts scattered over miles of free land....

That was a good view, he reflected. *Strange how memory does not come back the way it first was formed, in steps...it comes back, here and there, so that 100 months ago might have been yesterday....*

"Why did you leave your country?" Nori asked. "To flee shames?"

"Not so," uMubaya returned, shrugging. "I was tired of...of what was expected of me. Maybe. Doing sex, eating, sometimes hunting...talking about small doings every day...." Shrugged and frowned. "Men smiling when they envied and sought favor...quarrels over small things like who harvested from another's field or took a cow or...." Shrugged. "Waiting for war...dancing was good. Drinking and smoking magical herbs and dancing...."

"Dancing?" Nori considered that. "War and hunting and sex. Not so bad."

"Dancing was best. I would feel...hard to explain."

Around a bend screened by short, fat pines and thick bushes a welter of streaked, shattered light and shadow and rich sweet green and earth; then a sudden blast of sound that jarred uMubaya, startled Colin out of his inward reflections and brought a grin to Nori's normally set face.

A short, bow-legged man in black, baggy clothes with hair, the Zulu thought, like wind-blown underbrush, beating a wooden bell with a short stick while wailing something between a chant and cries of mortal pain in a rasping, metallic voice while a young, round-faced, slightly pop-eyed, ample young woman in (he didn't know yet) a Buddhist nun's habit swayed and shrieked in chorus. The din shattered the drowsy day's hot, heavy stillness. The monk's face was blank as an actor's mask.

As they walked the pair kept pace. Nori kept guffawing, holding his hand to his mouth.

"Quiet!" cried Colin. The volume increased.

"Are they possessed by spirits?" uMubaya wondered.

"Ah ha," said Nori, extracting a few mon from his purse. "A mountain monk and his *bikuni*."

"Eh?"

"A nun."

As she swayed, bent and shouted her ample breasts popped free from her loose kimono and lopped and swung which got even Colin's melancholy attention.

"What is she saying?" he asked in Spanish.

"She is like the women of the Spanish priests," Nori said. "As I have seen."

She made no attempt to cover herself. Moved closer to the Scot. They kept shrieking and banging.

"Better give her something," advised Nori. "Else they will keep following and praying for us."

"One of the monks we seek?" asked uMubaya.

"No. Independent mountain man. Give her enough and you can take her to the bushes."

After the next bend the road ran through a cluster of huts and then straight up the hill towards the temple whose fluted red tile roof showed through the heavy haze and dense trees. The religious pair had fallen back with their coins.

"These are good," uMubaya said, offering a palmfull of berries to Colin.

Colin took them, put one, idly, into his mouth, then let the rest dribble from his hand into the whitish dust. uMubaya was readjusting his head covering. Stocky Nori was marching ahead, wide-legged.

They look like drops of blood, Colin thought, looking at the berries that had clumped and scattered. He crushed some underfoot and paused to note the effect. *This country swims in it....* Shut his eyes, seeing her body, again. Her blood had spattered on the sandy pebbles where she'd lain, headless in the wet, gathering light.

"I long for a fight," he murmured, moving on in the heavy heat.

Ten

Takezo was tired of limping and now strode, evenly, back towards Miou's. He tugged the stuffing loose from his midsection and tossed it aside.

That servant girl at Hideo's, he kept mulling over. *A spy? For who? Why?....*

By the time he got there the sun was at noon and pounded the landscape into a blurry haze. Sweat streaked his face. He went up the bright white stone path to the porch and door.

Inside it was dim and cool. Miou wasn't in her room. He began discarding his disguise, then knelt by the futon and looked underneath: found an 8 inch, steel hairpin with a big black stone bead on the end. Frowned and held it to the light. No blood; clean and bright and sharp. Easy to grip and stab with.

What am I thinking? He asked himself, putting it back. Obviously she kept it for self-defense against a client gone violent. He'd heard such things were used by lady assassins and transvestite entertainers. Shook his head at himself. *Miou's best weapon is in her mouth....*

Back in his usual semi-slovenly yet clean clothes he went and sat in the shade of the porch and stared out at the sun-struck garden.

That ring, Chinese or whatever, might be Osan's but... He arrived at no conclusion. *The mother's actions were strange....Now, I have to locate the foreigners....*

Except he didn't feel like locating anything. Thought about the hairpin.

58

What am I thinking? Shook his head. *Miou crept out in the few moments I was around in back and killed a ninja with a single thrust and hid his corpse? Or he came in and she slew him there, then dragged him out?* Rubbed his eyes and sighed. *This makes my head hurt....*Odd that it seemed he was killed by a weapon like that, though. Tried to imagine it. Puffed out his cheeks and blew empty air at nothing. *Nonsense....Am I blind as well as dull?*

Wiggled his toes in the sunlight where his feet were out past the shadow of the overhang. Sort of pondered them. He had no better ideas, at the moment. Kept considering what he was going to do with the rest of his life.

While he was so usefully employed he heard sloppy footsteps coming around the side of the building. It was very quiet – he could hear a couple of faint voices inside, the tinkle of maybe cups or bowls being washed....The heat was draining...the humidity was dense and lay like a torpid blanket over the world....

I don't feel like going to find them, he thought. *I just feel like....what? Like....*Not a drink. No drinking until something was accomplished. *That leaves it open, Miou would say...where is she, now? Maybe at House Sanjuro?* She usually didn't like him to show up there. Not unreasonable. *What do I do about her? They marry rich men if at all....*She'd told him little about her life in the six months they'd been intimate. He assumed she came from a country family though her accent and manners didn't betray it. He believed she cared for him.

A shadow cut across his reverie. A small, unpleasant shadow contorting as the little man bowed repeatedly.

"You," said Takezo, laconically, "it's too hot to beat you."

"Master Jiro," said furtive Yazu, the petty thief and informer, who always made the *ronin* feel he should only be encountered in darkness or badly-lit inns. Takezo had once caught him stealing a purse and, in his sometimes random sympathy, covered for him, returned the item and won an informer and sometimes reliable friend. He had on a bamboo hat and slightly soiled off-white tunic.

"It's cool in the shade," Takezo reflected. "Maybe I'll beat you there."

"No cause, mighty one," said Yazu, starting another series of bows. "No cause. I have -"

"The new comb?"

"That rascal still eludes me."

"*You* won't elude *me*."

"Something was overheard…."

"Don't pause for reward. Your reward is your skin."

"I seek nothing for myself," sinking into a semi-kneeling position. "Yet I had to pay a certain fellow for this knowledge."

"Good. Deduct it from your debt. Now speak."

The samurai finally looked up at him. Yazu was fairly sure he was in no real danger. Some said Takezo was soft.

"Men were drunk at Sanjuro House," Yazu said.

"Amazing news," scoffed the detective.

"Where your woman works, good master."

"Is this your information? Reach some point." He felt sweat beading around his ears. Was getting irritable.

"Samurai were overheard. Talk about a prostitute who'd been killed and one said there would soon be another. Something to do with the slaying of Lord Hideo's unfortunate child."

"How did they know these things? Who are they? Meanwhile, you say they were drunks."

"What a drunken man says, though he slurs it, need not be false, master."

"What wisdom is before me. *Sensei* Yazu, enlighten me still more."

"You mock me, master. Yet one was heard to say that he had the commission to do the work."

Takezo stood up, scowling. Yazu prudently scuttled back a little in his almost permanent bowing position, fetching up partly under a berry bush full of flowers and bees. He scuttled a little forward, again, batting at the insects. His coolie hat fell behind him. He twisted his face from the sun, dividing it with a deep shadow.

"Ai!" he yipped, still slapping.

Takezo shook his head, grinning. Then scowled, again.

"Good work, killing women," he grunted. "Yet, what does this have to do with Lady Osan?"

"This was – ai!" Struck at a bee. "This was not explained." Scrambled back closer to the porch.

"Go listen some more," Takezo suggested, heading back inside to get his pack. He'd borrow a horse; stop at Sanjuro; ride the 50-odd miles to the seaside inn. Maybe *ninja* could walk 75 miles a day, but a horse was better.

Eleven

At the temple

It was hot but pleasant in the yard. The slanting sun divided the bamboo and clay tile roof, pebble paths and neatly swept earth.

The three fugitives faced about a dozen monks in dark robes. uMubaya loved the rich green and flower smells flowing in from the surrounding forest.

The abbot, a big, round man with thick lips and an easy, open smile, bowed and stepped forward.

"We seek help and protection, holy one" Nori said.

"Ah," responded the soft-looking holy one. "The clans wish to capture you for the killing. So much needless violence."

"Yes. How did you learn of these things?"

"Word can be swift."

Nori got it: the Yamabushi's close ties to the threatened ninja clans. The ninja's had the fastest communications network in the country. He had to assume they might have been shadowed.

"Yes, holy one."

"You are welcome."

Colin was scowling as the abbot came closer. The sun gleamed on his totally shaved head. The holy one said:

"You are the infatuate lover of the dead girl."

"I...we...."

"You are welcome here until the matter can be clarified."

"Not wish to stay here," he said in his still uncomfortable Japanese.

"Are you not free to do as you please?"

"No. He's not," interjected Nori. "He is a fool who would reject a kind offer."

Like, thought uMubaya, *the hyena whose mate brings him good scavenged meat and he says: 'No, I crave fresh' and tries to steal from the hunting lions....* Wondered if he could translate it into Japanese.

"Want go back...say my innocence," Colin affirmed, stolid and stubborn.

The Abbot smiled and nodded. Rubbed the top of his head, softly.

"Are you certain to convince them?" he wondered.

"Then fight and die as man."

"You'll die," put in Nori. "And Izu will be forced to kill himself. Wasteful and wrong."

"Perhaps we can help you," stated the Abbot. "Lord Izu has been a friend to us."

Then he went to uMubaya who hadn't removed his head covering yet. He'd been wondering if it were poor manners on his part to remain with covered face.

One thing he liked about these Japanese was their politeness. It was something he missed about home. There, the joke was, if you went to a hut for help getting a spear out of your back, you must first ask the occupants how they slept, were they and their family well....

"We do not fear your face," said the Abbot. "Though we have learned it is remarkable."

The black man showed himself and the monks took an interest.

"Greetings," uMubaya said. "I hope you are in good condition."

"You mean health?" the Abbot said, smiling, wider. "Your flesh shines like polished wood. I am fairly well. I hope you are well, too."

"Lately I've had..." Touched his belly. "Gripping...."

"Cramps?"

"Is that the word?"

"Some food, maybe, you are not used to. We have a good tea for that. We'll serve you some."

uMubaya bowed thanks.

"What does your religion teach?"

"That there are spirits and powers all around us that bring good or ill. That men must cleanse themselves of evil."

"So they must," said the prelate, smiling. "We will speak more of these things. And see how you practice the art of arms. We will be delighted to learn from you."

Nori was amused for the first time in uMubaya's recollection. Something to think about, he concluded.

Twelve

Now

Takezo was at the seaside resort of Mora. The day was clear and the oppressive humidity eased by the steady, onshore breeze. It was quiet at the inn at the end of the road where the murder had happened. He could see people swimming in the moderate surf; beyond, in the offing, frail-looking paper-sailed fishing boats, tilted and rocked.

Beautiful world, he thought, again. *But for the people in it....Ah, I am getting too bitter....*

He left the road and went into a cool ally where he put on clothes that suggested a well-to-do merchant. Hitched the horse and walked back to the main street where he found the bailiff, a sour-faced man who scowled for a smile. Mean, distrustful, petty type, Takezo decided. He'd left his swords wrapped-up in a bolt of cloth.

My life has been like a toothache, lately, he said to himself.

Standing in the hot sun he faced the stocky bailiff who was in the shade of the overhanging roof of his small, official building. The pony was nuzzling a bucket of water a few doors down. Some peasants were doing small-town things; a bony dog was chasing another.

A barefoot man with wide shoulders, high cheekbones and a face that belonged on a carved mask was sitting on a barrel in nondescript, gray and white commoner tunic and *hatachi* – a kind of apron-like garment. He struck the *ronin* as the causelessly hostile type...vaguely familiar, somehow....

"An exciting town," he told the bailiff who tugged his face as if he meant to extend his chin – maybe, Takezo decided, he believed the gesture made him look thoughtful. He had a cloth loosely wrapped like a turban over his narrow head.

"Ha," said the official. Often these men were expert in unusual weapons like the trident-like *jittu* used to disarm drunken swordsmen. This skill gave them a kind of petulant arrogance. "You think this?"

"Dull?"

"Ha. So you say."

Some days everyone you meet might be stupid, our spy thought, *and then you wonder about yourself....*

"I am looking for a place to come with my lady. Peaceful place."

"With your lady?"

Takezo sighed. It definitely was looking like one of those days when everyone you met *was* stupid.

"And my favorite goat."

"Goats in the inn? Ha, ha."

"It's a *shirabyoshi* goat. I dress it in fine silks."

63

"*Shirabyoshi* goat?"

That referred to a high-level courtesan with artistic skills, beauty and talent.

"It entertains me. You should hear it sing the 'moonrise,' song."

"You dress a goat in silk?" He turned around to look at the man on the barrel behind him. "You're weak in the head, I think."

The wiry man on the barrel just stared, expressionless.

"I heard a woman was murdered here," said Takezo.

"Maybe it was a goat."

"Look, I'd like to know this is a safe place to visit," said Takezo, the seeming merchant.

The bailiff looked up at the hazy sky; looked down and then spat a gob into the yellow dust and watched it roll into a dry lump.

"Go back where you came from," he said, judiciously, glancing back again. "You and your goat."

"You don't need visitors?" Takezo asked. "Business booms here?" He looked around. "Seems quiet."

"Quieter if you go."

"Did you kill all your guests?"

"Not too funny. Go away."

As Takezo had hoped, the wide-shouldered seated man got up and padded out of the deep shade over to them, standing on the boards a foot above the road so that the two of them looked slightly down at the *ronin*. The sun angle hollowed his face, under his high, deepcut cheekbones, into a skull effect. A slash had taken away part of one ear.

"Some left," the newcomer said, flat, expressionless. His face was abstractly hostile. "Some didn't."

"Do you own the inn?"

The man just stared. Takezo was sure he was dangerous. He had the blunt-eyed indifference, the impersonality of an executioner. There was a strange, almost familiar quality though nothing came to mind. He knew he didn't like him.

"Go away," he said, without heat. "The inn is closed."

"In summer?"

They both looked at him. The bailiff seemed to gain arrogance from the other whom he clearly deferred to.

"You heard him," the bailiff affirmed, with scorn. "Closed. Everything closed." Made a shooing motion with his hands. "Repairs. Come with your whore goats next year."

Takezo looked steadily into the remote eyes of the other man. He didn't like them, either.

"Did I ask the wrong question?" he asked.

After a long, narrow-eyed look, the wiry man turned and went back to his barrel in the shade. He sat and said:

"Farewell, goat-man."

"Have we met before, sitting-on-barrel-san?"

"I can't wait to forget you," was the retort. "*Sayonara.*"

If he'd had any doubts about the possible guilt of the foreigner this little interaction pretty much dispelled them. He recalled the saying: *The guilty conceal what no one is looking for....*

As he walked back to his horse he half-expected a s*uriken* or dart to come zinging at the back of his head; except he was just a merchant. A slightly crazy merchant. And it hadn't gone that far, yet. If he went back down the street to the inn, now, and asked questions…no point, one of these two would go ahead of him and say it was closed. It had looked a little too quiet in the first place.

He mounted and headed past them, still in the same positions on the porch boards: the bailiff, standing, giving a false impression of thinking; the other, relaxed, head tilted forward, hands on knees: position of readiness, the unconscious mark of a samurai, maybe.

About a quarter of a mile down the road he stopped a one-eyed farmer carrying two big yellow jugs on a yoke across his shoulders, heading towards the village. The man wore a kind of head rag, was very bony and kept sucking at his gums.

"What are you selling?" Takezo asked.

"Not for sale to you. For the inn." Started to walk, again.

"Wait. I heard the inn is closed."

"Closed. Ha. Who said that? The village fool?" Twisted his face, bird-like. The scarred lid drooped over the missing eye. Takezo thought it might have been put out in a fight or for a crime. Maybe this town was run by a criminal clan. Something to look into. "Too busy to talk to you."

"Maybe the girl's ghost is haunting it?"

The reaction was consistent. The man squinted up at him, pausing, not-quite-hostile.

"Eh? What girl?"

"The one whose head wasn't cut off," said the facetious Takezo.

But the reaction to that was excessive and left the ninja detective taken aback and puzzled. Because the fellow darted away, yoke rocking across his skinny shoulders, raising a dust with his flapping feet, as if he'd seen a ghost at that.

"No more talk," the man said, almost fleeing. "Busy today."

He sat the pony and frowned, watching the fellow recede into the dusty, humid day towards the haze of the village.

Maybe there is something in the water, he pondered, *so all their brains are shrunken or askew….*Wished he had a jug of something strong. He'd stop at the next collection of huts and buy some. Most families brewed their own. *I'll have to come back here…and not for the charming company…with their back to a wall they look over their shoulders….*

At the next collection of huts he bought a jug of *shochu* and discovered four men, including a monk, had passed through heading northwest. He vaguely remembered there was a Yamabushi stronghold in that direction; confirmed it and went on the same way….

Thirteen

At House Sanjuro

Miou kept seeing the blood spatters that criss-crossed the rosepale, silk-covered walls as if it were a mad attempt to shape calligraphic characters in wild "grass-writing" style, a message of death across the screen portraits of the women working there, her own image spotted from face to breasts.

She kept staring at the nude, slashed open woman her mind had refused to identify, at first.   The blood had fountained and misted everywhere.

She'd come to work and had to press and twist her way through the panicked, weeping girls and tense, curious male patrons, hearing the shrill voice of the number one woman repeating:

"An angry samurai struck her down…aiii…the beast…the beast…."

"Where has he gone?" asked a male voice.

She half-heard these things as she'd plunged into the charnel chamber.

"Fled. Ran like a coward," a girl cried out.

"I struck at him," another man's slurred voice. "Thus he fled."

Miou, staring at the starfished body, lying on its side, that seemed to be frozen, fixed while running, one arm outflung as if she had thrown the blood ahead of her in some unreadable attempt to scrawl a message.

Why? She asked herself, sick and angry. *Tanba knows...he must know....*

And then already turning, half-running through and around the others, down the corridor and back out into the sultry, oppressive night under stars swollen by the humid air.

Outside the gate she got into one of the closed palanquins that were carried by two sweaty men, tattooed, almost naked, with long poles over their shoulders. She climbed inside, gave an address and they started off at a slight trot, reminding her of the way a coffin barrel was carried. As they went she dropped the bamboo blinds on both sides and sat, thoughtful, as the cab swayed along the street, then turned up a steeper way.

She was thinking about the time when she'd first met Takezo. She'd been told to get involved with him. Though Takezo rarely said much about this sort of thing she eventually found out he'd tracked down and killed a member of a rogue ninja clan that had turned to outright crime - not uncommon during the civil wars that still went on in outlying provinces.

So, her job was to find out if the reputed *ninja*, Takezo, might be in the pay of some rival criminal organization, doing the work for the dead man's own clan or possibly a high-ranking criminal member, himself, advancing his own agenda. Her boss and lover, Tanba no Kami (Sandayu Momoichi) had instructed her in the stone and pebble garden of his Edo house on the hillside one cold, damp, gray autumn afternoon where they'd drunk hot tea, sitting on a cold stone bench. He wore light clothes, they said, even in the winter and though his house was luxurious, liked to alternate comfort with discomfort for himself and his associates: a kind of ninja moral principle.

'Learn what you can,' he'd instructed, sitting beside her, looking at the pale gray tile wall that enclosed this plantless garden. *'He may be of no importance but we can never know enough about others.'*

67

'Who spies on the spies?' she'd wondered, thinking about all the police and samurai, ninjas, informers that commoners said: "stayed close enough to help you wipe your behind."

'We do,' he'd said, amused, getting up, graceful, wiry, catlike and padding several steps over to the single, ten-foot, round pool in the center, full of lotus and lily, the only growing things in that barren retreat.

She didn't get up. Looked at him: slight, relaxed and deadly in his gray and black robe.

'Am I supposed to kill him?' she'd asked, showing nothing.

'I doubt that you could, from what I hear.' He'd stared down at the water where his reflection blended in blurry fragments among the green pads, fronds and flowers. 'You are, anyway, a reluctant assassin. Just find out what you can. I am told he is quite good-looking.'

'Ah. A love-match.'

'It's your duty,' he'd pointed out, looking down as if trying to focus on his elusive form and feature, blended away by the shadowy water and featureless sky reflection. 'No sense being bitter.'

'Am I bitter?'

'Find out what you can, beautiful one,' he'd concluded.

She'd stared at the blank gray wall. Then shut her eyes. Said nothing.

She'd waited for Jiro Takezo (one cold, wet autumn evening) near the cheap "rooming house" where he had one window overlooking a muddy canal in a tough district. It was full of gamblers, sake taverns, cheap restaurants, next door to a coffin maker and cooper whose hammering and sawing replaced, Takezo thought, the morning birds....

Miou purposely got soaked in the light, chilly rain, one tabi off, headdress askew, kimono torn. When he showed up in the deepening gray dark on the semi-deserted market street (that had shut down an hour before) she was ready.

He noticed her as he was walking close to the buildings under the overhang to keep out of the rain. He had a leather cape over his shoulders and wore loose, thick breeches and a buttonless shirt.

When he first saw her she was leaning on the side of a building with one arm, seemingly frozen in the act of staggering – then she reeled

68

sideways (he sped up his strides) and went down into the semi-frozen street mud. Was she ill?

He lifted her and sat her under an overhang out of the rain. Noted the condition of her clothing as she moaned and blinked and shivered.

'Drunk?' he'd asked her.

'Eh?' She'd sighed. 'A man attacked me...I fought him...ran away....'

'A thief?'

'What matter?'

'It matters if he took your property.'

He was on one knee over her. Her scent, in the wet, cold dirt and wood smell was indescribably rich, sweet and warm and he was reminded of lying back on crushed spring wildflowers and being bathed in fresh perfume. He studied her curving cheeks, small ears, slightly parted, perfectly shaped lips and eyes that seemed softly trusting, hinting at some total surrender: all this in a flash impression that included her runny and blotched makeup and two scratch marks on her neck that he had no way of knowing were self-inflicted.

'He took nothing,' she'd said, looking into his face as if to read it.

'Come with me,' he'd said. And she had.

Now she stared out through the wicker interstices at the outlines of softly lit buildings, the gardens between them widening as they went upslope into a wealthy area, bigger houses now often set back behind walls or fences.

They think I am weak, she was thinking, *and for him I am...it will end badly....*

She banged the knocker on the big, round paneled door in Chinese style with bronze characters for luck and happiness. It opened and, instead of a retainer, "Tanba" himself came out and stood beside her on the stone porch in the gentle light of one big golden lantern hanging above the door. She knew that meant he was aware she was coming, so she said:

"You honor me, Sandayu-san."

The moon was down, the stars softly bright in the humid air.

"Formal," he said.

His eyes were still as dark stones, she thought, and noted he was wearing a sword – very unusual. The lanternglow softly painted his angular, expressionless face on the night.

69

"You were watching me?" she asked. "Is there danger?"

"When is there no danger? Why are you here, 'Chrysanthemum?'" he asked, using her work name.

"Why was the woman killed?"

"Which woman?"

"Cherry Petals, at the house."

"Cherry blossoms are brief." He shrugged, moving slightly. Now the light was behind him and his features blotted-out. "What should I know of this?"

"What don't you know?"

"What? A great deal. We are surrounded by mysteries. I detest mysteries."

"She was killed horribly."

"There are few pleasant ways."

"Why was she killed?"

He grunted.

"You press me," he said.

She couldn't even see his eyes, now; not that it would have told her much. He turned his head again and took a step away from her, looking out across the dark garden to the dimly pale wall half an acre away. The lantern now showed part of his harshly ascetic expression as if it were being formed from the soft shadows.

"What can I do?" He shrugged. "I cannot help you."

"So. Do I need help, Tanba?"

"Just go, now, Miou."

"Please do not hurt him."

"Why would I? He has little to fear from me."

"Who must he fear?"

Another shrug. He walked to the edge of the porch and looked out beyond the wall over the small city in the middle distance…the gleaming lights…the stars….

"His enemies," he told her. "As we all must."

Fourteen

At the temple

The morning was hot. No wind stirred. The sun rose and was like an open oven in a closed room. No one had slept well except uMubaya. He felt alert and ready for anything.

70

With three fighting monks as an escort they went out the gate before the sun was much above the temple wall; they immediately stopped because a man was leaning against a thick plum tree, obviously waiting, a small horse nuzzling the grasses nearby in the golden, broken light. He had on a well-worn kimono, bare-legged underneath, and long, somewhat shaggy hair, a longsword slung over his back.

"Are we discovered?" uMubaya wondered.

Nori stepped forward, squinting, intent.

"I know this man," he said loudly. "Who can say *who* he works for?"

Takezo watched them come through the temple gate. Despite his disguise (the monks had re-stained his face and hands to a more Japanese hue) he identified the Scot at once by his build and movements. As uMubaya hadn't yet donned his beehive head covering that settled matters. He recognized Nori as a Hideo vassal and excellent swordsman.

Osan's strongly built former bodyguard reached him first, sun fragments winking over him as he came under the branches and sketched a bow which the *ronin* returned in kind.

"Who set you on our trail?" Nori asked.

The taller man shrugged and rubbed his chin, thoughtfully.

"I am actually not sure," he replied. "What do you think?"

They didn't say what to do except find them, Takezo thought. *I'm truly sick of everything…I need my bag of gold ryo and then to take her south to Honsho province…find a nice town not too big, not too small…maybe teach sword and write poetry…why not?….*

"I'm not thinking," Nori said.

The others came closer and waited.

"Yes," Takezo responded. "You are a Hideo clan samurai. Why would you think?"

"Why would *you*?"

"And I see you have no fear," the tall man said, looking at the group in the spreading, golden stillness of the heavy, hot morning. "Do you have children?"

"What?" countered Nori. One monk, the strong one uMubaya had dueled with, came up beside him. "A question? No."

"Neither do I, yet, I see now that I want them. I've been given some gold to locate you." Pointed with his chin. "And him and him. The man made of darkness."

71

"So you've earned your money. What more must you do for *pay?*" He said the word with a samurai's contempt.

Takezo chuckled and relaxed.

"Not fight the Yamabushi at their temple, for one thing," he stated.

"Do you mean to keep following us?" Nori wanted to know.

Takezo nodded.

"Yes," he answered. "I know he did no murder. I will travel with you."

"Where?"

"Back to the city."

They were all around him now, where he leaned, relaxed and easy, on the tree bole. uMubaya was impressed by his demeanor and took him for a man to be reckoned with. They stood there bathed in broken light and shadow.

"Is that where we go?" Nori asked, hand on swordhilt.

"There's nowhere else," the *ronin* pointed out. "Priests," he went on, "should a man not marry when he feels the urge? What was the Buddha's view?"

The first priest had a round face and a jolly look, with distant eyes.

"Oh," was the reply, "he might ask: 'what is it that marries?'"

"What is it that marries?" he responded, as they all started walking together. "Not the common sense."

This produced general laughter as they waded through the dust onto the road that headed back east. uMubaya got the joke with a little help from Nori. Colin didn't care.

"Who this man?" he asked.

"There are many points-of-view," answered the *ronin*. "Few favorable. My future wife thinks I'm a walking sake keg."

"A spy and assassin for hire," Nori added.

"Those are the good points," Takezo said and the round-faced priest laughed.

And that is how I will probably end, Takezo thought, with an internal sigh. *This time I'll play all sides, be cold as ice...take with "ten hands," as the saying is...no more drunken vows at night and half-measures in the morning....*

"And poet, it is said," put in the priest.

"There's the worst point," grunted Nori.

72

"Yes," agreed Takezo, nodding, grinning, as they marched into the gathering, broiling day. "I'm swearing off it." Rolled his shoulders and neck to relax them.

Fifteen

About sunset that day

Lorenzo Gentile looked into his brimming teacup and saw his lidded eyes reflected back at him in the rounded-off half of his face that showed there. When he'd first met her he'd been shocked that all her teeth were missing while her daughter had a perfect smile. His serving girl had covered her mouth and quivered with suppressed laughter before explaining that samurai married women blackened their teeth to enhance their beauty and wore short-sleeved kimono.

Hot drinks in this weather, he thought.

The Lady sat on her heels across the low table, a serving girl beside her who'd just prepared the tea. Issa had poured it herself to honor him.

"The more I learn about your daughter," he said, "the greater my admiration."

The graceful, long-limbed, aquiline-featured woman inclined her head, a picture of modest decorum, he thought, except for her eyes which, some said, had an icy wildness in them. The effect was to make you very careful in how you dealt with her. Well, the samurai women, he'd quickly learned, all carried a dagger which they used with skill to match any Florentine assassin. He'd been told that, after battles, these women gathered and washed the heads of important enemies to present to their victorious warlords.

"Ah, Gentile-san, we all mourn her loss. And, sadly, it may bring war."

"So I have heard."

"Gentile-san, why did you ask to see me? Is it to plead for your friend whose guilt is so plain?"

"My lady, if he is guilty of this hideous crime then it must come out."

"Ah," she said like a sigh, moving with that soft grace again belied only by her dark, remote eyes like those, he thought, in a portrait of Lucrezia Borgia he'd seen in Florence. "Has not that cloud already passed the moon?"

73

He hesitated…then got her meaning. He was slightly more fluent than uMubaya in this new speech, but still, subtleties were always difficult and these people depended on them.

He raised both open hands to his shoulders in a pure Italian shrug that she understood instantly. He glanced towards the west window where the red sun seemed to have broken like an egg over the mountains into a shapeless pooling of cloudy blood. The astonishing effect held him: the deep, bluish-green, shadowed landscape, the darkening night, the bleeding sky….

An emblem of this world, he thought, *all beauty and horror….*

Three weeks ago
Osan was in her room kneeling at a low table, brush-writing on a paper scroll with crisp delicacy, quick and even strokes running fluidly down the sheet. Like her mother she had finely chiseled-in features; unlike her, the eyes were large, well-opened and showed her feelings, her intensities and sympathies.

She faced the door, the long, low window on her right. Rain was falling straight down from a dark gray sky, pattering steady on the overhang and streaming from the gutters down several stories to the moat. The diffused light gleamed softly on one side of her face, blending it into an almost painted appearance like an exquisite porcelain doll. She wore outer and inner robes of faintly blue, unpatterned silk with a plain white obi cinched around her slender waist.

Her mother, whose eyes were long, very tilted, narrow and (as has been
noted) seemed unconnected to the rest of her – not even remotely so - as if an artist had sketched one person's face and used another's eyes. She slid open the painted doorscreen with the mysterious, moon-shot landscape (admired by Gentile) painted in black and white on the panels.

Issa just stood there motionless, tall, haughty and composed. Her daughter looked up and bowed.

'Writing things,' Issa said, without inflection.
'Greetings, mother. I hope you are well, today.'
'Sweet to hear.'
'You seem surprised, mother.'
'Surprised you paused in your incessant calligraphy.'
'I do not write for beauty. For meaning.'

'How bold you are.'

She stayed framed in the doorway, a dim, huge central chamber behind her, faintly lit by streaks of grayish daylight from high, narrow windows. The weak, soft glow blended away all but Issa's strong, pointed chin and long, slightly beaked nose which resembled pale, polished stone – accentuated by her shaved eyebrows, symbolic of marriage.

'Shall I cease writing, mother?'

Still as stone her mother replied:

'Write until your fine fingers stiffen and drop off. How many read your words?'

'Mother," Osan responded, thoughtfully, 'words have a power to gather meaning and make it solid as a brass statue.'

'Meaning?'

'From meaning, do we not find truth?'

'Or lies.'

'Because a true thing has been formed in words it may live long beyond the one who uttered it.'

'So, also, may not lies live?'

'How have I lied, my mother?'

'If you would please me, take the habit of a nun and offer the Buddha your silence save when holy sutras break from your lips instead of dangerous and disrespectful sayings.'

'How have I spoken ill?'

Osan set down her brush a little like a samurai placing his sword beside him.

'Your father is easily misled,' her mother told her.

'That is clear, else things would not be as they are.'

'You suggest I mislead him?'

'Only you know that, mother,' Osan said, shrugging. 'When my father asks a thing I answer as best I can.'

Issa looked, delicately, at the window where the rain was dinning steadily. The air smelled cool and fresh.

'He asks about the Chamberlain?' she wondered, too softly.

'He asks many things. The Chamberlain seems to favor bloodshed above most earthly pleasures, mother.'

'Daughter, more than ever, I believe you should renounce worldly things. More than ever, I feel the life of a solitary nun beckons to you.' Her mother seemed to be watching the rain. But, her daughter more or less

75

thought, who could tell what she was looking at. *'Chamberlain Reiko,'* she said, *'is our most trusted vassal. What can be said against him?'*

'What is your opinion, mother?' The beautiful girl picked up the long, slim brush and began writing again, not looking up. *'What do you want?'*

Issa turned back to her.

'What?'

'Perhaps I meant why? Why do you want?' Her graceful fingers worked the brush as if she were carving the sharp-edged strokes into stone. *'People who live for drink dance and sing but wake up sour and sorry. Those who live to eat awake swollen and strain their bowels. If I ask them why they want, what might they say?'*

Already turning to leave, Issa responded over her shoulder.

'They drink because what they want cannot be had,' she said. *'They eat from a hunger that cannot be appeased. Do not put yourself between the parched and starving and their ferocious need.'* And, as the last word, blending away into the inner dimness of the high chamber, voice barely audible over the rushing downpour, said: *'Remember, daughter, I am all appetite.'*

The Present

The stained light painted Issa and Gentile's shadows on the opposite wall, edges blurred and uncertain.

"My Lady," he said, not looking at her, "many of Lady Osan's writings are missing. Can they be found?"

"Who can say? Many of her ideas might have been better left in her mind."

Staring at the window he noticed the serving girl going out and sliding the door shut. He glanced over. On the door was a painting in red and black of Mount Fujiyama. He thought the line exquisite.

"Lady, might she have had enemies who struck her down and not the man who seems to have loved her?"

"You have many ideas yourself, Gentile-san." She shifted around the low table as smoothly and softly, he thought, as flowing water or wind. She was close to him, suddenly, her face in the blood red glow, eyes in deep, twilight shadow. "Choose among them, carefully."

"I hope to."

He looked back at the window where the red was curdling into near-black. Was startled to feel her hand touch his knee, hold a moment, then lift away as he looked at her.

"A gift," she said, picking up a red silk robe and handing it to him.

He was almost startled by the smoothness, the exquisite workmanship. Slightly baffled, he responded:

"Thank you, Lady. You are so kind."

"You must put it on. It is our custom with such a gift."

"I...."

She giggled, softly, like a sigh, folding herself into a bow like a drooping flower. Again, the eyes stayed apart from all her body-language. There was, he realized, an avidity showing there, a naked hunger....

"Behind the screen provided for you," she said, indicating one set catty-corner behind him. He nodded.

"Your custom," he murmured.

"Yes."

He nodded, again, getting up.

Che fa, he thought.

As he came back out he was barefoot in the long, watersmooth robe with just his linenshirt and Italian-style linen underwear underneath. He'd worn Japanese costume before, but nothing as light and comfortable as this. His long, bony feet made him slightly self-conscious.

He started to thank her and then paused because there was only one lantern still lit, she was totally nude in the dim reddish gleam, reclining on several silken pillows, smiling faintly, graceful and relaxed, the eyes still detached from everything else, but softer, this time and fixed on his.

She motioned him over without looking away. He was literally stunned by her beauty, wanted to speak, not speak, flee, stay...instead he dropped to one knee for physical and other reasons, managing to say:

"My Lady, I...."

"Shhh," she said motioning, then just touching his hand without having to change position. "There is no danger."

"But...my lady...."

"If I am your lady, I hope you find me desirable."

Her hands were very warm and firm and surprisingly strong and, as her long fingers caressed his forearm, his blood felt thick and thinking availed him little, as Takezo might have said, in Mongol paraphrase....

Why? Was the only thought he really had and didn't voice it. He may have said other things but there was no memory, later...not of words....

Sixteen

Yoshi's Promotion

Rubbing the welted scar on his nose, thoughtfully, Yoshi looked across the floor table at Chamberlain Reiko and indirectly at Captain Mori. They were outside on the polished cherrywood terrace, overhung and surrounded on three sides by dense 5 and 6 foot tall flower bushes, dripping with dark blossoms that, fallen, sagged into sourishsweet decay.

Sunset, shadows deepening as coagulate deep red seemed to actually spill over the leafy tops and drip through the broken spaces among the flowers so that the three of them were touched here and there by what might have seemed liquid spatters of blackening ruby.

Reiko nodded his head, almost imperceptibly. Mori was talking.

"It seems disloyal," he was just saying. "Troubling."

"A calm mind is desirable," responded Reiko. "Great things are developing. The fate of our people is at stake."

"Perhaps so," said the trusty captain. "But to betray one's lord is still treason."

"After success there is no treason. Many silk threads must be twisted together to make a fine garment."

"Are we tailors?" the captain wondered. "I have given my oath." He nodded, once, hard. "Twisting can make a knot no one can untie, I fear."

A dark stain of almost black red glow creased across the retainer's face as if it had leaked there from his skull. Yoshi just looked at him, waiting. The Chamberlain sighed and shut his eyes, as if meditating.

"You are brave and loyal, captain," he said, almost sadly.

"Why do you take this course, Lord Chamberlain?" asked Mori.

"For the sake of all," he murmured. Opened his eyes but looked at nothing.

The red had virtually melted away into the colorless shadows of twilight. The men were blurs.

"Whom do you serve, Yoshi?" Mori wanted to know.

"Greatness," was the response.

"Is not Hideo lord of all three here?"

"Silence," said Reiko. "It is dark enough, now."

Mori was already moving, twisting, left hand gripping his sheath (set beside him flat, as all were) as the right crossed over to draw, Yoshi already striking down from across the table and, like a cobra, Reiko's right hand locked over the captain's left wrist, turning the sword to delay the draw and hold him in place long enough for the arc of the clean, fast death blow that cleaved him neatly on a slight diagonal through his forehead and across his face, dividing him into two separate points of view, in a sense, blood and brainmatter misting over Reiko's cheek and catching one eye so he had to blink and wipe at it.

The body fell backward off the porch into the pool of shadows under the bushes. Yoshi grunted and sheathed his blade after wiping it clean with a napkin. The red in the leaves had gone black.

"Thanks to that drunkard, Captain Bitchumokami Yoshi," Reiko said, addressing him by his new title, "Izu will never kill himself and will be forced into war with Hideo."

"Yes. Takezo served his purpose. Now ...."

The two shadows sat there in the odor of blood and overripe flowers. The slain man was emitting a slight, sighing whistle as his lungs labored erratically.

"There is still the foreign ring, captain. Then the fool's head can feed the pigs."

Seventeen

Two days later the little party of fugitives, three monks and Jiro Takezo, the only one on horseback, were fairly close to the coast. On their left, to the north, medium-sized mountains half lost in mist, walled off the fairly flat valley area they were passing through where vision was limited by stands of bamboo, heavy brush and clumps of oak trees. To the right were lower hills and dense forest of maple and spruce. The afternoon was gray with whitish-streaked clouds with occasional, sudden bursts of light rain doing no more than puckering the road dust, bringing no relief for the steamy heat that left the sweat beading on their bodies.

Takezo kept wiping his face and swigging water from one of the jugs the monks had strapped behind his saddle. He was glad there was no direct sun. Colin was the most miserable being the least used to extreme, humid heat. It added a dazed quality to his brooding melancholy.

The *ronin* detective kept thinking about Miou. The problem of the ninja in her room who'd mysteriously been killed outside kept irritating his reason: something was wrong about it; she should have been more afraid; had she been hiding something under the futon? Whatever it was, when he'd looked later there was nothing…just the long hairpin….

I have that feeling and when I have that feeling I should act, he thought, *as when you think "better move that scarf" in a public place and don't and somebody takes it…I think she's in danger, too…involved in something….*

The road bent sharply through a misty, semi-swampy stretch of ponds and reeds and there was, suddenly, a low, flat, railless wooden bridge over a wide sluggish stream with a sign beside.

"What does that say?" uMubaya asked Nori.

"Village of Ota ahead," was the reply. "I can read pretty well."

uMubaya was thinking about women. It had been too long. He ached for the scent and heat of passion, the deep, thick need….

Takezo was still on the topic of Miou; and then it came clear, like a cold hand gripping his insides: she'd killed the *ninja*. She knew him. She was able to take him off-guard.

Am I mad? He wondered. *Could she…*even off-guard, a warrior could disarm a woman, even in surprise…*unless…impossible….*

Unless she were trained. Obvious. Or if he were in the heat of sexual passion. Worse….*But there'd been no time for that….*

Female ninja were generally recruited from the poorer classes. They were used to target men for information or to set them up for assassination. She was no samurai wife or child trained from birth in weapons (like the *naginata* favored by uMubaya) women like the legendary Kesa Gozen who, in battle on horseback, cut off the opposing clan lord's head and brought it back to her husband.

But she could have killed me anytime she pleased…but could she have killed him and made love to me?

"Strange," he murmured,

"What?" wondered uMubaya who was walking beside the pony.

A few drops of warm rain spit softly over them as they were just entering the village. Takezo spotted a typical lower-caste inn where a couple of old men were sitting on rice barrels and probably scratching for lice.

80

Rice and sake wouldn't be too bad, he thought. *I've abstained enough....*

"Time to eat and drink," he said, in general, gesturing at the tavern. Then to uMubaya: "What do they drink where you come from?"

The Zulu prince grinned unseen beneath his bizarre head covering.

"Water," he answered, "when we are thirsty."

"Water *gives* me a thirst," the *ronin* said back, dismounting, heading for the inn door. "Best for washing."

"There are different drinks for different thirsts," the prince said, following him as they all did. He was weary of wearing the mad basket on his head, but amused trying to imagine what that Masi princess would say if she could see him now.

Maybe 'improves your looks, Zulu'... 'never remove it and I will marry you'....

"Sit in the shadows," recommended Nori. "We will say you are from the islands of the Ainu and that you are a dark one. Who would be certain?"

"Sit in the shadows," Takezo took up, good-naturedly, "and, unless you smile, who could detect you?"

uMubaya chuckled and was glad to be free of it for the time being.

Nori looked thoughtfully at Takezo.

"Why do you want to help us?" he wondered.

"I was hired to find you," the *ronin* said, with a shrug. "No more. I'm not sure I'm helping you, anyway. I'm not so popular. People keep trying to kill me."

Nori grunted and nodded. They stood near the entrance.

"To find?" Colin asked.

"Yes," Takezo said, nodding and tilting his head to one side. "In any case, did you kill the girl?"

"I am Child of the Cat," Colin said coldly, in Gaelic. "We do not kill women."

"Eh?" wondered uMubaya, in Spanish. "What words are these?"

"The good tongue," he went on in Spanish. "My clan kills no women. Children of the Cat."

uMubaya liked that.

"We have a group," he said, "called the 'Lion Men."

"What do they do?" wondered Colin. "Is not the lion a huge cat?"

81

"Yes. You have to kill a lion after letting it almost eat you. You do this in front of a woman who laughs."

"Are there many members of this group?" Takezo wanted to know.

"Just one, at present."

"Surprising there aren't less," the *ronin* commented.

The Zulu was staring into the dull, still, oppressive afternoon where wisps of fog softly curdled on the breeze, blowing in gently from the swampy area just outside the village. Of course, he was thinking about her, again:

Heading north together into the dusk to lion country. Across the rolling, high-grass plains the moon rose immense, red and full just over the sparse treeline. He was looking for a good spot to build a fire and shelter for the night.

Her long, perfectly shaped feet were noiseless on the loamy turf as if she floated rather than walked through the pooling twilight. She undid her head covering and slung it around her shoulders. He carried the pack of blankets, dried meat and water jugs.

"What kind of hunter," she'd remarked, deadpan and not-quite-scathing, "brings meat to the hunt?"

"I am not seeking food, woman."

"True. You are seeking death."

"We will see."

"I will enjoy it."

Now, on the crest of a steep slope under a cluster of wind-twisted trees they sat down with their backs to a big trunk. The soft light was dimming into deep ruby in a world of shadows and hints...cries and distant chittering, insect sounds, screeches and faint yippings as nocturnal creatures began to stir.

Against the dying light her face was a dark, rich gleaming as if her features were being seen under deep, still water and her eyes caught the last color before all was night....

"You," he'd said, voice a little husky. "I want you." Put a hand, without intending to, on her bare, sleek shoulder and felt his heart quicken and desire thicken.

She didn't even bother not to move. Scratched an itch on the side of one knee; then began rubbing her feet as if he weren't there.

"I am in your power," she said.

"Are you?" Began stroking across her smooth, muscled shoulder then withdrew his hand. "I don't think so. It is I who am in yours."

"You are something different," she allowed, working on her feet.

Now there was only the moonlight as the disk cleared the low hills.

"I am a man, whatever you think. I will kill this lion and return you to your people, if that is your wish."

"Maybe they will kill you, if the beast does not. I can never be given to you."

"We will see."

She was now rummaging in the packbag.

"I am hungry," she said. "Let us eat. I think you will need your strength for the lion. If you manage to find one."

He looked at the moon that seemed, he felt, to gather a strange stillness into itself above the sounds, passions and hungers of the world. She gave him some meat and the waterjug. His roundish face was softly half-lit by the gentle light.

"Say what you like, woman," he told her, "I am content here, in your company."

Eighteen

At Izu's near Edo

Gentile was back at Izu's stronghold on the coast south of the city. He and Izu sat on folding stools by the beach at sunrise watching a duel with wooden swords. A newcomer was being tested for possible service with the clan.

The aspirant was young, stocky and strong. His opponent was wide and middle-aged, a first-rate martial arts instructor who fought stripped to the waist in breeches while the other wore a bright red kimono. Both were barefoot in the sand.

The Italian could see, already, there was a relationship between the style and line of the samurai masters and the artists. That was new. The dueling positions had a strange beauty; the fighters were more like dancers than the swordsmen of Europe. A dance of violence, beauty and death.

His eyes kept straying to the sheet of Edo bay, barely ruffled out to the horizon haze….His mind kept straying to Lady Issa.

'Why not indulge an appetite?' she said, he remembered. *'Whom does it injure?'* A point. *Maybe me, if her husband...of course, they're not like Italians...customs vary and I don't know enough to truly judge....*He smiled, faintly, remembering. *It felt very good...very sweet...yet, I was certainly being used...not such a bad way to be used....*

The wooden swords of the duelists clacked as they made a pass at one another, up to their ankles in the low surf. The onlookers nodded and made quiet, approving comments. Izu said nothing. Then he turned to Gentile:

"Well?"

Then looked back at the sparring pair. The bright sea behind the shimmering horizon made them dark blurs like shadow puppets, in mechanical irrelevance, half-eaten by the light....Gentile vaguely thought these things, mind still distracted by images of Lady Issa, her golden, sleek body moving gracefully over him, amazed by the incredible cleanness of her flesh, the sweet, perfumed and subtle scent of her genitals rubbed softly and maddeningly over his face....

She was going to be part of the painting, too, he realized. They'd brought him a huge wooden screen the size of a wall with the surface treated red, as he'd requested. He'd already begun a light ink sketch of the developing composition. It wasn't going to be very Japanese in style, he realized.

"Ah...well...." He started to say nothing.

Izu, watched his man catch the newcomers wrists with an upcut. The *thwack* made the audience wince as the young man dropped his sword.

"Well struck."

To Gentile's unfocused sight the half-melted fighting blurs had simply coalesced and separated. Wondered if that was how the gods (or angels) saw men: blurs hard to tell apart whose actions were violent and obscure. That was part of the picture, too. Thought about the fast-drying ink water colors they'd provided and decided he'd work fast over the sketches as with fresco.

"Your report," Izu asked. "What did you learn at Hideo's?"

"Ah...I sensed...deception there."

Izu liked that. Slightly creased his calm, bland, affable features with a smile.

"Amazing," he chuckled. "Well, how did you find the Lady Issa?"

"Ah...her child died horribly, yet...."

84

"She has a heart as cold as a snake?"

"I would not say that, Lord, I -"

"Would you say her heart is warm?"

"She made me...somewhat uneasy..."

"She is willful and takes her pleasure as pleases her. She is cruel in love but also generous. Like the tragic lady Ono no Komachi who became a nun because of her cruelty to her lovers." He chuckled. "Do your women not indulge themselves when it is possible?"

Gentile nodded and smiled.

"Yes, lord. They do, indeed. Many of them. But men are far worse."

"So women tell us. I need to know if I must fight or apologize with my life."

"You say it so lightly."

"I do not. Even knowing with the mind that life is a bubble, even then the heart does not rush to embrace the dark road. It is easy to say life is nothing when one feels death is far away. Or in old age when the body is a torment and the mind like smoke."

"Yes."

That would be there, too: the trapped samurai in the lower left corner (he saw it) his white robe a stain on the smoke that roiled from the burning earth in a landscape of flaming villages where steel-masked, mounted warriors fired arrows into fleeing villagers...as he drove the blade into his own belly his eyes would be turned to the viewer as if he saw the woman he loved...yes....

The screen has three parts, he thought. *A triptych....*

"When Prince Otsu was awaiting his execution in the morning, he wrote: 'There are no inns on the road to the grave – Whose is the house I go to tonight?'" The bland, oval face turned back to him, briefly, the eyes slit against the rising sun and mirroring water.

"Beautifully put."

Izu looked up to greet the approaching combatants.

"Yet, would he not have died as well in silence?"

"Ah, true too."

"How sorely did the lady grieve for her poor daughter?"

"Hard to say, sir." The Italian downtilted his long face and stared at the sand and tufts of swordgrass. "I think something is being concealed."

"Learn more. I need just enough doubt to let me fight back. Talk to Takezo, the spy. Tell him I need a grain of sand to tip the scales."

"Where is this man?"

"He'll find you if you look for him." The swordsmen were close, their long shadows almost reaching the clan lord and Gentile. "Improve your skill," Izu advised the injured one. "Then come back when you can defeat my monkey."

Everyone laughed at the reference to the famous sword teacher who'd had an aspirant face his monkey who'd been watching training for years. The student was defeated.

"Yes, lord," said the young man.

"Your name?"

"Sanada, lord."

"Meanwhile, Sanada," Izu went on, indicating Gentile, "go with this man and guard him well." Smiled. "And challenge every monkey you meet."

Nineteen

Trapped

The full moon was just rising over the dark sea. An unsteady line of silverwhite made a path through the easy waves to the beach.

A road, Colin thought, *for fairies or angels to tread....*

The seven of them stood on the sand together. uMubaya was a little apart, listening and watching. The onshore breeze and soft surf sounds obscured any noises coming from behind them among the dunes, moon-touched rocks and blotted shadows of bushes and scrub trees.

"There's a fishing village not too far south of here," the tallest monk, who rarely spoke, pointed out.

"Good," said Takezo. "We're going that way, in any case."

uMubaya cocked his head.

"I think we are found, again," he said.

Takezo held up his hand to freeze everyone in place. Reached out, as he had in the room with the ninja assassin, to sense what was around him. Grunted with admiration for the black man.

"You're right," he whispered. "Strip yourself and slip away. Important one of us remains free. "Follow the coastline. It will bring you to Edo. See Lord Izu if I don't find you there. My woman, Yoshida Miou, at the Highbridge inn on 4th River Street will help you. Go now."

The Zulu was already stripping and tying his garments into a bundle which he put in his beehive priest's head-covering.

"Cannot we try to fight?" he asked.

"Can't win. If they bring him back dead with you still free his guilt can't be proven so easily. A doubt is enough."

"I do not care to turn my back," uMubaya said.

"Well said," Nori put in.

"This is strategy," Takezo said. "Go. Samurai care more for honor than success. Foolish." That was from childhood ninja wisdom and his life had proved it.

By now dozen of fighters were closing around them on three sides, forming a loose crescent whose points reached the surf line. The Zulu went straight to the sea and half-crawled into the low waves, then walking in waist-deep water parallel to the shore, just beyond where the surf broke into gleaming foam.

He could hear shouts and the clash of steel blown back unevenly to him. He followed Takezo's instructions. He could see little against the blotting background of dunes and rocks. Moving on south the sounds were deadened into indecipherability by the shifting wind and crumpling waves....

Never spent much time in water, he thought. *Next I am sailing on the endless ocean...a king-to-be in a pretty dry country...now where am I?* Smiled and shook his head. *I like this Takezo as much, I think, as Nori...hope we live to drink and laugh...Takezo stands apart...not like the others I've met here...or anywhere, maybe....*

He half-swam, holding his headpiece and spear out of the water as the moon went higher and spattered the sea with shimmering pale coins and strokes of light. After a time he waded up to the firm sand where the foam traced brilliant curves and curls as each wave receded.

It was beautiful and it held him and made everything else seem far away and dream-like: the brilliant, silent heavens, the stars like shattered diamonds.

Of course, this brought back memories....

He wasn't asleep. The moon was high and round, pared and netted by the complexly entangled branches over them. They lay side-by-side, not touching, on the blankets with soft brush tucked underneath them.

"Mer'ce. Your name is beautiful."

87

"It is a name. The vulture is ugly. The antelope is beautiful. Do their names make them so?"

He puffed out a long, slow breath, as if at the moon, too.

"I will ask you a question," he told her. "After the lion."

"If I am in the other world with you, I may answer."

"You will be my queen."

"A king?" Her tone was faintly scathing. "Why did you not just take me, then?"

He stared straight up at the fragments of the moon that trembled as the light breeze stirred the branches.

"Then you might always hate me, Mer'ce."

"I might hate you, in any case. Know you no married couples?"

"You must say yes."

"That can never be."

"After the lion, who knows what can be?"

"You and the lion. You will be eaten and this subject will be closed."

"You will love me."

"I will sleep, now."

"You will love me."

"After the lion."

She sounded as if she were smiling. He stared straight up. Breathed out another long, slow breath and listened to the cries of hunters and prey and the droning, drumming din of ten thousand insects all around....

And even now, he was tangled in the memory of her long, exquisite legs and arms, her flared hips and lean, long torso, more graceful than a flower in the wind...perfectly shaped breasts, neck like a goddess, rich lips and deeply gleaming eyes as if the night itself had condensed into dark, misty jewels...and, still, it wasn't just that, either, it was what she said and didn't say, the mocking humor and all the mystery of herself that he didn't know...her days and nights and thoughts, enriched by being hers'....

"Aiii," he whispered. "I am a weak man. Enough dreaming!"

Then he dropped in one motion to his belly on the warm, wet sand. The beach was narrow here and back along the shadow of the dunes whose tops were moonbright something had moved along with him.

Takezo backed them all to the water's edge.

"To fight so many," he pointed out, "we're better off in the ocean."

"You have '*jitsu*' for outnumbered?" Colin asked.

"Run away *no jitsu*," said the detective. Nori liked that. "If you cannot run, make it as if you fought one man alone many times in succession. Then you don't feel outnumbered."

Nori liked that even better.

"Just make sure you kill him every time," he advised.

Some of the attackers now showed clearly in the moonlight. Drawn blades beaded silver reflections. He was trying to detect the *ninjas* who had to be there. Nothing of them would be showing.

One shadow and two men suddenly loomed up and the *ronin* drew and struck in one motion in a flash of moonlight without touching a single sword, just the sound of two flesh-impacts, groans and curses.

The sword moves by itself, he noticed, again, almost as if another had swung it. The old masters of the blade had said, in effect: when the technique melts away and one has no idea of swordsmanship, then the blade is freed. The blade but not the man. *Still, how would the blind bird know he is caged if he never tried to fly?*

"Into the water!" he reiterated.

A flicker of moongleam as a *ninja* loosed a throwing weapon that whizzed at his head; he deflected it with his sword. One of the priests was plying a humming chain and sickle and the spiked ball glittered as an adversary went down followed by the round-faced priest doubling up. Takezo heard the arrow zip and hit him.

"Surrender!" someone shouted. "No disgrace! In the interests of justice!"

"Let justice begin here!" answered Takezo.

They backed further into the soft tugging of the surf. The moonlight on the pale beach showed the action in blurry silhouette.

Too many, he thought.

The wounded priest knelt back to the water, shaft poking from his side. Colin slashed and grunted and fended off a pair of samurai. They could sense the fact that the Scot didn't much value his life and (despite all

89

the theory of the *buse*) they held back a little. Most men were ready to die at any time except <u>now</u>, say what they would. Takezo noted the effect.

Not caring, he knew, *adds half to skill....*

In his own case he was, generally, too busy or bitter or drunk to care.

"All right!" he shouted. "Wait!"

They were now in a line in the surf. Four of the pursuers were down on the sand. Nori was beside him, blade bending the silver light like a rill of water. There was a black crease of blood across his forehead in the monochrome illumination.

In the pause he'd created, Takezo's mind went (peripherally) to the great Chinese painter and poet, Wu Li who'd written somewhere, he was sure: "to understand bamboo, paint the shadow of the leaves by moonlight."

Black and white, he thought, *the night is rich with truth....*

"Surrender!" the same voice demanded.

"You do what you are told without question," Takezo called back. "Suppose your lord were a madman?"

"*You* are a madman," came back. Takezo thought he knew that voice.

"Is that Yoshi?" he inquired. "The one who dresses as a woman by the high bridge in Edo?"

"No time for nonsense," said the commanding voice. Yoshi, Takezo was now sure.

"Then what brings us here?"

Nori and one of the priests guffawed.

"Your lawlessness," the voice answered.

"I have a token from Lord Nobunaga," the *ronin* pointed out. "I am a staunch clansman, in a way."

"We will have to kill you," the voice repeated from the moonshadowed wall of men on the beach.

"If we quit will you feed us sweet rice buns, Yoshi?" Takezo wondered.

Nori nearly doubled over with laughter. His admiration for the infamous spy knew no bounds, at that moment.

The leader had come forward, his face a pale blur above his dark robes, framed by his basin helmet.

"No point in continuing," he said, quietly. "I am *Captain* Yoshi. Come with honor."

"With you, the killer of women," Takezo said. "Girls fall like rice to the sickle."

"Never mind your talk. Respond!"

"But I do mind."

"You need not kill yourselves."

"I want *you* to perform *jigai*," said the *ronin*.

This brought laughter on the beach as well as in the water because *jigai* was the ritual suicide of a woman. Takezo was surprised by the blocky Captain's new self-control.

"They want you all for open trial. No need to die," he offered.

With the surf breaking around their knees, Takezo kept them drifting south, the way the Zulu had gone. If they, somehow, broke out, they might meet up at the fishing village. He spoke just loudly enough for Nori and the others to hear him:

"We might be safe. Up to a point."

"What point?" queried Nori. "I think my head is not long for these shoulders, no matter what." Shrugged. "Life is a dewdrop in the sun."

"Brace up," said Takezo. "Now!"

He glanced up and down the strand, trying to spot those ninjas. Felt the day's warmth radiating back from the sand, smelt the sea smell with a hint of decay. Here was all this soft human flesh exposed to bitter, yieldless steel, bright in the silver light.

Except he never expected what came next as he lunged with the others at the men enclosing them at the water's edge. The wounded priest broke the arrow shaft and pushed it through even as he ran. Never expected, as they closed, that the enemy would drop back and then a blurring softness would close around them.

Shit of the 7 devils, he thought, *a net!*

His *katana* was already entangled so he drew his short sword and slashed with force and control – except they were steel-mesh links. They were all caught.

"Humiliating!" snarled Nori.

Takezo next curled himself up to maximize his freedom of movement and minimize his discomfort as the net was closed.

Appropriate, he thought. *Caught like fish....*

"May your balls decay," he said.

91

Twenty

Miou

She was taking the sultry air on the veranda of Sanjuro House. She was weary, bored and worried. She knew she'd been harsh with Takezo because she was guilty: part of her wanted to improve him; part of her wanted him to give her up. Loving him had crept up on her and it was frustrating. The sky was clear, moon and stars reflected on the wide, shallow stream that curled, broke and tinkled over mini-waterfalls under a low-hanging willow.

She was sick of her work…sick of so much. She'd escaped being a farmer's woman and become…what? A sometime entertainer, sometime whore….

A spy, she thought, *and worse*….She didn't like to think directly about some

things she'd done. *And I want to tell him*….

"I want to, once, open my heart completely," she whispered, as if to the moon and star-haunted stream, the softly swaying, silver-tinted willows. "Ah…I mock him, sometimes, yet he is so much freer than I…."

But it wasn't the willow or the purling water, either, that answered her.

"I'm afraid I believe that," a voice she knew well said softly. "But why do you share this thought with me?" He assumed she'd detected his silent approach across the thick boards. One of his nicknames was the "ghost," more literally, "the ancestor," which was a tribute to his wisdom as well as stealth. She knew him as a razor-edged man. She'd told a friend (without suggesting his name) that he made love as if stabbing with an *aikuchi* - short dirk used for hara-kiri.

At first she'd been fascinated and attracted to him. And flattered by the attentions of a man so feared and respected. Some said he had supernatural powers. Her fear of him, at first, produced a kind of passion. Later, there was more fear than anything…so she learned to act and fake.

"Sanayu-san," she said, knowing, not needing to turn. Sometimes she asked herself if ever in the throes of love while he spent himself inside her, would she ever be able to reach the blade or steel pin from under the mattress or couch and strike a mortal blow. She didn't hate him, even for how she'd been used and trained. It was more a reflex - as when you saw a deadly snake while walking through the brush.

"What do you ask me to do, now?" she wondered, still motionless, as if he *were* a viper, looking at the stream unfolding its mysterious beauty and feeling a remote longing beyond any words....Takezo was part of the feeling but not the subject anymore than the reflections or the scented air....

"Why ask that, Miou?"

She shrugged, slightly, whispered:

"Why not say it? You want me to kill him."

"I do?"

"Or betray him to his death."

"You are one of us. You come when I request."

"Like a beaten dog."

He was at her side, now, leaning on the porch rail. She kept her eyes on the slow current as if it mattered: the reflected heaven that (as a child) she often tried to touch. Once one summer she'd dived into still water that seemed, to a child as to a poet, the same as the star-shocked sky itself. Small and pale and naked in the foot-deep rice paddy, the village silent and lightless all around, lying in the warm, soil-scented, soothing wetness, reaching, when the wavelets died away, with small fingers for the wavering, reflected stars, coming up with loose and empty water spilling from her fingers....

Takezo, she thought. *My love...I am lost to you....*

"Was your former life so sweet?" he wondered. He'd wondered that before.

"Your father sold you like a beast."

"Once I was a free dog."

"Who is truly free? Maybe the Buddha."

His voice was gentle, almost soothing. Why need he speak loudly?

"Now I am sold to spying and murder," she said.

"A great warrior, when asked what he thought about what he'd been ordered to do, said: 'I have no interest in thinking.'"

"In what hell does he reside, now?"

"You have spirit."

"Like the dead girl."

"Strange how Toshiro died," he said, voice almost a purr, now. That was a dangerous sign.

She turned and looked at him, finally. He was compact, calm, watchful.

"Why was he in my bedroom?"

"One supposes a lady has her reasons."

"Amusing," she said.

"He was found, they say, in your garden."

"Was he there to enjoy morninglories?"

"Difficult to ask him."

She looked at his eyes. Just glints. Studied the water full of stars, again.

"Are you going to kill me?" she wondered.

"Should I? Are we not lovers? Who would cut down the flowering orchid he has himself watered?"

"Who truly loves what his tears have not wet?"

The lucent water held her eyes. She recalled Takezo's face when he sometimes held her after lovemaking: his relaxed, slight smile; looking at her and past her at the same time. She loved his dry humor and dry outlook, too. For all the violence of his life, she knew, he was kind and forgiving and regretted any hurt he caused. How many could that be said for?

Tanba no Kami Sanayu touched her arm, gently.

"I won't hurt you," he said, softly. "Just keep to your duty."

"Which duty, now?"

"Find the ring."

He knew he didn't have to explain much to her. She was very quick and he was proud of how she'd been trained. Her intelligence and independent nature was a potential problem but a sharp blade might always cut by chance.

"The one Jiro Takezo took from the murdered Osan?"

"Have you seen it?"

"No. He mentioned it. Said it was Chinese."

"Who knows. Find it. This will benefit him as well as you." He turned and kissed her forehead. "Believe me."

"Can you promise that, Tanba?"

"I cannot guarantee the workings of fate," he allowed. "I advise you concentrate on your job."

"Promise *you* will not hurt him."

She tried studying his eyes again, knowing it was futile.

"I will not hurt him," he said. "Though I wish he had never been born." He shrugged. "For simplicity's sake."

94

She knew he also had to consider the possibility that this Takezo might be running her as an agent of his own. He liked to say love was ever a weakness. Even mere sex.

A ninja in love, his father used to say, *is a three-legged horse....Loyalty should be enough....*

Twenty-One

The following night

Takezo was, literally, wrapped in thick rope. They'd leaned him against an inside log wall of a rough mini-fort on a rocky promontory maybe 20 miles along the coast from Edo. There was one window looking out over the great bay. The window wasn't even barred because it faced the sea side and was in an outbuilding. He could see the stars through his one good eye. His other was swollen closed, nose full of dried blood, lip split and his ribs ached from the kicks he'd taken from Yoshi whose orders reined him short of actually killing him.

He understood there would be more to come. They really wanted the ring. They'd let Yoshi enjoy himself but next time would be serious. How fragile their scheme must be, he reasoned, to hinge on so small a point. Well, he wasn't going to send them to Miou's where he'd hidden the deadly trinket.

Or how afraid they are, he said to himself.

Blinked his working eye at the stars because a chunk of them - in the shape of a man's head - seemed to be gone, and, despite his sick soreness, he was interested. Then wasn't.

"Don't block the view," he muttered.

He let himself slide down into a kind of stifled sleep where violent dreams jarred him...where Miou melted her body into his and then eyes, like ice picks, jabbed into his aching mind...there were flames everywhere and her perfect body was burning, charring, melting down into a tottering ruin....

And then he was awake and there were flames near his face, the heat and light blinding and there was a voice he knew beyond the flames:

"Why endure such pain?"

Takezo worked his lips, licked them, and muttered:

"This is normal for me."

"See what you have come to, Sir Jiro Takezo," Reiko said with false sympathy.

"I might have had a worse fate," the battered detective croaked. "We might have had the same mother and been raised in the same sewer."

"Brave growls from a caged tiger."

"I was born in dragon year."

"A non-existent creature."

"As you will be."

"Why did you betray your employer?" asked the chamberlain, moving the torchfire closer to his face.

"Did I?" he answered, wincing away from the heat. "Which employer? I lose track."

"You will suffer much before you die."

"How is that new?"

"You are eccentric. Give up the ring and you will be freed, in time."

"Is that time that goes forward or sideways?"

"What? Give up the ring and you may have sake. You'd like sake?" His voice was soft and concerned. He kept the flames close to the bound spy's face, the heat stirring his shoulder-length hair.

"I was hired by Izu. Or was it Nobunaga. Still, Hideo is in the soup I stir, too." Speaking hurt. His lips hurt. His head hurt.

The heat went away and there was just a glaring violet afterglow of Reiko's outline.

"I give you until the sun is well risen," the chamberlain told him. "Speak and
I grant you relief."

"You mean cut off my head? Will Lord Nobunaga approve?"

Something glinted: Reiko was holding up the golden pass the *ronin* had been given.

"You seem to have lost this," he told him. "Sunrise, anyway."

And left, the torchglow shaking his shadow around him as he went out the door and banged it shut.

"Who killed her, chamberpot?" he called after him.

The only reply was the bar sliding into place outside with a final clunk.

The whole story is in his sneaky head, thought the aching detective. *Maybe Issa's too....*

His consciousness was draining away; his brain hurt and his body felt like crumpled paper. And there was a sinking dread that hit him in a reflex of reasoning: if that Ninja had come to Miou's to kill him, Reiko certainly hadn't sent him. The chamberlain wanted him alive until he found the ring that didn't fit anybody....

And then he was onstage, long ago, a boy dressed as a girl while an adult, holding a sword, stood over him in formal samurai dress, music crashing, a single flute going higher in a kind of agony...and then his head was cut off...he watched it bounce across the pale boards of the main stage, hitting the name-saying seat and rebounding off the pillar of Shite, the Noh protagonist who often comes back as a ghost in the drama...the blood on the floor from the head formed a picture of a woman and he sensed she was dead and that he was, himself, the ghost coming back onstage and now soundlessly screaming, in a spirit's eerie wail, her name, over and over and over until he woke, shuddering in his bonds and there was again the window full of stars and a real voice (he knew it) saying in a shout-whisper:

"Takezo? Is this you?"

"Aaah," sighed the *ronin*, "who's Takezo?"

"It is uMubaya."

The blot shifted in the window, humped-up and was gone. The black man was beside him.

"How can you be here?" wondered the Japanese.

"I followed." He was already cutting away the ropes with a dagger. "One of the men in dark clothes attacked me."

"A ninja." The detective groaned and moved his stiffened arms and legs. "Pleased that you came."

"I believe that," the Zulu said with a quick grin. "He hurled sharp objects at my head." He helped the battered man to his feet, now. "They missed."

"Ah..." He hobbled to the window. Outside the sea glimmered; the wind and shatter of waves sucked away any sound they might make. "I feel...like a cart missing a wheel...."

After the short drop to rock and sand he went to his knees and swayed for a moment. uMubaya held his shoulders.

"Around the side, here," he said, close to his ear because of the sea noise. "There's a path down to the beach."

"Amazed you found me," said Takezo lurching to his feet and gathering the strength in his "belly," as *buke* liked to say.

97

"I follow like a hyena," he said. "An animal like a dog but rarely tamed."

"Ah...the best men are rarely tamed...."

They reached the surf which was much higher here. The dark rocks with the low roofed stronghold were out on the high reef. The ronin, turning his good eye on it against the moonshot background of low clouds and stars, judged it could be held against many by a few determined men. Torches burned along the 10 foot, steeply sloped wall.

Determined to do someone's bidding or for some muddily conceived, selfish purpose, to plot and kill and trick, he couldn't help thinking. *How we waste what we're given....*

"I need a sword," he muttered. "In a few days maybe I'll be able to swing it."

"Are you that injured?"

They were heading up the beach a little inland into the shadow of the windswept trees. The Zulu prince handed him a short sword which he thrust in his belt. He'd recovered the *naginata* he now prized above all other weapons.

"I exaggerate," Takezo said. "One of my few good qualities."

A few years ago he'd been in the middle of a fight with two very skillful samurai who'd trapped him in a garden. He'd been sliced twice already despite his superior physical strength and technique. Having come in a little drunk, he'd insulted one of them in a teahouse and was outside in the garden, paying for his folly among the spring blossoms and swaying clumps of bamboo. The setting sun threw soft, reddish light and shadows everywhere.

He thought this was where he was going to die and he didn't like that. Life seemed sweet as it faded away because all his skill couldn't pry one enemy loose from the other long enough to score before the other was attacking, again. This was new to him. They were too calm and precise without being the least careful or reckless. One of his teachers (he'd met on the ronin road) had said that someday his ability would get in his way and he would learn the truth or die on the spot. It looked like that was the spot and the day. He was tired, bleeding and discouraged. His sweeps, cuts, parries, evasions, witnessed by fighting men and commoners who were watching with general admiration for his style, were beautiful and almost eloquent as ballet; but the step and chop opponents who seemed so crude were about to defeat him.

He was tired as they closed in and he knew it was over. He felt he was going to die and he felt (though he was there) far away, remote, objective without any ideas about anything, without even fear or fury, and he moved, for a few moments, as if he were alone and fencing with shadows because he was already dead and so merely wordlessly curious about it. He looked at the rich, almost tender light, the hush of blossoms and the soft stirring of the spring air in the way he saw the two men ripping their swords at him and it all blended and he moved in that contented curiosity while his blade swept and stopped as naturally as an infant breathing and he had no idea what it might do next...except the two men rolled and ducked back, one already crease-cut across the forehead and the other with a razor-sliced vest and they were, incredibly, kneeling among the flowers and gathering darkness, saying:

"Sensei, we apologize for our rudeness. We hope you will teach us something."

"Can you walk well enough?" uMubaya was asking.

Takezo shrugged.

"We will float well enough," he said. "Have you seen the others?"

"I hid among the rocks here until night. I heard men talking. They said the monks were released on their word and that the blue-eyed demon was sent back to the city." uMubaya grinned, wide and bright in the moonlight. "They said you would suffer and be fed to the -"

Struggled for a word. Tried a couple and amused Takezo whose lips were in no shape to smile.

"Crabs," he said.

"That's it," the prince agreed. "What are crabs?"

"Reiko's children."

There were small boats pulled up on the beach just below the stronghold for the fishermen who supplied the place. Takezo knew the bosses would have to have their *sashimi*.

It was close enough to pre-dawn for there to be a fisherman working by the light of a lantern on a pole that bent his skinny shadow over the pale strand. As they quietly approached, black man first, any sounds they made were blown away by the prevailing on-shore wind so that by the time the stooped, almost fleshless, middle-aged man looked up it seemed a dark demon from some unimagined hell loomed above him, holding the sword-bladed, redly gleaming *naginata*. The man fell to his knees in the wet sand as the apparition spoke in strangely accented Japanese:

"We need your boat."

The fisherman's condition was not improved much by the sight of Takezo moving into the illumination showing one shut eye, cut and swollen lip and cheek laced with dried blood. The man quickly gave himself up for dead and softly moaned.

"You will be rewarded," said the detective. "I won't let him drag you to the first hell and eat you."

The following day the Zulu and the Japanese parted. With the wind behind them they'd rowed the fisherman's boat all day along the northern coastline of what in the future would be called Tokyo bay. Takezo had given the fisherman enough coins to buy two new boats. Since samurai rarely stole money (and had contempt for those who directly worked for hire) no one had touched his purse.

He'd drawn a simple map for uMubaya who was delighted, of course, and even made suggestions as they camped for the night on a beach of pure white sand literally walled by pine trees in a solid, dark mass. They put in at sunset. As the map showed they were now further north. They'd entered a fold in the bay. This was where, in the morning, the black prince would set out on foot in his monk's disguise to return to Osa village where the ninja detective was now certain Osan or maybe her body was hidden. As a monk in the countryside he would be left to himself and be able to listen and spy for signs of the young woman.

Takezo said when he dealt with some matters in Edo he'd meet the African warrior in Osa. He didn't explain because it wasn't logical: he was nervous about Miou. And he missed her in a new way. He'd had lovers; when he was an actor he'd had them like the lucky fisherman who'd burst his net. But this was new.

Twenty-Two

The winds were picking up and there were thunderheads out over the sea so he decided to walk the coastal road and leave the boat beached. The area was familer, a few miles out from the city. He sent the Zulu on a northwest road he knew would bring him close to the village.

Remembered a good inn he'd reach by nightfall that had a beautiful teahouse on the grounds. With the extra gold he'd been picking up, plus his generally battered state, he thought he deserved a little self-indulgence. A bath. Massage. Tea...sake?

When you don't drink, he observed, *blows hurt more....*

It was dark before he realized he'd misjudged the distance and was already in the outskirts of Edo. Without a pass to get through the checkpoints and too miserably tired and stiff to climb walls and swim canals, he went to a gate where he knew the guards. They passed him.

He was pondering the dead ninja outside Miou's room. There was some connection there which took him back to his miserable childhood in the clan.

I did well to flee, he reflected. *They kill with less honor than most of us....*

Remembered his nemesis Osa-kame. Saw his long ax-face, bending over him as he struggled to free himself from knotted ropes during a test. The sneering, teenage bully-face:

'You are weak. Pitiful. You ought to drown yourself like a common woman.'

'Osa,' he'd snarled back, straining to dislocate his shoulder and loosen the bindings. 'I will dismember you, you little frog!'

I did well...can she be a spy...an assassin?

Shrugged it away. Don't take yourself too seriously, consider the world.

Late now, the moon high, ducking in and out of prestorm clouds that resembled fish-scales he'd gone about half a mile along a canal and found the small house he wanted. Two lanterns glowed softly on the porch. He banged on the door and was let in by a dwarf girl with a big head and bowed legs who, after a start, recognized him through his bruises. She took him to the healer, witch and mistress of the place.

There's been too much drinking and getting banged on the skull, in any case, he said to himself, an hour later, lying on a hard mat as the middle-aged woman whose face was dominated by a long, sharp, pointed nose and a blind eye, that always reminded him of a cooked egg, fine wrinkles spiderwebbing her face, was engaged in rubbing him down with a slightly numbing salve. She was called Ri-ru. "You are ever in difficulties, Takezo-san," she pointed out, judiciously. "You should find sensible employment."

101

He sort of groaned, looking away from her and staring at the partly shuttered window of the low-roofed shop where the light was a general fuzziness. There was a composite smell of spices, medicines and flowery incense.

"Women like to tell me that," he muttered.

"Women are right, then."

She rubbed something across his split and swollen lip and he winced and grunted at the sting.

"Naturally," he said.

"Strong fighter," she chuckled. "You always come here when you fall from your horse."

"I fell -" he broke off as she put something searing under his cut and battered eye. "From my pony. My skills availed me little." Sucked in a deep breath. "What have you heard, noble Ri-ru?"

"Strong fighter, better if you go away. So many against you."

He grunted. The stinging was fading.

"Nothing new," he sighed. "But what have you heard, wise Ri-ru?"

"Lord Hideo is going to Wakishi shrine today to pray for his daughter."

"Mmm. That is Buddhist."

She sat back on her heels.

"The shrine is famous for its *chi*. All sects go there to seek holy effects."

He levered himself to his feet, stiffly. The aching was reduced and the potion she'd given him to drink with tea seemed to be building his energy.

"Give me more of the tea," he said.

"Crazy man. You should sleep."

"Have things to do. Give me tea and a prayer."

Ri-ru was already up and preparing what he wanted.

"It will wear off in half a day," she warned, "and then you'll be twice as weak."

He went to the window and peered out into the busy street. The sun's shadow cut it in half. The passers-by winked into and out of the light. In the middle distance was a high-arched bridge; because of the dip of the hill beyond it seemed to forsake the earth, arcing up into the greenish-blue horizon haze.

102

I have a very bad idea, he considered, *perfect for me....*

Twenty-Three

He was just leaving the grounds, pausing in the cool shade of a massive, low-spreading pine tree. He felt the strange cooling energy all pines seemed to have in addition to their shade. Many people felt it as a form of *chi.*

The thing about true poetry, he was thinking, apropos of Miou, a feeling engendered by the rich, invigorating scent of the tree, *you never say I love you or I hate you or show a need, loss or longing directly but through touching on things that make your own self seem petty, somehow....* Touched and stroked a smooth, slightly sticky bunch of bluish-green pine needles on a near branch, for a moment, *These needles are not sharp....* He stared at the busy street beyond the tile-topped low cement wall across to where a two-storied wooden building was under construction, the workmen, in colored loincloths with bright headbands, just winching up a stack of lumber. The hot, hazy sunlight left half the structure in angled shadow. *Not sharp,* he went on, murmuring, now:

"Yet they pierce my heart in the memory of their scent...."

"Sir," a woman's voice surprised him at his elbow.

"Hmn?" he reacted, looking down at a round, lovely face he recognized after a moment. "Ah, so it is you. I'm pleased to thank you again." He bowed, slightly as did she.

"It was my duty to assist you, in my small way, Takezo-san," said the serving girl from Hideo's stronghold who'd helped him get outside despite the massive jolt of alcohol in him.

"Your name?"

"Aika," she told him.

"Why was that your duty? You serve Hideo clan."

"I am close to Miou She loves you...we...."

"We?" He decided to press it, sensing she knew something. "Are you also a part of a ninja family?"

Her eyes told him no more than Miou's would have. They were nice, cautious eyes.

"That sir, would make me a spy, or worse," she replied. "A dangerous idea."

He brushed, again, at a ball of pine needles and felt the pleasant, tiny pricks.

103

"Aika, Miou's friend and companion in deception," he said, "I want her to be safe." He rubbed his long nose. "What do *you* have tattooed under your arm?"

"Tattooed, sir?" She seemed uneasy. "What words!"

"I spy things out. I have the eye of a hunting hawk." He kept a straight face, going on: "I miss nothing even so small as Mount Fuji-san. I detect things as subtly hidden as a festival parade."

"Ah." She smiled faintly, mainly with her eyes.

"I am matchless. Almost nothing fails to elude me."

"I cannot linger, sir, to learn more of your skills. You need to know that Lady Issa and the Chamberlain are secretly lovers and share many plans together that her lord is ignorant of. It appears the poor daughter had unpleasant words with Chamberlain Naruto Reiko just before she -"

"Ran away," he interrupted. "Interesting."

"And now is gone."

He took this in as he touched the branch and shook it slightly, watching the soft waves of massed needles sway as if there was a message there. He blinked and rubbed his stubbly chin.

"Gone where?"

We work so hard to be natural, he thought, tangentially, *to move with the grace of this tree limb...*

"I think you know, sir," she said. "I must leave."

"We are so clumsy," he murmured. "Our plots, our skills...I already suspect she is not dead. You need not hint it to me. Thank you twice again, young woman."

She was already moving, leaving the low-hanging shelter of the branches into the brightness.

"Yes. Thank you. Miou must leave the city," she said back, as she bobbed gracefully, short-stepping in a partial run and was lost in the busy street, moments later.

He had an idea: it appealed to the artist and the spy in him. He needed to confront the main players in this murderous drama so why not confront them *with* drama?

In the end, all men's actions become a play or tale, he considered. *We act these parts because we're used to them...it's clear I should run away to the mountains with her and lose this senseless way of life...it's all remembering and a mere blow to the head could knock me into forgetting*

104

and would I not become another man? A better one would be easy, with no shames remembered...a play, that's good....

Smiled and shook his head. Chuckled. Make them see something in an unexpected way. Maybe recognize themselves.

We don't notice what we really are until forced, he thought. *We live and breathe in the amazing air and notice little about it until a violence of wind knocks the world down or we're choking to death for lack of it....*

He went into the street, liking the idea. What he considered his dirty, bloody life was sometimes improved by poetry and pure sword practice; but the sword lost all beauty once you had to use it.

He headed to the watch house where Koba Taro, a senior policeman of his long acquaintance, former underworld chief and noted martial artist, usually could be found. Taro was now on the respectable side of crime - though he insisted he respected himself less.

*When I come back tonight I'll find the actors I need....I'm reckless...but I'm sober...*He passed a tobacco shop where two men were smoking long, metal pipes; pipes that could be used as deadly weapons by the skilful. These were as popular with the commoners as metal fans were with samurai for technically unarmed combat. He smelled the pungent smoke mixed with a whiff of incense and perfume from some lady passing in a closed palanquin, then, turning up the next narrower way into scents of cooking fish and hot steam from a public bath as he worked through the crowded street: high-pitched chatter of women washing clothes in tubs in an alleyway; laughter of a group of men gambling outside a sake shop....*Get her out of the city,* he reflected. *I mean to do that, in any case....*

Because he wanted her and she was always holding something back. He'd always assumed it was his "disreputable" ways; now he was starting to suspect it was *her* shadowy background that really stood between them.

Too much mystery in my life, he concluded, walking up to the open door of the watch house where an *ippuku* standing outside in black baggy trousers and long, black vest with pointed shoulders, nodded in recognition....

Taro sat with him on the porch in back overlooking a small garden with a nearly round pond, overbalanced-looking stone lantern, spiky, long-leaved bushes with pink flowers and a small willow reflected on the still water.

Taro was big, thick-necked and solid, with a pleasant smile and wore his topknot without shaving his forehead high, unlike samurai. Taro was a great fighter with offbeat weapons and bare hands.

They had tea after Takezo waved off sake causing the policeman to raise both eyebrows in silence. They talked for a little while.

"I'm changing my way of life," Takezo told him. "No more excessive drinking or recklessness."

"A woman's touch?" The big man smiled.

"My life leads nowhere." Takezo shrugged.

"You might have won fame where it would have helped," said Taro, judiciously, serious. "But you chose to serve Lord Yourself." Looked at the water full of hazy sky, swaying willow and flower reflections. "Naturally, one envies your freedom."

"But not the straw I lie in." Takezo grinned, liking him, as always.

"A man makes a choice."

"It only seems like a choice, later," the *ronin* remarked. "I really do wish time went sideways."

"A woman, for certain," chuckled the big policeman. "So, how can I risk my position, today? Or did you just come for my advice on matters of love? Want help with one of your haiku? In danger of arrest?"

"All of those," said Takezo. "But I'll settle for you risking your career."

Taro plunked a tiny white pebble into the center of the pond and watched ripples bend and break up the perfect surface image. Sighed.

"Of course," he responded. "When?"

"In two nights."

"I've heard your name come up." Looked at the *ronin's* thoughtful, faintly ironical face. "No need to mention you have strong enemies among the clans. They say you are, as usual, irritating people a sane man would cross a muddy street in new sandals to avoid greeting."

"I have to make a living." Sighed and shrugged and tossed down a fresh, hot cup of tea and felt the warm rush that brought the sweat out, instantly. Really wanted a drink, now. "Two nights from now, if you help me, maybe I can solve my problems and take a long vacation."

"If you live even two suns," the policeman said.

The tea helped but didn't take the edge off.

No disguise, this time. He stopped by the stable where'd he borrowed the horse and told the son (in the yard, this time shoveling grain into buckets) he'd left the mount in a village; said when he returned it he'd reward them well.

Then he caught a ride in a cart to the river where he took a poled boat upstream to the famous shrine.

Twenty-Four

At the shrine

When he disembarked on the long, thin dock, the air felt thick to breathe. Swords in belt, he stumped up the long, straight stairs that cut through the dense blue flower and red berry bushes. Halfway to the top, sweat beaded and itched on his face and neck while small, black flies clustered around his ears.

He went through the round arch in the low, red tile and white-brick wall into a bare white sand Zen-style rock garden, dominated at the far end by a 15 foot statue of the Buddha.

*I'll just present a bill and that will be that....*Because he suspected they'd try to cheat or even kill him. It wouldn't be the first time and this whole strange business was so convoluted and confusing he couldn't tell if he'd been hired by friends, enemies or indifferent third parties: the more he looked the less he saw.

And there was Hideo in dark silks with 4 bodyguards. He was just placing a prayer, written on bright paper, on the image's round, pale-rose colored stone belly. Incense was burning in several bowls, the smoke hanging, thick and slow in the heavy air.

To Buddha prayers were children's begging wishes, he thought, *and who can be enlightened by wishing? Who can be enlightened, anyway? These murderous fools? Takezo the sot and woman's plaything?*

The men watched him approach. He sensed they were serious and strong fighters. And there would be more in the area. This could be ugly; not like the funeral.

He stopped, not too close, and said:

"Lord Hideo, I am looking for a solid rock in the mist around me." He wiped his sweaty eyes with one loose sleeve. "Your grief seems real and becomes you."

Hideo was fierce and intent. His men were ready.

107

"So," he said, "you come as yourself this time, spy. Without your flute and eyepatch." He folded his arms. "You choose to provoke me at sacred moments. This is the last time. You will cripple no more of my men."

"In no case was it your order that endangered them, lord." That was true: when he'd fought the duels a few years ago, Issa had provoked the samurai to fight him; this time he was sure it was Reiko who'd sent them after the seemingly crippled musician at the cemetery. "I had no wish to injure anybody."

Hideo scowled. Blinked the sweat from his eyes. This weather dulled and irritated everyone. Fingered the curved dagger in his white sash, his only weapon.

"You came here to tell me this?" Shook his head.

"I don't believe you buried your daughter," Takezo said.

"My daughter?" His face was harsh as a bare bone with fury. "Madman. Kill him!" he commanded, then, as the retainers closed in: "Wait. Not on holy ground. This is intolerable. When next we meet you will die."

"Nevertheless," said Takezo, wiping sweat from his eyes, again, "there is a plot within your clan."

Stir the pot, he thought. *See what bubbles up....*

"Explain yourself."

"I think those responsible are close to you."

"Which men?"

Hideo acted like he was letting him sink deeper, the *ronin* noted, but was obviously interested.

"I don't know if they're all men," Takezo demurred.

The next reaction was extreme and showed the Lady Issa might be in the lord's thoughts.

"Fool!" he shouted, drawing the short blade and leaping forward except his guards moved faster and came between him and Takezo, everybody skidding a little on the slippery gravel.

As they moved to cut him off from the exit he automatically went the other way towards the statue and ran up the lotus-seated feet and legs, climbing onto the huge knees, then the massive, protuberant lap, kicking off his footgear for better traction and taking a stance, sword undrawn.

Furious Hideo tried climbing up after him but was restrained by his samurai.

"Why would I invent things?" Takezo reasoned. "I have nothing to gain."

He was hoping there were no bowmen in the retinue today.

The angry lord shrugged his men off, sucked in breath and controlled himself though his face stayed pinkish under the pale, faintly yellow skin poets (referring to women, generally) called *white*.

"Send for archers, my lord," one man with a thin, Mongol-like moustache recommended.

"Or short ladders to scale up there," suggested another. "His position is strong."

Hideo waved one arm. Called up to the unkempt swordsman: "Proof?"

Takezo nodded. Wiped the sweat from his face, again. The air was saturated.

"I will bring proof," he asserted. "When I do I expect payment."

"Money?" the Mongol-moustache barked. He was a tall, wide, tigerish man; serious opposition. He had a long jaw and big eyes, showing much white and bulging slightly like a Zen ink sketch of some fierce, Darumic bodhisattva. "Are you a merchant, man of rags?"

"I work for myself and have no *koku* of rice and stipend from the clan. I like to eat."

"I have heard you like best to drink."

"'Who could abstain altogether?'" semi-quoted Takezo from his perch on the Buddha's belly. He observed this fellow was a duelist with a precise manner and that it would be best to fight him in a disorderly way. "Still, you look well-fed, sir."

The fellow took a dull coin out of an inside pocket and flipped it up near the *ronin*'s feet. Hideo, clearly, allowed this man great latitude, doubtless the clan's reigning champion, Akira. He'd heard of him.

"Descend," he invited, "and I'll pay you more."

Takezo squatted down on his hams, like a farmer in the field.

"Not enough pay, Akira-san," he said, "to buy my services. I won't kill you cheap."

"That's true." The master swordsman grinned, unpleasantly, up at him. "The price would be *your* life."

"You talk like court ladies," Hideo interrupted. "Very sweet. Takezo, bring proof or Akira *will* kill you."

"My anus is already leaking with fear," the detective answered.

109

"A repellant picture," Akira responded, knitting the brows above his wide, bulged eyes. "Make sure to do your business before we meet."

Everyone laughed but Hideo whose scowl now looked like a demon carving.

"Bring proof," he barked, "and you'll get your gold! Say no names without proof. Make no hints."

"Yes," nodded Takezo.

They turned, almost as one, and headed for the archway, feet crunching the bright white pebbles, the hazy sun cast soft afternoon shadows before them. As they were going out, Akira turned back and leered.

"Don't keep me waiting," he called back.

"I long to please you," Takezo called back and heard Hideo's muffled disgust from outside.

"Saying a prayer to Monju, no doubt," the *daimio* said, with contempt.

Takezo chuckled, squatting there, amazed he'd come through without disaster, again. Shook his head. Monjushiri, patron saint of homosexuals, based on the supposition that the Buddha had been (as Shakyamuni) unnaturally fond of this disciple.

He went back downriver and dozed off while considering his next move. The potion tea was wearing off. He shook himself awake and realized he was hungry as the poled boat docked. Stopped for a bun at a small market area and hadn't taken two steps into the mellow, hazy late afternoon light when a bony hand at the end of a skinny arm plucked at his sleeve as he passed through a crowd of women going to market.

He felt no threat but gripped the wrist hard which brought a tiny exclamation from the little man he already was sure was Yazu of the underworld. Who else was so unaware as to touch an armed *ronin* without permission?

"What a pleasure," he said without looking at him. "Unexpected."

That made the nervous little man more nervous since "unexpected" behavior by a commoner to a warrior was grounds for instant death, in many cases. Takezo now looked sidelong at him, holding the bun in his free hand, chewing.

"Master," said Yazu, with a nervous look of triumph, "see what I have done!" Still holding on the swordsman took the proffered item: a golden comb set with jade. "For your lady. For your lady."

110

"Hmn. What about the girls?"

He released him and they walked together now, the sun muted and diffused by the breezeless haze.

There will be a great storm soon, he thought. *Maybe an earthquake to follow as in "My Hut"...maybe famine and fire, too...have we not earned it? Bah! The air sits like lead, today....*

And then in a flash he knew the ring had not been meant to fool anybody. It had been hidden on the corpse by someone in a hurry. Whatever Issa knew, she hadn't known that. Where did this plot end and what was the real point? For the first time he had an uneasy feeling that Miou's hints were real warnings; that this was something very big with stakes...who knew what stakes?

And why bring in poor Takezo? He asked himself.

"Which girls, master?"

"What?"

"You said -"

"The ring didn't fit. Who wears finger rings, anyway? It was put on her after Issa saw her. Had to be."

"Have you had something strong to drink, master?"

"Why do you call me 'master'?"

Yazu suddenly prostrated himself at Takezo's feet, causing people to drop away for fear the *ronin* was about to slay the skinny man for some offense.

"Ai. I wish my son to learn technique of fighting from you, great sir."

"Ah."

"If I succeed in all you ask may I not humbly request this? I wish to serve you as Cinzu served his lord -"

"Nonsense. Come on. You're attracting attention."

But he didn't actually kick him. That was interesting, he realized.

Yazu stood up, bowing, furtive but clearly sincere.

"I want to learn too so I can stand up against the bullies and -"

"No. You want to overcome your wife," the spy laughed. "Or have an excuse to hide from her."

"I swear, master, I wish to learn from you."

Takezo shook his head in wonder, grinning.

"It makes sense," he declared. "My disciple ought to be a petty criminal outcast. I will teach you the two-jug style of sake-do."

111

"You mock me, *sensei*."

"No. I mock *me*." Laughed. "Very well, pupil, go now to House Sanjuro and find my Miou who is called, there, Chrysanthemum. Give her this trinket and say I will come to her as soon as I can." He handed back the comb. "In any case, our debt is cancelled and you will now have a new one that you can never repay."

"You accept me, master?"

"Tell her to avoid going to work." He was serious now. "Not for the reasons *you* avoid it. Tell her I fear treachery. Do not fail me."

"Master, I will not." Yazu literally hopped from one bony foot to the other with happiness. "When I learn this two-jug style," he effused, "so will I defeat that fat Hachi from the inn."

"No question. Hear this: I saw a poster saying the actor Seki is in the city. Where are the performances?"

"Yes, yes. There was one already. Hitachi Theater two days past. I longed to go but could find no tickets."

"Steal, you mean."

"Master, I sincerely love the Noh. These folk of common taste and their Kubuki and puppets are -"

"You are all refinement, Yazu. When is the next performance?"

"There is another tonight and tomorrow. But the one tonight is closed because the great lords will attend." He nodded and clasped and unclasped his hands. "They say you -"

"Yes, yes. I resemble Seki. Go now." Grinned. "Pupil."

Yazu nearly bowed himself in half with frantic delight. He brandished the comb.

"I will not fail you, *sensei*!" he called back as he darted across the busy street into the market crowd.

Except he stopped dead as a broad-faced, stout, woman about 40 with small, stony eyes and a sternly set mouth, wearing a dull gray kimono loosely tied, blocked his way. The stony eyes were on his face. The smileless mouth showing one missing front tooth was moving rapidly. He had a sinking feeling.

"...and here you stand," were the first words he actually registered. He really hadn't had to listen to most of what she told him for years.

"Good news," he interjected into her first breath pause. "Good news!"

112

"Aha. Good news. You found honest work? My best robe has been redeemed at the pawnbroker's? Your older brother gave you back the silver coins he stole from his dead mother?"

"Now, Yoko, I -"

"Soon I'll be dead. Meanwhile your daughter's ribs are showing and your son was beaten by a fruit seller for theft! Good news."

Yazu hopped from one bony foot to the other. Still, she could tell he was genuinely excited about something. She was trying to deflect what she assumed would be another disappointment or a fresh absurd idea of her husband's. Which would it be, she asked herself?

It proved to be the latter as he cried:

"Yes, yes, I am officially apprenticed to a great swordmaster!"

"Ha, ha!" she laughed, the missing front tooth evident. "You're mad. Good news. Soon you'll be invited to serve the clan. Bah! Madman. Soon I'll be dead."

"But, my dear," he protested, backing away into the busy street in case she struck a blow at his head. "With real skill I can become a leader of -"

But that was too much for her. One hand went up, fist knotted. A few citizens had paused to watch the discussion develop.

"Leader of a pen of pigs!" she declared. "Soon I'll be dead and the dogs will water my stone! Fool!" She advanced on him as he backed up. "Idiot! Bad gambler! Poor thief! Shameful man!" There were tears in her small eyes as well as rage. There was hurt along with frustration. "Go to your *sensei* swordmaster Takezo Jiro, a greater drunkard than even yourself!"

"A man has ambition," he cried back, baited. "A man wants to rise!"

Yazu ducked behind a laughing *ronin* spearman who was eating a piece of fruit, bright sun glinting on his weapon's tip.

"Oh, how you will rise," she prophesied, gap-tooth winking. "You will be crucified on a tall pole!" He was already half-running to general laughter, feet slapping up the dust. "Worthless coward!" was her final opinion as he ducked into the shadow of the opposite street. She was crying, now, standing, shaking a little, shielding her eyes from the sun with one chapped, big-fingered hand.

Takezo went to his quarters. It was sunset and the small, second-floor room was full of soft, haunting rose-tinted light that made a square on the white wall. The shadow of a pine branch was projected there in a soft blur of needle-clumps and knottings and, for the moment, was as still and breathless as a painting….

Looking there, he felt a strange, deep, almost-longing – a longing for something he couldn't identify much less express – a feeling that flowed neither forward nor back: like a warm summer evening in childhood, the promise of rich, mysterious, unending life like a hush within and without…an outline from some world beyond the world.

He thought about her. With Miou, for the first time, no women from the past arose in his mind, as the Buddha might put it. She filled something that had long, long been empty; something that the boy dreams of and the man forgets….

Some things, maybe, children see before their eyes are ruined by seeing too much, he thought.

He sighed and opened the closet door and went back to the dull process before him. The almost imperceptibly deepening tinted light seemed to be sucked into the racks of clothing he kept there for disguises.

He had to stir things up.

Maybe I'll get paid, he said to himself as he picked out some very special clothes from his acting days.

He stepped outside to look at the deep fire of the sunset above the hills where the buildings were submerged in dimly glimmering shadow under an incredibly lyric, looping line of rose-white and dark clouds that crossed the entire sky.

There was a voice below him in the vegetable garden under his window. And the vague figure he knew was Taro, the policeman, stood there, looking up. His normal, strange life was back, again.

"Takezo," he called.

"Yes?"

"I have the actors you requested."

He could see them, two blurry forms well behind Taro in the rising tide of twilight. There was a sound of crickets and the trill of a bird in the solid obscurity of trees that lined the road. There was a rich smell of earth and ripening. The wet heat was steady.

"Good," he said. "I have the play."

By the time they got to the theater the sky was blanked by clouds with flickers of distant lightning, the faint thunder booming over the sea. He'd shaved his hair and darkened his eyebrows to look more like Seki and, under his peasant-style straw raincoat he had on an actor's robe and sash. His face was masked by a drooping hat and hanging cloth.

The air was leaden and almost stifling. Now and then a few big drops would spatter the street and low-roofed buildings. The four of them ducked into the alley between the theater and a busy teahouse and went around to the actor's entrance. Bodyguards for the nobles inside would be posted at the front and in the theater space itself.

"You better have authority, as you claim," Taro said, grimly amused, "or I'll be sleeping in a ditch and begging for rice."

There was one six-foot doorkeeper in back with high cheekbones, wide shoulders and squinty eyes. He reminded Takezo of the description of the murderer turned Buddhist monk in the "Three Priests" story where it's revealed that he'd murdered his companion's young lover for her clothes and lustrous, long hair. The big-headed young man looked bored, eating a bun and staring at the incoming lightning.

The saturated, heavy air made Takezo feel he was almost swimming up the two steps to the door. The laconic, lad, still chewing a bite, peered at him.

"Cannot go in here," he said in an unpleasant voice. The effort of speech seemed to make him yawn.

The *ronin* shrugged off his straw coat and flipped back his hat on the string, exposing his subtlely made-up face in the soft, uncertain, shadowy glow.

"Cannot?" he wondered.

"Excuse me!" the boy said, standing and bowing as Takezo and his companions went on past him into a corridor where he could enter the "mirror-room" unseen; the main door from there led directly onto the covered "bridge" to the stage, itself. One of the plays was underway and there were only three actors and two female assistants inside. One girl was preparing refreshments. The men were preparing for the farce that followed the formal drama. They were shocked to see him and his companions.

"Master," one actor, small and intense, dressed as a servant, said, "how can you be here?"

"I should have remained on the stage," Takezo said, reflective, looking around with pleasure.

"Of course," the second actor said, in disbelief. He was tall, thin, with a long and comical nose – his own.

115

"What a life I might have had as an actor." Let out a sigh of breath. The others looked nonplussed.

"You just were called "master,'" pointed-out the Buddha-bodied Sakura, already putting on a samurai outfit while graceful and delicate Rensai took up a woman's gown and a female middle-aged mask.

"Master?" the one with the nose inquired.

"What praise and admiration might have been mine," continued Takezo.

"Or what groans and catcalls," suggested Rensai, observing himself in the mirror, flouncing his hips, a little.

"You are almost a woman, anyway," darkly observed his fellow actor while the solid *ippukki*, Taro, grinned and seated himself before a mirror, pretending to preen.

"Meet me later in the garden," he offered. "I'll compose a haiku while you sing."

"This is not Seki unless it's a spiritual manifestation," said the woman not making tea. She was petite with smiling eyes. "I hear his sweet voice even now on the stage."

"Taro will protect you," Takezo said, absently, "while we give a brief performance." Looked at her. "Bring sake," he ordered.

"Who are you?" asked the long-nosed actor. "His brother?"

"I think this may be an assassination," said the other man, uneasy, sweaty.

Outside the thunder was closer and the booms clear though the heavy air remained dead and still. The girl handed Takezo and then Taro a square wooden cupful of wine. The others demurred.

"This is theater," declared the detective, emptying his. "We risk only displeasing the great lords with our poor play."

"As I thought," said long-nose, "a foolishly ambitious playwright." Shook his head. "I think you will suffer for this."

"I suffer already," said Takezo. "What's one more nail to a crucified man?"

"Ready," said Taro. "Hope you know your lines."

"We'll be fine. Just follow my lead. Improvise."

"Improvise Noh?" ejaculated the startled long-nose. "Impossible! You'll be exposed in the streets and beaten," he prophesied.

"They won't get violent," Rensai said, assuringly, "until he sings."

116

"You too?" said Takezo. "Musical taste is lost." He'd been listening to the play and knew the actors would now be leaving the stage through the rear "quick door" and, so: "Come on."

They followed him out onto the "bridge" that led to the main stage. It was walled off from the audience by a fine-meshed set of screens with two pines painted on it. You could see through it but only a featureless, blurry image showed.

He had a moment of nostalgia, at the sight of the red-lacquered pillars supporting the roof of the stage, the gleaming floorboards, the scents and sounds....

The audience came to attention as they emerged. The chorus and musicians (seated along the stage left) looked baffled as Takezo stopped and dropped a sack of coins, requesting them to play some well-known accompaniment music before taking his place stage rear off the bridge, at Shite's pillar. The 'woman' and the samurai with a demon facemask went front and left.

"We beg your indulgence," Takezo declared. "Something just for the great lords here present."

Takezo began to dance, falling right back into the slow, exaggeratedly graceful movements that had been his stage strength. The unsure but well-tipped musicians came in with a rattle and bang of drums plus a long, wavering, high-pitched, keening string note. Then he broke into semi-spoken singing:

"I am Lord Ill-temper, known to be honest and feared in battle. I am coming home from the wars where I fought beside the great lord 'Uniter,' who seeks calm and order in the land even if all must die to achieve it."

There was a stir in the audience at this. The musicians paused.

"What play is this?" someone called out.

"Is this the farce?" from another.

"I am the manager!" cried the manager from the audience where retainers were visible sitting on their heels in neat rows. "Are you ill, Seki? What happened to your voice? What is this? Stop at once!"

"Unheard-of, this talking," someone in the chorus wearing a gold robe just offstage right, shout-whispered to the man beside him in red and black.

Takezo heard a brief commotion and voices back in the "mirror room." By now the real Seki and then others had been cautioned into calm by the formidable Taro.

"No," said a commanding voice in the audience. "Let it continue."

"I am the wife of Ill-temper," spoke-sang Rensai. "We are forbidden lovers. My husband will soon be back. This is his trusted vassal, Chamberlain Pot. We have great ambition. What matter that the world is transient as a cherry blossom in May? The commoner may go to a birth in hell as surely as a noble. Better to drink good wine for one day than sour sake for life."

The devil-faced samurai embraced her.

"Fairest lady, our plans are laid. Our once hard daimio has been softened by peace and watery counsel. A samurai woman must be steel as polished as her man. Like the great Kesa Gozen, herself. Together we will control the clan for war and victory! We will unseat the upstart, "Uniter." First chaos, then our order!"

"Yet I fear my child had revealed suspicions to her father before she fled this great castle and took, in seeming disguise, to the outcast road. Only to be slain, her poor body found unrecognizable. Ah, my eyes burn to weep and yet stay dry for I am out of tears. I dread to think what evil rebirths await me!"

"We have agreed," expressed portly Sakura behind his snarling mask, embracing Rensai, again, "we must be cold and sharp as a blade from the 3 smiths of Bizen. What men call treachery is applauded when success is won!"

"That's an ill line," hissed Takezo under his breath. "Don't be so flowery!"

"Yes," responded Rensai as the wife. "Flowers are sweet but a samurai woman must have spiky thorns. "Uniter" who would eclipse us all must, himself, be darkened."

"You too," Takezo whispered. "Keep to the point!"

The chorus could hear his interjections and gold robe commented, with scorn:

"If part of a fish is bad throw out the whole."

"Still," demurred his red and black companion, "it has a certain literary style, I think."

"Bad fish style?" wondered the first.

"Imprison my husband but do not slay him," Rensai went on. "Later he may approve our deeds."

"Or, if things go badly, we can lay the blame on his orders," put in Sakura.

Not a bad point, thought Takezo, whispering:

"He's back!"

"I hear his voice in the garden," Rensai reacted, hand to ear. "I must await him within."

She moved stage left to Waki's pillar and froze. Takezo danced upstage.

"I am home," he explained, looking around. "On the road I met a priest who said: 'If the poor complain of poverty; if the rich rejoice in wealth, both are doomed to evil rebirths.' I mean to renounce this empty life. I will lay aside all ambition and pass the clan on to my chamberlain since my daughter is now dead and I have no son." He made formal gestures of weeping. Then noticed Sakura. "Chamberlain, where is my wife?"

"In her quarters, my lord. Welcome home."

"I would see you both. I want no more war. No more blood. There is no end to it. Lord 'Uniter' is pitiless but he is the best plug in a sinking boat."

And the commanding voice from the audience, again:

"Well put, actor."

Then Sakura stabbed his lord from behind with his short sword.

"I am slain," Lord Ill-temper cried, falling, as gracefully as he could. "Base treachery!"

It was mostly improvisation anyway; the semi-rehearsed material had been lost in the new turnings that developed. Takezo hadn't expected to get this far without some violent confrontation.

"As you fall into unending darkness," melodramatically added Sakura, "know that your child lives and is in my power! Know that the clan is mine as is your wife!"

"He wouldn't say that," hissed Takezo, under his breath. "This isn't a puppet show." Then, loud enough for the audience: "All grows dark...curse you, villain...may you be reborn as a jellyfish...aiii...I die...."

119

A commotion in the seats that wasn't approval crashed forward and then Chamberlain Reiko and master swordsman Akira leaped onto the stage as one, swords drawn.

"Kill him!" yelled Reiko, slashing at Takezo who glided backwards and pulled a silken hanging down over the raging chamberlain as Rensai and Sakura fled.

"The acting wasn't *that* bad," Takezo said, grinning, circling, watching the lean, wide swordsmaster, Akira, approach. "Anyway, Reiko, your shames are known."

Akira took one long swipe and, in the same blur, Takezo countered and shifted, then both stopped and stood there, thoughtful because when the *ronin* detective wiped his sleeve across his sweaty forehead it came away streaked with blood while the other, touching his ribcage through the slashed, baggy fabric, discovered he was bleeding a little, too. Nodded, impressed. Scratched around his drooping Mongol-like moustache with one finger.

"Enough!" called the authoritative voice from the audience as Hideo now stepped up onto the stage, squinting at Takezo.

"Akira," Hideo ordered, "step away." Peered closer. "*You* are Seki?"

"Ha," put in gold-robe from stage left, "this hack has no more *yugen* than a mouse has money. An imitator."

"The play was getting interesting," his fellow in red and black said.

"You are like a blind man praising a painting by touching the paper," the other responded. No one else was paying attention to them.

Reiko, disentangled now, had to just stand there: furious, sweaty, pop-eyed, flushed as his self-control was gradually restored and his face became a mask, again. Takezo realized the lord they all deferred to had to be Nobunaga or his right hand general Hideyoshi. He came up close to the stage without mounting it. Then the thick, mustached, features of the famous warlord looked flatly at him. His expression was about like the metal faceplate, the detective assumed he'd worn at the barn meeting, except fiercer. Takezo knew that in battle this warlord wore European plate armor.

"Give back what you stole, please," Reiko recommended.

Takezo, man of the theater, sheathed his blade. Rensai and Sakura worked their way, quietly, back to the bridge, shedding their costumes as they went.

"You found the foreigners," the warlord said. "Where are they?"

He didn't remember the voice but it had been muffled by the mask.

"Ask chamberlain Reiko, my lord," the detective answered.

"You deranged, drunken outcast," said Reiko. "Robber of the dead. Who will heed your mad words?"

Akira laughed, Hideo started to speak and the various actors, coming out of the mirror-room started asking questions.

"May I continue, honored chamberlain?" requested Nobunaga, very quietly which silenced everyone better than a blow from a club. "Sir, I doubt your play will bring you great applause. Was it needed? Why not have spoken frankly?"

"I tried that, my lord," the *ronin* answered, looking at Hideo.

"This play is excrement," said that lord. "What does it signify?"

"A stench. Ask Chamberlain Reiko," the detective suggested, again, with a jerk of his head. "Or sniff him."

"Insolent outcast!" exclaimed Reiko. "I will kill you myself."

"Quiet," said Nobunaga. "I am certain it is merely an attempt at art. Not likely to offend any but the discerning critic."

"A fool could see it is excrement," Hideo repeated.

"I needed you all to listen," Takezo said, noting, peripherally, the gauzy shadows of Seki and the others on the bridge. "Look, that foreign ring was put on the corpse supposed to be Osan. The question: why? What has become of her? If dead, where is her body?"

"Enough questions," said Hideo. "I warned you once, come back with answers or stay away forever."

"Give back the ring, then, or remain a thief," Reiko said.

"Maybe I don't have it, Chamberlain," Takezo pointed out. "Anyway, it didn't fit. Nothing fits." Takezo bowed, deeply, for once. "Please preserve the foreigners, if that is still possible," he requested. "I think a trial may free Lord Izu of any shame."

"We all wish to keep the peace," declared Nobunaga.

"No matter how much war it takes," Takezo added.

"Pretty true," Nobunaga laughed. To Hideo: "Where is the fire-haired foreigner?"

"Gone," answered Reiko. "Freed or escaped. My men are looking for him and the black demon."

"Do you think she's alive?" the warlord asked Takezo.

"I only know she was not the one buried in the cemetery of Achi hill."

"Who was buried, then?" asked Hideo, trying to take it all in.

The detective shrugged.

"A *shirabyoshi* or maybe just an unlicensed whore," he said, thoughtfully.

"Like your lover," Reiko put in, face utterly still and almost friendly, now.

A threat? Takezo asked himself. *I walk on a sword edge under a sky of arrows, anyway....*

The great lord gestured and Takezo came close to him, faces inches apart. He seemed human enough to the detective though his face was set like stone.

"You claim a token from me, actor. Important to know who gave it to you."

"You did not, lord?"

"I did not."

A high-ranking member of Nobunaga's entourage had come up and whispered in his ear. He turned and started to leave at once.

"'Uniter' has to leave," he said, over his shoulder. "My apologies to Seki and his troupe."

Behind him Takezo heard Seki's voice:

"Resemble *me*? Fools! The performance is in tatters!"

The relatively favorable critic from the chorus called over to the *ronin* as he was heading back to the bridge past Seki and the other actors – Taro had wisely chosen to wait inside the mirror room.

"How does it end? Disappointing not to know."

"Bah," said his companion. "What matter? A journey begun on a bad horse ends on a bad horse."

"The swordplay wasn't too convincing though," the first said.

Takezo turned around at the bridge and said back:

"We'll have plenty of chances to rehearse."

As he passed Seki and the others the long-nosed actor who'd predicted misfortune, in the dressing room, commented:

"Lucky. I was sure you'd be beaten but didn't expect anyone to really try and kill you."

"Wait until the next performance," Takezo assured him. "Blood will flow."

"I wasn't sure I followed the argument of the play," long-nose said, further.

"Follow it?" interjected Seki, as the *ronin* passed him. "One should run the other way from it!"

"We don't really look so much alike, it's true," Takezo said, going through the doorway into the dressing room where the young women just stared at him. "You seem older."

With Taro and the other two they went back outside past the laconic doorkeeper into the side street. A long series of lightning flashes cut the sky in half, bouncing wild shadows over the buildings and front garden of the theater.

"You never mentioned who would be in the audience," the big policeman said.

"I wasn't sure," Takezo replied, smiling faintly.

"Even a bad guess would have kept me home," Taro told him. "Your show wasn't worth a popped pimple much less anybody's life, *Zo*, even yours."

"Sakura was quaking," Rensai put in.

"Ha," said that round-bodied worthy. "When Nobunaga spoke you made water."

"Both of you were mute after the performance," said Takezo. "Remarkable for actors."

Who first hired me? he was wondering. *Izu knew nothing about it... not Hideo nor Nobunaga...I feel like a fish in a sea of nets....*

The wind kept gusting, kicking up dust and leaves into swirls. Branches soughed, lanterns swayed, tossing soft light and shadow everywhere. Rain spattered unevenly as thunder rattled and boomed closer. People were closing windows and battening them down. There was a little relief in the humidity, already.

He decided he wanted to watch them all come out after the show and see what he could see, so he sent Taro and the others on after giving the two actors the money he'd promised.

Went into the big garden that fronted the theater and stood on a small bridge over a stream: the landscaping was the wild woods style, dense with bush and clustered trees, complex paths running in and out of the virtual miniature forest.

In the uneven flash of approaching lightning and the lanterns swinging on poles marking the way he could see the path went on from the little, rustic bridge, bent left and right and went out the gate to the main street 100 or so feet away. Maybe 200 feet behind him, was the wide, enclosed gallery that surrounded the theater building. He could hear music and the muffled voices of actors, blurred by the shifting wind. His loose robes pulled and flapped a little around him. There was a cool, wet scent in the air, now.

And then a tall man came down the path from the building in strange tights, puffy, ruffled shirt and a slouch hat. He joined him on the little bridge. Obviously, this was the third foreigner. Must have come with Izu.

"You are from the lost ship?" Takezo inquired.

"Yes," was the reply as both bowed, slightly. "I saw you onstage."

"And you come to praise my skill."

"Most difficult to understand theater in another tongue, sir. I thought I'd take the air."

"Polite. Apparently, what we did was hard to grasp in any language." Takezo grinned. "You came with Lord Izu?"

"Yes. He has employed me. He said I could refuse. But...."

"Wise to say yes."

"I am grateful, naturally."

"The black warrior and the other man are your friends?"

"We met on the ship. They say you saw them?"

"Recently. We were captured. Co-rin was a prisoner. I escaped. I'm a troublemaker." Grunted. "Have you seen your ship again, sir?"

"At last glimpse it was foundering in the waves. As I was, myself."

"You saw it sink?"

"No. But it was surely doomed."

"Interesting."

Maybe the biggest mystery yet is what Nobunaga has to do with it? I think I have eyes that see no more than stones set in a carven face....

Takezo was now concentrating on the windy, wild-shadowed, blue-white, lightning lit garden landscape. A whirling gust rattled and

124

shook the foliage and the lanterns in a sustained *whoosh*. A few fat, warmish raindrops hit hard enough to sting.

There are men in the shadows, he thought. *Maybe guards*....He doubted that, however. *Feels wrong....*

A stocky man stepped from behind a 6 foot rock representing a cliff and came up the path towards the bridge as Takezo, with Gentile a few steps behind, moved to meet him. Inside, the music and drums were pounding and piping to some dramatic climax.

The gleaming blade in the man's hands seemed to flicker in the flailing light. Shadows shifted across his face, showing a long scar across the nose and cheek. Takezo knew him, at once. Drew in a long breath as the stocky figure stopped at the edge of striking distance.

"Ah, the bane of women," he said. "Are you as pleased as I am by this chance meeting? Clearly you cannot be alone, to come so close to me." He gestured Gentile to stay back where he was on the bridge.

I am missing something, here, he thought. *This place may be full of men...yet there are bodyguards inside and that Akira who's worth any 10 of them....*

"Maybe your time has come, at last, drunkard," declared Yoshi, the scar across his cheek and nose showing as a shifting shadow in the jumping light.

"Who set you on me the first time? Issa? Reiko?" Takezo still wanted to figure out who'd hired him in the barn.

Yoshi raised his blade, two-handed, over his head and moved to close. His opponent paid little attention. He was glad he was sober because the next gust of wind that shook the landscape also deflected the hurled *shiruken* so that it went just under his chin instead of hitting his neck and he knew there'd be another following up so he reacted by ducking off the path into the bushes, drawing and snapping a sweeping full extension clearing backcut at almost ground level that clipped Yoshi in the ankle, glimpsing the second hurled, star-shaped weapon glinting in the lightning flashes as it zipped through where he'd just been standing.

He crouched between a rock and a small pine, listening and looking, though movement was masked by the erratic, flailing light and shadow, the crackle-bang of thunder and the veering twists and bursts of wind and spatter. He could hear Yoshi curse and groan where he crawled, then limped back down the path towards the gate.

How many? He wondered. *Why?*

Was it an ambush for somebody else or an afterthought for him? He peered around the rock and made out the tall foreigner alone on the far side of the bridge, short cloak flapping around him.

A stream of warm light as the sliding main door opened and a small cluster of men came out into the gathering wind. He was sure it was Nobunaga and his retainers, maybe four or five men. They headed for the bridge where Gentile stood and he made way for them. Nobunaga may or may not have bowed as they passed – the light was too jerky to tell – and, as they reached the path on the side of the stream close to Takezo, samurai seemed to be everywhere, coming up from under the arch of the bridge where willow and low, dense oak overhung the water. In front of the *ronin* from under a thick flowering bush a ninja stood up with a heavy throwing dagger in each hand and as he went for the preemptive throw (about 15 feet from the target) the rain suddenly crashed down almost like, Takezo thought, a bathing vat had been emptied over everyone.

Takezo knew the ninja would try to close the distance and was up and running, crashing and splashing through the already saturated bushes and branches that whipped and tugged at him, so that as the wiry, almost invisible hooded figure in black made to snap the dagger into the great lord at point-blank distance, the detective struck and barely felt the assassin's arm resist the blade that sliced it off, seeing Nobunaga's expression in the streaming rain as they both turned to face new attackers coming on the path and out of the shaking, storm-blasted garden: faces, steel, lightning, shadows.

"Back to the building!" shouted Nonbunaga, his resonant snarl barely heard above the din. To Takezo: "Thank you. Dangerous people seem to protect you. Look into it. You are honest. Who can remain so?"

The rain was a massive, warm pressure, saturating him. Attacked from all sides, Takezo spun, fended and ducked, slashed up into someone's chest in a puff of blood and breath, glimpsing the foreigner, thin sword out, assisting the retreating men. In the wild light and dark moments through semi-solid downpour, a blade ripped past his shoulder. He blocked a spear thrust that nearly caught his thigh…stabbed into a shadow that seemed to form from the rain and heard a cry of pain…stepped on the *ninja's* severed hand and slipped, fell and rolled to his feet, just off the path, back to a tree, branches breaking up the downpour so he could see samurai going up the path past him in leaps and blurs and the commotion at the theater

126

building as dozens of armed men poured out in defense of Nobunaga who'd cut his way back to the porch.

Protect me, he thought. *Interesting...he's giving me something...maybe* his *protection too...who does he mean?*

The air was cool as he worked his way towards the street, staying just off the path where the water was hissing and spattering: foliage bounced and swayed around him; heard the banging of what sounded like a loose shutter, the muffled shouts and clash of arms, hollow thunder echoes...and then a sense that the attackers were withdrawing back across the garden.

He had to leave his dripping cover to go out the front gate; saw men hurrying down the path, far too many men; didn't want to climb the wall because anybody exiting the garden would be doing that too and who knew how many might be waiting on the other side. There was less lightning visible now with a cloud right overhead but the thunder went on pounding away. He was glad his soaked kimono was dark blue.

Maybe I should have gone back to the building, he thought. *If I hide and Hideo's men find me that will look bad and they'll claim I was part of the plot....*

He ducked through the slackening rain; the wind still twisted and gusted, wildly as he half-ran for the archway. The gate had broken loose and was slamming open and shut. He was almost out when a huge lightning bolt, so close it sizzled and ripped the air, blasted a tree in the garden. He felt his soaked hair partly rise and a stinging on his face and hands. In the lingering brightness made out Yoshi sitting on a rock, back on the wall, tying a rag bandage around his wounded ankle. He looked, up seeing the deadly *ronin* a few steps away, coming to finish the job.

Except, blade raised and ready, Takezo hesitated. He had time – the samurai falling back from the abortive attempted assassination were still just blurs in the misty, lightning-shot, now steadying rainfall. The air smelled of wet earth and green.

"I don't have to kill you," Takezo called over, sheathing his sword. "I can make up my own mind. Unlike you. Die another time, fool." Takezo went out the swinging gate, pushing it wider against the wind.

"You are the fool, soft-belly," snarled Yoshi. "Missed your chance."

Across the street, the *ronin* saw the blurry outlines of several armed men in doorways or crouching under overhangs. The seething rain dinned on the roofs and ran in thick streams into the bubbling mud. The storm front had passed over, the wind falling off, the rain coming almost straight down, at times.

Yoshi stared along the wall at the flapping gate. He was chewing his lower lip so hard blood was beading out and diluting away in the warm rainwater.

"I am captain now, openly, and much greater in secret. Kill all the fleas and none remain to bite. Kill the one my father still forgives," he muttered, almost bitterly, as if someone were listening. "I will rise high. Why not?" The lightning flickered softly, freezing the raindrops in semi-rhythmic beats. "Easy for monks and writers to criticize a man who seeks to rise. Bah. I will not swallow other men's dirt. I am not a puppet in a puppet show. Why should others stand above me? Because of the winds of time or the stars of heaven? The spurt from a father's cock? Bah. I will reach out and move the stars, if I can." Slammed his swordblade over and over into the bubbling mud as if the very mass of the earth itself offended him. "Bow to no one, in the end." Shut his eyes as other samurai came up to him. "That bum! I want to piss in his mouth," he said to himself. "He's a boil on my ass I'll lance."

Twenty-Five

That bum went quickly along the board sidewalk, too wet to care, barefoot because he'd lost his split-toed sandals in the garden. He was considering Miou. Some things about her didn't make sense and he wanted them to make sense. Lovers, he knew from professional experience, are like any true believers who want to make the facts fit the case. He was sure, for instance, that Hideo had proven to himself, more than once, that his wife was loyal and chaste.

And Miou, he thought, sighing, *is only the sweet victim of fate I want her to be...you look at what you want to see....yes, truly, I have eyes like a carved head of a man...better learn to focus soon....*

But he knew he couldn't afford that, either. He had to talk to her; he had to have answers because it had finally occurred to him that she might be a target, too; that, in fact, the dead *ninja* who'd invaded her room might have come for her and not him.

Four drenched men stood with a two pole palanquin that rested on the muddy street near the walkway. He was almost past it when he noticed the door was standing open: maybe the armed men in semi-concealment around the street were there to protect the occupant who might have something to with this aborted ambush.

He paused to peer in. Why not be rude? The worst they'd do is attack him and everybody kept doing that, anyway. It's was normal to try and kill Takezo.

I should wear armor to bed, he considered. *Not a bad idea....*

Two samurai came around from the far side of the vehicle and watched him. They had on yellow rubber raincoats which he envied – not that it would have mattered at this point. They didn't draw. Just stood there in the running mud.

"People who don't want to kill me," he commented.

"Get inside, please" one of them said.

It was dark inside. No movement.

"Why not?" he responded.

In a field of stones, he thought, *dung is a soft bed....*

He felt no threat so he got in and instead of wet mud smell there was perfume and a soft, female chuckle – not a giggle, he noted. The door was shut behind him and they started away. The rain was a steady drumming on the top.

"Waiting for me?" he wondered.

"How arrogant," the woman said.

The fading lightning flashes, screened through the lattice windows, showed her vague outline and pale silks.

"Are you kidnapping me?" he wondered, leaning back on the surprisingly soft pillows, trying to adjust his soaked clothing.

"Giving you a ride. Where do you want to go?"

"Fourth district." That was where both Sanjuro House and Miou's quarters were. "To whom am I so grateful?"

"Don't recognize me?" He heard a rustle of silks as she knelt closer. The perfume was a little cloying but, clearly, high quality. A soft hand touched his knee and stayed there. "You're so wet."

"Strange how it happened. With little warning, moisture fell from the heavens." He knew her now.

"And you, great warrior, were unprepared." She moved the material and gripped his bare knee. "Here." Handed him a towel cloth which he, gratefully, wiped over his face, neck and chest, and handed back to her. "I don't want it. Do your legs and feet."

"You're closer," he suggested.

129

"Do I seem a bath attendant?" she asked, tossing it hard over his face.

"No," he laughed. "You're Issa, the great lady. I let no one of lesser rank towel me."

She liked that.

"You will, generally, stay damp, Takezo," she told him, chuckling again, her hand back on his knee. That kept his attention. "In any case, I took you out of danger."

"Because you love and admire me. How did I miss that in the past? I had a silly notion you sought my life."

"Men are fools. And you are all man." She leaned over his lap, now, and opened his kimono, softly fingering his chest muscles. "I wish to help you."

"Why so generous?"

He just sat there, waiting for her to whip out a blade or maybe her nails were tipped with poison. He knew she was the real thing, a samurai woman equal to almost any man in combat. In Europe this would be improbable but in Japan, the refinement of martial arts and variety of weapons made speed and timing paramount.

"For selfish reasons," she answered, whispering, leaning in and gently nibbling at one of his exposed nipples.

"Is the ring this important?" he wondered, enjoying the softly sucking lips, the sweetly heated aura of her nearness, the scent less intense now.

"Take-san," she laughed, softly, "who can deceive you?"

"Any woman," he replied. *It's not just the ring,* his mind concluded, from somewhat far away as his consciousness concentrated into his body. *She's worried....* "What do you really want? Were you at the play?"

"No." She moved her hands down his torso and bit his lower lip, melding their breaths. "I think you are correct about my daughter," she whispered into his ear which brought an involuntary sigh and a more involuntary thickening stir in his groin. "I want your help. I will reward you."

"So you don't want the ring?"

"Unimportant. Something else."

She bit his ear, this time and he groaned.

"I'm a plaything," he whispered. That amused her, too. "You want this toy fool?"

She pulled her face a little back, saying:

"I have you already," she pointed out, one long-fingered, certain hand making sure down there. She was right, he accepted. He could see the glint of her penetrating, detached eyes in the fading, wavering glow of receding lightning, the thunder booms rolling lower, blurring together. "I want you to find my child."

Her hand kept him prisoner. Why not? It was all madness. For all he knew, even Miou was in this expanding net of shadows and intrigue. The next soft set of flashes showed her smiling and adjusting her hair in strobic fragments.

"Ah," he semi-sighed, cynical.

"I knew the body was not hers," she said, still drawn back like, he thought, a confronted viper. "If she lives. You must keep investigating."

"You are telling the flying bird to flap his wings," he said.

"Report to me, first."

"Ah." Just a sigh, this time, because her mouth encompassed him and it might as well have been Miou, so far as talent went. And it went a long way. "I'm..ahh…being paid, I…ahhhh…."

"Double, my sweet, wet, irritating, warrior," she murmured, then stopped her words with his craving, agonized, burning, helpless, hopeless flesh….

"My sweet enemy," he murmured, closing his eyes, pretty sure there wasn't going to be a dagger – yet.

The rain suddenly picked up but just spilled straight down, hitting as if to flatten the world.

"Ally," she said, around him.

"You don't have to do this…ahhh…I…I'd take just money…."

"I'm not doing this for you," she broke contact long enough to say with a strangely almost painful sigh as her hands gripped and roved over him as if about to claw for blood at any moment.

And then there was only the rain and the slight swaying as the bearers chugged on through the mud and he felt a bubble of ecstasy stir deep within him, starting for the surface….

At some point he dozed off….

131

Woke up, sweating, in silence, blinking at the brightness where the morning light streaked in around the blinds, painful and unwavering. He was alone and still in the palanquin. Since he hadn't been drinking things came together quickly.

He yawned and stretched and half-crawled out of the cab stiff from awkward sleeping. He decided his mouth tasted like unwashed socks. He spat and rubbed his eyes, looking at the shallow hillside where he'd been left.

Important not to think about last night, yet, he told himself. *Get a bath and eat and...see Miou....*

Something swayed, heavily, in the pocket of his robe and he didn't have to actually check to know it was a purse of coins. He'd been bought or sold or whatever again....

His eyes hurt from broken sleep. The air was pleasant, almost cool. The streets were dry except for standing puddles here and there. The rising sun was behind a line of fleecy, grayish clouds. He recognized the district and knew he wouldn't have far to walk.

He was taking a strange pleasure in wanting a drink and saying no. Smiled and shook his head like a waking dog. There was low morning mist softly flowing everywhere, folding and unfolding down the slope where the steel gray river *Oi* seemed to coldly smolder.

Twenty-Six

Naked but for their loincloths, the pair of tattooed coolies who belonged to the *kaga* were sleeping in a heap as if, he reflected, they'd been discarded like the empty sake jugs beside them. They were in the shade of a flowering bush where bees and small white butterflies were working the blossoms.

The morning air wasn't even cool, he noted. It felt as if the heat was stored in the earth the way it was in hearthstones after the fire went out.

He opened the small sack and saw gold *ryo*, again; estimated at least 20.

Shook his head and scratched his neck. Amazing generosity. He had enough, now, to take a few years off if he lived carefully. Get Miou and go to some distant province and forget this gathering intrigue – except he knew he couldn't because he'd be a plain thief, then. Either steal like a lord or be honest and keep your word....

132

There was a note:

"Takezo," it said, "there will be more when you expose the truth."

Didn't use her name, he thought. *Someone else probably wrote it, as well*....Considered things, as he started walking down the easy slope. *The clue is Mora village and those gangsters and the "empty" inn*....

He could always give the money back, too. Snorted. Improbable. Rolled his shoulders under his grayblack kimono. Wondered how often Issa liked to risk adultery. Obviously, she discounted any serious risk of paying the price.

As he crossed the street to House Sanjuro, the sun was higher and filtered by the heavy heat-haze. Still very humid; sweat beaded. He wanted a bath and to shave and pluck his scraggly beginnings of a beard.

He kept thinking about going north to the mountains he remembered from childhood. Crossed the garden, the brightness in his face, now.

Used to like summer, he thought.

Pictured the mountain forests, the cool nights and mellow days; waterfalls that creased and sparkled down sheer slopes into pools of mists...wildflowers, rich green, dense spruce and pine...clear, pure lakes shattering sunlight or awash with moonsilver....

Maybe I can send her ahead, finish my work...collect the rest of my pay...no more poetry for awhile, just taking with ten hands....

The Issa business already seemed like a dream – except for the weight of the gold in his robe. The sex, he reflected, had about as much significance as a prostitute's caresses in a public bath. The bath part he was now really craving....

She has a sense of humor, though, he thought, grinning, remembering.

The gardener was kneeling near the front steps, trimming a bush of deep red blossoms with almost jet black centers. The big namesake camellia trees lined the front and side walls of the corner lot.

The man's face was sweaty under a loosely knotted bandanna. He wore a trowel and various short, hooked-bladed cutting tools looped to the rope that secured his tunic. He nodded hello to the *ronin* who knew him and nodded back.

"Hot day," the man said, meaninglessly.

"Didn't notice," responded Takezo, wiping the sweat from his eyes.

133

The fellow grinned, brightly.

"Think she's inside, sir," he told him.

Takezo grunted and nodded and went up the steps into the relative coolness of the covered porch. Kicked off his sandals and gave his feet a perfunctory rinse. Passed a woman with a bundle of clean laundry on her head as he went into the dim corridor.

She was getting ready to go out. He stood in the already open sliding doorway and watched her in silence for a minute, kneeling at a bench-like table, tilting the mirror she'd been looking in so she could just see his reflection.

So alert, he thought. There was still that to get into. *Maybe as good a moment as any since time insists on moving straight ahead, today....* As opposed to last night sealed in the palanquin, sunk in softness and perfume. *Or when I'm drunk or fighting or...time has many speeds, that's well known...it races for the condemned man which worries me because I feel like it's racing right now....*

She cocked her head gracefully, without turning. Put down the mirror. Her underslip, was of the sheerest green silk. Still, on her knees there, she shrugged into an orchid-colored robe (almost as sheer) with immense, floppy sleeves.

He wanted to kiss her perfectly shaped, rounded and even toes where her feet pressed together. Like baby feet, he observed.

"How beautiful you are," he said.

Still not turning, she wondered:

"Did you sleep in the flowerbushes, last night? Or a house of whores?"

"I wasn't drinking," he replied.

"Was that my question?" She wrinkled her nose. "I can smell you from here. Were you disguised as a woman of the district?"

"I need a bath. I-" This exchange wasn't going to matter, he sensed, because she was worried about something else...was it him, as he hoped...or other business...."I have to finish the job," he said.

"I still think you should forget it, Takezo. Let the dead girl lie in peace."

"I still can't even prove she *is* dead."

She turned now, looked at him. She was beautiful. He was addicted.

"Osan," she said quietly. "An ill name, I think."

134

Osan and Moemon had been forbidden lovers of an earlier century and their romantic and tragic story was well-known. A kind of Japanese Paolo and Francesca, as Gentile had noted in his readings, they were eventually executed for betrayal.

There was the poem feeling, for a moment, and he stood there, abstracted, close to tears for an inexplicable sorrow and longing: a feeling as if they were already lost, dead, buried for 100 years, none left to even remember they'd passed this way, nothing more than the mark left in sand by a rill of water tossed from a broken wave running back into the sea….

"The moon floats on the passing stream," he said. "Teardrops of a god."

She sighed.

"Here you are again, Zo-san," she said.

"Do you wish me to be here?"

"The dew on the morning glory," she softly uttered, "is gone as if looking melted it."

He knelt and took her in his arms.

"What you smell was part of my disguise, last night," he lied like truth. "I want to go away with you. I love you, in fact."

She looked fiercely at him from inches away.

"I pretend, every night, to be shy and bending like a lily in the wind," she said. "That's a disguise."

"I know." Kissed her ear and whispered: "You were well-trained, I think. You are also talented."

She understood.

"Yes," she murmured.

"I don't care who trained you. But am I a client, a target, a fool or the one you care for?"

"Ah." She buzzed his neck with her lips. "The fool I care for."

"Love blurs the mind more than drink. You tried to warn me."

"Yes."

"I don't care. I want to go away with you. I don't care about anything. Just you."

"You know what I am?"

"I'm supposed to be a good spy. People pay me to find things out." He kissed her ear and cheek, adrift in her sweet scent. "You killed the *ninja*. Was he here for me?"

135

"No. For me, I think." She leaned back and away. "I'm not certain. They expect you to stir things up to their advantage. They don't want you dead, yet. But I'm not certain."

He sat down on the floor, looking past her at the hanging scroll between the windows depicting a snowstorm, bamboo and trees bending wildly, two people in wide, conical hats struggling through deep drifts. He shook his head and smiled.

"You were spying on me," he said. "Who knows what else."

"You should leave the city. Give it all up. In the end, you'll be killed."

"You too. Look, Miou, I have no cause to die for pointlessly. Neither do you."

"You have enemies. You should leave."

"Enemies? I thought everyone was so fond of me."

She went into his arms.

"Some are," she said.

"You think I'm a *heinan*," he murmured, holding her. Now he noticed how supplely strong she was under her smooth, soft grace.

He looked out the long window. Across the porch he could just see the tops of tall sunflowers swaying, slightly in the droning, late-morning heat. The thick air was rich with scents. He heard the gardener chopping at something with a hand ax.

"You're not an outcast. You're a true samurai."

"Samurai means 'to serve.'"

"You do," she said, kissing him with simple tenderness.

"I won't serve them. I still know too much and too little," he reflected.

"No. Too much. I think we're frogs hopping in the path of elephants." She sighed. "I have to go."

"Elephants have soft bellies," he said with a cold near-snarl, staring at the bright window. "I won't serve them. Not really. I won't take pride in not thinking or knowing anything but how to grovel and cut."

She held him softly closer.

"Yes," she sighed. "I know that. I love you, Ezo. I have to go."

"Meet a man?" He didn't even pull back, saying it.

"Yes. Business."

"I have business, too."

What had Osan written? He'd read something, once. She wasn't a poet, in his view, but her mind was a surprise: "The samurai becomes unfeeling when he is merely a slave who does the crimes he is ordered to do. Would they not slay the Maitraya Buddha if he comes again to this world in the flesh?"

Small wonder her voice has been stilled, he thought. *One reason, anyway...I know too much and too little and I love this sweet spy who takes my breath away and might, indeed, take my breath away, say what she will...who can guard his heart except a man of stone?*

She gently withdrew all the silk, softness and perfume from his arms and knelt back.

"I love you," she told him. "I want you to live."

"Which murderer do you work for?"

"No one, now," she said. Behind her was another scroll painting, in pink and palest blue, of cherry blossoms raining down from a branch in a gust of wind. "I want you to live."

"Business," he said, distantly.

"I was in a bad way and he helped me."

"Are you in danger, Miou?"

She shrugged.

"Not yet."

She stood up and he just knelt there looking at her, admiring the slightly downtilted face and graceful neck. Her eyes were right on him and were moist. He had an idea she might be acting; had an idea she wasn't. Wanted to keep holding her.

She's full of dreams, too, he thought. *She just won't show them to me....*

At the bottom of the scroll the petals were falling into a rushing stream like snowflakes, seeming to spin and dance in the bubbling current.

"When I've finished what I've started," he told her, "I'll come for you."

Stood up and hugged her again. She responded, absently looking past his shoulder at the doorway.

"That's good," she said.

"We'll take the money and vanish like two *ninjas*." Frowned. Thought about trust. If he couldn't trust her, what was the point? "I put the ring in your room. Leave it there. Give it up if you're in danger. Don't risk anything for it."

"In the false board?" She asked. He nodded, yes. "You test me? I won't betray you. You are the best man I have ever known. A young girl's foolish hope. If you are false then what matter how or when I die?"

He crushed her into himself so hard she gasped, a little.

"We'll be together," he said. "I'll come for you."

"Yes," she murmured, "you'll come for me."

He released her, not wanting to, and went out first. She watched him from the window as he crossed the garden on the bright white pebbled path. She was weeping.

My poor, savage poet, she thought. *You are so kind of heart that I would forgive you anything...for you, I might even forgive myself....*

She saw him turn and glance back and she bowed acknowledgement. Her tears made him seem an uncertain shadow in his dark robes against the bright path and background. A shade come back, she didn't quite think, to view the world he was no longer a part of.

Except I am the ghost, she thought. *None of it is real for me...I am trapped but who is free? The monk on the mountaintop runs out of rock to climb....*

"I won't serve them either," she said as if he could have heard her, watching him go out the gate under the massed red and white camellias. "Not again. I won't. Maybe I'll kill him." Meaning Tanba no Kami Sanayu.

I have lain with many men and yet, this one...I delight in his small sighs and even his snores fail to irritate....

She waited for the client. She'd never met him and didn't want Takezo to linger and maybe have to be introduced. The man had been recommended by the mistress of the house; she'd told Miou he was quiet and generous and liked to be entertained by soft singing and the Korean *samisen,* gently plucked.

He came in the afternoon and they sat in one of the private gardens in the inner courtyard, each with its own mini-teahouse. She found him dull. He seemed satisfied just to sit and drink, snack on and listen. She didn't recognize the clan markings on his green and gold kimono. When asked where he was from he named a place far north and west.

"Are you visiting here for long?" she politely inquired, at one point.

138

He was then leaning on one elbow, smoking a long, thin pipe she prepared for him. The sweetish scent of the spice-permeated tobacco blended with the "peach and apricot" afternoon incense that smoldered in a brass tray near the window, meant to enhance the pleasure of the smells from the flower-garden just outside the little structure. The hot, hazy afternoon was still, except for distant voices and the steady, spaced chirp of an unseen bird.

"Maybe," he said, neutrally, detached.

He made her uneasy. Reminded her, faintly, of Tanba without the feline sexual magnetism. She'd been trained to study everyone she met and make mental notes; look for special characteristics, weakness and so on.

She had a feeling this man cared little for love. Studied his face: pointed chin, high cheekbones, sharp-edged nose, eyes hard to see under bony brows. There was a sword-scar creasing one side of his skull where part of his left ear had been sliced off. A close call, she more or less thought. He was slim, like Tanba, too, medium but with very wide shoulders and big hands. He looked strong and had a careless manner more suited to a *ronin*, she thought, than a clan samurai. The damp, still air didn't seem to bother him.

"Is it ever this hot in the north, sir?" she asked, pouring out two cups of cool sake.

He shrugged.

"Play some music," he requested, seeming bored.

It seemed almost as if, she considered, he'd come there as a duty; like a pilgrim who is obligated to visit a shrine or historical sight. This piqued her, naturally.

"What music do you prefer in the north, sir?"

"Well-played," he said, sucked, gently, at the pipe; seemed not to be looking at anything but she couldn't be sure. "Music is purity. Humans are all corrupt."

"So said the Compassionate One," she put in.

"Buddha? Bah. Who can feel compassion for corruption?"

She inclined her head and picked up the stringed instrument beside her.

Looked at the hanging scroll on the wall behind him. It was a loosely brushed black ink sketch of a fierce-looking hawk diving at a small swallow-like bird, the black claws about to lyrically hook home.

This is strange, she thought. *Who is he?*

"Do you know the most respected Tanba?" she tried, starting to pluck a tune.

"Is he from the north?" was the flat, maybe, barely mocking response. She didn't like that, either.

"From many places, sir." Played and studied the drawing rather than look directly at him: the plummeting predator in graceful, strong, exquisite strokes. She thought of Takezo and had a sudden, strange feeling she might never see him again. The graceful music hung, muted, in the heavy air….Her fingers went still, involuntarily, on the strings.

We are all like that little bird, she thought, *almost in the talons of the hawk….*

"Don't know him," he said, looking out the doorway at the garden where a vagrant breeze tugged at a mass of gold and white chrysanthemums. A big crow dropped in a swirl of darkness and landed, gripping a rocking pine branch, its eye a dark glitter like a polished stone. "Just play."

Twenty-Seven

Later

The sky was dead black over the city. There was rain in the air, again. In the distance lightning flashed, softly, too far for the thunder to be more than a hinted quiver in the heavy, hot, tense atmosphere. Now and then a breeze stirred, vaguely, in the garden and seemed to die of its own thickness.

The client had left hours ago and she'd decided to nap in the tiny teahouse. When she opened her eyes the incense was out, the room was dark and a dim shape was standing over her where she was stretched out on the mat. She'd slept too long, she realized sitting up and drawing the long steel hairpin from her coiffure, just in case.

"Miou," a familiar woman's voice said.

"Oso?"

"Yes."

The pretty young spy who'd helped Takezo knelt there.

"Is he alright?" Miou asked.

"I know nothing of that. I came to tell you Tanba is supporting Hideo."

"Ah. Tanba has been to Hideo's castle?"

"Yes. But he met only with the chamberlain, as far as I know."

140

"No doubt." She replaced the deadly pin in her hair. "Hideo may know nothing about it," she murmured. "Please, good Ono, find my love. Tell him these things."

"Yes." Ono knelt. "Should I light a lantern?"

"No."

"But won't you see him yourself?"

Miou sighed, faintly. She was looking at the wall with the drawing of the striking hawk except only a faint, long whitish blot showed where the scroll hung.

"Maybe not," she said. "I have a bad feeling."

Because she knew she'd come to a fork in the road and could go neither way. She was out of choices. Tanba Sandayu was no longer sure of her and she was a danger to Takezo.

I can give myself to him, she thought. *I trust him...for the first time I feel close to a man and when he's inside me I feel like we're truly one person...for a moment, at least....*She felt, suddenly, cold and sick. *He dreams of going away and I want to go with him...and...Ah, I do not want to die, now...how sad....*

"Would this not be a betrayal of Sandayu?" Ono asked.

In their pale clothing they were formless shapes in the night. Detached voices, as if ghosts spoke, Miou thought. She felt strangely safe and comforted in the dark, though she knew it was a delusion.

"How do you betray a man who is on no side?" she wondered.

"Ah."

"I want Takezo to live. Forget his sword and write his poems. Tell him the money is where I left it. And the trinket men kill for." Sat in silence for a moment. "I want him to live in a beautiful place in the mountains."

Silence and darkness; the sound of crickets outside in the humid, still air...the other girl whispered:

"I am afraid for you."

"Go at once or I'll be afraid for you, good Ono."

"I...."

"Go!"

And the girl, with a slight rustle and padding of bare feet, was gone. Miou just sat there, staring at the long blur on the wall where she knew there was a picture. She imagined it, and then considered that was the way she imagined Takezo when he wasn't there. Smiled.

What you imagine isn't really anything, she said to herself. Sitting as if waiting, thinking about going away with him, trying to picture the most beautiful place she'd ever seen in the forests and wild mountains....*Always wanted to leave the country so much...now I want to go back...and be there with him...so much....*

"It's very sad," she murmured. There was a slight sound and a vague movement in the little doorway. "Ono?" she asked. "What is it?"

Except she knew it wasn't Ono and so the familiar, purring voice didn't really surprise her. She took a deep breath and stood up. Realized she'd actually been expecting him. In the distance there was a faint, wavering rattle and deep bong of thunder, again.

"*Okiku,*" Sandayu said, with a sigh. Chrysanthemum.

"You came yourself, Tanba."

She'd have to try it. Didn't expect to succeed but that realization was somehow soothing. She didn't have to worry about it. How long had he been listening?

"You were right," he told her, purring, "I cannot be betrayed. What you do against my left hand assists my right. That is the true art of governing."

Listening too long, she thought. *Ah, poor Ono....*

"You have no center, Tanba," she told him. Why not?

"What color is the chameleon?" he asked, stepping closer.

She made no useless attempt to avoid him; couldn't tell if his sword was drawn. Probably not. He probably wouldn't kill her himself unless she attacked.

"Did you slay that poor girl?"

"Maybe she assists my right hand."

"But you will slay me."

She could only see where he was standing by the faint luminosity in the doorway because he was in full black though she could tell his hood was open by his voice.

He could feel her strange indifference. It vaguely troubled him. Being what he was he wished to understand it.

"You think I will not?" he asked.

"I know you *will*." There was a shrug in her voice.

"You want him to live so badly," he said, sighed. "I warned you about love, *Okiku.*" Sighed again and she almost believed it. "Strangely enough, *I* want him to live."

142

"You can change colors," she said, "but you are always only yourself. How can you be expected to understand love?"

They were silent. He'd moved and she didn't know where he was, now: a shadow within shadows. Outside the faint thunder was lost in the swish of a breeze in the garden. The faint outline of the door was in front of her.

How good it would be, her mind said, *to just walk outside and never have to look back....*

Like when she was a child going out into a summer evening, looking with wonder at the gleaming, moonlit rice fields, taking in the rich smells of earth in the cool mountain air, bare feet on the warm soil where the day's heat lingered...

Then, a single day seemed like many and if you didn't sleep the nights seemed to have no end....

"Understand love?" Sandayu reflected. "I don't make swords but I use them."

His voice came from the side. His outline seemed to be partly blocking the vague blot of the long hunting hawk scroll.

"To die for nothing," she said, "is to have lived for nothing."

"Where is the ring?" he asked. "Don't pretend."

"That again. That's why Toshiro was spying in my bedroom."

"Is that why you put a pin hole in his head?"

"Because of some stupid trinket? No, Sandayu." She just looked through the doorway into the hush of night shadows. "Is it why I die?"

"You knew where it was and said nothing. That is betrayal."

"Stupid to die for a bauble. Why so valuable?"

"You don't know. Neither does the deep seeing Takezo."

She heard him sigh again and wondered if it really meant regret. She was already walking, not trying to see more than the hinted garden through the doorway, going out into the heavy, scent-laden night (not even pausing as a second shadow detached from the side of the little building) only paying real attention now to the wind in the leaves, following the curving white stone path that led to the main house, aware that both of them were now behind her...seeing a small sandal dark on the pale walking stone, obviously Ono's, and saying flat and loud:

"Coward!"

The laconic, almost bored voice she recognized from the afternoon, saying:

143

"This is what we do in the north."

She heard the whisper of the blacked, invisible blade ripping down between herself and death and her elevated awareness took it all in at once as if the striking sword were just a shadow too, that all these things were blurs and hints, insubstantial as the moon reflected in a pool...and she grasped it all with a speed and dexterity that seemed to fix the night, air and all movement in a dull, sluggish heaviness: we are all worlds in ourselves, her mind said, full of unknown wonders and reflections and we are cut down. We are always cut down.

They were both close behind her and in one movement, turning in a swirl of loose robes, the long pin already in her hand and striking; she felt it stab into flesh and bone, heard an outcry even as the shadow blotted at her with an infinite weight of massive, darkness and she broke like a reflection in water under a cold impact, no pain, just a strange shock and she felt herself seem to collapse into gleaming fragments and then melt like mist billowing into the night...the silence...the clouds of herself folding and unfolding over the flowers, trees...up into the night...silence...the moonstreaked sky....

And she saw Takezo (without memory of his name) and told him (without words) that she loved him and touched him with her meaning the way a mist touches...and was gone, the way mist is gone....

Twenty-Eight

Still later

Takezo was surprised to meet Yazu at the street entrance to the Sanjuro House grounds. In the light of the lanterns by the gate he saw tears in his new student's eyes.

"Why are you here?" the *ronin* asked.

"To find you, master." His voice was thick with emotion.

Takezo had a sudden, sick feeling.

"You achieved your purpose," he said.

"A terrible thing," croaked the thin, bent man. "I will go to the great father of the ward and beg him for vengeance!" Both bony fists were clenched and shook with feeling.

"What happened?"

"A foul thing, my master," Yazu choked out and then fell to his knees at the other's feet.

"What thing? Please speak."

144

"The great father will find him and then…and then…."

"You don't need the help of gang men," Takezo said. "Whatever wrong has been done you, Yazu, I will right it, if I can, as well as any short-changing *Tekiya.*"

Then he noticed a commotion by the front door and one of the women came out shouting and weeping. That was enough and he was already running up the path to the long darkwood porch.

He half-charged into the first room where two of the girls were crouched on the floor by the screen showing Mt Fujiyama in the spring seen through a flowering cherry tree, a gust of blossoms and petals unfolding on an elegant curl of wind over the brush-stroked earth.

"Where is she?" he demanded, with sinking horror, already sure.

Yazu had followed him in; the women just looked at him; the room swam and all he could see through blurry eyes was the six-foot image of the great volcano and pink glory of the blossoms in the air.

"So terrible," one was saying.

The other looked up and recognized him.

"Ai, Takezo-san!" she cried, convulsed with grief.

"Where is…" he started to say, already turning, going back outside, brushing past Yazu who was saying something, again, about punishing the "fool" who did it. Takezo distantly noted that he kept using that word.

He just stood on the porch under the starless, moonless overcast sky; wet, yet rainless. Heavy mist flowed over the long pond; wisps and twists of it brushed past his face, too soft to feel. Across the garden the phallic guardian stone stood beside the round, flat female stone in the foggy swirls. He thought of the two famous "married" rocks on the seacoast, wed, in ritual, by the villagers.

Lovers made of stone, he thought, *eat time….*

Because he knew and was just putting off going back inside. Because from this point on there were no more plans or promises and he wasn't ready to face that, yet either.

Miou, I never showed you…I never…I…Like Seki, I did a wondrous seeming but I never really showed you my heart, my…Ah, always when the day is gone we regret the wasted afternoon….

He felt Yazu behind him.

"Master?" he said.

"How?"

145

"Master?"

"How did it happen?"

"Ai, a fool. A fool in a cart." His voice choked and broke again. Yazu had, in becoming a disciple, despite Takezo's casual and cynical view of it, given all his feelings to his *sensei*. "In the street. Run down and crushed...ai...."

"Cart?!"

"Drawn, they say, by two maddened and foaming oxen the drunken fool was beating in a foolish hurry...they say...."

"Run down?"

"Crushed in the filth and mire...ai...."

"Killed by a cart?" His eyes were wide and there were no thoughts in his mind. "This is...this is...."

Shut his eyes. And then his stunned mind spoke:

There is no Takezo...what was Takezo is now gone...gone like smoke...time has eaten him too....

"Oh, master," said his bony pupil.

"Where is this fool?"

"Fled. After his cart passed over her. Master, I will seek out father Osihatchi who is related to my wife, that arrogant she-dog, and he will have the low-born rascal found, that *eta* toucher of blood, he will be found as surely as the hunting osprey finds the small fish!"

"Stupid comparison," gasped Takezo, breathing deep and uneven shocks while he thought his eyes would melt with burning. "Show me her." He couldn't say "body."

We're all bubbles...rising, floating... popping to nothing....

They'd laid her in a back room on the polished floor so the stains could be mopped easily. Her sheer robes were caked with mud and blood, twisted and torn.

He remembered the clothes from when they'd said goodbye in the afternoon. Incense was smoking in a brass pot beside a pair of smudgy candles.

He couldn't yet look directly at her. He aimed his blurred eyes at the doubled images of a vase with azaleas under the dark latticed window.

Not chrysanthemums, his mind said, remotely. *So she was called...flowers...flowers...what was the other one's name...killed here too...aiii....*

146

Held his head. One of the petals had fallen on the flower-table. His focus made it two. Shut his eyes and knelt beside her. She was cold. He knew she'd be cold. Yazu was in the doorway to the narrow room. One of the girls was crouching beside him. He heard her intake of breath as he opened and adjusted Miou's kimono. There were no slash wounds or punctures, he noted, in a professional reflex. A long bruise along the side of her head that could have been from any number of things, not excluding the flat of a sword or a flat stick but (he noted further, trying to hold off grief with observation) fit being struck, maybe, by the yoke and, in any case, there were the bloody tracks that crossed and horribly crushed her legs and her neck.

Ai, so much weight on...on her... he thought. *How cruel these marks....*

Her face was untouched so he couldn't bear to look at it at all. She obviously had been perfectly flat in the street on her back when the iron-studded wheels passed over her, breaking her neck and shins. Knocked unconscious by the first impact she'd made no effort to twist away. What must have been a hoofprint had badly bruised one hip.

He closed his eyes again and knelt there with nothing in his mind, now.
Found her hand and held it, shut in his own darkness....

The woman who ran the house came in while he was just sitting, crosslegged, still wearing his sandals while the rest were barefoot. He groped on his person for coins, staring wildly at her lined, over-made-up face.

"Please, see to her," he said. "I'll pay."

"Don't worry," the woman said. "It is taken care of."

Takezo blinked hard and tears broke from his searing eyes.

"Are you so generous?" he wondered. He knew he was clutching at things to think about to put off the real thing, the hollowing reality that was just starting to encompass him. The pain was waiting just outside his brief shield of numbness.

"A gentleman left gold," she explained, face turned away.

"Client?" Not that it mattered.

"He left no name. Just gold."

"So quickly?"

She shrugged, almost imperceptibly. He noted a muscle twitch in her cheek.

147

"I have lost…so many," she murmured.

He nodded, looking at the floor, now, aware Yazu had gone out – no doubt to look for "father" gangster. There were other people in the hallway; he didn't look.

"Yes," he said, "two young girls in a short time."

The woman shook her head rapidly and slightly.

"Three, now," she said. "Over a week ago one disappeared with no trace."

This was good. Something more to think about for a moment. He studied her face. The line in her cheek still pulsed with tension like a water-dimple in a shallow stream.

"Disappeared?" he asked. "Which one?"

"She was called, here, The Lily."

"Maybe she left with a lover."

"Maybe. But I've never known a girl to run away without taking her possessions." She shrugged. "Or stealing something."

He had the coins in his hand, now. Let them slide onto the floor.

"Anyway, I'll pay. Give him back his money."

Without actually looking again at Miou's body, he rolled to his feet and went through the doorway. On the porch he met Yazu who was just standing there. He was wearing the wooden practice sword Takezo had given him for training.

"Where is the cart?" he asked him.

I didn't see it coming, he thought. *I never see….*

Yazu held a lantern as they crossed the street from Sanjuro House. The sky was overcast. The cart was half-a-block away. The oxen were gone.

Takezo took the lantern and brought it close to each wheel. The blood was dried and red in the soft circle of light. He puffed out his cheeks and exhaled slowly.

"Who saw this happen?" he asked.

"I know not, master. It was reported by passersby, I think. Many people had gathered by the time I came here." He was agitated. "The fool ran away. All agreed on that. He seemed as one drunk."

The spy distantly appreciated Yazu's genuine sympathy. No doubt the gang boss, Osihatchi, would be able to track down the drunken perpetrator; what good would that do? He'd had enough of everybody's unsatisfying revenges, including his own.

148

"He matters no more to me," he told his disciple, "than the runaway bullocks."

Strange, he could not help but think, *only a single hoofmark on her poor flesh....*Charging animals would not pick their steps very carefully.

"Go away, now," he said softly.

"Master, I...."

"Thank you. Go. I'm going to have some drinks and need no one near me. Not this night."

Maybe not any night, he thought.

"I'll find out what I can, master."

Takezo grunted and sighed, just standing there, the paper lantern forgotten in his hand, the slightly wavering flame half-lighting both their faces in a gentle glow that blurred away marks of age, strain and even grief.

"Now time is done with me, I think," he told the bony little man. "It can move at any speed it likes."

"*Sensei?*"

He handed the illumination to Yazu. Looked at the glowing windows along the street. Thought about all the lives being lived as if death were far away when, in fact, it sat at every hearth.

"Still," he said, automatically because he couldn't help considering the problem.

"Yes, *sensei?*"

"Who was the samurai who slew the other girl..." He said the word bitterly. "I forget her name?"

"I do not know, sir. He escaped."

"How strange...so much is strange...."

His eyes were leaking burning water, again. His chest was thick with inexpressible feelings. He watched himself, as if he, somehow stood apart, wanting to scream and kill, blindly, as if fate could be found in a form that might be cut down.

And then his blade was in his hand, Yazu hopping back, lantern rocking light and shadow, and swinging as he watched, remote, his own cold and futile frenzy. He chopped through the spokes of the rear wheel, like an angry child, sword a chill, supernatural fang chewing up the mere wood, even the big, iron-studded rim, and the massive cart sagged.

149

And then he stopped, perfectly still. Because it was so obvious and he'd nearly missed it completely. A grim grin twisted his face.

"Sensei!" cried Yazu.

Suddenly a *okappiki* city policeman was there in his black and gold basin helmet, *jittu* ready, short sword and wooden *bokkuken* thrust in his wide sash.

"Stop!" he commanded. "What is this?"

"The mind goes on even after the heart has died," Takezo said, unenlightingly.

"Drunk?"

"No, no, sir," said Yazu. "He…."

"Like the lightning-struck pine that still stands, black and bare, against the chill, winter sky."

"Hmn," grunted the policeman, "Literary drunk. Sheath your sword and come along. No trouble here, understand?"

Paying little attention, the tall, wide-backed spy took Yazu by one arm and forced him to his knees.

"Lie between the wheels," he commanded.

"What's this?" wondered the policeman.

Yazu stretched out, understanding what his master wanted. He put his neck under the front wheel. His feet just reached the other one and he was at least as tall as Miou.

"Aiii," sighed Takezo.

"Both drunk," said the official. "Better come."

The *ronin* finally noticed him.

"Go away," he said. "Go talk to my friend Taro at the 5th district house."

That brought faint amusement.

"A good man. You know him? Has he arrested you?"

"A good friend."

"Hmn. A good man. He'll do you little advantage. He's been suspended for strange misconduct." Tilted his head. "Why are you angry at the cart?"

As Yazu stood up Takezo was already turning, heading back to Sanjuro house. He didn't really register what he'd said about Taro.

"Wait!" commanded the policeman. "Sheath your weapon and come with me!"

Takezo kept walking out of the lantern's soft, uneven ring of light. He wasn't anxious to go back in there but had to. This "*oka*" didn't interest him much.

The man drew his wooden sword, keeping the *jittu* in his left hand to catch and twist the other's blade if he should strike, then bang his skull or break his arm with the curved stick. This fellow was very good and had successfully disarmed dozens of samurai, drunk and sober.

Since Takezo didn't bother to turn and just kept walking along meditatively, wrapped in his gathering sorrow, the policeman simply chopped the wooden blade at the back of his head to stun him – except the target, not seeming to notice, took an extra half-step and gave the officer the impression he'd tried to hit a supernatural being formed of shadow.

Behind him the *ronin* heard Yazu and the officer. His disciple was saying, vehemently:

"See the blood, sir? Oh, don't trouble him! His woman was crushed to death on this very spot! A terrible grief for my poor master."

And the other voice, somewhat conciliatory, now, saying something Takezo didn't make out or pay attention to as he was crunching up the path to the building, across the polished porch and then inside, reflexively kicking his *tabi* off, this time. His naked *katana* was still in his hand.

The hall was empty and the head woman was just coming from the room Miou was laid out in.

"I've sent for the coffin-maker," she told him as he brushed past her. "I am going to Joishi temple in the morning to have prayers said and…."

She looked after him as he went into the narrow, room and skidded to his knees, head down-tilted, beside her crushed body in the dim, shadowy glow.

There was a fine-featured young samurai on the other side of her who looked with steady, muted fury at the intruder. Put his hand on his sheathed short-sword.

"What manners," he said.

He seemed familiar. Takezo was uninterested. Made himself look at the body, again. Sighed and nodded.

"It's so," he whispered.

"Coming in so rudely. Sword in your hand."

151

"Yes. I might have disturbed her," the *ronin* didn't quite snarl back. Looked at the blade as if just noticing it, then slipped it back into its lacquered sheath with a sigh. "Ah," he said. "Pardon me. Who are you?"

"Taramachi Sessu, impudent man in rags."

"So, impudent, well-dressed man," Takezo couldn't resist saying. "What was she to you?" Takezo didn't look at him. He was, again, putting off really looking at anything. "Something you paid for."

"Hmn. A fine companion. A good spirit. Intelligent." Studied the spy closely, hand relented from his *shogo* hilt. "Are these things that can be bought?"

"You loved her?"

"You do not remember me?"

"Sessu? I don't want to know you much less remember you." He held his face in his hands. "Leave me in peace."

Sessu took this in.

"I see," he said. "You loved her, too. I was in the inn when you trounced the fat gambler." He touched her hand where it lay at her side. Someone had covered her with a damask sheet. "She was supposed to meet me there."

Takezo glanced over at him. Then down at her covered body. There were a couple of bloodstains near where one of her small feet poked out.

Why not? Whose life is so simple? He asked himself, remembering him sitting in the corner while he threatened Yazu over the cheap comb. He'd wondered why she'd shown up there; she'd never actually said she'd been looking for him – which he'd taken for granted. *As if it mattered...aii...when was that? Years ago? Time has drained away behind me....*Except it mattered because he had to think about all the life she'd lived that he knew nothing about. There was a strange emptiness to that.

"She is not seven feet tall," he said. "Do you think she is seven feet tall?"

The younger man half-crouched upright, angry, again.

"What are you saying?" he demanded.

"Unimportant." Sighed. Touched her foot. "Miou...blood on your sweet flesh...." Tears suddenly rained from his eyes and spattered the floor. "She is much smaller than seven feet," he whispered, feeling a deep, involuntary shudder pass through him. "You see? You see that? Much smaller...very small....""

The other sank back to his knees, across the body from Takezo. Wiped a sleeve at his eyes.

"I don't...." he began.

"The cart was too wide," he said, voice dead. "They had to run it over her a second time."

And the reason, he relentlessly let himself realize, was probably because the first time it missed her neck and only crushed her legs. A miscalculation or intentional cruelty. What matter?

He was sick with anger and then he was just sick without anything.

"I desired her," Sessu said. "She did not let me possess her." Frowned. "What about a cart?"

"Did you get back your money?" Takezo wondered.

"What are you saying?" he snapped, irritated again. "I didn't try to buy her love. You anger a man. How have you lived so long?"

"It seems much longer than it is. I have problems with time." He sighed, staring at the two candles, thin, dark smoke sluggishly curling up like calligraphic lines spreading in the heavy air, suggesting words that were pictures...dissolving into hints and shadows...so many things seemed to have a message for him....

"You have many problems, I have heard, Takezo-san."

"I meant the money for the funeral. I told her to return it to you."

"I left none."

He looked away from the smoke; no messages there. Glanced at the fellow and knew he was telling the truth. Took another uncomfortable breath and scratched his chin where he needed a shave.

Who did? He asked himself. *Another man and so quickly....I'll find out from the woman here....*

"Whom do you serve?" Takezo asked.

"Lord Hideo."

"You must have sinned in a former life."

"And I trained in the Yoshioka school."

"Then I dare not fight you. Imagine your skills."

Sessu waited, alert and ready.

Takezo stood up and turned his back on her body and the samurai. He knew he was just himself, again. The lost, lonely boy, trained to extreme violence and deception who ran away and learned to dream in public, on the stage....

153

His master, Tengu Hiromachi, a solid journeyman actor, was sitting on the edge of the highly polished, cherrywood <u>Noh</u> stage, leaning his back on the first pillar and watching Takezo, in girl's clothing, wave a fan and gracefully fold to his knees.

Tengu rubbed his head with both hands. Hummed a grunt.

'Was that better?' Takezo asked.

'Worse,' was the reply from the stocky actor.

'This is as bad as learning ninja arts,' the boy said, giving the adult the feeling he might run away from this life, too.

'You better master something or you'll end a bandit.'

'Maybe that's not so bad, sir.'

'And die by the roadside or be executed in some hideous way.'

The boy just sat there and sighed.

'How can I be a woman?' he asked, frustrated.

'You cannot,' said Tengu. 'Or a man either. Not on the stage. On the stage you can only be a character made of words and gestures.' The teacher stood up resting one hand on the smooth pillar. 'Understand this: you must be like water taking the shape of what you pass over, reflecting what is around you and always know you are none of those things.'

'It <u>is</u> like ninja training,' the boy considered, staring out into the dim, empty theater.

'All beings act: the samurai to seem fierce and fearless, the prostitute to seem tender, the gambling-banker to seem a kindly friend, the tavern-keeper to seem concerned, and so on.'

Takezo liked that.

'Or the actor,' he jibed, 'to seem he has money to pay the bill.'

The teacher laughed and nodded.

'That is the highest art,' he said, slapping his hand on the pillar.

'But what is the difference, then, sir?'

'After a time the samurai cannot tell his own face from the ferocious mask he wears and the whore has forgotten the young girl's simple heart ....' He shut his eyes and sighed. 'How sad, young Take. How sad.'

'The actor, sir?'

His teacher was smiling again.

'He's no better. Maybe worse because he should understand. An actor who cannot tell himself from the part is soon locked away.'

154

Takezo remembered and felt a longing to see the old man again. Put it on his list of things that would never happen.

"Maybe all real love is first love," he murmured, not really aware he spoke.

"What's that?" wondered the samurai, Sessu, still on the floor by the body, looking up at the *ronin's* back where he'd paused at the doorway, lean and tall.

"Do you know who murdered her?" Takezo asked, not turning.

"Murder? What...."

"I don't really want to know why," he said, because it might be his fault.

"Why do you...."

"Hideo clan," scoffed Takezo. "Better call it Reiko clan."

He expected the other to leap up and draw or at least shout. He would have almost welcomed a moment of violence. He was surprised at the response.

"There is something," the man said, not loud.

Takezo turned and went past the body to the open window and parted the split light cloth curtain with a brush drawing on it of a flower more or less emerging from or maybe turning into loose, gracefully bold calligraphy. He leaned there, side on to the kneeling samurai without having to see her, listening to outside and in at the same time.

"Something?" he urged.

"I am loyal to my clan."

"Why mention it, then?"

"Bold to say anything you like."

The *ronin* shrugged. Outside was quiet. He heard the lady of the house out in the garden, talking and was answered by a deep male voice, then a higher-pitched one that might have been Yazu. The outside air was still, heavy and dead. Incense and candle smoke hung in the room. Upstairs someone was plucking a samisen, the mournful twang dull and distant.

"Yes, yes, some day I'll certainly be killed. Meanwhile, what do you mean to tell me? You've already said you're loyal."

Again, under-reacting, Sessu responded:

"Yes, I am loyal. But something is not clear."

Takezo almost guffawed, hearing that.

155

"Impossible," he said. "Please, speak or don't, but try not to mention loyalty, again." He could just see the young man, head hanging, caught in inner conflict. "If it might help, please explain."

"I told her the daughter ran away to escape something shameful and dangerous," he sort of blurted.

"Which daughter?"

"Osan. The child of my lord and lady." The young man sighed and kept his face bent as if bowing at Miou's body.

"You told whom?"

"Miou." He began to shake with soft sobs. "Maybe they killed her because of me."

"Why not kill you?" Takezo wondered, half to himself, hearing Yazu's voice saying something he couldn't make out and the woman saying: yes.

"I don't care if they do. I was drunk and spoke too much."

"Hard to believe that could happen," said the cynical detective. "Don't blame yourself too much. Miou had a way with conversation."

The young man stood up, this time.

"Careful what you say about her!" he hissed.

Takezo felt a little sicker, now, because it was possible. That was her job. He had a feeling whoever tried to pay for the funeral had a hand in her death. Shook his head and sighed. Sessu pushed his arm which normally would have been risky.

"Careful," said Takezo. "She had another background."

"Apologize," Sessu demanded. "Don't hint that she was a criminal."

"Not that. Not that. She worked for *ninja*." That stopped the young samurai. "What was the disgrace?"

"Always more to things than we see," Sessu said and Takezo bowed a nod. "A man, high in the clan – I do not know his name – was trying to force Osan into disgraceful...."

"Yes?"

"Relations."

"The chamberlain?"

The young man shrugged.

"Don't know," he said.

That would explain a few things, Takezo thought. *She was using the foreigner to reduce the effect on her clan...she didn't expect to be killed...if she was...still the question....*

He heard Yazu's voice and then his steps on the porch. He'd come in, Takezo was certain, and tell him the policeman had understood and relented, and did his *sensei* want him to help find the culprit.

Father Hachimachi, or whatever his name is, would be out of his depth here....

"Complicated," the *ronin* commented.

"I must go," said Sessu, heading out.

"I must drink," said the detective. "A lot."

"Is that wise? You seem to be in danger."

"I'm empty, young samurai," was the answer. "I must fill myself with something."

Twenty-Nine

On the quay at Edo

A half moon was rising behind long, thin clouds on the bay horizon. As cool a spot as would be found in the city. As Captain Yoshi came down the long dock he looked not-quite-furtively behind him towards the dark shadows of shore. His footsteps were soft on the smoothly weathered wood. The tide was coming in with a hint of decay.

The next to last moored boat had a long cabin which showed a faint, orange-red glow through slatted shutters. At the point where the steeply curved side made it easy to step on board, a big man was sitting on a stool, sheathed sword resting on his shoulder in the crook of his arm, outlined against the faintly luminescent sea.

The 50 foot long vessel bumped the dock softly, barely rocking in the light breeze and low waves. Lines and thick knotted rope, used to protect the hull in harbor, creaked slightly. The night was still. A fish struck at the surface with a soft, wet *pop* somewhere close by. Behind them on the dark shore among trees and scattered houses, someone was talking, words softened and unstrung by the soft sea sounds and uneven breezes.

The man stood up and bowed. His clothes were dark and showed no clan insignia. Yoshi responded and nodded his chin at the cabin.

"Inside," the guard said, looking past the Captain and the land's end to where moonlight was just touching the water with a spatter of silvery hush. "Beautiful here, Middle-Captain."

"No time for contemplation," Yoshi snorted, slipping off his *tabi* and stepping, barefoot, over the side to the smooth deck.

A little before

Inside the boat, Issa and Reiko sat at a floor table drinking warm sake, neither serving the other. He was looking, mainly, at the planked floor, the dull reddish lantern directly behind him so that his face was mostly obscured while hers was dimly lit and made unnaturally ruddy. The cabin was bare except for a rolled-up futon and some unopened cases. The air was close and wetly hot, in there. Both were sweaty and irritable.

She knew he was scowling and didn't much care. Tapped her golden fan softly on her knee where she sat her heels, facing him at a slight angle.

"Whose fault doesn't matter," she was just saying. "No point. If the ring was so important, why didn't you take it from him when he was in the castle drinking with you? Or when he came to the funeral and crippled our men?"

"Thought it might be a trick," he replied, not looking up, as if his dim shadow over the plain table might hold a secret. Shrugged. "Didn't want it to seem too important in case he didn't really have it and others were involved."

"You are so clever, Chamberlain Reiko." She didn't exactly mock him. Didn't have to. "I am but a foolish woman and have no idea, myself, of why it is important. Just a Chinese trinket you pretended belonged to my child."

"Yes, yes...." He sighed and stared at the empty, one-dimensional dark outline of himself that reached almost to her knees where the fan still made, slow, arythmic taps.

"You are so clever," she repeated, "that you have varnished the floor without leaving a path to the door." The fan stopped and she leaned towards him a little, eyes seeming amused while her mouth set into a frown. "I thought Osan was dead and I grieved...in any case, you have left me in ignorance."

158

"I was not told everything, my dear," he insisted, not lifting his long face. "Much was kept from me. And then this meddler, this miserable, worthless vagabond...."

"Who set Takezo on this scent in the first place?"

"Some devil," hissed the Chamberlain, clenching both fists where they rested on his thighs. "And, oh, that dog Kame, may he suffer evil rebirths, he gets killed and...."

"Why did she run away? I didn't chase her."

"Your daughter...." He shrugged his hands, then rubbed his face, raising his head, this time.

"She suspected us, my love," she said, turning her face so that half fell into shadow. "She declared she said nothing to my husband, but I think he suspects, as well."

This time Reiko raised his clenched fists to his face where they trembled, slightly.

"Thanks to that..." Shut his eyes. "And his idiotic play!"

"Maybe," she said. "But it is dangerous. I took this risk, yet you seem distant."

"That fool, Kame," he snarled. "Ahhhcc! That fool. Puts the ring on the dead woman for safekeeping. Hah!"

"Are you distant? Do you still care?"

"What?"

"Do you still wish to see it through to the end?"

"Of course."

"With me, to the end?"

Just then a knock at the cabin door. They both started, she said:

"Yoshi." Then: "Come in."

The door was already swinging open and the stocky samurai filled the narrow frame. He bowed, not-too-deeply. It was clear, though he was a clan captain, he had some additional power, acting like an equal. Takezo would have noted he was different from how he'd behaved in the presence of the armored lord in the barn.

"Well?" inquired Reiko.

"The plans go forward," said Yoshi. "With or without the ring."

"More risk," said Reiko, looking down at his shadow again.

"Afraid, now?" wondered Yoshi.

"Insolence," Issa put in. She was watching them both, narrowly. "Is this ring supernatural? Is Nobunaga not a mortal man that you need this

159

talisman to defeat him?" Her disgust and impatience showed. "My daughter ran away. Another is murdered and it's made to seem Osan."

"That fool, Kame," sighed Reiko, shaking his head.

"The fool was he who hired Takezo, in the first place," she offered with a sneer, sipping from her tiny sake cup and ignoring them both.

"You daughter's flight was fortuitous," her lover said, still brooding at the shadow of himself on the table. "A good way to begin action against Izu."

"Anyway," said Yoshi, still standing, which was a point of rudeness, "the foreigner will be tried and quickly executed. Then we move against Izu and his allies. Nobunaga will have to respond." Yoshi bowed with a jerk, rubbed the scar across his nose, looking thoughtfully at Issa. "Takezo will be dealt with."

"Yes, captain," she said. "Keep practicing and you'll master it. Meanwhile, where is Osan?"

"Safe," said Reiko. To Yoshi: "Keep looking for the ring. Takezo can't have hidden it so well. Maybe he gave it to his woman, the *yujo*."

"That was considered," said the stocky captain. "She was investigated."

"Questioned?" asked Reiko, looking at the other, now.

"Yes. She's dead now."

"Another dead girl," said Issa. "And still no magic ring? Is there a price in bodies still unpaid?" She opened and closed her fan with a snap. "Fools."

Yoshi bristled and glared.

"Insulting," he said.

She just looked at him.

"You serve our clan, for the moment, captain," she said, not looking at either of them. "Go, now, and kill more women or whatever you do best for your true master who, no doubt, is a manifest demon."

"As you say, my lady," said Yoshi, and went back out, half-closing the door behind him.

"Naruto," she said to the chamberlain, still not looking at him, "why did Osan run away? Even if she was in love with the foreigner she didn't have to go anywhere. Are we some rustic court?" Looked at him. "Why are you distant?" she asked, again.

He drank another cup of sake. Then again.

"No more mistakes," he said.

160

"I don't trust our 'captain.'"

"He's important. It's very big. We have everything at stake. Our heads, too."

She knelt-walked around the table and touched his arm, then his cheek.

"I don't care," she murmured, "so long as I have your heart. It's senseless, but it's how I feel."

He nodded, still downlooking.

"Don't worry," he told her.

"We'll end up suicides."

"No. Don't worry. We won't fail."

Thirty

Two days later

There were lines of blindingly bright light above him. Takezo was flat on his back in damp, acrid darkness.

He gradually realized the light was close to him...blurred...and the lines seemed perfectly even - which was incomprehensible – not that he expected to comprehend anything. The notion of comprehension was too remote for him to even find the word in his mind...if he even had a mind left to look in....

He was sure he knew his name but there was no hurry in remembering it; how important was that, anyway? What might it change? Something had a foul smell close by and he was a little curious about it...except he was still too far away and there were those bars of unbearable brightness....feeling shrewd, he shut his eyes...better...he sensed there were words for all these things but he didn't need to look for them, either, yet...because now there was a booming sound coming steadily closer...he reopened his eyes as it was banging right overhead, shaking the lines of light, then booming away, again....

The brightness hurt but he decided it was beautiful, fanning into his private dimness, suggesting infinite space and he felt very comfortable except for the smell which kept intruding like a hard lump in a mattress...and then the booming returned, coming from the opposite direction, then going and, as it passed, somehow blocking, spraying shadows into the sweet rays that bathed him in golden warmth...except it was too warm and there was the smell and then a voice, still far away, making sounds he didn't know were words yet...and then he did.

161

"Good morning Jiro Takezo," he said to himself with a slight groan, lying in a cramped, humid space in a stink of vomit. His own, no doubt. There was no mysterious world of light and dark because he was lying under a board sidewalk somewhere in the city and for how long was unclear.

Cheap lodgings, his mind commented.

The light hurt now. He winced. Things came back to him. Not nice things.

Had an inspiration: reached around the maybe two foot high crawl space until he located the jug that had to be there. He felt sly and more comfortable. What wisdom to leave the sake close at hand. And there was plenty of room to tilt it up to his lips. Not such a bad spot, he reflected, away from the bustle of the town and all the nasty things he didn't want to think about.

But only a trickle wet his eager, dry and cracked lips, not enough to penetrate the sticky, fuzzy stuff that apparently filled his mouth. Not good. Tossed the worthless jug aside. Thought hard – which hurt – and then knew where to get more.

The next problem was how to get out because the outside was walled closed by thick support boards and the ones above his head were solid. Well, he hadn't been born under there, so...pushed, then rolled on his belly and crouched up, heaved...nothing...

Panting, slightly, head throbbing, rolled onto his back again. It was very hot there, now, and the lines of sunlight were painful. No more booming, of what he now realized, had been passing footsteps.

Then he remembered his short sword; drew it and began prying at the planks....

Lorenzo Gentile and his quiet, stocky, dark-skinned young bodyguard, Sanada, assigned by Lord Izu, had learned Takezo had been seen in this outskirts area of storehouses where rice, grains, timber, dry goods, metal and so on were collected. No one really lived there besides watchmen and the tavern-keepers. Others mainly showed up to load and unload goods. Gentile thought Izu's advice: "Look for him and he'll find you," could have been better.

On the sunbright, weathered boardwalk in front of them a swordblade suddenly poked up from the planks, glittering like a mirror.

162

Coming closer they could see it was being used to loosen the wood. They stopped under the untreated frayed and curling overhang to witness this marvel. A moment later, with a slam from beneath, two boards popped free and clattered aside, followed by the bare head, dirt-smeared torso, arms and shoulders of Jiro Takezo. His hair was madly knotted, askew and greasy; his face muddy, unshaven for days, eyes puffy and, sitting there, breathing hard and sweating, seemed as if he were standing in a hole.

"Maybe," offered the bodyguard, "he's an earth devil."

"Is he nude?" Gentile wondered, vaguely.

Sanada shrugged. He was, typically, fastidious: shaved to the crown of his head below his topknot, neat and clean.

The *ronin* wasn't much interested in the blurry shadows observing him. He was getting ready to stand. Braced his palms and heaved upright, up to his knees in the sidewalk. Sheathed his *shogo*. Grunted, yawned and rubbed his eyes.

"Ahrhh," he more or less groaned.

Gentile was pleased to see his kimono was caught up around his waist so they were spared any intimate sights beyond the long, smooth upper-body muscles of the handsome, disheveled swordsman.

"We were told a certain Jiro Takezo is in this neighborhood, sir," said Gentile.

"That's exciting to know," the detective responded, planting one bare foot up on the planks and making the major effort it took to step up to the walkway where he swayed, ominously, for a moment.

"Are you well, sir?" asked the bodyguard.

"That's a good one."

"Are you Jiro Takezo?" asked Gentile.

"Never heard of him." He was concerned with the slight tilt of the sidewalk. He wasn't sure if it actually did have a slight tilt and didn't want to ask them. He took a couple of steps and went off the planks into the dusty street, trying to make it seem like it was all his own idea. "Anything to drink?"

"We have water," said the Italian.

"Don't want a bath."

"Sure of that?" questioned Sanada.

"We met in the rain," Gentile reminded him. "After the theater."

"I hate theater," said the terminally hung-over *ronin*. "Actors are boils. Audiences are the pus that spurts out."

The *ronin* grunted self-agreement and didn't quite wobble across the street and towards the corner. The area was nearly empty: just a single watchman sitting on a crate in the shade of a sagging overhang two cross streets away and a man in a bandanna with a stack of wood over his shoulder, trudging along.

He recalled an alley that led to a stable and then to a little shop that sold soggy buns and sake. The Italian and Sanada followed behind at a little distance.

"You are Takezo-san, yes?" Gentile called to him.

"Not sure who I am," was the reply, made without turning around. It was enough to walk steady and straight. "Maybe I used to be. Who cares?" Then he paused and swayed a little. "You speak better than the other ones."

"You found them."

"Lost them, too. Well, the fire-haired one. Lost him. Lost a lot of people in various ways." Started walking again, into the alley and around a short bend. The rich stink of the stable was heavy in the hot, wet air. "I'm bad luck." Rubbed his face. "I sent the black man away to be safe. Who knows? I'm bad luck."

"I hope not," demurred Gentile.

"The black one is very strong."

"He's quite muscular."

"When we say strong we mean talented."

"*Io capisco*. I see." They were side-by-side now with the bodyguard a little behind.

"You were trying to help Colin."

"Was I? My help can doom you." He spat except he was so dry there was no effect. "I like the black one better. Anyway, I'm busy, now. Where's that water?" Gentile handed him a small jug which he rinsed his mouth out with. Then he spat and made a face. "Now my mouth tastes worse."

They'd come to the little shop where ragged, stained and yellowing half-curtains and banner strips, written on in clumsy characters, barely moved in the sodden shifts of air.

"Sir," Gentile said, "why are you here in such a state? Lord Izu sent me to speak with you."

164

Takezo had a suspicion his skull had, somehow, been filled with thick, lukewarm porridge. Decided that was the best part of how he felt. He was aware of not thinking about Miou yet, not even letting her name form.

"Izu," he said, as they went inside. "Does he want us to watch the moonrise together?"

"Why are you staying here?"

"It's nice here," Takezo said.

Gentile paused in the doorway to glance around at the dilapidated buildings; a stack of broken barrels; an overgrown vacant lot; a skinny black and white dog sleeping in the dust....

"Very nice," he agreed, following Takezo into the dim, dank interior.

"So she's dead," the detective said, tangentially. "Who knows if she even loved me?"

They both sat on stools at a table about two feet high which was a rare pleasure for Gentile. Takezo rested his long sword against the side of the table and squinted at the shopkeeper, a middle-aged man with small mouth, eyes and nose. Sporting, the *ronin* decided, ten thousand tiny moles on the rest of his almost featureless face. For a moment he thought he might be having a drunkard's vision. The man looked with faint contempt at the disheveled swordsman and irritated curiosity at the oddly dressed foreigner. Takezo assumed the man's main business had to do with some kind of *tekiya* crookedness. There wouldn't be much of a steady clientele in a section like this, otherwise. The *tekiya* crossed the often blurry border between legal and illegal forms of rent collection, protection and extortion and, like the gamblers – *bakuto*, were known for their strong corrupt links with various forms of local police. Probably traded in stolen goods from the warehouses or something....

"Love, well...." began Gentile. "What man truly understands it?"

He was pondering Lady Issa. He'd stayed in bed with her, that night, until dawn. He'd tried to leave earlier when the only light was a single lantern in the far corner that shone through the fine mosquito netting enclosing the mattress in a kind of gauzy mystery. She seemed asleep. As he'd carefully moved to dress himself she'd said:

'A lover who bustles about and searches for his pocketbook, tangles his clothing and mutters to himself, is irritating.' She was quoting from a pillow-book.

165

'Forgive me,' he'd said, sitting back down beside her, thinking how formal even a night of passion could be.

She'd touched his lips with a finger.

'You are a tender man, foreigner. A rare thing.'

'Is your husband tender?'

'Don't speak of him,' she'd admonished.

One of her long, soft hands lay on his hairy chest. She was curling a bit around her finger.

'I...as you wish, my lady.'

'You are like a bear,' she'd informed him.

'Why did you....'

Her voice was a shrug:

'No question to ask a lady.'

He gestured, looking at Takezo.

"I understand very little," he said.

"Of women? Of love?" He peered up at the mole-struck face leaning towards them. "How about you?" he asked.

"You want prostitutes, eh?" was the response. "I can get them."

"A man who understands," Takezo said. "I want sake. To hell with romance."

"*La donna,*" Gentile pronounced, thinking about Issa. "ha(?) *sempre ragione.*"

"Sake," the host said and shuffled away.

"Cool," the *ronin* called after him.

"I have been with both clans," remarked Gentile. "As we say in my land: 'if the smell is bad, so is the fish.'"

"That's said here, too."

Takezo shut his eyes and saw her body again: the wheel marks...blood....Popped them open and blinked hard. Sighed, unconsciously. Then growled, slammed his iron-hard palm on the tabletop with a crash that sent puffs of dust up from the cracks. The proprietor twisted around behind his counter and another male face, peered past a hanging, ragged curtain marking off an otherwise open room in the back. The filtered, hot daylight coming into the musty place through open shutters and warped wallboards showed part of a bald head but left the features shadowed.

"Settle down," the owner called over.

166

The head withdrew behind the curtain again. Gentile wondered how many might be sitting back there. From the smell he thought maybe they kept animals at that end of the building.

The problem was Takezo's headache, the memory of Miou, the musty, heavy heat and the years of his life that had added up to this. Just then, he had the patience of a scorpion.

"Settle *yourself*, you ugly lout!" the *ronin* barked. "Bring sake and be still."

He knew that was unlike him. Sort of regretted it. Confirming his probable underworld associations, the man responded:

"Samurai bum. Who cares about you? Get out and rest in the street. You and your foreign devil, here."

Gentile noted the bald head was back peering through a parting in the curtain. And there was another face, too, this time. A long one with a thick jaw and a bush of hair.

Takezo grunted and dropped a coin on the table. Gentile's young man appeared in the front doorway, parting the greasy half-curtain there.

"Lord Izu hopes that you have discovered useful facts about the fate of Osan," the Italian said, ignoring the developing set-to.

"I'll discover some useful facts shortly," Takezo snarled, "if no sake is brought forth, insolent shop-man."

"Ha, ha," said the insolent one. "Take your coin and go, *eta*."

Gentile looked quizzical.

"Severe insult," explained the detective. "*Eta*. Unclean."

The two men Gentile had noted behind the rear curtain were now standing at the edge of this room near the counter. With a sigh Takezo got up and went over, sheathed sword in one hand. The man seemed unimpressed.

"Trouble, eh?" the man said.

"No," was the reply. "Just sake. I have a headache. Feel sick. I apologize for my bad temper." Jerked a bow. "Just sake."

The man shook his head. The other two had moved closer: the bald one was stout and powerful, the second was lean, weathered. Both sported tattoos like bands around their upper arms, one for each criminal offense they'd committed.

"Get out," said the shopkeeper.

Takezo sighed, again. Flashed out his sword with the blade reversed so that the dull side was poised over the man's shoulder. That way a blow could bruise, break a bone but not cut. The *ronin* chopped down, not hard with the idea just making a quiet point.

But in a practiced blur the small-featured fellow had a 3-pronged *jittu* in each hand and caught the easy downstroke in one, twisting it to lock the blade while he viciously jabbed at Takezo's face with the other.

A mistake, because he should have tried for the momentarily pinned forearm. He leaned forward too far. His target, waking from the remnants of his hung-over stupor, even as his left arm moved in that seemingly casual way and didn't seem as fast as it actually was, caught the shopkeeper's outstretched wrist, stopping the weapon a inch from his eye, simultaneously wrenching his sword free from the pin in a shower of sparks.

More good fighters among the Bakuto, he thought. *Small wonder Yazu wants to learn....*

He gave the man a punitive crack on the head with the swordhilt, noting that Gentile's young samurai guard had his own problems: his blade had been tangled by the bald man's weighted chain while his companion whipped his metal lozenge at his head. He had to go to one knee to escape the blow without releasing his sword.

The Italian had drawn the five-foot long rapier and flung himself forward in a long lunge and shout and got the tip into the bald man's armpit. The fellow dropped his chain and fell back, startled and bleeding profusely. He and his companion fled into the rear and could be heard clattering outside into the still, hot, heavy afternoon.

"What nonsense," declared the *ronin*, taking up a sake jug from behind the counter where the keeper lay sighing and muttering under his breath. "Come, we earned this."

Went back to the table and sat, heavily. Poured drinks for the three of them looking generally at the doorway where the brightness, gathered around the center-slit half-curtains, angled in the lower half of the door. Streamers of sun that slotted through the loosely spaced and warped wall planks made brilliant, golden blades in the dustmotes.

The bodyguard went and sat by the wall. They drank in silence, for awhile, Takezo occasionally studying the Italian gentleman. Lifted and studied the rapier Gentile had laid across the uneven table after wiping the tip. Nodded with understanding.

"Could penetrate light armor," he commented.

168

"You people fight in robes most of the time," Gentile returned.

"Not in battle. But light armor is best. It's all timing. If you are willing to die you can cut almost anyone."

"Ah. I am not a soldier. Though I was schooled in fighting."

"Think *I* am a soldier? Anyway, why are you here?"

"The murders of the women seem tied together."

"This is news already carved in stone," snorted the detective.

"The Lady Issa is troubled. She thinks you know more than you've revealed."

Her name made Takezo uneasy. A memory came to consciousness of her lips on his genitals as he rocked between waking and sleep, the soothing rain pouring over the closed palanquin.

"You are close to her?' he inquired. "Or is it common knowledge in the clan."

He noted the Italian's fleeting discomfort as he tilted back a full cup of sake before answering.

"Well, I..." he began. "Close would be...."

As he shifted himself in his seat a stray sunbeam touched the side of his face outlining his long, slightly arched nose and shadowing the rest of his head.

"Not common knowledge," affirmed Takezo.

"No," agreed the other man. "She suggested I ask you and...so...."

"Hmn," grunted the detective, dismissively. "I wonder how long I have been drunk? I had a hope, you see..." Gentile realized a deep feeling was surfacing in the Japanese. "Well, a hope...to live a life that...but now it is all so trivial. Makes a man sick." He raised a fist but didn't pound the table as Gentile expected. "In the pond dead leaves gather...time takes autumn's form...." Poured and drank another cup. "If I could challenge time, you see, my friend, I'd cut his head off!" Takezo hissed. "He has taken everything...everything...." Shook his head like a wet animal. "I'm supposed to be clever and yet I cannot duel with time...why, money to me is dog dirt...." He chuckled. "Issa's a whore," he concluded. "Sells herself for power."

"Sir?" murmured the Italian, nervously.

"Miou was not a whore...very subtle and commanding distinction...Miou had no price, you see?...Human life is food and drink

169

and love and dogdirt....Reiko's a bigger whore than anybody. He sells himself for...for...." Couldn't find the words and he shouldn't be even close to drunk, yet. Not really. Or maybe, he vaguely conceived, the wine just unlocked the madness and fury that could smash down reason's door by itself....

Gentile would later note in his journals how powerfully these people suppressed massive feelings. There was an obvious comparison with the Spartans. Maybe their violence was so extreme because they were imprisoned by the custom of closing them in.

Ah, I wish I could have discussed these things with Osan, he thought. The idea that he'd slept with her mother created a strange feeling of unease and, yet, pleasure that he had, somehow connected with her – absurd, of course, but a feeling is a feeling. *I am like this angry man, here,* he reasoned on, *in that I have tried to contain myself...pitifully trying to think my way through what I should have only felt...and so I slept with Issa wishing it were her child while pretending to myself it was not so........*

He wished he were working on the painting. More and more he'd find himself visualizing the composition, the characters.....He'd blocked in the general area where Osan would appear. He wasn't ready to sketch her in but knew it was going to be a stylized figure, maybe like the Madonnas of earlier centuries....

Issa, too...he saw her lying voluptuously, golden body naked and in stark, almost metallic color as if her flesh were wrought from smooth and perfect precious metal, her face a mask with eyes like actual jewels...above her would loom the storm that seemed to rain blood in scattered gusts, the storm that whipped and whirled around the fighting horsemen and soldiers on the black, hellish battlefield where the lone samurai (a spot of purest white like a fading gleam of hope and purity) stabbed himself to death.....

He shook his head, swallowed more wine, and chuckled at his own absurdity.

Takezo glanced at him, grim and blurry.

"Will those men return with others?" Gentile asked, practically.

"I hope so," said the *ronin*. He considered the Italian. "Suppose she isn't dead. How would you like that?"

"You mean, Osan?"

"It's how you say her name. I noticed it."

Gentile waved his hands.

170

"You believe I love a dead woman?" he exclaimed.

"It's how you say her name." He held his sake cup up to his face and squinted at his reflection, featureless and partial outline that, he dully thought, needed to be filled in. "Anyway, I love a dead woman, myself."

"I see."

"They murdered her….they murdered the others…." Sneered at the half-empty cup and the hint of him in it. "Is this a life for a man?" Set the cup down, carefully, as if it mattered. "I don't know how to feel…we had plans, you see…plans…."

"Don't you want to find out who are the killers?" He was remembering something Osan had written – which he did all the time. Something about once men get into the habit of killing, people can be crushed like insects in a garden.

He realized there were others like this bitter, grieving man whom he could speak with about these matters but he often found himself imagining conversations with Osan, a kind of almost literary conceit, he realized.

"I know them," Takezo replied, staring at nothing, now. "So many to slay…."

He knew he liked to think killing was always forced on him. Maybe it was. He wasn't sure, anymore.

An excuse that won't fool the keepers of destiny, he thought. *Ah, the sword sticks to your hands, once you pick it up….*

He stood with a slightly wobbly violence, staring at nothing. "Maybe I might have saved Miou," he murmured. "But my stupidity is nearly perfect. I have labored on it."

The Italian stood up, not sure he followed Takezo on all points. The bodyguard, Sanada, offered them water from a hanging jug and everyone drank deep. It was tepid but clean-tasting.

Takezo noted the shopkeeper had crawled out of the room and was gone. He assumed they'd sent for reinforcements – or even the police, depending on where they actually stood among the criminal groups.

Sanada had found a tray of buns covered by a cloth behind the counter and passed them around. They were stale and spongy but Takezo was hungry enough to eat three, munching as they went outside into the bright, cloudless heat. The street was empty except for the black and white dog still sleeping in the shade across the way.

Sake for breakfast, he thought. *Still, I'm not so drunk…*

171

He wanted a bath more than anything else. Was considering sobering up. Wondered what that would be like. The foreigner was talking but he didn't really listen. Vaguely liked the man because he was obviously sincere.

"Will you continue?" Gentile repeated.

"Sure. Like a stone rolling down a hill. What else can I do?"

Takezo told him where to leave messages for him and watched them go back down the alley to the main street, picking their way around the litter and empty storage barrels, crossing into and out of light and shadow; the lean foreigner with his strange sword and the compact samurai who was a perfect example of what they were bred to be: taciturn, incurious, fearless and intentionally stupid....

Whereas I remain a fool, he thought, *despite my best efforts to be wise....*

He went to a cheap bathhouse near where he lodged. The women who ran it knew him and weren't likely to distract anyone with their beauty. He felt improved. Except he knew Miou would have been buried by now and he was going to have to go to real emptiness....

The bathhouse was four posts and a roughly thatched, pitched roof over wall-less raised boards with four big wooden tubs into which the women poured steaming water while you soaked, then doused you with cold. Takezo had never been crazy about the cold part but in this weather he was almost looking forward to it. The sole customer, he could enjoy the view across the tanner's sheds, the backyard of a small stable plus a few feet of dry earth and a cracked stone lantern in a clump of tired-looking, pale flowers that hinted at what once might have been a garden.

Whatever he'd said to the Italian, he had no real plans beyond going to Miou's grave. The idea of revenge didn't mean much: he was weary and sorry and nothing was going to make him less sorry....

He cupped water onto his face and sat with eyes shut, up to his neck. When the eyes re-opened, the nodding, serious, intent, nervous, pale, bony face of Yazu greeted them peering around the side of the adjoining well shed. The rest of the small, wiry fellow appeared bowing, wooden sword thrust through his sash. He came, spryly, out of the brightness and approached Takezo. The sword was too long for him and tended to slip so the point tip-tapped the damp boards as he walked. The *ronin* had to smile.

172

"*Sensei*," he ejaculated, "sorry to be so rude but I have discovered a fact."

"What? That no other can piss for you?"

"No, no, *sensei*. I…I saw father Osihatchi and…"

"Was he well? Has his sleep been untroubled?"

Yazu frowned.

"I know not. He seemed in good condition, sir."

"Thank heaven for it." Takezo raised himself and now knelt waist-deep. "Please, get the cold bucket over there."

The skinny man virtually scuttled with pleasure, darting to the wooden pails, hefting the biggest and then swaying under the weight, came, wobbling, and heaved the cool water over his master's head and shoulders.

Talkezo gasped and exhaled.

"Villain!" he snarled. "Ah…hhh…." Shook his head. He never got used to the shock.

"*Sensei*?"

Breathing normally, again, Takezo asked:

"What about Hachimachi?"

"Who?" Then Yazu got it. Looked pleased with himself, even gloating a little, the detective noticed, as he answered: "The Father was deeply concerned about the sorrow that came to you. He does not think she was run down by a drunken fool, as was given out."

Takezo nodded.

"I know," he said, quietly. "She was murdered."

"So the Father thinks." Yazu was obviously pleased at having the ear and attention of great and powerful men. He looked thoughtful.

"Is this your 'discovery?"

"No, master." He leaned over the huge tub, serious and concentrated. "Father Osimachi told me who struck down the prostitute, 'Cherry Blossom.'"

Takezo took this in. He knew what was going to follow. Sometimes time was the river and you the wheel and it passed and just turned you.

I have spilled much blood, he said to himself, *maybe enough will wash itself out….*

"Kill a man, bad or good or indifferent," he said, "and another comes in his place. In that sense, killing is pointless except for its own sake; make up whatever fine story you like."

"*Sensei?*"

"You did well, Yazu. You did well."

"Thank you, master."

"The best thing is to run and hide." Shook his head. "How few have the talent and strength for that."

Yazu didn't try to really understand. He'd accepted that his teacher was an extraordinary being disguised as a drunkard who liked to say too much or far too little. He shrugged.

"I'm pretty good at that, master."

"It doesn't count until you're good enough to win."

He stood up and left the tub. One of the older women came in and chuckled at the sight. She held a worn, clean towel.

"More cold water, Takezo-san?" she inquired.

"Spare me," he replied.

"Want a bath?" she asked the disciple, looking at him as if there could be no doubt, handing the towel to the swordsman.

"No," said Yazu. "I'm clean in all my parts, woman."

"Ha, ha," she said. "I count myself fortunate not to encounter them. I see enough strange things in my trade."

Takezo laughed. Then went cold, empty and serious again.

"Do you know where the grave is?"

"Of Cherry Blossom, master?"

"No."

"Ah. I'm sorry, master. I can show you."

"Good. You show me tonight. Meanwhile, who does the 'Father' say is responsible for the Blossom?"

The bath woman, exited, at this point, as the *ronin* had already paid. Takezo began dressing himself in his worse-for-wear kimono.

"A bad samurai. Very bad. Very feared. Treacherous as a snake. A poisonous man who works for one, then another. His sword, they say, is evil." Which was like saying: his soul.

"I don't require his credentials," said Takezo. "Where will I discover him?"

With both swords back in his sash Takezo turned to Yazu.

"Draw quickly and strike me on the shoulder. Now!"

He drew his own short sword at moderate speed. Yazu hesitated, then struck, leaning away from possible retailiation. Naturally, the master barely moved to avoid his half-hearted blow.

"Yazu," he declared. "I can improve your almost non-existent skill 10 times over before we leave this spot. You value your life too much. Think about your woman and all the miserable days you've lived. Consider your probable future. Do this continually and we'll practice again."

Thirty-One

Lorenzo Gentile left word that he would meet Takezo at the graveyard that night. Then, uncomfortable, the Italian went to see Issa so she wouldn't think he was avoiding her.

He was at the castle by sunset and sent a message he actually was able to write himself. He'd already been told his calligraphy was surprisingly good. He liked the Chinese brush they used for writing and pointing.

The rocks and miniature trees were already blended together by the thickening twilight. Fireflies were staining the humid air with streaks and curls of lingering greenish gold as if, he imagined, something inexplicable was sketching a message on the gathering night. Somewhere there was a faint, pinging tinkle of water.

He sighed.

There was no way to have refused her, he reasoned.

A woman from Issa's retinue, carrying a red lantern, came up the path. Her exaggeratedly delicate, mincing steps made the light and shadow of her coming seem to flicker rather than sway.

She bowed deeply and handed him a note, holding the soft light so he could read the long, sharp-looking characters.

"Eh," he sighed. "*Momenta, signorina*...." Concentrated...got it. It was a haiku, naturally.

The ice in the pond, he translated, *jewels in the moonlight, too cold to wear*....

"Will you reply?" she asked.

He shook his head and let his hands rise and fall back on his knees.

"No," he told her.

Delicately done, he remarked to himself. *I've been dismissed in verse*....

175

Outside he met Sanada the bodyguard and went into his leather bag. Removed 5 "Puffer"pistols and tucked the heavy, charged Wheelocks into his wide belt. The sun was well down, now. The stars were big and soft-looking in the wet sky.

"Take me to the burial place, Sanada, please," he requested, "where Takezo went."

At the first checkpoint Sanada pulled out a pass sighed by Hideo. Then they followed a curving street that joined the road that went up to the hilltop where the detective had attended Osan's supposed funeral, uninvited and in disguise.

The moon hadn't risen yet. In this suburb, long, low houses were set back screened by trees and walls; lanterns shifted their glow in the warm, easy breezes.

At the last checkpoint at the city limits, the big policeman, Taro, blocked their way after the *yoriki* already let them pass. He was in his official basin helmet and gold and black clothes.

"You saw Takezo, the swordsman?" he wanted to know. He didn't seem pleased.

"Yes," replied Gentile. "We are going to find him, now."

"I will come with you."

"How did you know we were coming this way?" Gentile wondered, as they started walking up the long slope away from the city. Sanada the taciturn bodyguard held a pale, moon-colored lantern and led the way.

"You are as difficult to locate as a burning building," Taro told him.

"Ah. Of course. My appearance. Are you a policeman? A friend of Takezo-san?"

"Aha. Both. Sometimes. Neither today."

"He went to the graveyard."

"A good idea," grunted Taro. "Saves expense."

Thirty-Two

Akichi Cemetery

Less drunk, Takezo was still walking on balloons, putting each foot down a little too carefully, stepping over imaginary obstacles. The earth was uneven and loamy between the grave markers.

176

The full moon was above the horizon, fat and intensely red, reflected in the great bay visible from the hillside, the water seeming still as a sheet of dark glass.

Like another bloodstain, he couldn't help but think.

Her grave was the only fresh one in the section. He stood near it. The moon's sanguinary gleaming shown on the stone and wooden grave markers; tall pillars with mini pitched roofs on top that always reminded him of tiny houses. As a boy, he'd imagined a race of tiny people with tiny ideas and problems, weapons and small lives living there, hiding when people were around, active at night when almost no one visited the territory of the dead....

The rising moon half-shadowed the mounded earth and hinted the shapes of trees, bushes and artifacts, all twisted and blurred by his tears.

"Silent, empty ground," he half-whispered. "A road to a gateless wall."

I'm so sorry, his mind dinned. *I should have seen it...I let myself believe you were safe because you said you were safe...fool!...so sorry...I believed I had time...time...like a man working hard in a dream to finish a task that awake does not exist....*

He gripped his face with both, long, powerful hands and puffed out a rending cry as if through the dull, heavy flesh itself, flushed and agonized:

"Unseeing fool!"

He let himself fall forward over the grave, fingers now clutching into the warm, damp soil.

"My plans," he whispered, not-quite-sobbing, into the muffling earth, "had no more...no more substance than...than the schemes of a madman by the roadside, twisting his fingers in the air to give shape to nonsense...."

Oh, Miou...Miou...am I just the drunkard, at last, swearing at night how he'll recover his lost life...recover his lost riches...dig up buried honor? Recover lost face?

He lay still, for awhile, just breathing, unevenly.

"All we were," he murmured down to her, "has unraveled like smoke....I was blind...my eyes two empty holes in a stone head...."

He arched back to his knees then sat on his heels as if at a formal meeting with the dead. The moon was well up, now, and had gone to silver, the subtle tones spilling unevenly over the burial ground.

Die, he considered, *and the dreams must go on...asleep they seem solid...without the body they will* be *solid for the body deadens everything, I think....Would I see her, then, or just dream her?*

He drew his short sword and angled the blade to glitter and break the moonlight.

Kill yourself or go on and kill them...either way, you die killing...and how can you be sure of even the dreams? Or of darkness, either...or 10,000 rebirths to come? Small wonder samurai are trained to avoid thinking too much....

"I love you," was all he said, this time.

He just stayed there with eyes closed, not even thinking. That was good because he heard the bow twang behind him and the *whuttt* of the arrow as his body threw itself aside as if jerked by an unseen cord.

Rolling onto his back below the level of the mound he stared around into the night's silvery hush, wondering how many were out there. Shut one eye to eliminate a slight double blur.

The next arrow would have to come from within his field of vision. It did, well-shot. A flicker of movement he sensed as much as actually saw. He deflected the shaft with his short sword.

It was pointless to wait there so he rolled up and over the mounded grave, vaguely thinking how if he died now he'd be near her. The brilliant moon and thin streaked, illuminated clouds flashed around twice before he was down the far side in time to catch half-a-dozen men in dark clothing, not *ninja,* crouching close to him with drawn swords and long poles with jutting hooks to deflect or even trap swung blades. They'd just emerged from a screen of bushes and pines.

This section of the cemetery was closed by a high wall with a single gate back behind him. No point trying to lose himself in the night this time since there were probably men hiding everywhere, inside and out.

Must have been waiting and here I come, mumbling and weeping like a woman....

In an almost child-like response he rolled at them, then, almost under their feet, leaped up with both swords drawn. He stabbed the short sword into a spearman's foot, cut the shoulder of a swordsman whose downslice bit the earth. Went behind a thick-boled tree as a spear *chukked* into the bark. He was angry, now. Where he'd been grieving he now spit fury – icy fury because they were all so stupid, because it was stupid not to pity and care but instead just do murder.

178

There's no rain for you all to hide behind, this time, he thought. *Or me, either...maybe we finish it, now....*

His awareness seemed detached from his actions like the still eye of a typhoon. He moved around the tree to whip his blade across the face of the next attacker and then shatter the spear of another who barely flung himself aside in time. His mind flashed: suppose he could kill all the retainers and then all the captains up to the rulers, themselves, it would be like trying to empty a river with a bucket and, anyway, most of them wouldn't understand whether what they did was right or wrong because, always: "Duty is a mountain, life a feather...."

He wiped blood from his eyes as he cut into the heart of a man he could tell was a good swordsman and the warm spatter hit his face. Spinning back out from the clump of bushes, he jumped up on her grave, blade upraised in the bright moonlight.

"Come on," he cried, "if you savor death!" Another arrow zipped past and missed. "Come closer and maybe you'll hit something."

Several goaded samurai broke from cover and charged the mound. Someone called for more archers. The voice sounded familiar.

This caused laughter out there and a hissed curse from Yoshi...there he was, limping out of the shadows to the delight of the detective. The moonlight brought out the roundness of his high-shaved head. It was too dark to see his scowl or his scar. He raised his sword high.

"Orders are clear!" he cried. "Destroy this shit-pile in the shape of a man!"

"You call for your own death," Takezo observed, to more laughter. "How strange."

Samurai charged the *ronin* from front and rear as Yoshi moved cautiously forward. The night was a glittering hush. The weapons glinted and flashed silverbright. The air was thick, warm and sweet with perfume, green scents and the dark richness of the earth.

Part of Takezo's being looked on as if he were standing still, immersed in contemplation while the rest of him danced into combat, again, in the slowed-motion where time seemed to be ineffectual and he was free to move: each shift, each position determined by fate's choreography so that even his drunken looseness and inexactness became a natural advantage, a new skill exposing the clumsy weaknesses of the angry, struggling shadows closing in, striking at him.

His sword whipped around like a child swinging a stick at the air, relaxed and unplanned. He accepted he'd probably be tangled in a steel net of doom, sooner or later, but paid no attention to that observation. The dance was everything. There was no objective or outcome that he imagined because that part of his consciousness was taken up with the still stars, the wild moon and the surrounding shadows that seemed to form and dissolve around their flashing steel: the beauty absorbed everything else.

So he waved the blade as if it were imaginary and he cut down waves of attacking dream-figures and the groans, shouts and curses seemed to come from some unconnected, remote waking place where blade slashes and impacts were all part of the dance he was watching unfold as his body spun and stepped and new figures kept springing up and striking at him....

For an instant, the glitter of steel in the persistence of vision resembled an almost decipherable calligraphy slashing doom's meaning into the lucent night in complex sweeps and blots and stops....

He was just present, angerless, fearless, caught in an indescribable purity of rhythm where time did seem to change around him like a stream now fast, now whirlpooling, now spreading and slow, now paused in a backwash....

He had a sense that he would just dance out of this world into whatever oblivion waited through the opening gate into night and forever....

He'd circled back to her grave into a sudden pause. Just the sound of skreeghing insects, gasping breaths and groans in a world splashed by untarnished silver staining leaves, stones, woods, pillars, metal and men: living, dead, dying.

Takezo was almost sober, waiting for the final wave of steel-fanged shadows to sweep over him and drown him in darkness. He noted bowmen nocking arrows and figures closing in around him; shocks of sound that seemed unreal, blood itself was a colorless shadow. One, two: pause; then three, puffing blasts that popped the ears with three gouts of orange-red fire and a disproportionate roll of smoke suddenly covering half the scene blotting and dimming the gleaming night....

One attacker had fallen, flopping sideways over a grave, trying to crawl in agony, holding a hip shattered by a pistol ball. The inexplicable blast of pain shocked the man into a un-samurai-like keening.

Another ball had hit a wooden gravepost cracking it in half while the third shot missed everything. Instantly Takezo charged the men nearest him who were just starting to blur into the powder smoke.

The flashing moon-sketch of his blade cut so neatly that he had an impression the men just dissolved into blurred heaps as he disappeared into the acrid, reeking, heavily spreading cloud. On the far side of the unintentional smokescreen, Gentile was leveling his last two loaded pistols at a samurai who'd come through the smoke, firing point-blank, both shots good, the heavy caliber balls knocking the man down as if he'd been hit with a 12 pound hammer.

He recognized Taro and the bodyguard, Sanada, flanking the open gate. There was now almost enough smoke to suggest a burning house. The attackers came on, into and out of the drifting fumes as Gentile and the *ronin* fell back towards the gate. The Italian had his rapier out, now. A samurai struck down overhand and was briefly impaled by the five-foot long blade in the throat. He dropped backwards, gagging and spitting blood as he vanished in the obscurity.

A few tried to cut them off at the gateway. Taro and Takezo moved at them together, the spy almost nonchalant, actually more aware of the night, the moon gleaming on the slowly thinning gun smoke of the opponents.

One lunged behind his spear at Takezo and stabbed a coil of smoke, throwing him off balance as the *ronin* swayed slightly away from him. Taro had a three-pointed trident-style *jittu* in each hand, the central point a thick-bladed dagger, and caught a swordsman's side slice at his torso, locked the blade with his left hand weapon and slashed the fellow's forearms with the other, without really breaking stride so that they were already in the gateway.

Takezo gestured with his sword and stomped his foot with a *kiai* shout and several fell back from him. This cry from a master warrior's belly had been known to seemingly stop or deflect attackers as if they'd been touched physically.

The four of them were now covering the gate, Sanada on the extreme right, Takezo on the extreme left. The smoke was gently and slowly spreading in their direction on the wet, heavy air that made hard breathing harder. It was perfect cover and reminded him of the sudden fog that had concealed them at the village.

As they backed to the gate another wave of samurai came out of the smoke and they clashed violently. As he cut the nearest opponent across the short ribs, Takezo peripherally noted Yoshi limping to the attack against young Sanada. He further noted that the young bodyguard was a good swordsman but Yoshi was better. Sanada ducked away and was in trouble except that, in a brilliant move, Gentile stuck his blade in the ground and drew two more pistols. Led by Yoshi, most of the attackers fell back into the obscurity with no way to know they weren't loaded.

Outside they were crossing the moonwhitened road, kicking up dust in pale gouts when an arrow hit Sanada in the base of his skull and poked out a foot through his mouth. As he stumbled, Taro held him, saw the wound, blood (just a dark stain) drooling over his teeth and lips and let him continue to silently crumble onto his side. The policeman followed the other two into the dense darkness of the forest on the far side.

And then he took over and led them, down into a deeply slanting declivity, picking his way among closely spaced trees and hanging branches, then coming out into an open sweet-smelling stretch of tall pines. The air was clean, cool, almost electrically crisp under there.

"Where are we?" Takezo asked.

"An old smuggler's way back to the city," Taro replied. "We pick up and follow a river that flows into the *Oi*. No gates to pass, that way."

Now there was a soft whooshing rush of water. They scrambled down a loamy embankment and started following the quick, looping river.

Takezo paused and dipped his face into the cool flow. His head felt better and the exertion seemed to have burned-off the alcohol. He had a feeling things were going to move faster and faster from here on. Drank and wet his hair. The other two were seated on a fallen tree trunk where it lay half in and out of the foaming river. The steady water-roar softened all other sound. The moon was directly overhead.

"I am grateful," Takezo told them, standing up, amazed to be unhurt.

Taro leaned his face at him, half-silvered from above, topknot puffed-out and twisted like a dog's tail.

"I'm in plenty of trouble," he said. "I came to warn you, anyway. Late."

Gentile was reloading pistols. Takezo picked one up and weighed it in his hand.

"Interesting weapon," he commented.

182

"If I go back to honest crime," said Taro, "I'll get some of these."

"I'm sorry, my friend," Takezo said. "I didn't wish to cause you problems."

"Oh ho," scoffed the big man. "You didn't." shook his head. Behind him the foamy silversheen of water hooked around a sharp bend and vanished into the overhanging tree shadows. "I have a family. They developed bad habits, like eating and living under a roof."

Takezo nodded. Taro and Gentile stood up.

"Yes," he said. "I'm sorry. I don't have those problems."

Taro touched his shoulder.

"I know, my friend," he said, sympathetic.

"I feel like a man nailed to a tree," Takezo said. "I take small delight in the view before me."

"What do we do, now?" asked the Italian, pistols tucked back in his belt. He looked at the *ronin* whose back was to the luminescent water, a tall outline, featureless, one side of his long face lit by the bright moon. "That poor boy."

"We're all poor boys," the *ronin* said.

"Ah," demurred the Italian, "still…violence is irrational. Nature moves towards harmony, as in your exquisite paintings. Murder is jarring ugliness."

"You come from the land of peace and reason?" wondered Taro.

"You have me there," chuckled Gentile, shaking his head, no. "But the enlightened mind expresses the truths of the soul and brings harmony and…." Shook his head, again. "Sadly, ideals are mere dreams."

"Here," said Takezo, "the harmony of the spirit has a sword for a tongue." To Taro: "Two ways to benefit you, Taro," he said. "I sent the black man to Mora village by the sea."

"Where the girl was killed," confirmed the policeman.

"Maybe." Takezo shrugged. "It's run by criminals. You can arrest them and the crooked magistrate and so look good."

"Or join up?" Taro didn't quite laugh.

"Or make yourself boss. Kill them, cripple them. Scare them."

"Why?"

"They have it coming. If I had time I'd go there now, myself."

"What about uMubaya?" put in Gentile.

"The black one?" asked Taro.

"A good man," affirmed Takezo. "He's in disguise and hiding out. Wants to help his foreign friend."

Taro moved so the soft silver light was almost directly in the other's face as
he turned to look at the two of them. The subtle glow smoothed away all strain and harsh lines, so it resembled a silver sculpture of some bodhisattva, or, as the Italian thought, the hinted mask of an angel with a sword in his hand; a Michael.

"Why?" Taro repeated his question.

"Whatever you do there," was the answer, "it will help expose them. Like crawling things under a rotting board."

This man has a purity, Gentile thought. *Small wonder he is so troubled....*

"Alright," said Taro. "Now one for you." They started walking again, carefully, following the twists of the rushing river. The bank was stony, damp and a little slippery. "There's a nasty, known killer low-life been getting drunk for two nights at the Old Moon Inn. A spy for criminal families. Powerful protection. Dangerous. Pays well for young boys, I hear." Shrugged. "Anyway, there were complaints to the watchhouse."

They were passing in and out of deep shadow, now clear; now lost in darkness. Suddenly the earth downslanted steeply and they had to dig in their heels and backtilt. They were at the edge of a thin waterfall that vanished, then reappeared a hundred feet below, spilling into the moonlight and puffing out into a cloud of mist over gentle hills where the soft, colored lights of houses showed they were at the outskirts of Edo.

"Why mention this nasty fellow?'" Takezo wanted to know.

"He has muttered things about the dead women. The *kosho.*" Meaning licensed prostitutes. They were all almost running, now, as the slope steepened, voices jarred. "You can't miss him."

Takezo grunted, concentrating on his footing, bracing quick steps on rocks
and exposed roots, briefly gripping low branches and thin trunks as moonbright and shadow blurred and blotted past and for a moment, in a long stretch of steep darkness going down faster and faster where steps were blind and feet found their own footing, he felt the deep fear that there was about to be nothing under his *tabi.*

At bottom (racing full tilt out into a gently sloping, open field of wild wheat grass that swooshed around their legs and flowed in shadowy

184

waves as freshening breezes ebbed, gathered and quickened) they might have been three boys on some lost summer evening, exuberant in the warm richness of the moon-charged night.

And all three kept running a little longer than necessary: for no reason except the knee and thigh-high grasses whipping past felt so good.

I'd like to just keeping running....

Thirty-Three

Colin had a big, angry bruise covering most of his left cheek. Blood caked in his nostrils.

He faced a high, narrow window barred with wrought-iron where he was seated on the polished floor of a small room. He assumed he was at Hideo's stronghold. He expected to be put to death.

"Come all this far," he muttered, in Gaelic, through his stiffened lips and discovered he must have bitten his tongue, too. Spat out a gob of partly clotted blood. It sat like red and black wet mud on the bright, stainlessly smooth wood. It gave him a dull satisfaction.

His arms were bound since he'd pummeled the guard the night before who'd come with food and water. Worked his sore mouth and could tell he'd lost at least one tooth.

"I wasn't here but a short time," he muttered, stiffly, "and see what I come to...."

His weak Japanese had pretty much collapsed, altogether; but he understood when they said he'd soon be punished for his crimes. The consensus seemed to favor beheading.

His arms were bound in front of him. He was tired...ached all over...leaned back on the floor and shut his eyes...

Thirty-Four

Takezo and Gentile stood at the open door of the Old Moon Inn. A sweaty man in a loincloth lay with his feet on the porch and his face in the dirt. He smelled like urine.

Inside the smoky room someone was erratically beating a prayer drum that resembled an oversized tambourine without the metal jingles. Deeper, drunken voices de-harmonized a dirge-like tune. A woman shrieked with laughter, a jug crashed to pieces near the doorway, chips glittering out in the smoky light while someone cursed, seriously and with flourishes.

185

"My kind of place," he told him. "Like you, I'm in love with a dead woman."

"I told you, Takezo-san, that is untrue. I do not...."

"The difference is, mine is truly dead and must stay in the spirit world." He took his arm and they entered into the stinging air and din as some gamblers roared a response to a play and the woman laughed again. "Until a rebirth where, if she is blessed, we will not meet again."

With her I always believed we had a destination, he thought. *Time died and the road ended...like at Satta Mountain where Tokaido highway meets the sea and many drown who think they are on solid ground....*

"I never really met Osan," the Italian said.

"What matter? It's all there at once or not at all." Takezo shrugged his hands. "I'm always thinking about time," he went on, really to no one. "Don't know why."

Feeling another bite of emptiness, he wanted a drink even more intensely. He felt hollow as he squinted around the dim interior: most of the lantern light was concentrated along the rear wall above the gambling. There was an open fire filling the low room with smoke from burnt pork, seared fish and smudgy candles here and there topped by cheap incense. It smelled, overall, of bad perfume, sweat, mildew and rancid sake.

"Wait out here," he told the Italian.

Because he'd instantly recognized the one he was looking for.

At least I was in disguise that day, he thought. *Maybe I'll get by....*

He crossed the crowded room, stepping over a sleeping man, circling around two brightly dressed prostitutes and then was standing in front of the mask-faced, wide-shouldered killer who was seated, back to the wall, on a slightly raised platform with a floor table and sake in front of him. A garish color scroll painting hung there showing a stiff-looking goldfish and a lotus blossom the color of decay.

The light from the blazing brazier flared and dimmed as fat dripped and smoke billowed. The reddish light shook and wavered over the grim swordsman's pointed face, hollowing and unhollowing the bony features. He didn't look happy about anything and wasn't as drunk as advertised. This looked like another fight. He wondered, abstractly, how many more times he'd be lucky as well as good. Took a long, sighing breath in and out.

186

The man didn't look up as Takezo knelt across the low table from him and carefully rested his long sword beside him on the worn, uneven boards.

"Forgive me, Kame-san" he said.

"Give a reason."

"I'm poor. Looking for work."

"Am I a great lord?"

"Work is work, Kame-san."

The fellow gave him an up-from-under look.

"Who said that as my name?" he asked, half his face seeming to fill and empty with the smoky light's halations.

"Aren't you well-known?" Takezo responded, shrugging. "People say you're worth talking to."

"Go away." Kame-san poured himself a cup of sake and drained it without offering. All he was showing was a faintly mocking smirk.

Takezo noted two tough-looking thug-like men seeming to casually take positions on both sides of him, maybe 15 feet away. He sensed they weren't going to let him leave.

"I like it here," he said.

"Go away, anyway."

"I'm hurt."

"Like a girl. Some say you're pretty as a girl. Maybe you are a girl."

"Maybe you don't like girls. Do you enjoy killing them?" said Takezo. "Look, Somebody-san, my guts are hollow as a gourd. I need work."

"Eat one of your goats."

Takezo nodded and smiled, faintly.

"Nice to be remembered," he said.

"I want to forget you."

"I was in disguise, that day. I'm a master of disguise. Looking for a man who owed me 10 ryo."

"You were overpaid, no matter what for. Master of irritation. Go away."

The wide-shouldered killer seemed bored. He knocked back another drink. No signs of being drunk, yet. Probably wouldn't be.

"Did you say 'go away?" Takezo chuckled.

187

The other seemed even more bored. The detective noticed the two men were sitting to his left and right. Both sported greasy, drooping, thin moustaches. The uneven light blended them into the background of noise, bad music and intense gambling.

"Why don't you sing and dance for me?" Kame asked. "Maybe I'll let you blow my flute."

Takezo's patience was about played out. He wasn't getting anywhere, anyway. He knew he was missing something. Kame was pushing far too hard and wasn't worried.

What am I blindly missing, this time? he asked himself.

"Why did you kill Miou?" he asked. "She had nothing for you to steal."

The seeming boredom was gone. Kame looked up and set down his cup of wine.

"Kill?" he asked, neutrally, as his hand went to the *shoto* in his sash.

"Time to say something."

Takezo felt the two men readying themselves. Here it was, again. He hoped the Italian would stay clear, this time. Already liked him and didn't want to lose him.

"Say something," Kame sighed. "Give up the foreign bauble. I say that."

"The ring," Takezo said, mocking. "It's nothing, now. Everybody knows the story. The ring proves nothing."

"It's nothing, yes. So give it up."

"Better question: who pays you? Reiko? Who?"

"Who pays *you* to be stupid and a failure at your work?" Smirked, again. "We know you were an actor. A girlboy."

What am I missing, here? He doesn't serve Reiko, not directly...that feels all wrong....

"If you can defeat me," said the detective, feeling a little sick at heart, "just tell me and then defeat me. What's the harm?"

Kame was furious and cold. He was a hair from drawing the blade.

"You," he said, quietly, just audible over the background sounds of voices, hissing fat, plucked music. "You could not even protect your whore. You think she was run down by a cart."

"No, I don't. But now I know the rest."

188

He's stalling to let them get ready, his mind said. *I spoke too soon but at least I'll have his head....*

"You know very little, Takezo," Kame said and his amusement was real. "So many questions with just one answer. We were waiting for you."

Because he'd missed that, too: a drunken assassin bragging about slaying women. All they had to do was make sure Taro or Yazu heard and the bait was in the water.

And so comes Takezo the fish, he thought, wryly.

The men were already in motion, on their feet as Kame drew in a glittering flicker, fanned blade hissing as the detective tilted back and the terrific cut just missed his throat. The two thugs closed in, simultaneously, brandishing swords. Striking down at Takezo who stood flatfooted, this time, and blocked both cuts with one round sweep in a flash of sparks.

Think of attacking, his mind almost chanted, *conceive of defense, and you are already defeated....*

He frog-hopped over the table, sword first like a fang, and cut at Kame, as the room began to clear out, people scrambling and shouting. His wiry target ducked aside and whipped back a missed stroke. The bony assassin was very, very strong.

One of the thugs was just a blur in the smoky, erratic light as he tried a lunging stab and Takezo's blade seemed to whip itself back and under and caught the man's lower ribs. Chopped through.

Kame came back, quick, low and deadly as a cobra; Takezo stood totally unmoving, sword leveled waist-high in front of him. Kame stopped short, too talented, himself, to press into the *ronin's* fearsome stillness.

The other thug wasn't so aware and tried to cut down from behind, his opponent seeming almost trapped being so close to the wall. Takezo backed into and under the stroke and stabbed his blade under his own armpit and into the fellow's chest, still watching Kame. That was that.

The assassin had his back to the flaming brazier where the pork had blazed up into fatty fire, surrounding him with flame-wrung smoke as if, Takezo poetically flashed, he'd just stepped through the gate of Hell. The whores and patrons who'd hadn't run out (not counting the drunks on the floor) stared while the owner, halfway to the fighters, was yelling for someone to get the *okappiki*.

At this point, Takezo wasn't even not thinking: more than ever, it was as if his body could itself see and respond at once; aware of everything

189

without fixed focus. Something had suddenly altered his technique, again, as when he'd nearly died in the tea garden. Now he knew each outcome was already inscribed in unfolding time. The one who wanted to win would lose. Time felt fluid and collected around his sword and himself; now he could move into and out of it at will. He'd never felt so remote, so detached from consequences. Smoke, fire, shouts and flashing blades were gestures, soft, vague breezes affecting nothing that mattered - perfectly still at his center as if composing a poem in a garden.

Closing with Kame another, huge thick-bodied man with massive hands holding an iron staff he plied like a baton, moved in on his flank. He went near Kame to tempt a stroke but the other fell back again and edged behind the flaming grill so that he spoke out of the fire and oily smoke from the burning flesh.

"This is too big for you to understand," Kame said.

"Why?" asked Takezo, again. "By whose command? Whom did she hurt? My poor love."

"You don't understand the powers involved. The destiny of our people is at stake."

So it wasn't for pay...but why did he....

Takezo edged nearer, starting to move around the smoke and stinging heat. His eyes teared as Kame circled with him. The massive man with the iron staff was closing slowly, still out of range.

What do they think I know that's so dangerous? This fellow says nothing and never will...a fanatic, a ninja actor, not a low assassin...maybe high in rank....

Unexpectedly, the massive man hurled the twenty pound rod in a single snapping motion and it whirled at the detective like death's scythe, tearing through the fumes and should have shattered him.

Except he couldn't tell himself from his sword or his opponents or even the side-spinning staff of death because time belonged to him and he dance-stepped through and past and the bar took down the brazier, meat, sparks, wood and charcoal spraying across the room, igniting curtains and setting Kame's kimono afire.

The innkeeper screamed for buckets as everybody conscious fled. Kame beat at the flames then poured a jug of sake on himself as Takezo came for him, not even looking at the squat man who was now coming with a stool. He faced Kame as he struck behind and cut the man's hand off at the wrist, dropped stool banging to the floor as he screamed and

190

staggered back. Flames now chewed rapidly left and right across the walls and flowed across the dry wood of the ceiling. Paper screens whooshed, burning almost instantly; straw matting crackled and curled.

Naked and half-naked whores and customers were coming down the stairs as smoke poured up in their faces. Outside someone was banging an alarm bell. The owner's voice was yelling for help.

Flames beaten out, robe smoldering, Kame, hemmed in by Takezo and the explosive fire, charged and slashed with terrific speed and desperation. The detective blocked two cuts, ducked a third and just sliced the shorter man's back as he spun away into a spume of smoke, seeming to briefly dissolve into shadow and reform into substance on the other side.

They were in the center of the room, now. Kame was circling to keep a support post between them. Takezo pressed him. It was hot as a baking oven in there. The flames had already enclosed three walls. One of the sleeping drunks leaped and stumbled madly, rebounding off a partition, hair ablaze, then reeled though the front door.

"Killed that woman," he snarled, breathing a little hard, more from emotion than exertion, "for the destiny of our people?"

Takezo kept him cut off from escape. As he ducked behind the stairs a naked couple came tumbling down, coughing and shouting. Takezo dropped back in front of the door and waited as the flames burst and spurted, everywhere. He couldn't see far into the room, now, stinging billows of smoke filling the place and pouring out all openings. Straw and paper walls went up, explosively.

Kame came out of the choking clouds, eyes tearing, coughing, sword upraised. The heat was nearly unbearable.

"Madman!" he yelled. "Finish this outside!"

"A taste of the hell-world that awaits you," Takezo returned, holding his ground in the doorway, blinking and wincing as the furnace-level heat blasted at him in the sucking draughts.

"You still fight like a girl!" Kame yelled, tossing his sword aside into the flames and coming forward, unarmed, out of the roiling smoke and fire. "Act like a man, 'Peony-boy,'" he sneered, charging, hands open. "Fight me!"

Takezo, for once, was surprised enough to break his unfocused concentration. He hadn't heard that nickname since he was 12 or 13 years old. The associations weren't pleasant. And to make it worse, he suddenly realized who "Kame" was: the squinted-in eyes, bony cheeks, truculent manner.

Osa...yes...he got skinny, his mind said. *Incredible...Osa!*

He hesitated, wanting to ask questions except the desperate fellow-student was on him, inside his sword's arc and they locked and spun. As the room reeled around them, in the blasting heat, the moment was a slowed nightmare....

"I could always beat you, Girl-boy!" hissed his childhood nemesis as they bounced off the doorframe, then went down and rolled outside, choking and struggling.

"Osa," Takezo snarled. "You still smell like monkey-shit!"

"You're out of time," Osa-Kame hissed in his ear.

He had to release his sword to avoid the supple, wire-strong choke hold bony Osa was putting on him and his outflung arm sent it sailing into the yard. Osa had his old schoolmate facedown on the board sidewalk in front of the door, the heat and smoke gusting out as the fire peaked towards a crescendo.

"I'll put it in your ass, Girl-boy," Osa promised over the flameroar. "The way you always liked it."

Then the roof fell in and the impact and gush of sparks, flying fragments and unbearable heat sent them rolling, locked togther, off the raised planks into the street where the crowd was falling back. Men with buckets were already soaking the neighboring building – the nearest other one was across the street.

Yazu had shown up and the little man was armed with a short sword. He and Gentile moved into the blasting heat to assist but Takezo waved them off.

"Stay back!" he commanded. "This is for me alone!"

Chunks of blazing wood were all around them as they levered, punched and kicked at one another, then rolled over a burning board that set both kimonos alight. They flung apart, ripped clothes off, facing each other, now, in loincloths, hair wild, blackened with soot and dust, blood on both of them, fire geysering and spilling all around. Battling, the Italian flashed, like a beautiful, trapped human spirit versus a razor-faced demon formed from conflagration itself. Even there the painting in his mind took new form: this battle witnessed by a goddess-like Osan showing stern compassion and sadness....

192

Takezo realized he'd never defeat Osa hand-to-hand; too slippery and inexplicably strong. He saw his sword a few yards away, the hilt sticking out from under a mass of smoldering rubble that glowed like a charcoal fire.

The detective ducked past Osa, going for the blade, diving – except the ferocious opponent, seeming all sharp bone and relentless muscle, quick as a ferret, slammed on top of him again, driving his face down almost into the hot coals. Takezo's hair started to smolder. The blinding, searing redness seemed to bake his skull. He felt the terror of childhood again, the binding, suffocating agonizing weight of the bully and murderer.

Yelling with pain he clutched a handful of redhot wood in his free left hand and scattered it over the clinging, strangling killer's bare torso and in a spasm his body literally flung Osa off his back. He groped for his blade, blinded by tears from the heat and gritty smoke as the other rolled over in the dust, screaming curses, getting the flaming chips off himself, then, in a blur, stood and knocked down Yazu and disarmed him in a single motion.

Then the seared, charred-looking killer, crossed the few yards of wild flame-shadows and wind-billowed smoke to where Takezo, clawing at his eyes with his burnt hand, was still trying to find the sword he'd almost reached. His fingers kept perversely missing it even as Gentile rushed in past the stunned Yazu, rapier out.

Osa was first and the short sword was already coming down to stab through the detective's exposed back when he went still inside again and he gripped the hilt and drew the now glowing blade from the steeping coals, blinded eyes shut and running tears down the sooty cheeks as if he wept like an avenging angel for the world consumed by blood and flame.

To the Italian it looked like a wide-shouldered, bird-legged, cadaverous shadowy demon leaped and squatted on the air, striking down with a supernatural fang of doom. But, on his knees, the blinded *ronin* arced the glowing blade up and under so fast it seemed a semi-solid red fan of flame, intercepting the fiend's neck so that his body dove on into the coals, the impact spattering them into a whoosh of new flame as his head hit, bounced and rolled to the side, rebounding from one of Gentile's boots.

The heat pressure from the crumbling inn was so intense Gentile felt like a hot hand was pushing him back. He took Takezo under the arm and helped him up. The *ronin* swordsman was still touching his face. He had a little blurry vision left; enough to locate the head and lift it by the topknot; but he was burned under both eyes and could feel the seared flesh swelling.

Squinting at it up-close in the smudgy, flailing flamelight, it seemed eyeless in its hollow shadows and the gaped mouth was a wordless, dark cry. He kept the hot sword out to the other side. His blistered left hand seemed to be clutching a ball of agony.

Now you answer my questions, he said to himself.

"What will you do with this man's head?" Gentile wondered as they fell back to the crowd in the street. Yazu came over, looking for his sword. He worked around the roasting body, shielding his face from the heat. The stink of burning flesh sickened him. He found the blade and scurried away.

"I knew him," Takezo said. "A long time ago."

"*Sensei,*" said the bony pupil, joining them, their wild shadows shifting and jerking around them. "You are burned. And you weep. Let me take this evil head and practice my downcuts on it."

"Nevermind," was the answer. "I need it."

Osa, he thought. *Well, why not...time sped up and floated you ahead to wait for me....Osa, you were the devil of my fate...I never got to ask you why you always hated me...maybe I can ask Yoshi why* he *does.....*He now was weeping through his tears, thinking about Miou because Osa had been part of killing her so the question had become: who did he really serve, Reiko, Nobunaga...and then was sure it had to be whoever Miou, herself, had been forced to work for....*And the ring, business...again....*

"Your poor eyes, *sensei,*" said Yazu, hoarsely. "Let me get a poultice from the healing woman and -"

"I'll shave my skull and put on black robes like any *Zato.*" These were blind men who dressed like Buddhist priests and made a living from various skills like storytelling or music.

"Not easy to join those guilds, master," Yazu reflected. "I know a skilled acupuncturist who might help -"

"I'll be a traveling singer," his master remarked. "I'll sing joyful songs of spring."

194

Yazu just looked at him. They were passing through the crowd onto the main street which became the Tokaido Eastern Sea Road and ran hundreds of miles along the coast to Kyoto.

The dour, blocky tavern owner and his big-bosomed part-time prostitute wife, barely covered by a torn and scorched, sashless kimono, followed them for a little way cursing Takezo and waving their arms. Then the woman charged with nails outstretched, robe open and fluttering in the breeze, eyes wide and furious in the changing, reddish light.

"You demon of shit!" she cried. "Who will pay? That inn is our life!"

"Go away, witch," said Yazu, brandishing his short sword, stopping to block the couple who were followed by a younger relative, holding a *bo* staff.

Head in one hand, sword in the other, Takezo was being partly guided by the tall Italian and took little interest in these matters. He was thinking about what he had to do, now.

The snarling woman was almost on him, when Yazu stooped and picked up a semi-dried cowflop muffin and scaled it at her. It caught her in the neck. Spattered and stuck.

Disgusted, she wiped at it, then slipped on another and went down on one round side. Her husband and the staff-wielder came on. Yazu stood his ground, stooping, firing off three more dung pies, one glancing off the innkeeper's rage-distended face, shutting one eye.

"You die for this!" he fairly shrieked over the background roar and cracking of the blazing building, wiping at the befouled socket and then careening on at the skinny apprentice as his armed companion moved to flank.

Gentile turned to watch and Takezo managed to get a blurry view by tilting his one semi-functioning eye at the flame-lit skirmish. The infuriated wife was stooping and wildly hurling cowflops herself from the steamy collection by the roadside. Her aim was poor and she succeeded only in hitting her husband in the back which he hardly noticed, having drawn a dagger and made several cuts and thrusts at Yazu.

Yazu, never easy to grasp or strike, avoided them as well as the sweeping pokes and blows of the staff. As his master had taught him, he took a stance and shuffled calmly forward, sword leveled waist-high, between the two men who now hesitated. The short, curved blade gleamed in the flickers of red-orange.

"What is death?" he exclaimed. "Mere illusion."

"Ah-ha," sneered the innkeeper, "a bodhisattva."

The younger man with the staff could bear no more and leaped in, aiming a round blow at Yazu's angular head.

"Here's a sutra!" he yelled.

The counter sliced the *bo* in half. Then Takezo's stooped, skinny student and petty thief, in the same motion, whirled a sidecut at the innkeeper, just missing him as he stumbled back behind his outstretched dagger.

"Illusion!" reiterated Yazu. "Life is a shadow!"

"Well done, I think...." murmured *sensei* Takezo, twisting his head to try to really focus against the background of billowing dark smoke and seething flame. As he went a few steps closer, still holding Osa's head in one hand and the naked sword in the other, the sight proved too many for the two attackers and they fell back at a half-run to the delight of much of the crowd. Gentile was grinning.

Yazu stood, posed, sword above his head, savoring his triumph, trying to look detached. Unexpectedly, the wife lurched back into the scene, both hands laden with turds, and managed to come behind the victorious swordsman. Takezo saw only a smoky blotch of movement, tilted his head, again. Gentile shouted a warning but, instinctively, in Italian which had little effect.

So the roundly naked, coldly frenzied and furious lady clamped both hands, like the stinking paws of some cacacophic avenger, over poor Yazu's face and filled most of his head's orifices with shit.

Yazu twisted and turned, slashing, accidentally shoving her to the ground where she sat, then laughed and cursed with the fearless joy only a baited and outraged woman can display. His previously victorious sword was waved in vain all around him.

Gentile sank down to one knee, shaking with silent, pre-laughter which soon exploded into sound. Takezo couldn't quite make it out but heard the gagging sputters of his student as he blew out his nose, spat and vomited from his mouth and clawed at eyes and ears to expunge and free his head of packed vileness.

"Aaaahhh!" he cried, sagging to a squat and puking with singular violence, his sword forgotten in the dust.

The innkeeper, himself, simply sat down and in the light of his burning livelihood, roared, uncontrollably, with hooting laughter.

"Ahhccc," coughed the defeated one, on all fours, spitting straight down and shuddering in massive spasms.

"What?" wondered Takezo, squinting, cocking his head.

Gentile got up and took his arm, again, avoiding the head side. The sword was cool now, anyway.

"*La Donna*," he pronounced, shaking his head and grinning, "*e sempre la vincha.*"

"Eh?"

"Women always conquer."

A little later, after Yazu had practically drowned himself washing in a rainbarrel, splashing and wiping his face clean, they went on. Takezo had very little vision. His eyes hurt, were nearly shut, now, and there were only blots and shadows with scattered specks of relative clarity. He'd sheathed his sword and had put the head in a small leather sack he'd borrowed from a standing horse. The sky was overcast and there was distant lightning out over the bay. The wind would suck first from one quarter, then another. There was a sense of something immensely gathering. Dogs hid. Horses were restless. Gentile felt it.

"A storm coming?" he wondered.

"A storm, yes," replied the *ronin*.

"This head, Takezo-san," he asked. "I do not think he will tell you much."

"Wrong. He will have a great deal to say."

'Peony boy,' he thought. *Time brought me a revenge I never sought...and if he knew who I was then others know....*He shrugged. Could he be in greater danger, in any case? He'd forgotten...or had he? Shrugged, again. *Did I recognize him and not recognize that I did? That makes no sense, yet....*Because he'd always dreaded that memory and wondered, suddenly, if he'd really run away from that as much as the *ninja* training. He'd defeated Osa and now held his head by the hair in his hand as he walked, the topknot just protruding from the small sack. Takezo tilted his face almost like a blind man to find fragments of focus with his scorched and swollen eyes.

"Where are we going, *sensei*?" wondered Yazu, now recovered from the dung-battle, sword in his sash and almost strutting like a boy playing samurai. He was a little uneasy because he feared being asked to carry the head.

197

He saw they were approaching a checkpoint at a bridge over a small canal. In the overcast night, the light was all from scattered lanterns and fluttering torches.

"You know where Ri-ru lives?"

"The one-eyed witch-woman?"

"The same."

"Yes. But, *sensei*, why don't you bring this unhappy head to a shrine and calm its troubled spirit?"

"Seems happy enough, to me," the detective said.

"Yet a troubled spirit is said to haunt those who had a hand in...."

"Better beware the wife of that innkeeper than the dead," Takezo advised.

"Do you intend to bury it, Takezo-san?" asked Gentile, chuckling.

"I can't bear to part with it," said the detective. "I have things to ask it. My fellow student." Twisted around and found an almost clear spot of sight: saw the street and the guard at the bridge ahead, lit by the shifting light of two torches set above on the gatehouse. The stolid figure seemed to shift back and forth with the restless shadows. "Lead the way to Ri-ru's."

Peony boy, he repeated to himself. *We hold time in our memories except time decays our memories, too...what's ever to be trusted?* And there was the memory:

Because it was dark and hot and he'd gone alone to the little mountain lake's edge to swim. He'd already stripped and waded a few steps out on the stony, muddy bottom. The stars were bright in a moonless sky. The still, dark water was full of gleaming reflections and tree-shadows as if the earth and sky had sealed together. Frogs and nightbugs made a strangely soothing, undulating din.

The air was heavy but sweet. He smelled pines and flowers. It was good to be away from everybody. He often slipped off like this to swim out, float and drift, silent, alone, feeling comfortable as if he really lived there, was at home there and could drift where he pleased....

Another swooshing step and then thumps and violent splashes behind and beside him as he turned to face blurred shadows and was instantly hit at the knees and tilted backwards and then the shadows fell on him in massive, overwhelming weight and he was knocked flat on his back and under the surface, shouting bubbles, water burning up in his nose,

198

*choking for air and struggling as they dragged him onto the rocky mud
shoreline and flipped him over, facedown. Pebbles ground into his face
and the mud was sour with wet decay.*

*There were three of them in full ninja suits and he knew they were
teenage and it was no training test because one had to be Osa (he knew the
strong, gripping, wirelike fingers and bony shoulders) whose name he kept
snarling until his mouth was pressed into the sour muck by a hard pair of
knees (another held his legs) while Osa lay on top, breathing hard and
muttering; then, while he writhed and twisted on the mud, smearing
himself and tearing his skin, gagging and spitting the foulness from his
mouth, he felt what he took, at first, for a stick poking at his buttocks, then
some rubbery implement, the pressure on his back shifting around, Osa's
voice panting with effort and something else, too, saying:*

*'Hold still little flower...' Laughter around him. 'What kind of
flower are you, pretty boy?'*

*'Peony,' another said, laughing, holding his legs as he kicked and
twisted on the mud and rocks and stink. 'He's your peony-boy.'*

Thirty-Five

The Trial

Colin sat on the ground with bound arms in the brilliant, hazy, hot,
shadeless walled yard. Two guards with spears and wide, conical straw
hats stood behind him while the magistrate, other officials and clan
dignitaries (including Hideo, Issa, and Reiko) sat up on the long porch in
the cool shade of the overhang. There were more people seated on folding
stools under umbrellas on the shimmering, sandy enclosure.

When the accused looked up, sunglare and sweat blotted at his
vision and the figures above him were featureless. His head throbbed.

Being used to the ponderous injustice of English law applied to
Scots and the quick, violent tribunals of the Northern clans, the Japanese
system of harsh, rigid military law seemed almost reasonable. At least
there was a presumption, not of innocence but some interest in the facts, in
hearing testimony, weighing the words of high and low alike.

His arms hurt; he was numbed and cramped.

I came a long way, he thought, *to die in this bonnie fucked
place....*

He didn't feel much about Osan other than wishing he'd never
seen her. It all seemed long ago, lost in blurs and batterings.

199

So he didn't look up when the magistrate of the seaside village of Mora came out onto the blindingly hot sand to testify about finding the body and how the two foreigners and the retainer, Nori, had fled at once. The man stood there, tugging at his chin and described the headless girl lying in the garden outside the inn and expressed his view that the Zulu was a demon though he had not actually seen him.

"Where Nori?" Colin suddenly asked, trying to focus on the shapes above him.

"Be quiet, barbarian," said the judge, harshly.

"The traitor, Nori!" declared Reiko, scowling.

"Speak when it is your turn," said the judge whose big, dark robes with exaggerated shoulders gave the Scot an impression that his head was tiny. "Where is this man?"

"The traitor was left dead on the beach, judge-sir," Reiko answered. "You'll have to ask the crabs and gulls his present whereabouts."

The authority frowned and looked, unsympathetically at Colin.

"Unfortunate," he said. "Who is left here to testify?"

Reiko briefly recalled the scene at the beach near the small fort where Takezo has escaped with uMubaya. They stood on sand slapped smooth by the unending waves after the priests were released and Colin was carried off to Edo in a prisoner's net-closed palanquin. Nori understood his position.

"Unbind me, Lord Chamberlain," he'd requested.

"Amusing," some samurai had said.

"Want to go, eh?" Reiko had asked.

"A sword, please," asked stocky Nori.

"Know you're a traitor?" Reiko, gestured that he be untied.

Nori knelt there; behind him the water broke, muted and steady against the softening, off-shore breeze. The round moon was going down in his face, fat and reddish over the western mountains.

"I leave no regrets," was the last Nori had said as he tore open his kimono, baring his torso, taking the dagger, putting the point to the side of his belly. He looked only at the moon, cut about in half by a distant slope.

Reiko had turned away as the blade dimly gleamed in the samurai's shadowy movements as he stabbed and ripped himself open with a sighing gasp....

200

Issa, who'd been staring across the bright yard at the red-lacquered gate to the street, noted a commotion as guards, a crowd of commoners mixed with *ronin* and idle samurai surrounded two women and two men. She noted the outlandish costume of Gentile as he seemed to guide a dark-robed, wild-haired blind man holding a sack in one hand. She almost smiled despite misgivings and anxiety because she was sure it was Takezo in some absurd disguise and so there now was likely to be some entertainment mixed in with law and bloodshed.

They came up to Colin and faced the magistrate, their shadows blurry and dark as the hazy sun was reaching noon. There was silence for a moment as the viewers absorbed the surprising, disturbing sight of a one-eyed witch in white, a foreign devil in bizarre garments with a sword like a 5-foot food pick and a *ronin* in a torn kimono with burnt hair, swollen eyes and stained with char as if, Issa considered, he'd made a ridiculous effort to disguise himself as the black man.

Earlier at Ri-ru's

It was pre-dawn by the time they'd made their way to the witch's place. Takezo's burns hurt and both eyes were swollen nearly shut. He wanted to bathe and sleep at the same time. Everything hurt.

There were no lights. Yazu knocked and called out. After a few minutes the tiny hunchbacked woman peered through the spaces in the shutters.

"Go away!" she said. "Or you'll be cursed!"

"How would I be able to tell?" said Takezo. "*Uni,*" he went on, using her nickname, "it is Takezo *Zato*. Call her and let us in."

"Who?"

"Open, fool!" cried Yazu. "My master is grievously hurt!"

A lantern light shifted inside and showed through various spaces and then Ri-ru's voice:

"He never comes here when he's well."

The door opened inwards as Takezo said:

"I'm never well. You miss nothing."

"It's nearly sunrise," the dwarf said. "Who are these men?"

"Go back to sleep, Uni," the witch said, holding the lantern up to see Takezo and Gentile as Yazu peered around the doorframe like a curious monkey, blinking at the light. "May the merciful heavenly beings protect us," she whispered. "What has happened to you?"

Takezo staggered past her and groped his way to a stool he barely saw.

"Forgive me for not washing my feet," he said. "I need rest." He set the bag with the head down. It clunked on the smooth wood that gleamed darkly as the lantern moved.

Her lined and bony face, twisted to her good eye side, came into the light she held and to his blotted and focusless vision she seemed disembodied.

"You've been burned."

"There was a fire," said Gentile from outside the light. "And bloodshed."

Uni, the dwarf servant, was in the darkness across the room, looking on.

"A hunchback came here looking for you," she told him.

"Eh?"

"He was old and bad-mannered," she went on. "A cripple. Said it was important. Said he knew you."

Takezo nodded.

"Interesting," he said. It had to be old Momo, Hideo's doorkeeper. The lord of the cellars he'd cracked on the skull. "Any message?"

"Look at your eyes," said Ri-ru. "You really fell from your pony, this time."

"Might have been worse."

"Ah," she sighed, getting up. "Said the monkey who dropped into the cooking pot: 'At least I won't die without food.'" She was already across the small room, opening a cabinet. "I'll make a balsam for your eyes." To the small assistant: "Since you're still here, boil water for steeping."

"Yes," said the other, bobbing her head as she lit a second lantern, then turned to the fire. The flints clicked and scraped out sparks as she rubbed them.

"What did the man say?" Takezo repeated, shutting the one eye that worked at all. Groaned, internally, as sleep dragged at him. He decided he felt like a gangrened foot. Wasn't really that interested in the latest news from the castle.

"He was irritating," she reported. "He said someone...I don't remember his name...a samurai...." She worked over the fire, blowing on the coals.

202

"He said Yoshi," interjected Uni.

That woke the detective up a little.

"Maybe so," Uni went on. "Anyway, he said to say…ah, I have it, he said to say this Yoshi had brought him another dead woman."

"One with her head on," Ri-ru added.

Gentile squatted beside Takezo.

"What might this mean?" he asked.

"Old Momo?" wondered Yazu. "Pretty strange." He stood, nervously, partly in the glow from the lanterns and small fire where Uni had set a pot to heat.

"He further said," put in Ri-ru, dropping some scented leaves and chunks of perfumy stuff into the water, "the information might be useful at the trial today at the chief magistrate's on 2nd Street. The great lords will be there."

Takezo took a deep breath. Gentile looked at him, up close, deep, dark brown eyes troubled, his face tired and world-weary in the uneven light that lit barely half of his features.

"Trial? Could it be?"

"Yes," said Takezo. "It must be." To Ri-ru: "Do what you can for me. No sleep tonight. And I need your help with my chief witness." To Yazu: "Go, seek out Momo find out what he knows and then come to the trial. Not long after sunrise. Go!"

Maybe I have them, he had to think. *Maybe….*

At the trial

The witch woman knelt and formally set down her "conjuring box" on the sand next to Takezo who'd taken the testifying position near Colin. He held the sack in one arm. For effect he'd refused to wash or neaten his hair and he was still wearing the ripped, bloody and burned dark blue and black kimono. The salve had partly opened his left eye and by tilting it like a bird he could sort of see, though the people in the shadow of the porch were pretty much outlines blurred together. He recognized Issa, Hideo and Reiko among the others.

"Who called you?" the Judge demanded.

"Hachiman, god of justice," replied the *ronin*.

"Fool. That is the god of war," interjected Reiko.

"Maybe the same," he replied.

"Who is this witch?" asked the judge, a little uncomfortably.

203

Ri-ru stood there while her tiny assistant dribbled water over the leaves she'd put in her box. Ri-ru's hair was wild and long under a black headband and she kept her bad eye aimed at the judge – which did little to put him at ease. Her face was expressionless, painted white with thick makeup, almost the same tone as her plain, unpatterned robe. She might have been in ghost costume for a play.

"Who is this?" someone asked. "The ghost of Masakado?"

"Don't use such names!" cried the judge, for fear of drawing the famous and cursed spirit.

"She will speak for a witness in this matter," declared Takezo.

"Which witness? You?"

"No, another," said the dramatic detective with a flourish, bending and lifting the head out of the sack by the hair, displaying it. Colin strained to see. Hideo stood up and the judge leaned forward. If they'd been Christians, Gentile considered, they'd have been crossing themselves. Takezo held it up to Chamberlain Reiko. "He misses his friend," he declared.

The magistrate considered the two faces before him.

"Hard to say which looks worse," he pronounced.

The head's jaw hung slack with dried blood around the lips, that with the sooty, seared skin, charred hair, protuberant cheekbones and madly staring, bulged eyes created a demonic, rapacious, furious look hard to match. The worse thing noted the court, was that Takezo's own damaged and disturbing head was alive on his shoulders, speaking and moving.

"You cannot escape from here," said Hideo, still standing.

"Do I seem to want to?" Takezo responded, noting that Reiko hadn't lost any composure at the sight of the late Osa-Kame. Tilting his eye around, he stepped back close to the bound Scot who was taking an interest. "Let the witness speak!" the *ronin* declared, dramatically. He wished his face didn't hurt. Wished he could see better. Shrugged. There'd be no fighting his way out, this time; but, without Miou and the illusion of a future, he was just going on, anyway, out of an almost abstract curiosity about what number time would roll him next.

"This man always fills the air with nonsense," said Hideo. "An insult to the court."

"He's no doubt drunk," put in Reiko.

"Thank you for your kind help, my lord," said the judge. "Please sit and permit me to continue." To Takezo: "Now, you, enough foolishness. Whose head is this you so disrespect?"

"Let this witness speak out," the *ronin* said, brandishing Osa's noggin. He could see Issa was smiling, slightly. "He was an evil man, lately repentant."

At which cue the witch twisted around, loosed her long hair and began to twirl in place as if she were trying to screw herself into the ground as her dwarf assistant, Uni, set alight incense and waved it wildly in the air. Ri-ru began to keen and moan softly, then loud...then soft...then a sudden shriek, high, ululating, ending in a gagging cry. Gentile noted the audience was having all its superstitious strings plucked. He felt a little smug, standing, one hand on hip, head tilted, every inch the Renaissance rationalist.

Crooning softly, now, Ri-ru sank to her knees, body vibrating, head flung rigidly back.

"Speak!" commanded Takezo.

"Aiiiiiiii!" cried the witch, now medium. "All is darkness!" She stood rigidly, head backflung. Her voice became a deep, hoarse groan. Uni waved the incense. "I see gleaming frost everywhere and demons of hard ice with holes for eyes! Aiii! I freeze!" She began to shake. Ventriloquism was one of her many skills and, even expecting it, the effect startled him. "This is the Hell of the Red Lotus!" the head seemed to growl, in agony.

Most of the audience was stirred. Several had pulled out prayer beads. Even the Italian man of reason seemed suddenly uneasy.

Takezo moved his blurred area of sight over the witnesses and noted Yoshi, for the first time, standing just behind Hideo. Decided he'd better watch him.

To cover his nervousness, the magistrate asked:

"Your name?"

Holding the head up high with both hands, Takezo squeezed the jaw joints to make the gaped mouth move as the flat, raw voice responded:

"I was called Kame, in life. Now I am no more, alone in the freezing darkness of hell! I who showed no compassion now am tormented by fiends made all of ice! Aiiiiii!" She flung herself back flat and flopped like a beached fish.

This produced general uneasiness; except Yoshi seemed almost amused.

205

"Yes, yes," the judge hastened to say. "A dreadful fate. How pitiable. So, Kame-san, what can you add to these proceedings?"

Yoshi's smirking, noted the detective. *He's in on secrets....*

He dropped to his knees beside Ri-ru, keeping the head aimed at the judge. Tried to keep his semi-focus on Yoshi; had an idea.

He lifted the head high while he bowed his own to the, now, softly writhing medium.

"Say," he shout-whispered, "Kame was also called *Osa*, a homosexual friend of Yoshi. *Yoshi.*"

"Osa," she instantly roared, the hoarse, flat, violent voice seeming to come from the moving, dead jaws. "Osa the homosexual was my true name. Sweet Yoshi can tell you."

The stocky new-made captain's face reacted in a twitch of anger and surprise. The judge shook his metal fan.

"There is precedent for this," he declared, touching his small chin with one small, delicate hand, "but the seeker of truth from the world of the dead must be known and vouched for. Who knows this woman?"

"I know this *man*!" cried Yoshi, stepping forward, still with a slight limp, Takezo noted, with pleasure. "He puts lies even in the mouths of corpses!" The scar that creased his nose was red with fury.

"Improper," said the judge.

"Sit down!" ordered Hideo.

Reiko still just watched, sitting on one side of Issa who was smiling, slightly, fan covering one side of her face as she moved it. Gentile saw there was a lotus flower design on it in bright red.

"You're running out of time, drunkard," Yoshi said, sitting back down, scowling and folding his arms.

"No," answered Takezo, "I have a keg of it at home."

"Ay," said Colin to him. "That face...know face....Damn my clumsy tongue," he said in Spanish to Gentile who asked:

"What is it, sir?" in that tongue and heard back:

"I saw that man. Drank with him at the village the night Osan died."

Gentile translated but was silenced by the magistrate.

"Speak when it is your turn. This is a place of law and these outbursts will be punished!"

"What will you do to the dead man?" Takezo wondered, standing up now (a little unsteadily) head a swollen, thick, raw ache and pushing the

206

ruined face at the people on the platform. At which cue the bass, flat, harsh, raspy voice spoke again.

"Rrrrr!" it growled, jaw moving at which Issa covered the lower half of her face with the bright fan and the Italian was sure she was shaking, ever-so-slightly, with amusement. "I murdered women. I…I…." The medium thrashed, good eye rolled up into her head, foam at her lips; the uncanny voice still seeming to originate in Osa-Kame's mouth. "Hideo was betrayed! The *seisho*, Lily, I killed her and hid away Osan. It is her body in the young beauty's grave! Rrrrrr….aiii…." She flung herself around, raising a cloud of fine sand that shimmered in the unrelenting impact of the near noon sun. "The torments of Hell surround me…aiiii!"

Issa wasn't laughing, this time. The fan went away from her face. Hideo scowled. Reiko was perfectly still except one finger tap-tapped rapidly on his gold and red silk embroidered knee.

"He's making the mouth move," ejaculated Yoshi, "while she utters nonsense."

"Disgraceful," echoed Reiko. "Another stupid performance by a bad actor."

Hideo frowned and said nothing. Issa had folded her fan and tapped one palm, gently, with it. She was looking at Reiko who wasn't looking back.

"Who can identify this?" asked the judge, pointing to the head with his gleaming, gold-lacquered fan. Everyone looked at the lidded, shadowed eyesockets, jutting cheekbones, old scar tracing across one partly missing ear, the gaped mouth full of darkness in the pallid face.

A Hideo samurai stepped forward and knelt with a bow before the judge.

"Two years past, my lords," he declared, "that fellow served in our ranks. He left, deserted, less than a year later. I don't recall the name he used. He kept to himself. Some suspected he might have been a spy but nothing was proved."

Yes, a spy, Takezo thought.

The magistrate stood up in his full, dark, shiny, peak-shouldered robes. His small hat sat like a decoration on his bald skull, the small, delicate fingers of one hand pointing at the *ronin* detective.

"Too much confusion," he said. "Trial is postponed for one week. The body of the dead woman to be exhumed and examined. If you have made sport of these proceedings, your name and image will be posted with other outlaws and you will share their fate."

"My image as I look now?" Takezo wondered and Issa smiled before her hand reached her mouth to cover.

"You will be punished."

"The body has no head," Reiko put in, maintaining rigid calm. "And must be decaying. What is the use? Not even her mother and father could -"

Except he was interrupted by a nervous, somewhat shrill voice from the side. Everyone turned other than the witch who still lay prostrate, writhing very slightly.

"There is a way to tell," said Yazu, stooping in deep bows, keeping his face down so that he presented only the top of his narrow, bald head to the officials and spectators.

"Now who speaks?" said the frustrated judge, looking hard and long at the skinny commoner. "You? I think I know you. Have I not sentenced you to be beaten for false swearing and selling bad goods?"

Yazu went to his knees on the ground in a complete kow-tow.

"A deception, lord magistrate," he insisted. "I was shown rice free from mold when I received the load! The truth was hidden from me."

"I recall there was meat involved, as well."

"More evil tricks, lord magistrate."

Hideo was shaking his head.

"Where did he steal that sword?" he wanted to know.

"Well…what have you to say in this cause?" the judge pressed on.

Yazu peered up from under at the notables.

"Lord," he said, "the whore 'Lily' is known to have a tattoo of that flower on her body. Near a spot I won't mention."

Takezo was now trying to focus on Issa's face, whenever the fan moved aside. He found it hard to register what had happened between them in the palanquin that night. It had melted like an uneasy dream on waking. He wondered what she might really know about the death of Miou. Had a feeling she'd been left out of a great deal. And she hadn't spoken, yet.

He now let the head dangle at his side, resting against his knee; studied Issa's husband through the blurry shards of his sight. The man kept looking at his wife and scowling every time he did. Reiko held himself still while Hideo seemed ready to erupt.

Then Issa said:

"It seems we should discover if my daughter is buried there."

Reiko still showed nothing while Hideo slit his eyes and looked hard at nothing.

"I agree," said the judge. "Too much confusion, otherwise."

"Confusion?" exclaimed Yoshi, sarcastically from the back row. "This business is tangled like a nest of snakes."

"Yes snakes," said Hideo, looking at his wife who had just stood up and leaned out over the porch edge.

"Ask it," she said, pointing at the head, "ask it if my daughter is alive or dead? I care little who is buried there if it is not she. Where is my child?"

Takezo stood up and held this piece of the late Osa-Kame up at arms length towards her. A few flies now flickered around it.

Why is Hideo so angry with her? The *ronin* wondered. He was swaying slightly in the terrific sun. He wondered that Ri-ru hadn't fainted in her exertions.

Reiko suddenly stood up.

"All nonsense!" he shouted. "Lies!"

As if on cue Yoshi shouldered forward beside him, snarling.

"This outcast criminal brings disorder everywhere he goes!" he exclaimed.

"Did you know this dead man?" the magistrate asked, looking closely at the outraged samurai. Takezo moved the head from facing Issa to Yoshi now.

Yoshi moved back from the bony, gaped and sooty countenance.

"No," he said. "It's a trick."

Ri-ru thrashed and the head spoke, hoarse, raspy, violent:

"He lies! We plotted together with …."

But Reiko, with supple speed, drew his short sword, made an accurate slash and split the face in two leaving the *ronin* holding (as he stepped back) what might have been two demonic masks, one with the mouth downsagging in a halved frown; the other seeming almost to be trying a smile, exposing long, uneven teeth. The effect wasn't good.

"Trained as a butcher?" Takezo said, insultingly, throwing both pieces point-blank into Yoshi and Reiko's faces, unpleasant stuff from the opened cranium spattering other officials and onlookers.

Outcry, commotion as Hideo men milled forward clashing with police. Ri-ru and Uni the dwarf melted away as Yazu stood at his master's shoulder, drawing his blade. Gentile tried to get to Colin but was blocked while Yoshi and Reiko made straight for the *ronin* detective with plenty of backup. Hideo just stood there, brooding, wiping some of Osa-Kame glop from one forearm.

Hand on his katana hilt, Takezo crouched and moved his head around trying to keep blurred track of events in the violent contrast of glare and shadow as the judge shouted:

"Stop at once! Disgraceful!"

Which wouldn't have done much to discourage the infuriated clansmen already clashing with the *yoriki* guards had not Hideo bellowed, shaking his fist, as all his pent up rage and suspicion was relieved by the powerful thunderclap of *Kiai* from his mouth:

"Enough!" They stopped. He stormed over to Reiko and Yoshi. The judge knew better than to object to anything at that moment. "Dig up the grave," he said, ferociously, face a little too close to his chamberlain's. "Find my daughter, her body or herself. No discussion." Glanced up at Issa who nodded, with downcast eyes - for once, Gentile noted. Then to Takezo: "I want to have a prosperous, honorable world for my family and clan. Like Lord Nobunaga, I want peace and orderly life." He stepped closer, ignoring Takezo's bare sword, peering from barely a nose away. To the dizzy, seared and battered detective, the coldly raging, frustrated lord, seemed to take form through undefined, bright and dark blurs, face a mask carved in steel that somehow softened and hardened at the caprice of his damaged sight. "Because of you, spy, where all seemed tragic but correct, there are shadows and doubts. My mind is poisoned with confusion. Maybe you did what you said you'd do so I cannot kill you. We will see. But I don't thank you."

Turned and stormed away across the sun-blasted yard, bright robes shimmering, followed by his entourage, ignoring Issa and Reiko who stood in the deep, bluish shade near Yoshi and their bodyguards.

The judge shook his fan at a ranking policeman, then pointed with it at the two halves of the head where they lay on the bright sand, turned in almost completely opposite directions with their opposite expressions, saying:

210

"Get a priest and bury that! We don't need cursed spirits in the place of justice. The cursed living are enough." To Takezo: "I thank you even less than Lord Hideo, disrupter. Now this sorry business drags on."

Takezo gestured at Colin who was being led away, still bound, to the adjoining jail through the back wall gate. Kept his face cocked to where he could see the big-robed outline of the judge and a blurry hint of Issa and the others at the border of one of his uneven patches of vision.

"If it was not Osan then he must be freed," he said, gently touching the swelling around his eyes. "Lord Izu should be informed."

"Are you blind?" asked the judge.

"Not altogether," was the reply. "But the less I see, the clearer things become."

Two police guards in black and white with shiny lacquered helmets were depositing the divided head into a wicker basket with a lid, without much relish for the task. The judge took it in, glanced back at the group still near him in the shadow of the overhang, then said:

"If your supernatural testimony and that of this one" indicating Yazu with his fan, where he stood uneasily beside his teacher, "- proves false, you will be in trouble."

"Me, in trouble, lord magistrate?" the *ronin* remarked, twisting a blot of semi-sight more towards Issa, Reiko and Yoshi. None of them were saying anything. None of them looked very comfortable. Yoshi seemed the least concerned which Takezo thought might be interesting if his skull hadn't seemed full of hot needles that were being hammered in by the sun while his body almost shuddered with exhaustion. He didn't want to drink or eat or think: just sleep, this time.

"And that witch, too," the official concluded, turning away.

"A few more twists and the puzzle comes apart," Takezo said towards the gallery. He was feeling suddenly far away, faint and maybe delusional, "There are, as they say, clever fish who eat the smaller one in front even as the biggest one swallows them whole." A little giddy as it all caught up with him, he chuckled, dry and almost maniacally. "The dead man told me this." Then he wrote something with his sword in the sand with a quick, casual swirl of the tip, and smiled as if he'd just expressed a great truth, then started away, sword still drawn and catching the brilliant, burning light, Yazu beside him, putting his own bamboo hat on his master's head.

It all comes back to Osan and that stupid ring, he thought. And it was well-hidden. He'd assumed ninja experts would have searched his and Miou's place. It made sense that she was able to kill the man that night, he suddenly realized, because he wasn't there to hurt either of them but to look for it. Someone wanted it so quiet she wasn't told. His mind went on despite his utter dull, exhaustion. Miou might have known the assassin. It made some sense. Not enough. *The ring and the rest...I just don't see it...why did Osan really run away...it wasn't for love of that fire-haired barbarian who can't speak six words of Japanese...because I never see anything Miou is dead and so maybe I don't deserve eyes....*

"What did he write?" asked Reiko, not looking at either Yoshi or Issa.

The policeman holding the late Osa-Kame's divided head in the basket, peered at the scrawl in the hot sand and gave a shrug of contempt.

"Looks like the character for 'big,'" he said.

The previous night

Hideo came into her private bedroom where she lay naked on her embroidered covers behind the soft, subtle misting of the mosquito netting, the scene glowing in the light of an oil lamp and two soft green paper lanterns. At her a feet a small naked girl was giving her a pedicure while a second paid naked courtesan was dipping her small hand in a honey pot, then crushing berries and letting Issa suck and lick the sugariness from her delicate fingers while her other hand did sweet service between her long, beautiful legs. Issa had what was sometimes called a Northern, "Chinese" beauty.

Hideo stood near the curtain and just looked at her blurred and softened through the mesh. She smiled.

'Will you join us, my lord?' she wondered, not quite mocking, not quite serious.

'I've had enough of such things,' he said. 'I have no need to exceed the pleasures of Paradise.'

'You wish only to watch, my lord?'

'No. I wish only to say this: do not betray me.'

'My lord?' She was genuinely puzzled.

'I don't mean with lovers,' he said. 'Do not betray me.'

'You think this?' She moved aside the sweet-stained little hand from her mouth and looked at her husband through the fine mesh where he

212

had just turned his back so that he was a blur and a shadow to her. Her lips were blotted with the jam. The soft light gleamed on his black sword sheaths and golden robe. He was looking without focus at a dim, old scroll painting of a monkey in a tree full of blossoms throwing a fruit at a tiger crouching under a crescent moon.

'It's unclear,'' he said. 'There are shadows in the shadows.'

Thirty-Six

uMubaya's interlude

The big African prince had followed Takezo's directions and came, at length, to the seaside village of Mora. He'd left the main road and followed a horse and foot trail along the wooded hills that roughly enclosed the flatlands in a rough crescent. Through breaks in the dense, moist forest he could look out over the farms and glimpse the distant village itself in the humid haze and shimmer of the seacoast, about three miles away.

He worked his way down all afternoon, following a cool, zigzagging, rushing river, until he came to the outskirts of the farms where the water spread out into a wider, slower flow, twisting into bright branches intercut with irrigation ditches.

At the edge of the thick masses of leaves and underbrush, in the cool shadows speckled with hazy spots of filtered sunlight, he stripped and went in the water up to his waist, reveling in the cool, foaming push and sweet, clean fragrances, the sun and deep green shadows on the stippled surface. This reminded him of home, of a place he liked to go alone and purify himself after the blood of a battle by ritual washing, a strong stream that fed the river called Thukela where trees grew thick on the slopes above the sand and brassy, olive colored plains.

He wondered if he would live to leave this incredible land. If he told the tale at home they'd be sure he'd been taken to a world of sprites and spirits. Not so far from the truth, he reflected, standing there, waist deep, refreshed, looking downstream and out across the flat landscape to the sea. From here the land haze and cool surf mist turned the collection of small houses and fishermen's huts into featureless, pale nubs with touches of green and black.

He was thinking about hunting. Wanted to test himself against this strange wilderness. Realized how much he'd missed things like this.

All the rules, he thought. *Even their fighting has more steps than a dance...this is good, here...very good...but I must do what I can for red-hair....*He grinned and shook his head. *And that mad warrior drunk more than sober....*He shook his head and laughed aloud. *There's one who stands up to fate's blows – even if a little unsteadily....*

Wondered what Takezo was doing, if he'd gotten back to Edo without more bloodshed. He was a man, he considered, worthy of true respect. He couldn't know the respected one was, at the moment, in the middle of his warehouse district binge in the city 60 miles distant.

Later he took a nap in the soft shade and woke as hazy sun was settling towards evening. He got up, packed his monk's robes in the beehive headpiece and hung it on a string behind his back, spear in one hand, and followed what he took for a game trail at almost right angles to the stream and roughly parallel to the open country just below. Wearing just the loincloth was comfortable and reminded him of home.

He trailed the animal which he took for an antelope by droppings and tracks almost to dusk, partly circling around the crescent curve of the hills. He came out into a huge old bamboo grove, some stalks two hands thick around, going up out of sight and spaced like pine trees. He was down about to the level of the farm plain.

He wasn't too concerned about actually finding the creature because even the pretense of a hunt was better than just semi-wandering based on vague instructions about what to do when he reached the village. A man's actions were supposed to have some purpose.

So when he came over a sudden, steep declivity he wasn't actually much excited by the sight of the buck, its antlers just fuzzy stubs this time of year, in a mass of cut brush, branches and mounds of rotting grasses from some farmer's ground-clearing, chewing, and looking around with big, liquid eyes, body all white-dappled brown.

He stopped and just looked. To his right the big stream flowed rapidly in a wide curve, powering a watermill about a quarter of a mile away. He could pick up the creaking on shifts of breeze. The late sun slanted steep and mellow.

He crouched a little and cocked his spear. Wondered if the *naginaga* would fly true. He'd never really tossed it. Thought about Mer'ce, naturally. Smiled.

214

A man can imagine her comments, he said to himself, amused. Wished she were there to make them. How weak that was. *I'll never see her again,* his thoughts said, bitterly. *This creature is so graceful...* And refused to phrase: "like her." *I do not wish to kill it...I am not hungry....*

"Why must I think of her?" he murmured, shrugging his massive shoulders. "How weak."

Worse, he was trying to imagine her village from her descriptions. She'd called his country "bare and spiny." She'd pictured hers as lush, rich with green and brilliant blossoms.

They were lying awake, side-by-side, on the soft hillock under the low, wind-twisted tree as the brilliant, full moon had now dropped off from the night's silvery noon. They had not touched. The nightsounds chirped and droned on. Stars crusted the sky.

'What is it like there?' he asked, looking up at the incredibly lustrous sky.

'Why do you care?' her voice wasn't unfriendly, he thought. 'You will never see it.'

'You don't know that.'

'My father's main village is in a valley. Many trees. Farms. There is a river there full of fish and snakes and water beasts that could eat you in a moment.'

She'd snapped her finger to indicate his consumption. He smiled. Liked getting her reactions and opinions.

'Sounds crowded,' he jibed.

'They'd make room for you.'

'I have been in battles where the spears flew so thick -'

He broke off and sat up because he'd heard it: a low, purring snarl and cough down the easy slope in the moon-softened brush that partly enclosed the hillock. She'd heard it too. He loosened the rag that tied his two spears togther. She was squatting now, alert, long arms resting on her knees.

'We should strike a fire or climb this tree,' she said, casually.

'Let him come.'

'At night?' Expressionless.

'The moon is bright.'

'Great hunter,' she said, studying the deep, detail-less shadows under the silvered bush, 'your spears are too big and clumsy.'

215

One was a long throwing spear, much heavier than the ones used by her people. The other was the famous thick-bladed Zulu hand-to-hand weapon. The longer one in his right hand, other in his left, he crouched to his feet and started moving carefully down the weed-grass slope, listening and keeping his eyes unfocused for better night vision.

'Climb the tree,' he whispered.

'You better climb it, yourself,' she told him.

He knew she was right, this was not the time; dawn or sunset, not in the middle of the night. But her actually saying it made it impossible. She might have just mocked him, he decided, to his death.

He felt very exposed in the moon's brightness, his shadow softly clear on the knee high, rough growth, undulating ahead of him.

Fool, *he thought.* Go back and wait for morning....

It felt as if his body was holding back against the seeming downflow of the slope itself under him so that time rushed forward and he was instantly far too close to the menacing shadow of the bushes and he heard her calling out to him from up behind.

All irrelevant because the shadows lunged out and formed a big, liquid-smooth silvery shape exploding almost instantly into a growling leap all too close too sudden too fast to even take in so that, instantly, his arm had whipped away the long spear at the center of the tinted dark blot of bright fangs and claws and it vanished as if the night or phantom beast absorbed it; then snarls and hot, raw breath in his face and terrible rips of pain along his sides and across his back and he went down only aware that he was about to die, of incredible weight and massive movement, the moon rocking in the sky, the crushed grass, the metallic taste and the feral smell of blood...and his free arm pumping of its own volition, stabbing the spearblade, the "sword-on-a-stick," into the vast, suffocating mass that beat down, crushed and ripped and shook his soft and fragile flesh...his arm stabbed and stabbed and stabbed...and then, as his consciousness drained away into the shadows, there was just the blur of the moon...and then it shook...melted and went out....

"Go away," he said, in Zulu, to the stub-horned buck and maybe to his memories, too. "I do not need you."

Spear over his shoulder, he strolled towards the animal who took him in with a long, soft, incurious look, then simply bounded, flowed away around the tall mounds of cut grass, upslope and blended into the sun and

216

shadow speckled forest edge as if dissolving into that intense green and gold.

uMubaya stopped and turned to his right into direct sunlight, feeling something, instantly expecting attack, a missile or a charge because he knew, even before his squinted eyes finished adjusting to the soft, uneven brightness, it was a human watching him from partly behind a mound of wheatlike grasses.

When she stepped out he was surprised and a little excited, too, because it was a bare-legged woman wearing a white, diaper-like tunic, hair caught up in a wide band into a brush effect not unlike the women of his people.

They just looked at each other. She had a pretty, round face and solidly curved body showing, darker than the Japanese he was used to. He was instantly thinking about how she might feel under his hands.

She didn't run away as he approached. He made a Japanese-style bow which she returned. Up close her unmade-up face was a little roughened from exposure to the sun.

"Are you mortal?" she inquired.

He flashed his smile at her. He liked doing that because it seemed to have a shocking effect among those where noble married women actually blackened their teeth to seem to have none.

This one giggled, without covering her mouth, something he couldn't know would be a social gaff in Edo. Then she smiled widely showing large, fine teeth.

"A black demon," he told her and she giggled again.

"A poor hunter," she put in.

"Even here," he said with a sigh and a headshake. "Women tell me that. Princesses." He didn't know the word and said it in Spanish which failed to enlighten her. Then tried: "Great ladies."

She liked that.

"Yes," she said, joking. "My father is *daimio* of the village."

Later, night, the moon a thin crescent in the blurry sky that hinted more rain. They could see it from where they lay side-by-side in the loft of the laying-by barn, stretched out on soft sacks of millet. It smelled musty and sweet and uMubaya felt totally relaxed for the first time since he'd been washed up on the beach.

"No one comes here at night?

217

"Only to do what we did, maybe."

He touched her with friendly intimacy.

"Why did you, I mean, with a demon?"

"Why not? I have never seen your like."

He grunted and looked at the moon, thoughtfully. Memories.

"My people hunt and fight," he told her. "Like others." Chuckled. "In the dark, who can tell one from another?"

She gripped him low.

"Here's one way," she said, giggling.

"Pause for breath," he said, grinning. "But all peoples I have met seem more alike than different, in the end."

"Well, if they hunt in your fashion your people must often go hungry." She giggled again.

"I didn't want the beast," he explained, touching her, absently.

"The woman who tells you 'no' is always unpleasant-looking."

He chuckled.

"You recall someone to my thoughts," he told her, looking at the moon.

"Someone who teases, dark sir? They say I tease too much."

He shut his eyes.

"My name, though you have not asked, is uMubaya. What is yours?"

"Unimportant," she murmured, "unless you see me again. What is your second name?"

"One is enough to know me by." He yawned and stretched. "What is yours, in case I do see you again?"

"Kimi Teasing," she told him, not giggling this time, now touching him down where it mattered. She put him, he considered, in a grip few men could break. "Enough foolish talking," she concluded.

Dark followed day followed dark...bright, hot, harsh...his eyes felt filmed over, sticky...there were glimpses of blurry, bright blue fragments above him leaking through a network of twisted, sharp, spiky finger he sometimes recognized were thorns...when he'd try to move, tearing, agonizing stiffness would rend his body and he feared those spiky hands were gripping him...his heart would race, rapid and light, breath rasp into his dry, raw throat...then an inexpressibly soothing coolness would touch his cracked, sore lips and trickle into his mouth...then light

218

and darkness...he would burn with thirst and gasp for air... violent shivering shook him, terrible cold...cold...twisting, wild images of fangs and fighting, blood and pain, mad dancing and feasts and somewhere lost among bright and dark and freezing and burning and terror and despair there was something wonderful that was no more grounded or certain than the rest, yet more solid, somehow, a sweetness and musk that sucked a strange, painful gathering of independent, itching, irresistible need into his body, knotting itself into his loins while his hands groped like a newborn child's at the breast, to somehow seize the sweetness...his body thrashed for relief and ecstasy amidst all the hurt, spears, swords, screams and blood and lost, lonely emptiness that welled up like a vast, shifting painting in the fever of his mind...he felt her and knew it was she...heard her cries...smelt female richness...then fell into imageless night...and then woke and was alone in a thorn bomba *she'd enclosed him in for protection while his wounds healed and sick heat faded...finally, days later, blinking and wincing against spikes of sun stabbing into his consciousness through the brush he saw her impassive face, the V cheekbones, the proud-held head, himself too weak to do more than rasp at words, her voice saying:*

'Farewell, brave man. I must go home. I will always think of you."

Later, the moon was gone from the open space and only the stars, intercut by long, straight, silvered clouds showed. The drone of nightbugs and chorusing frogs was almost a roar.

He'd fallen asleep and, as he woke, the dream overlapped and he was back there on the veldt under a waning moon that seemed to melt in silverwhite blurs through the netted thorn branches of the bomba where'd he'd been lying in fever and stiff pain for unmeasured days. Since it was part dream, it suggested meaning and seemed clearer than mere memory: the earth was soft under him (like the bagged millet he presently lay on) and his fever and soreness had seemed to melt away and gather in the suddenly rock-hard center of his body as the graceful, long-curved female outline descended over his arched and aching groin and sat them into a single flesh welded together by agonizing sweetness...he knew what it meant (in the dream now and in the fever then) because the two times had been welded together. It was as if he'd been made of liquid so that his entire being flowed up from the feet and down from the head and poured out into the graceful weightless shape straddling his loins that was also

219

himself and an emptiness, as well, infinitely suctioning him away as he was trying to fully wake up now and the fever then…gasping and blinking, sitting upright in the barn, the Japanese woman stirring slightly beside him, traces of dawn showing at the open high door beside them, a single, soft, big star in the subtly lightening eastern sky….

It happened, he thought. *It must have happened…I remember…I remember her leaving me there when the fever had cooled and I was still weak as a baby goat….it must have happened…or did I dream it only in the heat of my brain? I'd have to ask her and even then I'd have to believe her….*

The memory of a dream or the dream of a memory, he didn't quite put it. And this haunted him, too. He lay back down and looked at the star that he didn't know was a planet. At some point his eyes closed again….

There was a dreamless blotting-out and then the loft opening was hazy and bright and he was lying there, alone. He rubbed his face and sighed. Sat up.

Did I dream this, too? He asked himself.

He could see over the edge of the opening across flat, flooded rice paddies to where the wood and thatch homes clustered beyond the watermill. He supposed she went back to her hut and family.

He liked this woman who hadn't given her real name or asked for his. Sensed that it made it less real for her but no less exciting. Smiled. She'd been more than real in his arms: the fluid touch and musky scent, soft outcries in ecstasy's helplessness…trying to press himself deeper and deeper, to pin her there as if she, somehow, were melting away beneath him….

Memory is not here, he reasoned, again thinking about Mer'ce and the troubling dream of the moonstruck, South African night. *Many nights and moons ago…here is here….*

He stood up and dressed himself in his monkish disguise. Outside, the fresh sunlight reflected on the rice fields and stream, the high blurry clouds still pinkish. The air smelled of earth and green and was still almost cool; but the heat was already gathering.

There was a ladder up to the opening and he climbed down. At bottom there were red and black blossoms wedged in a crack between two boards. He knew she'd left them. Smiled.

He entered the village an hour later. He was dressed the same as the first time but assumed most monks looked like other monks. He passed the bailiff's where Takezo in his merchant's disguise had discussed bringing his imaginary goats to the inn. The barrel the late, wide-shouldered and mocking Osa-Kame had been sitting on was still there. No one was outside.

He went into the first sake and bun shop he came to on the main street which ran straight down to the beach where the inn overlooked the ocean. The surf was a steady whooshing hiss; erratic on-shore breezes brought a salt-scent and touches of coolness to the sunbright-side of the thoroughfare.

There weren't many people out yet. A boy was currying a horse behind a rude fence; an old man and woman on a porch were mending fishing nets; a stout, barefooted woman was toting two jugs of water on a pole across her shoulders, singing to herself.

Inside he sat at a table facing the haze-bright street through the unshuttered windows.

The medium-sized, average-looking, greyhaired shopkeeper was a little uneasy. He'd asked if the blessed monk actually had coins to pay or did he mean to bring out his begging bowl. uuMubaya put out a few of the coins Takezo had given him.

"Priest," said the man, peering out into the street, nervously, "don't bother with this village."

"Do not?"

"No good."

"No good?"

"Where are you from? The far South?"

"Yes," said the Zulu.

"Thought so. I have an ear for accents." Pursed his lips and studied the other. Yawned and showed big, yellowed teeth. "Take off your headpiece."

"A vow," explained uMubaya.

So saying, he popped open the visor-like hinged flap and poked a ball of rice and meat into his mouth. His hands were covered by light gloves. Then he made a drinking motion and the man poured him out *sochu* from a jug. The big African liked it. Tossed it down and let it burn.

"Good," he said, holding out the cup for a refill which came – along with a confidential stream of words and bad breath.

221

"Some priests don't drink. I don't trust them. How can you show compassion for sinners if you don't share the sins?"

"I have many faults," agreed uMubaya, leaning away slightly as the man went on, moving even closer and almost whispering the smell that the Zulu thought must be a rotting tooth.

"This is a bad place, Holy One." The shopkeeper squinted one eye nearly shut and nodded. He was now so close uMubaya couldn't focus on his face; not that he wanted to. The prince was trying to remain polite. He twisted away to give the impression he was bringing his ear closer but the smell seemed to gather inside the headpiece.

"To eat and drink?" uMubaya sort of answered, losing the thread, somewhat.

"No, no. This village. Not good, Holy One. All gamblers. Crooks. Killers without pity."

He kept looking over his shoulder, automatically. The black man had noticed this habit in others and had sort of grasped the alien concept of a society where police spies often overlapped criminal informants;, where every clan and crime family had spies and police duties to help suppress, not local crime, but the threat of uprisings that could flare up in city and country and rage for years....

uMubaya grunted. Leaning back away from the breath while he took another drink through his "visor."

"I heard a noble woman was murdered here. Her head cut from her body."

"Better not talk about that," the man said, kind of leering. "They don't like it. Big trouble. Covering up a big mistake."

While the Zulu understood what Takezo wanted, the complex and obscure interactions of these people eluded him, at times, so he cut to the point:

"Some believe the woman is here and not murdered."

"Hidden?" The man seemed surprised. He leaned back in his seat and the breath relented.

uMubaya made a shrugging gesture. This seemed to be pointless and his mind reverted to the farm woman, her strong body, intense hands gripping and kneading him. He half-decided to go back to her village and find her.

That would be good, he said to himself.

222

Thirty-Seven

At the estuary where the river had widened and shallowed out opening into Edo bay, the sluggish current was presently negated by the incoming tide so the long shadows from the moored fishing boats masts seemed to lie perfectly flat as on a sheet of polished glass. On the far side were spindly docks and low buildings just starting to cohere and blend into the hazy dimming as the sun hung hot and yellow-red, falling over the edge of evening. The brilliant splashed sunglare on the water contrasted the rest of the river into a purplish, faded blue.

Takezo stood a few feet into the almost unmoving water on a semi-firm mix of sandy mud and smooth pebbles. He was in a loincloth, sheathed katana in his hand.

He was facing out to sea. The reflected light hit the flat shoreline in softly shifting, wavy patterns of brightness. His shadow stretched, angular and exaggerated, over the rocky, weed-spattered beach and up over the high-tide embankment about 25 yards further on.

The heat was steady and oppressive. He could scent the dead fish lying at the water's slightly undulant edge in pale and silver bloat.

He glanced at Yazu wading out to him, *bokkuken* over his shoulder, "live" short sword sheathed in his sash. He'd been promised a lesson; having put the dung defeat by the tavernkeeper's wife aside, he felt pretty good about his martial improvements. That morning he'd made the point fairly strongly to his fierce and fearful spouse.

He and his young son were working together in the small, fenced-in space behind his modest house. The afternoon was bright and steamy. For a week they'd been turning the weeded lot into a garden. He'd even dug a short channel from the stream where the women washed clothes so that a thin trickle just made it to partly fill the shallow, 5 foot around rock-lined pool he'd dug.

Today they were planting hibiscus bushes wheedled from a landscaper who owed him a small gambling debt. Since the battle of the inn, he'd been taking a more aggressive stance among his fellows. And the keen shogo in his waistband had to be considered.

'Goldfish,' he said, peering into the somewhat murky water swirling sluggishly into the tiny pond. 'That's the thing.' His bony, intent face looked back at him from the dull, brownish swirl, dim and blurry. "I know a man in 1st street who-'

'Think you're a samurai?' his wife wanted to know. 'Crazy fellow. We've been eating millet and mouldy rice for weeks and you construct a garden that looks worse than a weedlot.'

'Nevermind, woman,' he responded. 'I have plans. The sensei *promised me gold* ryo *for my work. Consider that.'*

'Ahha,' she reacted, 'that tramp. When has he seen a metal penny? Don't talk to me about him.'

'Guard your mouth, woman. He's the best swordsman in Edo. Maybe in-'

'My robes are frayed. This child-' indicating the boy, '-wears worn-down sandals of cheap hemp. He-'

'Mother, Takezo-san promised to instruct me, too,' said the sleek, soft-looking, big-thighed lad with rather feminine pectorals. His mother always made sure he got sweet buns every day.

'Quiet!' snapped the bony little man, standing up and striking a samurai's pose, fists on hips, narrow, bare feet gripping the earth with long toes, suggesting a bird. His confidence was real and she felt it. He stepped over to her. 'Woman, busy yourself. My son and I are working together. After this comes sword practice.'

Oh, she knew she could have stabbed him with scorn and tossed a pot or two at his skull; she didn't want to because, even if futile, there was a gesture of hope there like being lost in the country at night and seeing the soft light in the distance that might be the inn you're looking for. It had been so long since she'd believed anything, ground down by the dull, automatic cynicism of poverty and disappointment.

So she almost smiled as she reached up a jug of water from the shade of the porch.

'Thirsty work,' she said, noting that he flinched, slightly, thinking she might dump it on him as she held the jug out. He took it, clearly surprised. Her expression was a kind of shrug. 'Save some sword practice for tonight, husband.'

Oh, she didn't really believe it, but the hope felt good. Maybe that was enough. Maybe it was just a moment or maybe a change was actually coming....

He took a drink, too careful to risk saying anything else. Nodded with satisfaction and handed the cool jug to his son.

'Boy, in this existence we don't get many chances,' he told him and her, too, not checking if she were listening. Stared, reflectively, at the

224

little world they were making there. 'Can't do much about much. A man lives with one eye over his shoulder.' The boy nodded, serious. 'But do what you can do with a whole heart. Master something and when they take all else away you still have that.' She'd stopped partway back inside and was just looking at him. 'Master something and you don't die in vain.'

Takezo watched a shadowy flutter of minnows around his feet, stopping and going in instant, synchronized flashing. No humans could imagine such precision. How did they signal, instantly?

He was about to share his observation with Yazu the way he might have with his pet dog – if he'd had a pet dog.

The bony, excitable student was already speaking, saying:

"Master, master, important news!"

Not looking at him Takezo swept a leisurely stroke with his sheathed blade at Yazu's head not hard enough to do more than stun him. The splay-legged little man reacted well, ducking forward and under (hard to teach) so that the impact was too close to the hilt to hurt, glancing off his back and shoulder. His own counter actually creased his teacher's leg. A "live" sword would have made a shallow cut.

"Impressive," he told Yazu, stooping down and splashing some cool water over his face. Peered at his fragmented reflection on the broken surface.

That's how I really look, he thought. *The face of my soul....*

"I did as you instructed, *sensei*," said Yazu. "I surrendered my love of life. I cling no more to-"

"Ready for the mountaintop?"

"Yes, *sensei*, I can feel my mind turning away from worldly matters." He looked into the hazy distance where the river opened into the ocean. Their shadows lengthened, side-by-side on water and beach as the sun inched down and slowly dulled to red. "I see myself meditating with sword in hand and-"

"Sounds like you're holding something else in your hand," Takezo commented, straightening up from his disturbing image on the water. "But you're changing, maybe a little."

"Yes. Even my wife has been...."

Takezo smiled.

"Yes," he said. "When people even think you have money they want to make you loans."

225

Stared through his shadow to the shallow bottom and remembered when he was a boy, swimming in the lake, going underwater, sinking through the strange, reversed rays that seemed to radiate from the bright, sandy bottom as if the sunlight were spraying up among the swaying fronds in spreading, soft beams.

Decided to wade out and really swim underwater. Maybe he'd forget a few things for a few minutes. Tossed his sword to his apprentice. Started heading out.

"Hold this," he ordered.

"Wait, master. Hear news. Father Osimachi discovered what you wanted."

He looked back, up to his knees.

"Yes?" he asked.

"Discovered who paid poor Miou's burial expenses. I approached him. He responded."

Takezo sighed, not moving. Because whoever paid knew she was dead far too soon. Whoever paid did it maybe from mockery or even shame. And to make a point, too, for all he knew.

I see this through or else commit seppuku by sake...it isn't even for revenge, just to finish something in this nasty, ugly life of mine that goes on and on from one corpse to another until, I swear, I could walk on bodies from here to Kyoto....

"If you don't tell me I won't have to do anything," he said.

"Master?"

"I want to write poems about time."

"Master?"

"I want to swim to an island and think about nothing."

"A certain island, master?"

"Just speak. Who was it?"

"A man you know. The samurai Yoshi."

"That fist-full of shit?" Sighed, again. Deeper. "Of course. It was mockery. I let him live twice. How weak of me."

But he wasn't the killer, that's part of another trap, I think....

"Yoshi paid the madam of Sanjuro House, master."

"And he will know the true culprit. He is at the heart of the big, great plan or plot or sickness for the good of our people." He clenched both fists and shut his eyes, hard. "It's so important it can only mean endless slaughter. It's such a blessing it can only mean pain and misery

226

without end." Opened his eyes, blinking at the blur of sweat and tears, his back to the now dull red sun that was melting into the cloudy horizon behind him, silhouetting him in the reddening water. "It's big and important, Yazu."

"Ah," breathed the little man, reverently holding Takezo's heavy blade. "I don't doubt it. But Father Osihachi said it is unwise to press further in these matters."

"He said that, that sage and revered criminal?"

His eyes were still prone to blurring since the duel in the flames with Osa-Kame. He tried to focus out to sea where long, inky black clouds spread across the horizon. Extreme-looking weather.

Another temptation, he thought. *Another grain of rice for the silly bird to peck as he follows the trail they left him until he comes into the trap...I think this has been from the first day...too late to stop....*

"Yes." Answered Yazu, shifting from foot to foot, waist-deep in the water. "So he said. Too dangerous to keep on."

"How can I not, then?" Blinked and rubbed his uncertain eyes. "I need to talk to him. Arrange it."

"Yes, *sensei.*"

Their shadows had now blended away into the general dimming of the day. The sea was deepening to purple. On the sea horizon the dark clouds seemed thick as paste. The sunset was gathering into stunning red over the city.

"Looks like a storm on one side," he said, "and blood on the other."

A few hours later

Night in the city. Takezo followed Yazu into a low-ceilinged gambling den, full of tobacco smoke, bad music, strong incense, shouts, songs, laughter, whore's perfume, spilled sake on wood and cooking food.

They worked their way across the main room into the back area closed off by a dingy curtain with the characters for "private" scrawled on it. They went through. On the other side an immensely squat guard in black kimono sat on a low stool, back to the wall. He seemed to recognize Yazu but otherwise seemed as responsive as a bag of rocks.

"Father" Osimachi and two of his men were sitting on their heels at a low table laden with cold food and sake. A big, dull red lantern hung

227

over the table on a cord, coloring his bald, oily-looking head and sinking all but his long beaked nose and heavy brows in shadow.

Takezo knelt to face them, sword laid beside him. Yazu stood, uneasily, at the outskirts of the ring of illumination. One of the criminal boss's henchmen was smoking a long iron pipe, the smoke hanging low and thick in the stagnant, wet air. The effect of the hot coal colored light struck the *ronin* as a scene of shades in some Buddhist hell.

Men are just men, his mind said. *All of us....* Yet, lately, more and more, some people were, somehow, truly dark like the shadows on the stagnant smoke.

He noticed an unadorned wicker screen behind them and assumed there would be a bodyguard or two behind.

"Takezo-san," said the big-nosed boss, nodding a slight bow that winked his nose into and out of the light. "Pleasant to see you."

The *ronin* snorted a laugh like a cough.

"Oh, no doubt, thank you," he said, bowing back.

As the non-smoking cohort pushed the sake jug across the table, Takezo said:

"'Father' Osimachi, I want to press further. Though I thank you for your concern."

"Press what?"

"I have another question for you, 'Father,' and beg your knowledge be bestowed on me."

"Well, ask, then, sir."

"Yoshi, the dung-beetle," Takezo said, "since one cannot tell from his robes, what color is his loincloth?" Which was to say: what was his true allegiance?

This is an obvious trap, Takezo decided, watching, concentrating and feeling no substantial threat in the room. *Obvious makes it subtle....* The boss chuckled softly with about as much mirth as a man with a toothache. Takezo took a drink of sake. It was thin and had too much wood in the taste. Cheap stuff.

"Why did you come here?" the boss asked, mildly, almost abstractly.

"Because you suggested I press no further."

"Of course." Bowed an inch, again. "Is Yoshi so important to you? I doubt it."

"Who is his true master? And don't say Hideo."

"Yes, yes, we see your cleverness."

"You see more than I do." Poured and tossed back another cup. The second was always much better. It tingled with promise. "Can you assist me?"

The man behind the nose that poked into the light spoke almost soothingly.

"Takezo-san, there is a man who can answer your questions. I can send you to him, tonight."

The detective smiled. Looked into his sake cup as if some answer lay there and saw only the reddish shadows of the lantern like a tiny pool.

"I like this trap," he said.

"But, Father," put in Yazu from the background, "you promised no deception!"

"Not so bold, runt-man," one of the lieutenants at the table said, harshly.

"There's no deception," said Takezo. "It is all far too plain." Took another sake. "I trap myself because I have to go on looking at things even when there's really nothing to see." The third drink was even a little better. He felt relaxed and easy. He almost liked these silly, self-important plotters who were the least pieces in a game of *shogi*. Gestured with his head. "Who's behind the screen? I hope it's Yoshi or Chamberlain Chamberpot."

Someone guffawed. Osimachi didn't. He raised a cautionary hand.

"No point in bloodshed. In the end you'd perish. Even the greatest swimmer must drown in a lake of mud." The hand dropped back out of the light. "You will be brought to him safely. No treachery."

"Excellent," said the detective, standing up and thrusting his *katana* back into his wide sash. "You're not really going to tell me anything. Annoying. Maybe I'll go tomorrow. Come, Yazu. Too many promises here."

"Go now," said a woman's voice he knew as she came around the screen and moved into the dull reddish gleaming. A shock: Issa, hair up in a perfect bun pierced with silver needles, wearing water-smooth shimmering silks, looking like a high-priced courtesan, came around the table through the hanging smoke that flowed around her tall body. She came so near her long, aquiline face was breath close and again those long eyes showed something he couldn't read. "You are thinking," she murmured, "that maybe I wasn't born a great lady."

"It would explain some things," he murmured back. "If you were born a whore."

"Not born one."

She smiled but didn't kiss or touch him. He was surprised but not enough to be off guard. In the main room the music, talk, yells dinned on.

"And your secrets are safe with these noble men," he said.

"Perfectly."

"Because you're all part of it."

"It?"

"The big thing. The great changes in the world. Maybe the restoration of the Emperor. You have to kill a certain number of girls for it to work."

"Understand this, roughneck, I love my daughter. I wish her no harm. She fled and I don't know why. I'm grateful to you for showing that she may be alive."

"They opened the grave."

"Yes."

"And it was the girl with the lily tattoo?"

"Yes. And there's more you don't know."

She stepped aside and he had a fleeting impression this was a moment in a play except there was no chorus to explain and comment on the drama. He waved his hand in front of his face at the smoke that was really thickening as the seated man puffed continually at his pipe: Osimachi and the others looked almost like cutouts blurred and depthless in the tobacco fog.

And then, for the first time, he was so shocked he staggered back half a step, blinking, staring through tearing eyes at the graceful, beautiful woman who'd, as if on cue, come out from behind the screen. As she came through the haze towards him his heart pounded and his mind said *It's a spirit...it's a trick...it's*....because it was Miou...*but it's so smoky...impossible*...and then she was close and it was her face...*clever makeup...ninja tricks*...and she spoke, saying in what might have been her voice:

"My love, I still live!"

Dropping to her knees before him and he knew it was nonsense but had to watch himself lose his concentration because hope overwhelmed it and, in that instant of wanting to believe, gave Issa the time to whip one silver hairpin from her coiffure and stick it into his neck.

Globefish poison, he thought, already feeling dark numbness shock his blood and brain, face and neck tingling as the drug-like poison began to shut down his nervous system, his breath and the floor came up on a tilt to pound into him – except he didn't feel it and only was aware of what might have been Yazu shouting something too far off and blurred to understand and a close, fading whisper, that could only be Issa, saying:

"I have come too far to turn back, poor Takezo. I too am on the wheel of fate…"

And then the smoke and shadow closed in and covered him completely, pressed him down, pressed him flat as if darkness were a vast weight and nothing moved. What could move? Time had stopped….

As Yazu saw his master fall he drew his sword and struck a pose, blade over his head.

Life is nothing, he kept saying in his head.

"Traitors!" he said with his mouth. "False-swearers!"

Issa turned to him, silver needle in her hand, beautiful clothes rustling, eyes remote and introspective.

"Calm down," she recommended. "These are matters beyond your understanding."

"I understand you slew my good and wise sensei. Evil woman!"

He was chill with fear and felt flimsy as when struggling in a dream; still, he didn't retreat. Kept his sword upraised. Then made a feint as if to strike her with it though he had no real intent. His legs felt watery but, still, he stood there, suddenly thinking about his garden, his son and himself patting the transplanted flowers in place with care around the murky little pool; his wife coming out with a big bowl of soup for them all to share….

He had an impression Issa moved as if a gust of supernatural wind blew her and she was, somehow, behind him and he tried to turn awkwardly in the smoke and shadow and felt the needle jab the back of his neck. From far away he heard his sword drop and clatter…laughter…his flesh became ice and he knew he was falling and had a remote impression that when he hit his body would shatter like a sheet of frost…saw only the garden and tried to say something very important to his wife and son except there were no words for it or sound either…very important…he wanted…just wanted…a great sadness because there was no sound and then he felt himself shatter and there was no garden….

231

She dropped a sack of coins onto the floor table in front of Osimachi. The *chukk* impact rang the wood with an almost musical tone.

The song of money, she reflected walking past them to the back door that opened out into the garden yard. *What is the true price of what cannot be bought?*

"Be careful of him," she said behind her. The fact that she said it annoyed her. It wasn't necessary. "As was agreed," she went on anyway. "Thank you." Her thank you was almost a threat because she was irritated and guilty, too.

The false Miou was following her. She stopped without turning.

"My Lady," the girl said, "please, do I return to my job, now?"

"You mean you want your money. Your services were bought."

"Please excuse me, Lady."

"He is a good man," Issa told her, "not really for sale, though he takes money."

"Yes, please."

"My head hurts." She stared at the open sliding door out into the overcast night, not turning. "My insides are tied in small knots. I feel like my life is all mistakes."

The sickness of the woman's moon, she said to herself, touching her abdomen, unconsciously. *I must control my judgment...the smoke in here chokes me....*

"Yes, my Lady."

"Go," she said. "Your madam has the money you were bought with."

"Yes. Thank you." She bowed at Issa's back as she went through the door.

"I've been bought, too," she murmured, to herself as she went outside into the hot, thick, heavy-hanging air. She breathed hard and deep. "Not for money. Maybe far worse."

I like him too much, she thought. *I wanted to seduce him to prove...no, not prove...maybe because he's not one of them, eager to bow and beg favors...I hated him the way a woman hates what she most wants...no...needs....*

She looked at the backs of the buildings across the half-hearted sketch of garden: a few bushes, a few flowers, a few rocks all overlit by too many lanterns, she observed, all soft shadows and warm pools of light.

232

Reminded her of a festival. Inside the mumble and shouting of gamblers, the shrill interjections of women, clash, bang, laughter and curses was a screen of sound behind her.

I like to take a man by his strength and bind him...lead him where I please...I use him but am I not still a whore in the morning, unpaid, unlike that child we just hired to act and betray? She snorted with self-contempt. *There's pleasure in feeling the power of a whore and imagining you rule men....*

"All I rule are web-weaving, shadowy, greedy...."

She thought about Takezo.

Dirt washes off some of us...washes off him....

She stepped off the low porch, looked down into a softly bright stain of red lantern light on a razor-edged rock surrounded by sagging, long-stemmed flowers. Her feelings went one way, then another. She unconsciously slipped a hand beneath her underslip to check her loins for wetness. She hated when the blood ran thick and warm down the inside of her thighs.

"Aiii," she sighed. "It is so difficult...." Shut her eyes. "Difficult to find balance." *My child,* she thought, *hopes she will express something whose truth will stun the world into sense...she chases false ghost light, but she is brave and, like Takezo the Spy, she is unsullied....*"I am cruel to such people since they lay bare my shames."

She dug her fingers into her face and then ripped her gold-sandaled foot in a slashing kick at the flowers and left a shattered swath.

"I sicken of doing wrong," she hissed. "I sicken of greedy men and I sicken of myself."

As if no time had ever intervened her memory was darkness where a twisted rill of pale candlelight, softly wavering, in a big black night where formless terrors gathered. She was a child and that air was cool on her pale, naked body and the big, massive, sweet and sour smelling shape that by day was the lord she was, at times, presented to and the semi-hard poking thing pressing at her lips, big, harsh hands vising both sides of her head, pushing her into it, filling her mouth and throat until she was almost gagging, afraid to breath, hearing his moans and wild curses that she didn't know were curses.

Because later there were strange men (a roar outside she didn't know was battle) and shouts and screams all around her in the small

233

fortress where she'd been born (she was just nine) hands on her, lifting her, carrying her away to a slave existence....

"Beast!" she said, standing in the garishly overlit and unkempt garden. "I live still and you are dead. Did I not find your grave, some years ago?"

Her retainers had waited outside the walls of the famous cemetery. Alone in her cold fury, she'd pulled her undergarments aside and squatted over the sunken mound and made water as if it were poison, an acid of hate that could corrode the very spirit of the dead man.

I am too vengeful and unforgiving...my heart is stained with hate and may never be washed clean...yet....I must control my life...without this clan I am a slave again and what fate for my dreaming child....

"Takezo-san, I am sorry. So sorry. Maybe you are a purity. I stained you. But you are, I think, pure and corrupt at once." She shut her eyes. The world tipped and swayed, a little.

I can't look back...I won't be a slave again...never...nor will my child....why should I not rule these fools?

Tears squeezed out of her eyes. She just stood there. The garish lights. The blank, overcast sky. The faint, rotting scent of dead flowers.

Thirty-Eight

Most of it had to be dream. Opening his eyes did no good because the darkness was utter, the air stale; he'd try to move...the darkness was solid and curved around him. Next, vivid brightness as if he were watching a living painting, a giant hand scroll unrolling before him with city, town, countryside, mountains, rivers and sea flowing past...people suddenly coming to life, moving, all at a distance until, instantly, he'd be close...wherever his numbed fingers touched there was the unyielding curve closing him in behind, in front above – he had a fleeting impression before sheer, numb weariness dropped him back into what might have been sleep (unless the black confinement itself were that) that when he pressed his hands a few inches over his head there was some slight give...maybe that meant something...maybe not...and the painting came back to life, again, and there was a woman lying flat on her back in the gray wash of early morning light, mist gathered around her in dark, dew-wet bushes, lying on sandy soil in a bright shock of blood, headless and he tried to move, to act, to speak...but he was high up above a battlefield, next, horsemen clashing in a violent storm, the dark clouds themselves

234

seeming to shape themselves into twisting, lunging, stabbing, striking riders treading on piles of dead and dying...blurs...blackness. He tried to stand and push his way free against the unyielding, hard, smooth circle that trapped him as if he were in a lidded jar...then the scroll was back, moving and there was Miou with her broken, bloody body walking like a puppet on a string upheld and moved by moonbeams...holding out a ghostly shimmer of silver, silent, beseeching eyes full of silvery tears, holding out the shadow of the ring, lips moving but speaking only in shadows....

And he heard his voice or some howling wordless rasp of agony; there was only the hard, stifling jar-like prison as his mind said:

*This is all that's left of the world....*He tried to smile into the numbness of his face. *Wonder what time it is....*

And then he was rising higher and higher over the vast, unrolling scroll until all the pain, lust, love, longing and mad violence were just shapes, colors and lines like a picture without a subject leaving only the essence and gesture of human life...and he soared so high, now, it could have been just curds and kneadings of smoke....

The constant tilt, bump and rocking kept jarring him back to the black confinement of his barrel-shaped environment. The numbness was lifting and he started to seriously, though weakly, struggle and push against the section above his head that gave slightly.

The air was fetid, humid, hot and hard-to-breath; he was conscious enough now to imagine he might have been buried alive – no – the rocking motion told him he was moving but he was suddenly sure he was in a coffin being carried to the graveyard.

A nice revenge, his thoughts said.

Redoubled his efforts, straining, not really aware of how feeble his struggles were until, suddenly, they were still and cooler air flowed down over him because the lid was gone and his hands barely reached above the rim of a hogshead-like coffin. He was panting, the beaded sweat rolling off his head and face.

After a few breaths he gripped the rim with fingers that felt like fat Chinese sausages and tried to heave himself up. He got far enough to glimpse overhanging trees and a pair of torches, swaying slightly in the heavy, nearly windless air.

He heaved again, hung a little longer and this time saw what he thought for an instant was a statue of an armored man. Looking straight up there were shadowy pine branches and flat, blank dark sky. He knew it wasn't a statue.

His lips were tingling, hard to move. Forced in a deep breath and tried again.

This time he got up enough to rest his elbows on the lip of the coffin-barrel and hung there, blinking to help adjust his eyes to the bright flame.

There was a grave dug among the marker stones with what he assumed was his sword thrust into the earth as when a samurai dies in the field. There was what looked like the same suit of armor and the same mask he'd met in the barn, how long ago? It seemed very, very long ago. Time had sucked away days like years, like dead leaves down the river....

He stared at the blurry outline that seemed to be alone. Assumed he probably wasn't.

"Well done," Takezo grated. "You got me, once more."

He remembered Yoshi and Captain Mori. Remembered the two of them standing over him in Miou's garden as he came awake into headache and a sick stomach, the mellow morning sun hurting his eyes whenever he peered out from under the sleeve of his robe at the two of them standing over him. He couldn't help but think that if he'd said "no" then, she might still be alive.

The first mistake engenders all the rest, he thought. *My parents made it by having me....regret isn't so vain when you have nothing else left....*

"No so hard," the muffled voice said with a metallic vibration.

"And now is when you tell me if I don't give up the ring I go into the hole you dug over there. Or first you offer me gold."

The numbness was draining away by tiny increments; he was still far away from any level of effectiveness.

The metal-muffled voice seemed amused. He was close and the bright torch lit the silvery faceplate. Takezo could see his own gleam and shadow-eaten reflection there distorted to seem all mouth, chin and twisted cheeks without eyes.

"Maybe the offer is your woman back," the voice said.

"Who was the actress?" the *ronin* almost spat.

"Maybe the dead girl was the actress and your grief was senseless."

Takezo knew he was being played, again.

236

"You," he said with full contempt, "who are you playing? You're not Izu. Not Nobunaga nor Hideo nor Reiko. Too intelligent to be Yoshi. Maybe you're a woman with a deep voice."

The numbness really was fading. He started to gather himself to leap out. Go for his sword by the open grave. What were his odds, anyway? Keep talking a little longer, he decided.

"I respect you," the other said and there was almost a kind of purr in it, Takezo noted. "So you still live. I want you to come back."

"Back where?"

He tested his legs for standing, started to squat upright, got past shoulder-high and then they weren't there and he went all the way back down with a thump, banging his head.

"Too soon," the voice said. "The drug takes time to wear away."

Then the mask was leaning in over the rim, the bright torch halving it with uneven shadow.

"Come back where?" the *ronin* repeated.

"To your clan. To the life intended for you."

A night of surprises, he thought. *By the Holy Beings, maybe I'm near the end of all this obscurity....*

"I have no clan. I have no life." Heaved again and this time, straining on his arms, stayed almost upright, face so close to the mask he could smell the warm metal. "Show yourself."

"Show you something else." He stooped down and stood back up with a severed head in his hand. He thrust it forward as if to touch the detective's face. "The hole is for him. Talked too much."

He recognized the young samurai, Sessu, who'd loved Miou, too. The torchlight showed him with lidded eyes and a sad mouth.

"He's pretty quiet, now," said Takezo.

The other half-turned and tossed the grisly artifact in a soft looping arc at the hole. It hit and bounced, dropped into the pit blackness.

The detective got all the way up, this time, and rested on both palms.

"Rejoin," the tinny, firm voice said, coming close, again, the frozen metal fury inches from the battered, bleary, numb, weary flesh face. "Hear this: you are strong and valuable. There will be a decisive war soon. The upstart Nobunaga, enemy of the worthy people, will be crushed. He will die even before his armies collapse."

"Are you a soothsayer, Mask-san?"

237

"Before the first arrow flies we will own victory." The torch was close enough for Takezo to feel the heat pressure. "The world will be overturned as if a great earthquake had struck and the great castles will be brought low while the lesser will rise, triumphant. There will be a new way of life. You can be part of this. It is your place. You can be part of destiny or die a slave with the weak and stupid!"

As the speaker got fired-up the muffling effect of the mask increased the distortion of his speech as the metal rattled and vibrated. Takezo missed a number of the words which sounded like coughs and retchings of air; he got the gist.

"You will rule?" the detective asked. "Will you unmask, then?"

The man stepped back, torch in one hand, other on his martial hip. Behind him the flames lit the lines of tombs and grave markers.

"Takezo," he said, calmly. "If I show myself to you I'll have to slay you. I don't wish that. Come back to our clan. Yes. Our clan. The one you fled."

The finger poked his brain, as usual. Then he had it:

"You waited almost 30 years to reclaim me? Touching. Why didn't you tell me when you gave me gold ryo."

"Bah. You know better."

"Miou told you. She worked for you. You had her murdered. I think you're the butcher behind it all."

They were both silent. Takezo was about to try to spring out and go for the sword. It was probably hopeless. But his disgust was getting the better of him. In the distance there was a faint booming of thunder.

He heard the other sigh inside his silver helmet. It was strange because nothing showed, not even a careless movement as if, the *ronin,* thought he *was* a being made of iron and steel. The torchlight made shadows in the gathering mist. He realized it must be close to dawn.

"Consider well my words, Takezo."

The detective just stood there, waist-deep in the coffin, too angry and disgusted to even react.

"You're going to make war," he said, sadly. "You will kill everybody. Do you drink blood? What *are* you inside that stupid suit?" Waved one hand. "I don't really want to know." He shook his head. "A new world. But can you do it without the mighty ring? You haven't said much about it. I'm disappointed. Don't you worry that I'll go away with it?"

He was ready now and wondered if the other knew it. He could feel the strength come back into himself. He had things to do and places to go.

"You are always watched," said the muffled, purring voice, calmly. "I brought you here to demonstrate the stupidity of your life. And to offer you a new one."

He paced away, into the mist, holding the torch. A sudden stir of wind fluttered it and the one stuck on the pole by the grave. Takezo got his leg over the lip of the coffin barrel and stood on the loamy earth. He headed for the grave and his naked sword.

"This is all theater," he called after the armored man, half-running, drawing the blade from the dirt and reflexively wiping it clean as he followed him, out of sight now, just the flamelight winking between bushes and tree branches. The thunder sounded a little closer and there were soft shakings of lightning in the distance.

Wobbling a little, he managed a run, cut around the graves and stones, ducked under low-hanging branches and came out abreast of the torch. The sluggish fog filled the branches and closed him in. The torch was stuck into the earth and he glimpsed the armor glinting faintly maybe 20 feet away behind the wet, gray mist-curtain.

Takezo leveled his sword and moved carefully forward, trying to feel the man's strength. Felt nothing.

"Draw, butcher," he said. "Maybe you'll win." Silence. The outline came a little clearer, standing still, under a twisted pine tree. Then the voice, muffled, this time, by fog and damp earth so that it seemed to come from nowhere:

"Look around you," it said. "This is what your life has come to. You stand ignorant, alone in the dark of a graveyard."

A roll of mist thickened and gave the impression the figure was retreating. Takezo instantly charged, was on top of it and slashed down in a single terrific burst of movement aware that it was futile, as the blade sliced through in a spray of sparks with barely any resistance. He drew a breath and sighed.

Worse than a bad dream, he thought.

Because the armor had been suspended from a limb and he'd cut it in half. The suit had crunched to the earth while the helmet hung there, mask divided in two, swinging. The fog stirred and roiled softly in the pre-

239

storm breezes. The torchlight behind him cast his shadow on the gray air, bending and shifting.

"More stupid theater," he said, breathing in and out slow and hard. "You won't even try to kill me. I'm worthless dead and you are merely worthless. *Ninja*."

"Reflect on your life," said the virtually directionless, blurry voice. Takezo knew the trick: cup your hands and talk into the ground. "You stand almost on her grave. Take time and reflect. She was one of us. She was sent to learn your secrets. She weakened. Come out of the dark where you stumble like a blind man."

Takezo just stood there, staring at the swaying pieces of the helmet and mask. Then he shut his eyes and held one hand to his face and shook his head. He'd already half-guessed even that and had half-buried it.

Ah, he thought. *It's more than true...my love, my love, I saw nothing...nothing....*

Thirty-Nine

Mora-by-the-sea

uMubaya went upstairs to the sleeping loft where the bad-breathed owner was letting him spend the night. He said he liked having a holy man around. The big African wasn't tired but had decided to wait for darkness before poking around the village. Or maybe go back to poke around the farms. Smiled at the idea.

Some more poking. He thought.

Later, the sun was just setting over the hills. He watched it through the wood-barred window that cut up the exquisite, washed-out orange and pink streaks.

He'd about concluded that dreaming about Mer'ce was like a sorcerer's curse. He tried to concentrate on the farm woman opening herself up beneath him. He stretched out on the cheap, rough straw mattress, looking at the window that was a magical painting in the rough wall of the rough room.

Regardless, he found himself thinking about how the same sky was above both of them, that, even now, she was doing whatever she did, maybe eating or laughing or stringing beads for a dress....

He shut his eyes and drifted into fantasy, mixing up the farm girl and Mer'ce in memory and dream so the barn and the thorn *bonba* were one and the exquisite, blended naked body sat down on him in the dimness, melting the thin Masai, himself and the resilient, obliging Japanese together....

"Did I mate with her or not?" he said, in Zulu, frustrated, opening his eyes and seeing, as the paling sunset light faded in the little room, a young woman's face peered at him above the open trapdoor where the stairs came up. She had a pale kerchief knotted over her head. Her features in the dimness seemed long, aristocratic, very fine. He almost took her for a spirit with a harried, haunted look.

He thought he knew her as she crouched up to floor level and knelt-walked into the sleeping area. She wore a pale, hempen robe and had particularly long, graceful hands.

"So the spy-who-drinks was right," he said, not loud, sitting up. "You live."

"I slipped away," Osan said. "You're growing a beard."

The Zulu rubbed his chin, nodding. The last light glowed pale, pale rose on the wall behind him and showed part of his dark face. She was like an evanescence exhaled by the twilight, lovely, he thought, and unreal as one of their misty paintings of misty things.

"There's been some trouble over you," he said, dryly.

She inclined her head, gracefully.

"Which grieves me, uMu-baya-san," she said.

"Are they looking for you?"

"Not yet. One of my guards likes to drink and dozed off. They don't worry about me escaping. Who would assist me? Most people in this region are one criminal family."

"So I heard."

"I saw you on the street earlier. You are a very big priest. What happened to Cor-in and Nori?"

"Nori I do not know. Colin is captured and may be beheaded for your murder. I was sent here to look for you."

"Strange choice," she said, thoughtfully, bowing slightly, again. "You speak even better than before and it has been less than a month since I was taken."

The room was nearly dark, now, the barred window a vague luminescence.

"I was sent here by a spy, Takezo," he said. "Many things have happened. Few good."

241

"Ah. I recall him. My mother dislikes him so he must be a friend. Will you help me to reach Edo, Ya-san?"

"This is why I have come." He mused, a moment. She was a vague blot kneeling close to him. "You are tall," he pointed out. "You wear my clothes and headpiece. It's dark. I'll find something else."

There was a commotion outside. He squinted through the window into the already dark street. Torches and lanterns were spraying and shaking light as several clumps of armed men moved rapidly, spreading out into alleys and yards, calling out to one another. An obvious search.

He got up and went past her kneeling at the open trapdoor.

"I think your guard woke up," he said softly to her; then called down into the shop, keeping his face back from the candlelight that gleamed up the stairs. "What's the noise?"

A customer had just come in. uMubaya could see he was a big man in dark kimono and a conical straw hat. He called up:

"Looking for a man. A big black devil from some devil land. Up to no good."

"Black?"

"Black like charred wood," was the response.

"Have you seen this devil?" asked the shopkeeper just out of the Zulu's view.

"No," said the newcomer.

Outside there were suddenly footsteps on the board sidewalk and the gruff voices of men wanting to seem fierce, uMubaya thought. One man burst in the doorway, torch flaring as he held it up to scrutinize the interior. He wore a sword, breeches and a wide-striped tunic. He was missing an ear and front teeth.

"Seen anything?" he demanded.

"I see you," said the big newcomer; he had no weapon visible.

"A black demon?" asked the shop owner. "How do you know?"

"Eh? He was seen by a farmer crossing the fields." Shook the torch around so the flame stuttered and ripped the air. "Better not hide him. The Boss would boil you to death."

"Why would I hide a devil?"

"I see something! Who's up there?"

"A Buddhist priest."

Screwing up his face in almost a comic scowl, the man started to rush up the stairs, saying:

242

"Saying sutras?"

Except the big man in the hat reacted before the African had to, snatching him by his sash and yanking him back down. The torch dropped, the shopman scurried to pick it up and the one-eared criminal drew his sword with a great flourish and swept it sideways in a flat cut; a dagger-centered *jittu* was instantly in the big man's left hand, catching and locking the blade, while his right struck the scowling face with an impact, the Zulu thought, like a coconut hit by a club. The gangster smacked the floor with a whump and less teeth than before. His feet kicked, fanning left and right.

"Come on, foreigner," the victor said, slipping his weapon back under his robe. "I'm Taro. Takezo sent me."

"Good," the reply from the shadows above. Outside the voices and footsteps
had moved off. "A moment."

And almost at once a smaller priest in uMubaya's baggy robes and wicker headpiece startled the shopkeeper who was crouching with the torch in one hand, the smoke curling and filtering out through the wide spaced planks of wall and ceiling.

"Un. What's this?" he wondered, then hopping back as the massive, muscular, ebony prince in just a white loincloth came down, gleaming seven-foot *naginaga* in one big fist. "Ai!"

"Delicate hands even for a priest," said Taro, looking at Osan in the voluminous disguise. "So you found her."

"She found me."

The policeman was already stripping off his outer garment.

"Put this on," he said. "It's moonless dark. Our best chance is to follow the beach south towards the city."

uMubaya grinned, looking at the man on the floor as he shrugged into the robe.

"I know that beach well," he commented.

Taro bowed to Osan.

"Reverend one," he said, smiling. "Bless our journey."

"Amusing," she said through the wicker. "It appears I am indebted to Takezo-san. He must have reformed himself and achieved sobriety."

Taro liked that. He led them out the back door and, after holding up a cautionary finger to the shopkeeper, he said:

"Sobriety? Please do not insult my esteemed friend."

243

As they went out the back into the dark yard they could hear him yelling out the front door:

"Over here! Over here! The devils were just here!"

As they worked their way around small trees and bristly bushes, then over a low fence, she said:

"We must get to Edo and help that poor young man. It is my fault. I should not have used him as I did."

"Did you not love him?" inquired the Zulu as they reached the sandy, scrub brush area that bordered the beach itself. The wind was steady, onshore, rich with sea scents and washed the voices behind them into the distance. They moved quickly because there were already torches showing back where'd they'd come from.

"No," she replied. "I am ashamed. He was my excuse to run away. I should have stayed."

"He cares much for you," uMubaya said, thoughtfully. "Whom do you love?"

"I have not loved," she replied, "the way you mean. I sometimes think I am like the 'grasshopper girl' in the story. She thought only of studying her insects until a handsome captain stopped by her gate having heard how strange she was."

"A tale," responded the Zulu. "I like tales."

"I'll tell it if fate permits us peace and time. I am skeptical of that."

"You are like this girl?" he asked as they ploughed up and over a dune, stiff reeds brushing brittlely at them.

"Ah. I study my grasshoppers of thought, but where is the captain by the hedge to stir me with a poem?"

"Ah, ha," put in Taro from just in front. "She should have stayed with her bugs. Love brought her sorrow."

"Nothing is more certain," agreed uMubaya. "But sorrow is not all of it."

"What is all of it?" inquired the girl as they now crossed the wide beach towards the retreating low-tide shoreline. "Were a man or woman born deaf, dumb and blind, they could love only what they touched. What would love be for them?"

Her eyes were wide, distant, looking out where the moonsheen came and went on the dark sea before them.

Taro shrugged, looking over his shoulder back towards the village.

"Can't say," he responded. "There's smell and taste, too, anyway."

They went out quite a distance through tidal pools and ridges of sand, much further, uMubaya realized, than the night Takezo and the others had been captured.

Every time I visit this village, he thought, *people want to kill me...when this is over maybe I will explore the hills and forests of the south...*Grinned. *Get to know more farm women....*

The retreating surf broke in slopping hisses, almost viscous, rills of bubbles faintly visible as the withdrawing sea strung seaweed and other detritus on the slightly curved shoreline. There was a faint fishy scent of decay.

I've come in a circle, the black man thought. *Where do I stop?*

Faintly, against the wind, there was a fresh outcry where the inn stood behind the wall of dunes. Out over the sea there was a distant, muted quivering of thunder and faint, shapeless pulsings of lightning.

Looking back, the twinkling lights around the village might have been part of a festival. Osan threw back the basket-like headpiece and breathed deeply.

"I fled," she said to no one in particular, "to save, I hoped, bloodshed. But what is promised by karma is fulfilled one way or another."

Forty

At Izu's castle – same day

In his chamber, Lorenzo Gentile was wearing a green and red kimono, pacing in front of the wall-long painting he was working on. His only set of European clothes was wearing thin and was being washed. The third story room had excellent light, shaded by an overhang. He'd been painting, with mixed results all afternoon, waiting for word from Takezo. He'd just received permission to visit Colin in jail at the magistrate's building.

At the moment, as the sun set behind the city, he was pacing without looking directly at the sprawling sketch and daubs of color that covered about 15X6 feet of red silk screen. He'd glance over then away. He knew this work was obsessing him and seemed, somehow, as real as or more real than the wild and bloody events he was embroiled in.

245

Her face was still a featureless outline and he was starting to think he'd leave it that way. A mystery. Near the center was another mystery: a cloudy whirlpool-like effect swirling from the mouth of what could have been a severed head or a giant mask of fury, sucking in Takezo, tapping with his naked sword like a blind man, clothes whipping forward in an occult wind, dead men around him, a slim woman holding his free hand from behind, struggling to hold back, holding her the little fellow, Yazu, then uMubaya, naked, a spear defiantly over his head, a warcry on his lips...then other figures...he wasn't sure yet, the line like medieval depictions of the dance of death...others, maybe himself...Izu...Issa for sure....

He stood still and sighed. He'd never worked on such a large scale and yet it felt compressed...he wanted the action to vividly burst out at the onlooker...wanted the pain and need...the love that was a fire in the blood....

He went to the window. The red orange cloud line on the horizon, the pure, darkening blue looked washed clean, the white edges gleamed. He fingered, then opened the little leather pouch on the string around his neck that Takezo had given him. Took out a ring. Turned it, the dark red, flat stone glowing faintly in the fading light.

Interesting, he thought. *This is so important...this was hers'?* He held up his hand. *It looks like one of mine...so much blood and pain for this?*

Then an idea was there: he began toying, twisting and squeezing around and under the setting.

Let us see....

Forty-One

At Hideo's

Takezo decided it was now his turn. He'd been a practice dummy, target and pigeon for the hunting hawks. Now he'd ask the questions. Painful questions.

So he was standing, this time, in full ninja costume, just his eyes a hint through the rectangular opening in the black, black hood.

The bright moon disk was sailing in and out of long, undulant, narrow clouds that suggested a slight curve as they flowed from north to south in a circle maybe hundreds of miles across. Erratic hot gusts stippled the viscous-looking moat surface.

"Dangerous, if it comes this way," he said, thoughtfully.

Yazu bobbed his bony head in agreement, in his normal semi-crouch. His
clothes were dark in a baggy attempt to look *ninja* which his master was too kind to discuss.

"Yes, *sensei*," he semi-whispered. "It seems unwise to risk-"

"Were it wise I would have nothing to do with it." He loosened his shoulder with a stretch and roll. "I'm really too big to make a good *ninja*."

His pupil was staring up at the tilted, sheer castle wall faintly luminescent in the off and on moonlight.

"So high," he said. "And-"

"Hand me the jug."

"More, master? I fear that-'"

"Are we married?" He took the jug and inhaled a long, long swallow of the sweetish, lukewarm sake. He already had that easy, relaxed, slightly floaty feeling. "I never come here sober."

Without warning he drew and slashed with his short sword, making sure the edge would be checked just short of his disciple's head. The steel had been blackened and was invisible; but Yazu melted aside with a kind of awkward ease and drew his own gleaming blade.

"Good," said his master, re-sheathing. "You had no time to do anything but be natural. You saw without seeing. That's the whole secret. Keep practicing but don't try to practice that." The moonlight softly winked off and on as the clouds flowed overhead. "Stay concealed and wait for me."

"What can you achieve here, master?"

"I owe the lady Issa a pinprick and Reiko a question." He went into the water, softly and swam quietly with one hand, holding the sword above the surface. He winced at the rank smell of decaying vegetation and muck.

About half way up the cliff-like wall his fingers were getting sore from gripping the climbing hooks. He hadn't done this in a long time. He was sweating in the sticky, close air and the gusts of wind were picking up and tugging at him.

I've had better ideas...maybe I've never had a worse one....

The stones were big, wide with just enough space for toe and hook-holds. He groped with a foot, then eased, inched up and caught the next edge above, swinging free a second and feeling like he weighed 500

247

pounds. Sighed and grimaced. Caught a glimpse of the moon to his right gleaming on the vast, dark bay.

Good thing you're numb, said a thought.

Up…another…another…scrape…grope…pull….He noticed the day's heat radiating from the wall, the warm rock smell….

"I'm too heavy to go back this way," he whispered, finally getting his arms inside an open, unshuttered window. He hoped it wasn't full of swordsmen.

There are, sometimes, defects in my planning….

Clambered in, not as quietly as a passing shadow; at least nothing banged or rattled as he eased himself into a dark and silent chamber.

Actually, he admitted, *I don't have a plan….*Crouching across the darkened room to where a side door faintly showed; the painting on it suggested big, shadowy flowers, maybe chrysanthemums…*and, judging from my past plans….*Gently moving the panel open until he could peer into a corridor lit by a single, dim reddish lantern at the far end showing another closed door…*better to have none….*

This was the Chamberlain's floor though he didn't know which way his quarters were. His face felt thick and hot and pulsed as his heart slowly slowed. He blinked his sore and foggy eyes.

He withdrew his head as the door opened and two men came out, silhouettes against the greater brightness behind them. Their voices were hushed. He recognized both of them: Reiko and Yoshi.

He shut the door and pressed himself to the wall. If they came in he'd kill Yoshi and subdue the chamberlain – the problem would be noise. He'd have to strike instantly in near-blackness.

The voices were just outside the door and the men stopped walking.

Forty-Two

On the beach

"This way," said Taro as the three of them went north heading out on the low tide flats close to where the still retreating surf was breaking among massive rock shoals, the beach itself a blur of shadow on their left, the village falling behind: faint, soft lantern light, flashes of moving torches, shouts and commotion faint and wrung away by the uneven gusts of the gathering wind as the rising moon went into and out of the long undulations of rainless clouds that had suggested to Takezo the extreme

248

rim of a great, cyclonic storm out at sea. "They'll expect us to go downcoast," the disgraced policeman concluded.

"How do we get to the city?" Osan asked. "As this is the wrong direction."

She took off the wicker basket head covering and let it dangle from the string down her back.

"Fishing villages all along the coast," Taro explained. "Use a boat."

"Why did you come here?" she asked, stepping over a long, narrow tidal pool. Something scuttled near her feet into the water.

"For my health," said the policeman.

The sand was wet and firm. The surf, a little distance out, was crashing heavily. Osan was noting the time between the crashes.

"We'll have to get a boat quickly," she said. "There's a very big storm out there. If it comes this way soon we'll never make it."

"Then we'll take horses," said Taro.

They were close to a jagged ridge of rock, a reef at high tide, featureless and vague, darkly gleaming, then fading as the moonlight came and went almost regularly.

"Wait," said the Zulu, quietly.

Out of moonshadow a small figure suddenly staggered into the silver glow from around the edge of the rocks. A woman. She took a few steps forward, then fell, arms outstretched, into a shining pool, splash water glittering around them.

uMubaya bent and turned her onto her back, tugged her to drier sand. A shadow passed over and away: they could see her pale clothes were dark stained and slashed. She'd been recently wounded, fatally.

"Poor woman," said Osan. Bent closer: "Who hurt you?" she asked.

"Can't be far off," uMubaya put in, scanning the shadowy shapes ahead, the pale gleaming surfline.

The woman was middle-aged. Her eyes were closed, mouth full of night and uneven teeth, Blood drooled as she rasped out:

"Samurai...came killed...fishermen... children...everyone...."

"What was the village's offence?" asked Taro. Not just families but whole town could be held responsible for perceived crimes.

"No, noo," she strained to say. "They...they...."

"Peace," Osan soothed. "Save your strength."

249

The dying woman's eyes went suddenly wide in a shock of staring as the moon brightened. Almost colorless, blood-caked lips moved in her suffering face, smoothly painted by the subtle, silvery tones.

"Bad things…" the woman managed. "Stupid…want boat…we offered boats…many boats…no good…stupid!" she virtually spat it out with a gob of blood. "Take boats…don't kill us…wrong boat….'

At the jail

Through the wooden crossbars a guttering torch that threw more shadow than light lit the tall Italian. He faced Colin. The feeble illumination created a sketchy impression of the powerful, battered Scot who was leaning on the latticework, thick fingers gripping through the squares.

The only guard was outside so they were alone. The cell room was narrow and clean.

"Well then?" asked Colin in Spanish.

"It is not clear," the Italian said. "Osan was not in the grave. She may live."

He still had trouble with that idea. Saying it seemed strange. The idea that he might see her again was exciting and, yet, troubling.

Perhaps *she could pose for the picture,* he thought. *We could discuss…many things….perhaps that Takezo fellow is right and I love…but how can a man love what he does not know…he then loves something born in his own mind….*

"Who did I see, then, so bloody and fair of form?" Colin asked.

Gentile shrugged.

"They say it was a prostitute," he replied. "Do you love her?"

Colin just stood there, leaning towards the bars on the stretch of his arms.

"They're going to cut off my head," he said. "That's what I think about. I don't know what else is left in me." He sighed. "I wish…I were back at sea."

"They have no excuse to kill you, now."

"Ha. They have law."

"Yes," murmured the tall man with the big, sad eyes. His fingers, unconsciously, twisted the ring in his inner, silken pocket. "But I think they'll have to free you, friend."

"They'll free me," the Scot said.

Then Gentile's fingers went to the bauble. The answer hit him. It had to be right....

Back in Hideo clan stronghold

Reiko and Yoshi had stopped outside the sliding door but didn't open it.

Leaning into the linen-covered panel, Takezo listened in the dark room, blackened short-sword drawn in one hand.

Maybe, since you see so badly, he told himself, *you will learn to hear*....

"The cursed boat has not been located," Yoshi was just reporting. "All who had information seem to be dead. Every method was used to question the living but to no avail. The fishermen. The pirates that were left. That fool Kame, in his arrogance, struck down the pirate chief, thinking the ring would be enough."

"Yes, yes," hissed Reiko. "Then he puts it on the corpse of the whore like a Chinaman in love."

"He'd already courted her," said Yoshi, with perverse amusement that coldly angered and disgusted the eavesdropping spy.

"He was a degenerate," snarled the chamberlain. "A dim-brain. A..a...."

"The men are ready. The time is at hand. There can be no turning back."

Reiko's voice was dulled and disturbed. Takezo could hear fear in it, as he said:

"Meanwhile, if we lose, the great *ninja* will slip away into the shadows and we will die alone. Death is nothing. Life is sweet. I have risked my whole life to rise to where I belong and ride this skittish horse of state. I will not serve the stupid. A new world is before us and the blood of those who resist will wash our feet."

How would you know the stupid, to serve them? Takezo sarcastically wondered. *How to tell them from yourself? I'll see you drown in blood, not wash in it....*

"You expect to be *Seii Taishogun*?" Yoshi inquired. Neutrally.

"Who better?"

Takezo nearly laughed. He wanted to bang their skulls together.

"With your consort?" wondered Yoshi.

Reiko's voice showed discomfort as he shifted the subject:

251

"The girl remains safe?"

Yoshi's voice had a shrug in it.

"At last report," he said. "She is unimportant, now."

"Yes, to you women matter little. Unlike the ring," Reiko said with barely suppressed fury. "Not all the master *ninja* in the province can find this single thing and wrest it from that drunken, insolent outcast. He must have given it to another. All who know him closely should be arrested and tortured. Half-boiled alive and taken out and put in again and again." This pleasant prospect enhanced the chamberlain's speech with a kind of dreamy quality as if he could actually see it: the victims thrashing in the bubbling water as their skin blistered and sloughed off. He sighed, savoring the vision.

"Hmn," uttered the captain, judiciously. "Maybe when he learns of this his slit lips will open."

Interesting how others see you, the *ronin* thought, amused. *My lips are well-shaped....*

"When we capture him again," Reiko said, "he will suffer."

Useless to kill them, Takezo reasoned. *But what does the boat have to do with the ring? Madness....*

"The Mongol 'slow death,'" offered Yoshi. Cutting and cauterizing someone a tiny piece at a time, starting with the first joint of the pinky.

"Not slow enough."

"It could take weeks."

"A thousand years would be too short for that shameful wretch."

And then there was a newcomer. An almost blissfully confident, smooth voice – could this be the "master?" Kill him and to hell with loose ends. He had no client. He was serving only fate and the memory of love.

"No question of failure," said the almost jolly voice. "The unholy one will be overthrown."

Reiko grunted. Takezo knew that grunt. And the voice wasn't the *ninja* boss in the graveyard, either. Better to listen.

"If you monks stop fighting each other for half a day," the chamberlain hissed, "maybe there'd be some progress. That and the cargo of the accursed foreign ship." He sighed. "My two wishes for the deaf gods to hear."

So it didn't sink, Takezo realized, at once.

252

"You have a cargo of faith," the monk's smooth voice said fluidly. "Worth more than weapons of steel."

"When you renounce the world must you renounce your brains, Abbott?" Reiko wondered.

"Ah ha," put in Yoshi, "they will pray our enemies to death like En-no-Gyoja."

"Take not such a name in vain," the prelate said, uneasily, "lest his ancient and undying spirit form from shadows in some lonely place and stop your foolish heart with hellish chill."

"I respect all spirits, good and ill," said Reiko.

"Bah," uttered Yoshi. "Men are skin stretched over bone. They die like leaves in autumn. Where are the spirits of leaves, priest?"

"Leaves are neither gods nor men," rejoined the happy voice. "You-"

"Pray this, captain Yoshi," interrupted Reiko, "that your master is sneaky enough to destroy the 'unholy one' and make things much simpler."

Must be Nobunaga, Takezo the spy, concluded.

"Any man, high or low, rich or poor, priest or sinner," Yoshi said, coldly, pointedly, "can be assassinated. Safety is a dream that death wakes you from."

"Yes, yes," said the cheerful Abbott, "you are closer to the Buddha than you imagine."

"I too believe all is nothingness," Yoshi said with contempt.

"That is a false view," the buoyant voice went a little stern, "you-"

Cut off again by Reiko:

"Enough nonsense," he said, nervous, angry. "We all agree on what must be done. Do it." They were moving away now, and Takezo pressed his ear to the door panel. "After the assassination fails. After the ship is not found. After the priests squabble to the brink of doom, we must still find a way to win."

They agree, quipped Takezo, *on poking boys in the rear end, why should not Yoshi and the monks agree in all things?*

They were moving away. He carefully cracked the door a few inches. They were back down by the lantern, going around the bend as he slipped out and followed, padding along close to the wall as he'd been taught. Blend in shadows, know that you can't be seen.

That's a good one, he thought, wobbling slightly out from the wall, starting to lose the voices. Peering around the corner they were about 50 feet down where another single lantern shone faintly behind them, stretching their weak shadows along the corridor.

"Tomorrow, at the second trial," Reiko was saying, "we have witnesses to swear that the foreigner killed the *yujo,* Lily, to cover himself and with the connivance of that Black Devil raped and kidnapped Osan. All this was learned from the dying confession of the traitor, Nori."

"Ah," said Yoshi with approval. "That explains the body and makes the crime much worse."

"Such evil is ever the result of human lust and delusion," said the Abbott.

Delusion? Delusion? Takezo nearly spoke out. *You want to wash the world in human blood in the name of the Compassionate One?*

"The Black, who has so far escaped justice, took the innocent child for his own pleasure and by now may have killed and eaten her, since such wild men may be capable of any atrocity."

"Better and better," agreed Yoshi. "These crimes cry out for blood."

"I have heard of such Black Devils," the Abbott added in. "They are the rebirths of monstrous men and supernatural fiends."

"Further," Reiko went on, "the tall, pale foreigner was set a spy in the house of Hideo by ever-scheming Izu. This at the behest of his puppeteer, Nobunaga, whose hand fills his empty shape and moves him as he pleases."

"Curse him," said the prelate. "What a union of wickedness."

What a union, the *ronin* sighed, mentally, *of shit, piss and poisonous vomit....*

"As your master has agreed," Reiko went on, pacing a step or two before the light, his faint shadow shifting near where Takezo crouched and overheard, "we will all have many, many men concealed around the magistrate's. In a fit of just rage, Izu and his people will be slain. War will soon begin."

"Yes," breathed Yoshi. "Yes."

"With or without the ring being discovered." The chamberlain sighed. "Well, Abbott, go and prepare your monks for war. Captain Yoshi, I'll see you at the trial."

As the monk went down the stairs into dimness, Yoshi's silhouette moved closer to the chamberlain who had begun to mount the steps to the next floor.

"Bad news," he said. "The girl ran away from the village." Reiko's response was to breathe deeply as Yoshi continued: "She must not return here."

"I sense that miserable *heinan's* hand in this!" snarled Reiko.

"By horse or boat, she could be here at any time."

"No harm can come to her! Have men posted at the castle, Izu's and at the magistrate's. See to it! Bring her to our boat."

Quick thinker, Takezo acknowledged.

"Yes," said the captain, heading downstairs without ceremony.

Reiko paused a moment on the steps. Then called down in a soft shout:

"No harm! Be certain!"

Takezo heard no reply. He was thinking, as he moved quickly down the corridor after Reiko, blackened sword drawn:

Like to not kill anymore...maybe I'll stop tomorrow...take a vow....

At the next landing Reiko was closing the door behind him in a room just off the stairs. Coming closer Takezo could hear a woman's voice. Cupped his ear to the wood. Issa was just saying:

"So you spare me some time? How kind."

"Things are in turmoil."

"Yes. There is deceit everywhere."

"What are you implying, woman?"

"You weary of me."

"Not true. Not true." He sounded very tired to the spy who felt like a ghost condemned to imperfectly overhear the trivial, dull and commonplace shames of the living. "I feel...well...."

Their voices faded as they moved to some other part of the room. Going partly up the next flight of steps he saw he could swing himself up to the rafters of the dropped ceiling. Sheathing his blade he managed to do it, and crept flat out over the paper ceiling on the wide timbers. He could make out their conversation, again.

"Future?" she was asking, sarcastically. "If we fail there will be none for us."

"I don't wish to disgrace my lord."

She didn't quite laugh.

"How noble," she told him, with great control. "You think you can dispense with me and rule alone."

"Nonsense. We'll rule nothing if we divide our purpose." He was sighing his breaths, almost directly under Takezo as he, obviously paced back and forth. "I am not cold, my love. There is turmoil."

"There is deceit. That I love you, Reiko, is the deceit I practice on myself. The heart, if you are cursed with one, makes need seem reason and wins all arguments."

"I say, again, I love you. Nothing is changed. I have none but you."

"I think *you* have none but *you*. I am wanton and willful but my heart is not easily given. Like the whore in the old tale."

His voice receded as he went to the door.

"You say all this," he said. "Not I. Meanwhile, your husband will return tomorrow for the trial of the foreigner. We must be discreet. We must work as one."

"So you leave me, now?"

"I must. There's too much at stake and much to do by morning."

"Ah. Yes. Be warned. Do not betray me."

"Foolish. I love only you."

And went out. Takezo thought:

My poor noh play now writes itself...in blood and farce....

As he eased himself back across the boards he turned around in the almost black space and cracked his head on a supporting post; pulling back, his knee missed and his leg went through the paper ceiling. Unbalanced, he clutched for the unseen post, missed, and rolled through, hitting on his back with a slam that bore little relation to the catlike, noiseless drop of a ninja.

Nothing broke and his head hit just hard enough to stun him. There was a dim, tall, outline looming over him, depthless, a dagger coming down that a moment later, still trying to find out how to move himself, he saw was a shadow on a bare paneled wood wall that might have been a brush sketch except it was moving and then his growing focus included two smoky oil lamps set on either side of a futon. Then he raised his head far enough to see Issa bent over him, her long dagger, glinting the dim, red-orange light as it pressed just above his genitals. Any other spot and he would have blocked and swept her down.

"So poor a spy," she said, with easy scorn, "ought not to reproduce himself, in any case."

Forty-Three

On the coast

Between the in-and-out moon and the gusting glow from the burning fishermen's huts they could see bodies lying along the beach. uMubaya counted about a dozen before they came to a long, narrow fishing boat pulled up just clear of the low, slapping surf of this cove. The wind was hard and steadying, blowing south and a little west towards Edo.

"How stupid and sad," said Osan.

Taro shrugged.

"Always," he agreed. "Yet, what can be done? This is man's way."

"I am a sailor," said uMubaya, studying the craft. It seemed sound. Strangely, he'd just realized he really *was* a sailor and not just a prince of warriors.

"Blood and the curse of blood," she said. "This sickens our land."

"All lands, lady," put in the Zulu, leaning his massive shoulder to the boat and testing the weight. It gave, slightly. "We can launch this." Grunted as Taro moved beside him to help. "In my country," he went on, "a warrior who spills blood must purify himself for days before seeing his family again."

"Ease in killing makes death slight as a mortal wound struck in a play," she said, looking at the dead in the dull light of the middle-distance flames that wobbled shadows as the soft and subtle moon painted the scene.

"You have eloquent words for anything," remarked Taro. "Can words move a boat?"

"Words move all beings. The words of Buddha can enlighten. The words of a fool can bathe the world in blood."

What point, she thought, *to be reborn if only pain and grief turns time's wheel? Like someone rushing out of freezing winter into a burning building....*

An hour later they were scudding down the coast at a good clip with the wind almost at their back. The slim craft was stable and quick to the helm, slicing across the angled and growing waves. No lightning

257

showed or thunder echoed, yet; just a gathering surge as the tide began to turn and the wind pulsed, uMubaya considered, like a leopard toying with a hare.

Looking at the vague shoreline, the scattered lights like soft stars, Osan thought about what she had to do with really no idea of what was actually going to happen.

Should not have run away, she said to herself. *Caused more suffering than I sought to avoid...I longed to complete my work in peace instead of facing ugliness and now my father's house is threatened as civil war smolders...*

"Ahhh," she sighed, watching the vast, obscure darkness of the country flowing past in the changing, insubstantial moonglow....

Gentile

He was back in his chamber with all the lamps and lanterns lit. He was wearing just a loose kilt skirt, sweating, blinking, rubbing his beard, colors staining, smearing his fine-featured face.

I am like the astronomer who, entranced by the glory of the heavens, cares not where his feet fall until he trips and the dull earth hits him, he thought, stepping back to consider the unfolding shapes that seemed to be growing out of the saturated brush-strokes.

Somehow the pain and violence, treachery and vile intentions became a pure design the way the spiritually polluted world itself might be viewed by an archangel or some other timeless god as pure composition, utterly beautiful.

Overall, the sky was darkened with towering, glossy-looking clouds, black-red in places, showing lightning streaks, with gaps here and there where sunbeams broke through like spotlights highlighting a stage scene. On each panel main figures repeated. On the first, still faceless Osan stood tall with a brush and scroll in her hands looking towards the viewer...middle-distance showed a road lined by groveling peasants in bright clothing as a long, elaborate procession passed with captives or prisoners yoked together, seeming to form their shapes from a swampy mist or blowing smoke under the lash and kicks of masked, armored men...a headless woman lay in an exquisite garden of pink and white blossoms accented by her blood...there was even Takezo, in torn and burning clothing, eyes swollen shut, dueling with a man made of smoke

258

and flame, skinny Yazu kneeling, arm flung up heavenwards as a sooty rain poured down....

All that and the blank spaces. The blank spaces worried him because he was blank, himself, looking at them...and the still, hardly touched, final panel.

He went and leaned out the open window overlooking the fairytale, almost too-precious city.

"Storm, fire and blind war," he murmured. "That's the third panel." The blanks had to be filled, somehow, with moonlight, romance and poetry. It all had to balance: the more extreme the grotesque agonies of existence, equally extreme must be the wonder. "Balance," he whispered.

Italians have so little, as persons and so much as a people, he considered, amused. Rubbed his face and eyes. *Reason is wishful thinking....*

"She must be like me," he whispered. Smiled. "Someone must." His hair was tugged by the thick, hot, unceasing wind. He could hear banners snapping and popping down below over the low, soft humming soughing. "It seems she lives so she must be...somewhere...out in this same night."

He had no idea where to look for Takezo. He wanted to show him the apparent secret of the ring. It seemed trivial. Seemed a kind of *haiku*.

Maybe only here, he thought, *could so much blood be shed over* a poem....His mood was still wry. *In Italy, the cause would be cheese and pastry....*

The moonlight faded off and on across the choppy, white-flecked dark bay.

"They say the storms are coming early," he said out into the windy night. "But, perhaps, they are always on time."

Under the knife

"I mean you no hurt, lady," Takezo assured Issa, trying to add sincerity to his pain and trepidation.

"I mean you much," was the unsettling reply, "assassin and spy."

"Ah. But I am your ever-obedient Jiro Takezo."

"Then I mean you still more. Unmask." He did. "I should have known you by sheer clumsiness alone."

The knife blade stayed where it was.

259

"My private parts displease you?" he inquired, tugging off the hot, confining hood.

She didn't quite laugh.

"Worse are known," she said.

Her humor reminded him of Miou. He blinked, hard. His head pulsed, dully from the blow and it had been a long time since his last drink. He was sure there'd be a jug somewhere in this surprisingly bare chamber, not an aristocrat's private room so, obviously, a place to meet Rieko where few would think of looking.

"I'm not angry because of the poison needle," he told her, trying to read her face; with the light behind it was mostly shadow. "I learned a great deal as a result. I met the great one." Sighed and rubbed his eyes. "You don't trust me. I meant to come in the main gate but I never have much luck seeing you, that way."

"This way is far better. You should try it from a higher ceiling, next time."

"Hmn. How fickle you are. I'd like to both sit up and keep my manhood." Sighed, again. "Maybe. Anyway, you gave me money for my services. You recall that morning?"

"Did I receive them?"

"I couldn't tell you much because I knew nothing." She pulled back, folded herself onto her heels and set the bright knife beside her. He sat up, staring at the two candles framing her from behind, painting in just the outside of her face in gentle uncertainty. Her eyes were obscured.

"Now you know something, Takezo?" she inquired.

He realized he was seeing her in a different way. It wasn't that they'd been intimate because, really, they hadn't; they'd merely had sex – if memory served. It was her surprising vulnerability with Reiko that had affected him.

"Let me ask you one thing," he responded. "Why are you so deep in this mad and confused plotting? Why conspire to betray your rightful lord? You are too mature to chase wild dreams of the heart."

"You mean old," she returned, deadpan. "What is the age? Have you passed it?"

He sighed and rubbed his face and head, shaking it, slightly.

"Alright," he muttered.

"Life is too hard, Takezo. Stubbornness can destroy us. I mean no harm to my husband. In great matters to choose wrongly is ruin. I wish my house to endure. It was dearly bought."

He nodded, reluctantly.

"And your stubborn husband will stubbornly cut his belly to keep his oath."

Shook his head. "Do you all really think you'll undo Nobunaga with some 'magic' ring?"

One eye on her and the other on the doorway. He half-hoped the chamberlain or somehow, Yoshi would come in and make life simple for a moment. He realized he was starting to treat her as a friend. And he had to respect Hideo. Whom did he now serve?

Maybe I'm working for everybody, he had to think. *Interesting....*

"Some Chinese wizard claims the ring is from the gods, once worn by a divine warrior in ancient times." She shrugged her hands. "Who possesses it cannot be defeated."

"Shrewd Reiko believes this?"

"So he says."

The spy rubbed his back and hoped he'd find a masseur tomorrow. Knew he'd be black and blue.

"There's nothing like pursuing a sacred vision to blunt all pity and sense," he said. "Since I'm supposed to have this talisman, how dare they oppose me?"

"You can't know its secret," Tapped the dagger softly on one silk-covered knee.

"How can they be sure?" he wondered, standing up, feeling the twinges as new pains manifested around his spine. Grunted.

"Theirs is the side to choose," she said, "in any case."

"I better go. I have people to kill."

"You're a great fighter," she said, amused, "but not a man to enlist for cold-blooded work."

"I can improve," he said.

"Why? Because your lover was murdered?"

"Because of many things."

"Don't kill mine."

"Which one?" he wondered.

He saw she was amused but serious.

"The one I love," she told him. "Remember I just spared you."

261

"Only my manhood, lady. A thing that always points me to fresh troubles."

"Take off that outfit. You'll never get past the extra guards. There's a threat of war." She stood and came over to him, dagger at her side. He thought about climbing back down that wall. Started undressing. "All your guile and skill will avail you little," she concluded, not-quite-not laughing.

He grinned.

"My arrows will miss their mark and I'll topple from my pony, great lady. But won't it be worse at dawn?" he asked.

"I will get you out, Takezo-san." She came close enough for him to see her ambiguous eyes and take in her subtle perfume. "Do you still have enough gold to serve me a little more?"

"There's nothing to buy, my lady. For either of us."

"Ah."

"I think we're like people falling from a high place. We have time to cry out or think and watch." He shrugged. "How quickly the ground arrives."

He stood there in his loincloth, now, sweating all over in the thick air.

"Find my child and bring her back," she told him. "Whatever else you do, do that."

He nodded.

"Yes, lady," he agreed. "We both need to ask her things." Bowed. "You surprise me."

"Maybe I am a bad woman but I love my child. I cannot help the ways of my heart anymore than I can stop the wind by wishing."

"I understand."

He moved so more of her long, oval, smooth face showed in the weak illumination.

"Or the burning in my body," she continued.

"Yes, I itch myself, sometimes. But, you know, it was a nasty trick. Using that actress." Going back to the Miou imitator. "I cannot do much with my heart, either."

She looked at him and seemed quite guileless.

"It might have been she," Issa said, "and you would have been certainly slain if you'd tried to leave that place."

"You thought only of my well-being."

262

"I need you because no one controls you."

She looked demurely down. His impression was that Issa demure was like a basking cobra. She sat again and then uncoiled onto the futon, silks swishing in a soft hiss. It was hard not to think about that golden flesh barely covered.

"What were you before you were a great lady? What clan? Or might you have been a merchant's daughter mounting on steps of silver? I'm insulting but I can't control it." He leered a grin. "Like the burning in my body. Or my windy heart."

She laughed and supplely stretched. He felt she was too good and too deadly to be a farm girl and far too free to be a samurai's offspring. Didn't like where that was going, either: please not another ninja woman. Again, he felt like he was in a play where he wasn't sure of his lines and had half-forgotten the plot.

"You think I'm some kind of spy, too?" she asked, as coy as a viper could manage. She moved and a line of flesh showed honey-pale, diagonally creasing down her long torso where the robe just pulled away a little. "Bolt the door, Takezo and let us beguile the time a little. While we, as you deeply observed, fall from a high place together."

He breathed slow in and out. Outside the wind had picked up again and puffed and whistled; the pressure shifting wavered the twin lamps whose soft shadows caressed her.

Yes. Let time lose itself for now.... He went to the door and slipped the bolt shut. *As every soldier knows, great causes and battles recounted in one dramatic sweep, are always dotted with pauses and sleep....*

"Sake?" he had to ask, coming back and kneeling beside her, feeling the inevitable thickness in his throat, chest and loins as if the blood swelled and slowed, letting himself succumb, again. She turned to him, eyes close and clear and, of course, seemed no more connected to intimacy than if she were pondering a coup in a game of *go*.

And then her mouth, hot breath stunning and overwhelming his ear with raw intensity, whispering:

"I burn, you see...I burn with hunger..." Her teeth closed down hard on his ear, then neck and he winced but he didn't pull away. Sighed with excitement and sweet defeat. "I am all appetite," she whisper-hissed....

263

Forty-Four

Storm Before the Calm

Issa actually escorted him to the moat at daybreak, with two servant girls, and it caused no stir at all. He'd left the sword inside and had only a short dagger under his outer white and blue robe ironically featuring chrysanthemums. His long hair was gathered up and fell straight behind. He'd done his own makeup, eyebrows shaved and drawn in on his forehead. She said that he'd break the hearts of the guards.

So he minced along as he'd been trained and nearly perfected long ago; a too-tall, wide-backed, striking, acceptably graceful woman with a nose enough like Issa's to pass for a relative. Their garments fluttered in the hot wind that seemed to have fallen off a little, uneven gusts stippling the sour-smelling moat as the sun rose behind a wall of dark clouds.

"Sure you don't want me to stay on as a court maiden?" he asked.

"No," she replied, smiling. "Your beauty would detract from mine."

Looking up he could make out the curve of a vast storm-pattern in the clouds. It wouldn't be long.

"I'll be back when I know more," he told her.

Which may be never, he thought.

"You cannot stop the war," she said after him as he crossed the narrow bridge. "You might as well find Osan." She followed a couple of steps. "I want you in my service."

"I'm too beautiful, lady," he said over his shoulder. "I'll be back, though."

"Stay off the ceilings, next time," she advised. "And hide yourself because they think you have the ring. I don't wish them to torture you to death for spite."

He guffawed and shook his head, liking her, again. It annoyed him but he kept liking her. It made him try to understand her point-of-view. He realized she'd never told him, in the hours they'd just been together, where she actually had come from; never answered the question she'd put herself: "Do you think I'm a spy?"

No point in caring, he told himself. *It goes nowhere....*

It wasn't so far to the front of the Pine and Crane inn to tire him walking like a woman in those restrictive garments. As he tilted along across whirls and puffs of dust and straw from the street he passed a group of disheveled and bleary-looking young men, the well-off scions of merchant families or lesser nobility - probably just turned out of some whorehouse. They looked him over as he went demurely past, head downtilted. He didn't respond to their comments; the last one he heard he thought was: something...something "......but big feet."

And then he crossed the dusty, unfenced and unimpressive yard to the steps and sagging overhang of the inn that creaked with every turn and push of wind. He glanced back up at the sky: where the blue showed it seemed wet and clean. You could feel the storm. Every dog he'd seen was still, chin on forepaws and few birds were flying.

And there was Yazu sleeping with his back to the outside wall in the shelter of the thick-barred fence that ran close to the front of the building, sheathed sword tucked in the crook of his left arm, samurai style. His ragged-toothed mouth was open and the *ronin* detective half-expected a couple of flies to circle up from it. His bare legs poked out from his tunic; his snores were uneven, racking and seemed to presage suffocation.

*Wonder if his wife has a lover...he certainly doesn't ...yet he has a son...*Miou came to mind. *Aii, if only she had gotten pregnant, maybe we might have....*

"Nonsense," he sighed. "Think like that and you have to get drunk."

Stood over his sleeping pupil. Adjusted his partial veil. Reflected on the fact that Yazu's skill had been improving.

*Useful in a land of killers....Well, what next? Look for the girl, again? Warn Nobunaga? Hah. If he needs me to protect him he's doomed...talk to Hideo and sink in embarrassment? What? I don't even feel like cutting down Yoshi, he didn't kill her...and endlessly scheming Reiko's like my brother in shame, now...*He knew he was just circling around the real issue: find the ninja lord. The master of shadows. The one who'd used her and betrayed her to a dog's death. Find him and sleep in peace. Maybe. *That damned ring...they don't want to take on Nobunaga without it...she's right, they'll boil me alive for spite...and if I give it to them they'll probably be kind and cut off my head...I can't defeat them all even without the ninjas who've spared me serious attention so far...you can't defeat everybody...I better get it back and try to buy something with it...*He hoped a plan was starting to form; waited for a flash but nothing much happened. Yazu snored. The wind gusted and turned back the leaves on the surrounding trees, showing the lighter green; dust and bits of stuff lifted, swirled in eddies and dropped back down.

He stooped and gently started to ease his pupil's blade free of the black-lacquered scabbard. He felt it was a teacher's obligation.

Surprisingly, the little bony man reacted without even opening his eyes, levering the weapon free, rolling away and kneeling up with the glinting tip aimed at what he took for a tall woman in fine clothing.

"Beautiful lady," he said, "have a care!"

"*You* be careful," was the reply in a moderately successful fluty voice, "or I'll steal your heart instead of your sword."

"I am a married man, lady," Yazu returned with some conviction.

"No surprise. You're a fine-looking man." Tried a hand-stifled giggle with mixed results. "Has your house no back window?"

Yazu took that in. Cocked his head and showed a slight smile. Scratched one ear, thoughtfully.

"But, lady," he cautiously said, "I am not of your rank."

"Ah," returned Takezo, nodding his head, trying to be delicately bold. "Passion is reputed to cross over all boundaries, good sir."

The little man, sword re-sheathed, came closer with almost a swagger. Takezo lidded his eyes, he hoped, coyly.

"Well, beautiful lady," he said, "I suppose these are the kind of things that happen to swordsmen."

A twist of wind sucked his half-veil aside, his exposed face drawing Yazu into ambiguities.

"You seem…well," he groped.

This is a good disguise, he considered. *Lets me see life in a new way, too….*

"It's Takezo, master of deception," he explained, looking over as maybe a dozen mounted men in armor trotted by, followed by half-a-hundred spearmen moving at a run, dust filling around them, blowing to the side.

They're really getting ready…in the end, all wars are fought just because someone wants to….

"Amazing, master," Yazu had just said. "I was deceived."

"More amazing that you reacted so quickly. Maybe you're learning something."

"I try to concentrate on the hollowness of life, master," he responded, standing up and resheathing his blade. "Life is a candleflame in a strong wind."

266

"Something about the sword induces bad poetry," Takezo commented.

"If a man strikes at me I tell myself his blade is a mere straw."

"By the time you tell yourself you'll be split in half," Takezo advised, looking after the troops that were now lost in the dust of their passage.

Trouble with a sword is you can't cut anything worth cutting...try slicing despair or lust or loss to shreds....

"The city is full of warriors," Yazu said. "Something's up." He cocked his head. "Strange to talk to you in those clothes." He scratched his ear and yawned. A fat bald man in white and red wearing string-tied straw sandals came out and glanced at them then at the sky, adjusting the pouch at his belt. "I worried, master, seeing you high on that dreadful wall like a bug. Yet here you are." The man looked over, wincing at a puff of dust and, obviously, wondering where the "master" was. "What follows now?" Yazu concluded.

The man went on into the street stepping around some fresh horse droppings. Two small women passed holding straw bags trailing bright ribbons with writing on them, the ends fluttering in the wind. A closed palanquin jounced along, swaying. An open chair came in the opposite direction bearing a beautiful young girl in green silk holding up a stick with a paper head on the end, the round face, fierce mouth and the bulging, staring eyes of a Dharuma Bodhisattva...

"What, indeed? What...I stumble blindly along. Eyes wide open and vacant of any light." He rubbed the side of his neck and felt the sore bumps where her teeth had fastened. *Hungry?* He said to himself. *No more than a wolf in winter...The things we do and say "well, why not..." How indulgent...She wants her clan secure yet runs more risks than a one-armed spearman in a battle....*

"Master, look," Yazu pointed towards the fairly busy street.

The pale skin and beard were unmistakable. The tall, lean Italian was dressed Japanese in a loose, dark, zigzag printed big sleeved shirt, floppy, pantaloon-like knickers bound just below the knee. He had a *katana* and his rapier stuck through his sash. He had two pistols underneath lost in the billowy folds.

He flicked a bow to the woman he didn't know wasn't, and addressed Yazu:

267

"You serve Takezo," he said. The little man nodded, glancing at his disguised master. "Greetings, Miss."

Takezo downtilted his head and spoke in the fluty voice:

"Thank you. I know that clever spy, sir."

Gentile studied the exquisitely made-up face.

"You should wear a mask, Takezo-san," he said.

"Ah. Master, he sees through your disguise."

The *ronin* detective shrugged, a little sourly.

"He has an artist's eye, Yazu."

"Your features are striking," said Gentile. "And I've studied them. I came to find you. About the ring you gave me."

"They all looked at the street as more horsemen crashed by, scattering the pedestrians. Dirt flew and dust billowed. The trees and bushes shook and whooshed as the wind picked up, again.

"I hope you threw it into the sea," Takezo said. "It's a curse."

I need sleep, he thought. *Can't go home...even if I stay dressed as a woman....*

"It's here," said Gentile, taking out the unimpressive-looking piece of jewelry and holding it on his palm. "It is not a curse, it's a poem, I think." His long, delicate fingers popped open the flat, dull-red stone to expose a hollow with a rolled-up paper fragment folded into it which he shook into Takezo's hand. "There. It makes little sense to me."

The *ronin* unfolded it and read the tiny characters written in red ink. Not many.

"Bright fish...three docks...last ship...no masts...golden lantern." Looked up; blinked his tired eyes; went back to thinking about how to find the master *ninja*...then went back to thinking about nothing...

All at sea

It was going to be close, considered uMubaya, as the narrow-beamed skiff plunged and twisted as the waves bounced them closer to the visible dark rock jutting like fangs from the shattering waves, spray blowing back in the wind like smoke.

He and Taro strained at the oars, facing forward, digging in violently to port. The Zulu's massive muscles cracked and wrenched, eyes vibrating with strain. Osan crouched calmly in the dipping bow as the rock fangs ripped past, mad foam like drool, seaweed like writhing snakes. She held on, composed, in the flopping, tent-like monk's robes.

268

The deadly bite just missed as they reeled, broached and tilted up and over one of the suddenly huge waves that had been showing up for the past hour – additional evidence, beyond the curving clouds overhead and the deep, wet, gray churning horizon, of a massive storm rolling closer to the coast.

At least, uMubaya thought, *with Osan back, Colin will be freed....*

The city was visible now, blurred-over by the fogging spray. Another boat, a mile or so ahead, was rocking wildly, mast kicking back and forth as it rushed towards port.

Gods of these yellow men, support us, he more or less prayed, as they surfed down the far side of the massive wave that wasn't quite breaking this far out. *Include too the Italian and Colin's Christ spirit and great Unkulunkulu to bring us safely in....*

Taro was behind him. He glanced back and saw the strained, unhappy countenance of the powerful policeman, flecks of vomit on his face and loose shirt.

The Zulu knew how that went and turned away. He'd been sick for almost the entire first month at sea.

A Week Ago

In deference to her rank, Osan had one of the best rooms with a double door to the corridor and a single door opening onto a tiny garden of rock, sand and a few scrubby bushes with sharp, hard-looking leaves and a little rock fountain that barely gurgled a trickle.

Unable to sleep, she'd gone out in her pale slip during the recent full moon nights and written by the brilliant silver light, staining the ghostly paper with dark, fluid symbols.

Freedom, *she wrote,* is but appearance like the masks of actors or the seeming water in a dry, hot plain that is only dust. The moonlight here is the same that falls on those imagining they are not prisoners. Yet, are they too not bound? Still, the perfect sky and moonlight, the distant sounds of the sea, the whispers of the wind frees me from all the walls men or myself can build around me...

And then she'd stood up and walked around the little area, pausing by the far wall that had no building behind it. She inhaled the sea air and touched the smooth, damp stone and wood, reflecting on how some barriers were palpable and others of the mind.

269

'In any case,' a voice was saying on the other side, as one who delights in giving the news, *'the farmers are ready to revolt.'*

A deeper, tough voice responded:

'Yes. And the fishermen in a panic because of raids. The blame falls on local lords. They'll think about nothing but survival. We have brigands and ronin, thousands of them, attacking villages all along the coast between here and Edo. Tanba says the moment for war is approaching.'

'I think Lord Nobunaga will have much to...'

And then they went on, their conversation was lost in the shifts of breeze and sounds of crickets. She'd understood enough. Looked up at the moon and ice-point stars, her lovely, calm face lit as by magic light.

'I think I'd like to stay here,' she whispered – because all the ugly, senseless, savage things she hated were about to unfold; and she'd have to confront Reiko, her mother and father...open wounds - cut new ones. She sighed and leaned on the wall. *'But I cannot stay,'* she finished.

On the Water

The narrow boat reeled and pitched as the wind picked up, again and quartered around.

"I have to warn my father," she said into the splash and rush, hanging on. "I was silent too long."

Back at the Pine and Crane

Inside, at a floor table, the three of them were eating rice balls and pickles. Yazu and his master were taking sake; Gentile was content with bitter tea. The wind sucked steadily around the windows and door, fluttering the curtains as the sunlight outside went off and on in the almost regular rhythm of the passing clouds.

Takezo, in his female disguise, was attracting attention because of the "castle" quality of those rich, brocaded robes. The tavern keeper, who knew him and Yazu well, was talking with a sleepy looking, round-faced whore as he cleaned up the serving counter across the good-sized room.

"Look at that *uchigi*," she said, meaning the unconfined, flowing outer robe that spilled around the *ronin* detective. "Were it night I'd ask Ichiro of the Allys to snatch them from her for me."

"Ho, ho," responded the owner, stacking cups, "you think he'd do it for a taste of your charms?"

"Why not?" She frowned a pout. "What are you saying?"

"What man who's already full can be tempted by rice?"

She tossed her head and looked back at the table.

"That one with the beard," she said, "he's queer-looking."

"A foreigner," shrugged the dour man. "Maybe Korean."

Takezo had spread out the little piece of rice paper on the dull, battered table near a sake spill. He poked the tiny puddle with a forefinger and drew the characters for boat, then fish. He got nothing back. His brain felt like morning porridge.

Gentile was looking at the round-faced *yujo* beside the tavernkeeper. He thought he might use her face in his picture. Her age was obscure, face wary, puffy under the eyes...something in her features he couldn't read, a secret, knowing quality that might have been, equally, merely dullness, the dullness of the routine of life rolling over her like a millstone. The changing light from the window lit the side of her face so that it seemed to float from vagueness to solidity.

At what point is it she? He asked himself. *At what point is it merely an effect? How much paint would be enough to show the truth?* Shrugged.

He shut his eyes and tried to imagine the presently blank, soft, romantic sections of the triptych. He wanted to go back and work on it. Because the mystery was waiting there; what would he find, what would the shapes and hues and hints reveal as unexpected forms emerged from the confusion of what he tried to see?

His legs felt cramped from floor-sitting. He shifted and scratched an itch on his knee, losing the thread of his thoughts....

Yazu looked up as two men in loincloths came in from the back where they'd obviously been sleeping it off. They were all yawns and bleary eyes. One had such thick thighs he waddled, the other was blocky, muscular, with a stringy beard and thin moustache. The bony outlaw-turned-pupil knew him. Uneasily touched the hilt of his sword beside him on the worn floor. That helped. He repeated to himself like a litany that life was but the shadow cast by a flame, wavering, uncertain and easily blown out. Still, his heart was beating a little fast and his appetite was instantly gone.

He hoped the man, called Toshiro, door guard for a neighboring brothel, would, somehow not notice him. A matter of 20 *mon* and a disputed throw of the dice.

271

The tavernkeeper brought them a bucket of water and they splashed their faces, grunting and spitting. The covetous prostitute was still vaguely observing Gentile since he'd glanced at her while she softly poked a fair-sized boil that graced her jawline under one ear.

Takezo was intent on the "poem" he'd decided was a message, maybe a *ninja* code.

Here's the great secret, he thought. *From the ring worn by a god....* Shook his head and tapped his fingers on the table.

"What shit," he ejaculated.

"Eh?" reacted Gentile.

Yazu was concentrating on trying to hear the conversation across the room. Toshiro was saying something like:

"...a fine high-class slut...with that weasel...."

He didn't look up as the gangster padded heavily over, yawning and stretching. Then the muscular, nearly-naked man bowed ponderously to the table. His eyes were small and narrow, nose a twist of sallow flesh. He had the skin of a man who didn't spend much time outdoors.

Takezo barely noticed, still straining his brain at the fragmentary message – if message it was. Gentile bowed back while Yazu kept twisting his lips together combining frowns with winces as Toshiro spoke:

"Good day." Aimed his expressionless face at the little man. "An armed weasel. Dangerous."

"Insolent," retorted Yazu. As if surprised by the force of his own words, he stood up, feeling a little floaty but determined, holding his undrawn sword.

His *sensei* took note, now, tilting his head in a reasonably feminine manner: noted the newcomer's face was set in a sullen mask.

"So," Toshiro said, "here I stand unarmed and you wave a sword at me and talk from the belly like a samurai."

His hung-over half-naked companion shuffled closer on his absurdly thick legs while the whore and the owner looked on.

"What is wrong?" wondered Gentile, alert and tense. He wasn't getting used to these sudden, violent confrontations. He'd never known such touchy men, not even Sicilians.

"A matter of money," explained hard-faced Toshiro. To Takezo: "You are lovely, iss. Why associate with this weasel?"

Takezo rolled his eyes. Never a surprise. He remembered his own dealings with his now disciple.

272

"A matter of lies," Yazu said, with almost convincing force, gripping his blade tight, like an irritable swordsman.

In the past he would have run by now, his master thought, smiling, faintly. *Have I but given the horse soft sandals and done him no favor?*

"A matter of a broken neck," quoth Toshiro, squinting and semi-crouching. "And that blade will be sheathed in your skinny behind!"

This entertained the onlookers considerably. Takezo intervened:

"Good sir," he soothed in the unnatural, high-pitched voice he was affecting, "I understand perfectly. We'll resolve this matter easily."

"But master," cried Yazu. Caught between showing relief, anger and pride, suddenly, Takezo realized, he was starting to understand the contradictions of being a warrior. "I do not owe this malediction –"

"Master?" overrode the vastly underslung second player who now loomed over the table, glistening with sweat and stinking of sour brew and mouth-breathing sleep. He peered at the Italian.

"You his *sensi*?" he wanted clarified, for some reason.

"Eh?" Gentile responded.

"Yes," said the companion, "he teaches him dice-cheat *jitsu.*"

Takezo inhaled a big cup of sake in a somewhat unfeminine fashion.

"What handsome men," he fluted. "Don't injure these poor fellows. Come back later and take tea with me. Thank you."

"Oh ho," said Toshiro, "I don't see tea in your cup, unlicensed one."

His companion chuckled. The girl at the counter giggled behind her plump hand. The owner frowned.

"No trouble in the place," he said. "Go outside for argument and insult."

"Unlicensed?" asked Takezo, taking a fresh pour of rice wine.

"Better be careful," insisted Yazu, ready to draw, a little giddy, heart working hard, alone in his little island of inner agony.

"Outside," reprised the tavern-man. "Toshiro, Koji, do you hear?"

"Unlicensed *yujo*," inquired the girl, giggling again, "where did you steal such finery?"

Toshiro sank to his knees and sat back near Takezo.

"I like a big woman," he set forth, reaching for a cup.

273

"Are you invited?" the Italian wondered, flushing a little with irritation. "I weary of broils," he went on in his language. "I wish to paint and explore the wonder of the world, not spill blood at every turn."

"What gabble is that?" asked Koji of the vast hams and thighs.

"I know most of your speech," responded Gentile, in Japanese, "partly because it's usually limited to expressing violence." He knew that wasn't true but said it anyway. He was angry, now, for the first time. He'd had enough nonsense, pride, face and false face, as he put it to himself. "There's so much worthwhile in life and all you want to do is fight all the time."

"Go away *sensei*," sneered Toshiro, shifting a little closer to the charming lady, as he perceived it. "Let's have a drink." Scrunched his face up at Yazu who was still standing there, uncertainly. "Pay me my money or go away," he concluded, turning back with a gap-toothed smile, to Takezo.

"I owe you nothing," protested the skinny gambler. "You shame yourself to claim it."

"You are a delightful fellow," the disguised *ronin* detective said. "Have a drink. I will come back later to see you."

The delightful fellow put his hand gently on his wrist and Takezo brushed it off coyly, he hoped. He wanted to sustain the role so *ninjas* wouldn't be able to track him from there. He also liked the idea that he'd defused the situation.

"You have a strange voice," said Toshiro. "But tender skin."

At which Koji of the massive underpinnings began to vibrate with laughter.

"He's a sissy dressed up," he guffawed. "Roll over and he'll plug your rear end hole for you!"

At which the whore's giggle became a near shriek of joy and the tavernkeeper squinted hard and long at Takezo. Toshiro's ardor was instantly choked as he groped for the suddenly doubtful beauty's breasts and managed to discover the steely chest under the flowing, expensive robes before he was brushed away, again, this time hard enough to topple him sideways – no mean feat.

He leapt up into a squat, red-faced, furious. Takezo took up his food picks and poked a last pickle into his mouth. Gentile stood up beside Yazu.

"Queer!" Toshiro shouted. "Let's view your cock and balls!"

274

He dove for the *ronin*, snatching at his outer robe, having learned nothing from the way he was levered over a moment ago. He was met by a pick hitting his forehead with a crack that made the onlookers wince, leaving a round, bloody spot that, Yazu thought, looked like the third eye of the bodhisattvas.

Toshiro sat back on his heels, both hands to his shocked head as the rest watched and Takezo rose, gracefully, and bowed himself and his companions out the tavern door, not neglecting to toss a few pieces of money behind him. He had the ring and the scrap of paper in one hand.

They stood on the porch in wind that had definitely picked up a notch or two. Pedestrians were gripping their hats and shielding their faces from the gusts in the street. Takezo was thoughtful, holding his fluttering, chrysanthemum-patterned *uchigi* around him.

"Gen-tile-san," he said, "it's no poem. Must be code." Shrugged. "Who can tell? Either I give it to them or destroy it."

"Code, you think?"

"Bright fish," he quoted, "three docks…and so on."

Yazu leaned close, looking past his master into the dim interior of the tavern, half expecting an attack. The wind shook the overhang and sang along the eaves. Leaves rattled.

"Bright fish?" Yazu wondered aloud. "Three docks. *Sensi*! I know where that is."

"Where what is?" Gentile asked.

"On the waterfront," the little man said. "I can take you there."

Forty-Five

View from the sea near sunset

They weren't going to make the dock area, uMubaya decided. The current and shifting wind was driving them onshore short and north of the main coves and piers. Another big wave had just lifted them really high and he could see a bright, white beach backed by lines of dark pines packed shoulder-to-shoulder.

The city was sinking into a reddish-gold haze, deepening as the sun melted itself behind the long, undulant, cyclonic clouds. Taro was still green but kept working the oars. Osan was just holding on, head bobbing on her graceful neck. She was considering how to approach her father and thinking, as they crashed up and down through the hissing spume that stung her face and blurred her vision, how the blood-red sunset, the deep,

275

burning richness, seemed to be consuming the entire darkening horizon, as if the land were melting and sinking into a vast furnace....

"I'm a bad swimmer," Taro shouted, the wind sucking away his words.

"We'll make shore," called back the Zulu. He didn't bother to mention his own negative aquatic skills.

"Look there!" cried Osan, pointing to the city.

They didn't hear her; didn't have to because in the deep twilight shadows where the sea had blended away seamlessly into the land it seemed as if the molten sunset had, somehow, burst up from the edge of the city in a terrific ball of flame, flinging a shattering fire over hundreds of suddenly blazing buildings, burning fragments going up and up and arcing out over the water that reflected the violence, hissing down like fireworks as masses of smoke, sinking and roiling heavily in the twisting winds, covered the dockside area.

It was silent as the stars, Osan more or less thought, and then they heard a muffled crack and boom like nearby thunder, wrung through the uneven gusts.

Those houses burn like dried leaves, the Zulu thought.

And then there was no time for thinking because the waves were starting to break as the shore sloped into shallows. Taro cursed. uMubaya shouted over his shoulder:

"Get up on the next wave."

Backed off on the oars and the policeman followed suit, not really having heard him. The black man had learned this technique landing on strange shores in longboats: they held the craft on an angle so it would ride up the reverse slope of a wave...then row hard forward to catch and hang on the breaking crest.

To the prince's surprise it worked the first time and they were surfing in, falling down the front as it kept sinking away under them; moving fast enough to slow the wind at their backs as the beach and wall of pines, red-lit in strips by the staccato clouds, came up at impressive speed.

Osan was looking back at the spreading flames maybe five miles across the bay. The massed smoke, underlit by the explosively spreading fire, was pumping up, blowing out, down drafting under the last dribbles of sunset that seemed like clotting blood.

276

Is Hell come to earth? She asked herself, soaked with spray, tilted between heaven and slamming sea, watching what might have been the first spark of the world's general conflagration and deserved destruction....

Somewhat Earlier

Yazu had gone home and come back to rejoin Gentile and his teacher. His wife, amazingly altered, had fallen on her knees and begged him to stay home, citing the coming storm, the rumors of war; then saying she'd seen a diviner who'd read the stars and the cracks in a tortoise shell and determined that he, Yazu the Reckless, she said, was in terrible danger, surrounded by bad and ruthless men, that a great disaster loomed over them all and devils were gathering in shadows all around.

She'd clutched his legs and since she was heavier and stronger than he, he'd struck and levered at her with his sheathed sword to pry her loose, shouting that his honor and loyalty forbade him to desert his master.

'That drunk who uses you like a toilet stick!' she exclaimed, weeping, face down in the dirt in front of their house, hands groping for his long feet which he kept just ahead of her fingers as she heaved forward. The wind blew dust over them both. A few neighbors looked curiously at the tableau. 'I beg you, husband, you are needed here not going to certain death with a madman all mock!'

'And fear, too,' he yelled back, stepping forward. 'Want me to shame myself?'

Stepping forward was an error because her wide, strong, work-hardened hands got a good grip on his lead ankle.

'Stay with us!' she cried. 'Your son needs a father.'

'Release me,' he just said, not struggling this time. 'I won't go back to what I was.'

So she just let go and he stood there. The sun, past noon, was regularly blotted and freed by the flowing, curving clouds. In effect, they went into and out of the light. She stood up, furious, frustrated.

'You are no great fighter, no samurai, not even a boss's captain. They will step on you like a worm on the road.'

'I know that, woman. But this is the better way. I had no face for anything but cowering and sneaky ways.' He stamped one foot. The wind fluttered his baggy "knickers" and loose shirt.

277

'No more. No more. I'll shut my eyes and die but never cower, again.' A cloudshadow covered them and then was past and the baking hot, humid sun went on like a back-mirrored stagelamp. *'Never.'*

So he came back and the three of them worked their way down to the waterfront in the late afternoon, the wind blowing the heat around like an open furnace door.

Takezo was still in the fancy women's clothes; Yazu had picked up his master's *katana* from his place next to the coffin maker and held it for him like a squire.

"There," said Yazu, pointing at a street signpost which said: *BRIGHT FISH.*

"Ah," breathed the *ronin*, nodding, making little effort to seem feminine, at this point. "Which dock?"

There were men, here and there, securing moored boats, tying down cargo, hatches as was usual in the face of a serious storm. No one paid much attention to the three of them.

"Maybe this way," the little pupil said, his *sensei*'s longsword over one shoulder. He grimaced a frown and spat towards the water, the wind breaking the spittle into a mist. "Master," he said, suddenly, "that evil-faced criminal lied."

"Which one?" Takezo wondered as they picked their way around barrels, rolls of rope, logs and small boats drawn well up on shore. The curved clouds blotted and wiped dimness over the steeply angled sun, going down behind them and stretching their shadows right out over the water, thinning and thickening as the light changed.

"That shitlump Toshiro, master. I owe him not a *mon*!"

He didn't scuttle much anymore, Takezo noted. Didn't look over his shoulder so much. The good side of learning to kill, the detective reflected.

Sandals on the horse, he said to himself. *I've made him afraid to run and hide and given him unnecessary ideas instead of armor....*

Gentile pointed to another sign stuck on a post at the foot of a long plank dock with fairly large boats moored alongside.

"Doesn't that say *'NUMBER 3 DOCK'*" he asked.

It did and they went out on it behind their long shadows. The sun was tilting down towards the hills, still gold but tarnishing as if the clouds rubbed the brightness away.

Even in this protected cove around a bend in the bay the swells were lifting and twisting the wharfs, moored craft creaking and scraping their sides. The cloud-cut light seemed to synchronize with the beat of the waves.

The planks tilted and rolled enough to make it interesting. They had no way of knowing that the high decked craft about midway out (maybe 200 feet) was the one often used as a rendezvous by Issa and Reiko, where Yoshi had met them, recently.

"Now what?" Takezo asked himself, aloud, his embroidered robes phut-phutting in the steadying onshore wind. He looked around, getting no ideas.

"What was the rest?" Gentile wanted to know.

"Last ship...something ...golden lantern," the *ronin* detective answered.

They came near the end of the long pier. The last ship was so big it stood higher from the rocking water than even a Chinese junk and was mastless, roofed over with tented cloth.

No masts, he quoted, mentally.

Looking at it, Takezo found it odd that the sides seemed to undulate slightly as it rolled, scraped and yanked against the tensed, strain-creaking lines that held it close and fast to the pilings.

Bends like it might be made of straw or paper, he thought. Puffed out his cheeks and furrowed his high forehead, holding his colorful flowing cape close around himself. *Strange....*Each time the wave surge drove it up into the timbers the impact was clearly massive compared to any of the other boats: the thick ends were being splintered and gradually rubbed away. *The sides bend by the rail and yet the hull is shattering the dock...it must be full of stones....*

"Look, master!" cried Yazu, pointing.

As a cloud-shadow passed the reddened sun broke through and glinted on a big brass lantern, bright and polished, visible where an overhanging flap of covering across the deck had pulled away.

In the end, Takezo decided, *it is always something ordinary or silly or pathetic that turns the key and opens the door....*

They walked to about amidships.There was nothing like a gangplank or even a visible break in the strangely flexible rail section of the maybe fifteen foot high side, there, where it curved down in a long bow-bend. Timing the rise and fall he was just able to jump up enough to

279

catch the top of the rail before it pulled away under his hands and he came crashing down in a rattle of bamboo sticks and torn fabric.

He banged his head on the bulge of the hull but kept his footing on the swaying planks, despite the wind.

More ninja tricks, he was sure. *Why disguise this ship? So no one will know what it is or what's in it...profound, Takezo...the ring leads here and...*Paused because he thought he had it. Part of it.

"Was this your ship?" he asked the tall Italian.

Gentile frowned.

"Ours had..." He frowned and touched the curved, weathered, darkwood hull as it rolled up and then slowly back down, chipping at the dock. "Tall masts and a different shape...but this is covered...."

"The masts may have been shattered and cut away," said Takezo.

"Ah, here!" said Gentile, peering up under where the *ronin's* fall had rent the covering of the false side. "The *gunwhale!* Eh! Look just below the rail." There was a square hole, just visible. "That's where the cannon poked out."

"Cannon?" queried Yazu, leaning close.

"Big guns," explained Gentile. "Powerful. Can smash down walls."

Takezo grunted and nodded.

"Yazu," he said, "I'll toss you up. Then you pull me after."

"This must be the *Santo Pedro,*" the Italian concluded. "Why is it hidden here?"

"Why does the assassin wear black at night?" Takezo responded, picking up the light, slim man and, in a graceful twist and strain, hurled him up towards the railing.

At Hideo's about the same time

The *daimio was* still in his traveling clothes: yellow and black silks pointed-shoulder vest and baggy balloon "knickers." He was standing in the rock-garden where Gentile had received the dismissive poem from Issa. His expression was set in a grim mask. He tapped an iron fan against one knee, looking past his wife who was seated on a low, stone bench.

Above the shelter of the long stone wall the tops of tall pines were swooshing and flexing their long, dark needles. The deepening sun-red seemed to coagulate in the branches.

Chamberlain Reiko was standing near Issa under one of the blank, darkening walls. His head was tilted slightly forward as his lord spoke:

"Let me say this. I have pledged my loyalty to Lord Nobunaga." He considered the chamberlain who showed nothing readable. "This means no trouble with Izu or anybody else."

"As you say, lord," Rieko responded, bowing a little.

Issa seemed uninterested, looking up at the swaying branches over the blank, dark wall. A maidservant knelt close to her.

"The wild days are done," declared Hideo. "*Gekokujo* is intolerable." Meaning when the lesser would betray the greater. "Understand this. We will be true *samurai*, not bandits."

Reiko revealed no discomfort. Nodded a bow.

"Yes, lord," he agreed. Issa glanced, sidelong, at him. "Tomorrow is the second trial of the outlander."

"What nonsense. If my daughter lives why has he not been freed?"

"Grave doubts arise, lord," explained Reiko. "We don't know she's alive. Just that she was not buried here. Witnesses say the Black Devil and the traitor Kendo Nori, kidnapped her."

Hideo cut an even deeper frown into the set stone of his face.

"This twisted business," he snarled, "sickens a man. Armies of brigands, backed by certain clans and shadowy groups, are, even now, raiding villages and outposts. The *Tokaido* road is unsafe, again." He shook his fan like a blade. "Nobunaga already has men in the field, moving up the coast to support our allies."

Reiko nodded again to mask reacting. Further sweat glistened on his forehead. He might have been the monkey reaching into the trap whose bait was irresistible.

"That's good, lord," he said, reassuringly.

"What of that crazy drunk with the talking head?" Hideo wanted to know. "What new latrine has he uncovered?"

"Bah," said the chamberlain. "Maybe he drowned in a barrel of *sakekasu.*"

Wine dregs used to make pickles.

"Mistake him not for a fool," Issa spoke up.

"Fool or not," declared the *Daimio,* looking at his wife for the first time, "he is dangerous."

"He uncovered the false burial of our child," she went on to say.

281

"My lady," interjected Reiko, "he is no more than a man who wakes in the dead of night and, groping in the blind dark, finds, by chance, a coin on the floor and then imagines himself a seer."

"Does not luck prevail over mere skill, Chamberlain?" she asked.

"Enough," commanded her husband, holding his fan in both hands now, level across his chest. "You begin to sound like Osan, however." The cold anger that had set his face so hard was making him more impatient. He looked first at one, then the other. "When the smoke clears we will see what the fire burnt."

Reiko barely managed not to wipe his forehead. A salty sweat drop beaded down into one eye and blurred his vision slightly.

His lord was walking towards the archway that went inside, feet silent as shadow steps on the flat stones.

"My Lord," he called after him, "ought we not take counsel?"

"Counsel? Ho," Hideo replied, not turning. "I go in search of good luck to outweigh my poor skills."

"Which skill, my lord?" his wife wondered blandly.

This time he looked back; paused in the shadow of the arch. The late light fading and dimming gave the impression that still objects in the garden moved, slightly.

"Which indeed, wife."

Went on, his form lost in the dimness inside.

Reiko went closer to her, wiping his face with his sleeve. She didn't quite look at him.

"Weeping?" she wondered.

"Eh?" he said, distracted, frowning and blinking to clear his sight. "We cannot wait any longer. No time left."

"No brains left," she added.

"He suspects," Reiko whispered, checking behind him.

"Some brains left," she amended.

"Nobunaga is on the move."

"It seems so."

Otherwise still, he clasped and unclasped his hands. Then wiped at the sweat, again. He needed to see Tanba. He never discussed that side of things with her. After tomorrow there would be almost no time, he decided. The wind picked up and moaned in the walls, the pine tops above the wall sloshing back and forth, detail-less outlines, now, as the light died.

"The storm is nearly upon us," she observed.

"In every sense," he said, clasping and unclasping his hands, not looking at anything. "I think we've been betrayed, my love." He said that consciously, to gauge her mood.

She didn't seem one way or the other. She was actually thinking that maybe she'd gone wrong.

"That might be true," she responded. "But I don't think so. My husband doesn't like to hear any voice but his own."

"Or his daughter's."

She inclined her head.

"Yes, my love," she said, expressionlessly, "that is so."

The wind picked up...then softened again....

At the ship

They found a prepared unlit torch; Yazu took firestones from his pouch and they had light as the three of them went below decks.

"This is called the 'forecastle,'" said Gentile. "I have never actually been down here."

It smelled wet and salt-sour. The cargo door was padlocked. A big padlock. The door was thick and solid.

"Looks Chinese," opined Yazu, poking his pinky into the outsized keyhole in the hand-sized chunk of iron.

"You've seen a few locks, I don't doubt," Takezo concluded. "Well, I have a key. Stand aside."

"It is not Chinese," stated Gentile.

Takezo drew his short sword and took a two-handed grip on the 3 foot weapon. Stared, indirectly at his target. He'd have to graze the door with the tip to cleanly strike the U-shaped piece of metal that fit into the body of the massive lock.

"But it's too thick," objected the Italian. "The blade will chip."

"There are other blades," said Takezo. "Yazu, hold it up straight."

The little man was uneasy and held the base of the lock with two fingers as if he were being made to touch a cobra. Takezo concentrated, preparing to hit with all the mass of the world flowing up into him, feeling it gathering an instant before he actually let the blade explode, guided by his incredible wrists and hands. His student shut his eyes.

Chop, spark, crack! The lock swung free, as Yazu simultaneously pulled his hand away. For some reason this amazed Gentile more than all the dueling he'd witnessed- because the steel wasn't chipped and the cut

283

had been made as easy as a breath. The blade glistened in the wavering torchlight.

"A good sword," commented the *ronin,* pushing the door open.

"Brilliant, sensei," applauded the pupil, relieved.

Gentile stayed astonished. The blade had sliced through the inch of metal as if it were bread.

Inside, the headroom in the passageway was about five feet – so that even Yazu had to crouch. Both sides of the walkway were lined with stacks of muskets.

The torch showed the passage probably went the almost length of the vessel. Each side was filled floor-to-bulkhead with stacks of muskets. Gentile estimated there had to be four thousand if there was one. Was this the cargo intended for China? In the hands of trained troops what would these weapons do to a bow and arrow opposing force? He'd seen them used once in a battle before Padua and. When either side tried to close the massed fire tore soldiers to bloody shreds, a single shot sometimes ripping through two armored men and half a horse.

He tugged one free, hefting the very heavy piece of brass, wood and steel. Between the stacks of arms there were bags of 60 caliber balls capable of making fist-sized holes in human flesh.

"Ugly things," he said now, with disgust.

"So," breathed Takezo, "it comes clear. Now it comes clear."

"But what can this mean, *sensei*?" Yazu asked, holding the torch.

His teacher shrugged, crouching over to a hatch in the floor, yanking it open and reaching back for the torch, which he poked down the opening into the pitch blackness.

"What do you see?" asked Gentile.

"Barrels. Many, many barrels. Like a warehouse full of sake."

He went down a couple of steps and pried at a lid with his dagger. He came up with a handful of black powder he didn't immediately recognize, a lot of it streaming through his fingers. Held it close to the torch and it flared, in a hissing burst that seared his hand and face and he banged the burning end against a barrel and coals dropped down into the shadows where it had just spilled.

So he was already turning, starting back up, yelling ahead:

"Go out! Go out! Run!"

"What?" asked Gentile.

"Just run!" he shouted, shoving the tall Italian; Yazu was already in motion.

They bolted at a crouch out the door, then up the steps to the deck under the canvas tenting. But Yazu slipped and reeled back against Gentile who bounced off Takezo and kept running; the *ronin* fell back partway before he could recover and sprint for the hatch opening just above him. Levered himself half out of the opening as the first explosion propelled him like a soft, giant hand up and out, setting fire to his silky outer robe and spinning him so the puffing rush of flaming chips and impact seared his face, stinging particles tearing into his eyes and he knew he screamed, soundless in the blast, barely aware of the fabric whooshing into fire.

He blindly stagger-ran, fell over the rail and was partly caught on the dock by Gentile who cushioned his fall, then ripped away his burning garments leaving him in loincloth only. Then he took one arm and Yazu the other and half-dragged the stunned detective along the long dock as the ship gushed flame. It was about fifty yards to the first row of wood and paper houses.

Not looking back, Gentile said, more than once:

"Jesus Christus, regnum angelorum!"

In partial shock, Takezo was getting his legs back. He knew the pain in his eyes was really bad, this time. Really bad.

"Fire is....is not my friend," he mumbled.

His lips hurt, too. His whole face. There were redhot tacks hammered around his sockets and one more in each eyeball.

Bad, his mind repeated, *very bad...this...this is...now I've done it....*

He could feel the heat from the mass of flames at their backs, a pressure distinct from the wind gusts; heard the surf crumbling into the beach, distant shouts and alarm bells being struck; the tilts of the ground...and then they stopped.

They were maybe 100 yards from the dock area when the bulk of powder blew. The impact was an almost soft shove that knocked them over a raised road into a canal as a ball of fire rushed over them, burning fragments spraying down like meteors over the trees and houses.

"Ave Maria," cried Gentile. *"Grazia plenum!"*

Yoshi and a few of his men were sitting their nervous horses in the yard of the Pine and Crane tavern as the gradually building gusts filled the air with dirt.

The stout man in red and white clothes, who'd left the inn while "Lady" Takezo and Yazu were outside, was standing on the low porch, addressing them with some authority.

"He's disguised as a woman, now."

Yoshi snarled and nodded. Rubbed the thick scar that cut across his nose with one hand while the other yanked at the reins.

"So," he barked from his belly, "finally he reveals his true nature."

"They were tracked to the waterfront. Not too difficult, Middle Captain. They are well-watched."

"Where?"

"Bright Fish and Number 3 Dock."

Yoshi was already turning his mount, with needless violence. He was a knot of frustration and anxiety. The way to victory and greatness was open. No time to hesitate.

"Ride men!" he commanded, cantering out into the street in swirls of dusty wind, galloping as the warriors strung out behind him, pedestrians scattering, clothes flapping in the warm gusts. "His luck has run out," he muttered. "Now he's finished. Rip him from the world like a bad tooth from the mouth."

They were, maybe, half a mile away when the ship exploded and Yoshi instantly grasped the import. Tanba had provided a demonstration with the ten muskets the pirate captain had given them as samples before the rescued, battered, mastless Portuguese ship had been hidden. The late Osa-Kame had been well cursed for foolishly trying to get the goods with violence rather than the promised gold, creating needless problems. Kame erred further thinking the ring a mere identifying token.

Yoshi had witnessed the demonstration where three condemned criminals had been dressed in armor, given spears and told they'd be freed if they could charge through a line of ten men with muskets, from thirty paces away. The desperate characters had rushed forward behind their long spears and got very close before the volley was fired and the lead balls, in a gout of flame and smoke, literally shattered them. It was clear what masses of them could do to unprotected troops and charging cavalry.

286

It was clear that Tanba had a weapon that would alter warfare and break his enemies. Except, now, he didn't....

So Middle Captain Yoshi knew what the terrific fireball that shook the earth and obliterated the docks and boats probably was, as their horses reared, bolted and bucked as the riders tried to hang on. And he raged:

"Repellant dung-stink!" Virtually shrieked because he knew with a sinking knowing that it was Takezo. None other – even as flaming chunks of wood and torn metal arced like shells into the flimsy buildings all around. "Arrrr! What filth! Wouldn't let me kill him! Wouldn't let me kill him!"

Weeping with anger he and his men rode away and around the bend of the bay in a wider arc than that taken by the *ronin* detective and companions who were on foot, hugging the shoreline as they fled.

The fireball fluffed up higher and higher in roiling smoke over the already burning city as the deadly and growing winds came to bear like great gears of fate, bending the massive cloud like a striking fist above the buildings caught in streams and torrents of racing fire....

The baffled leading the blind

They struggled across the canal and climbed the far side. Takezo in his loincloth, led by Gentile with Yazu out in front. They went along the shoreline of rock, sand, rough bushes and contorted pines. The red-orange glow shifted with the veers and twists of the wind, the curdling clouds now stretching, thinning then balling up, the mounting, wildly-spreading fire running in rivulets, streams, rivers of flame up towards the heart of the tinderbox city, fireballs staining the sky and falling like cannon shells.

The heat, even at this distance, pressed at their backs. The massive surf slammed into the shore.

"Edo is burning up!" Yazu cried out over the general roar, as if he'd just realized it.

To the blinded Takezo there was just noise, wind, heat, spray and the incredible needles around his eyes and cheekbones as he struggled over the uneven combination of rock, mud and damp sand as the world shrank into wobbling earth, pushing and crashing as he stumbled into the wall of spikes that jabbed into his face. For the first time he really considered ending his life.

At least, he thought, *I cannot do any more harm...so many have died because of me and now this!....One more blind action and maybe I'll set off an earthquake and sink our island....*

"Aiihh," he voiced, gripping Gentile's long-fingered hand. "Yet, all my actions will be blind, now."

"What's that?" the Italian asked, leaning closer.

It will be all mistakes and so...no harm will be done...because....

"What is time to a blind man," he asked, "since he sees nothing move or change?"

"Try to be calm," said the other. "We will get clear and rest. Then..."

"Then. Yes. Then." Takezo had a thought. He had many thoughts; at the same time, he had none. "Miou," he said like a sob. "Ai, my Miou...."

"We'll hide and rest."

The *ronin* tried to concentrate. At least this was a kind of goal.

"Where are we?" he asked.

"By the sea," said the Italian. "It's all fog and smoke. Can barely see."

"Be grateful. You are like one who barely lives and I a breathless corpse."

"Ai," cried Yazu, falling back, "there are shadows moving ahead."

Takezo heard sounds of horses and men shouting.

"Samurai or bandits," he declared.

It will be good to die but I do not wish to be mad, he told himself. *I must think carefully....It's the pain...worse than a fever...twisting my senses into unsupported conclusions....*

"Samurai, master," said Yazu.

And then a voice he knew well, over all the other sounds, saying:

"Here he is! Here he is! Ah, by the gods. By the gods!"

Yoshi. That had to be bad. That had to be the bottom of bad....

To the sticking place

The same sunset that made a dark corpse of the earth and the sky a waterspill of burning blood, filled the window of Hideo and Issa's lesser audience room, called *Moon and Mist*, on the first floor of the castle. They were both kneel-sitting at a floor table, a tea service being laid out by a serving girl.

The double doors slid open and a retainer bowed himself in. He was stocky and nondescript. He bowed over to his lord and lady and handed Hideo a scroll message. Hideo read it, glanced at his wife whose detached eyes were looking at nothing, then said:

"No answer. Go."

As he left Issa gestured for the girl to follow, taking up the pot and preparing to pour, saying:

"My lord, are you still determined to support the upstart rustic?" A reference to Nobunaga's country samurai roots.

"More to the point is that he supports me. If an emperor were drowning, would he not let a lowly fisherman pull him from the sea?" He looked around the bare, highly polished room. There was one immense screen in three parts all done in black, white and gray with misty hints of mountain-like outlines, groups of probable trees like coagulations of some primal smoke, a tiny, melting hut, all under an oversized, clear, perfectly round moon. "You have other matters to concern yourself with, woman. Where is my devoted chamberlain?"

She looked sidelong at him, teapot poised.

"So," she said, "you meant to chastise?"

"Do you have cause to fear it, woman?"

"Ah, my love," she replied, "who has not some small shame or other?"

"Who has not?" He wasn't really looking at her. "You, who have face like a mask of brass. What might shame you?"

"Rumours." Teapot still poised, the polished metal glinting dark red in the sunset glow from the window. No lamps were lit and sourceless shadows began to pool around them and blur their outlines and slight expressions. "False ideas."

"I feel the unseen hand of age on me," he said, looking straight ahead across the imperceptibly dimming chamber at the wall where a triple rack of sheathed swords glinted darkly. "I'm sick of ambition. I want to fight to protect and not to take. What use is a world of treachery?"

She poured two cups, delicately, her pale, loose blouse seeming to concentrate the dying light. There was a distant rumble that might have been a single bang of thunder.

"Men will ever betray from fear or for advantage," she pointed out.

"Unlike women," he snorted.

289

Hesitated, then handed him his cup. She had almost intentionally spilled it.

Too late to turn back, she thought. *Anyway, he hates me as it is and after we both reawaken he will hate me the more....unimportant, if we succeed our clan will survive....*

"You are harsh, today, my lord."

"I think that drunkard's half-conceived play haunts me with truth, lady." He held the hot cup, remembering Takezo on the stage playing the murdered lord. "I have covered my sins like a cat his droppings."

And then, looking at her in the last light that left those ambiguous eyes with ambiguous hints, he raised his cup to his lips as she followed suit and they both drank deeply. She couldn't look at him. At the window the sunset's dark red seemed to have flared brighter. Seemed strange.

Next the double doors slid open and Reiko bowed himself in like, Hideo thought, a character in a puppet play.

"What a delight to my eyes," Hideo said.

The Chamberlain came close and bowed again; stayed down.

"Lord," he said, "are you unwell?"

Because the Daimio had broken out in a sweat, blinking, rubbing his face.

"The room swims," he said, thickly, breathing hard. Stared at her as he went down sideways onto his right elbow. She was sagging, herself. "You whore!" he snarled, feeling his heart racing as he fought to keep conscious. "As I feared..." He groped for his sword but, instead, went down flat on his face in slowed-motion as if he sank into water or a dream. The last thing he saw was her sinking gracefully onto her side, and her voice, saying:

"We will sleep...just sleep, until this is...is settled...for the good of...."

"Treacherous whore...." He thought he might have said...or was it just the rushing of waters that covered him, now, and was carrying him away into the thickening dark...

She held the tilting floor with both hands, watching Reiko as the drug lapped at her conciousness.

"Where are ...*ninja*?" she asked, in a gasp. "You cannot carry us alone."

"Plans are changed," she heard him say, kneeling over her fallen husband, jerking his head up by the topknot in a gesture of unspeakable

290

rudeness and contempt. His helpless and violated master actually managed to struggle and froth curses. "I will have discovered this treason," Reiko went on, "in time to save only *your* life."

And through the dimming world where things moved slower and slower as if running down, she saw the shadow of her lover raise his shadowy sword and strike at her shadow-husband's stretched-up neck once…twice…three times before the blot of head parted from the blot of body in a mist of colorless blood as the last light failed and Reiko's voice, far away and substanceless:

"One cannot strike half a blow! Only the dead can be trusted!"

Suspended

Someone was coming back from somewhere…he was coming back…there was no name yet or thoughts or words, yet….The quasi-memories were mixed in bright and dark together at the same time as if all were motionless as a painting where swords were frozen in mid-stroke, bird's wings never flapped, the moon stayed still among fixed clouds and flames burned forever without consuming anything….

He felt he was a *he* and there was a name…somewhere…that didn't really matter yet…call dung gold, if you liked, but where would you spend it?

Like the babe lapping honeyed milk at its mother's breast so Takezo, still nameless to himself, drank deep of an incomprehensible bliss as if he existed without shadow, edge or blur because there was nothing to contrast anything with so while nothing was solid, nothing was empty either. He didn't want to leave the milky softness…sweetness…silky feelings unfolding like perfumed gossamer under a child's questing fingers…And then there was what, in a world where time moved and things took solid form, would have been a memory:

Wild wind pushing stinging specks that might have been dust or sand, voices that were wordless barks; impacts that set fire to existing pain…and then something lifted and moved him and he floated, arms and legs pulled out and then, at full stretch, a new agony became the only thing real and wild confusion smothered down on him, massive and there was a pounding that shook everything, a monstrous iron hammer slamming down as if the weight of the world hit him….

'Here hang until you rot, how I wish you might never die.'

291

And he was reborn, full of knowing, with a name for his pain and pain maker. So there were words, again, "Yoshi" the first.

Is this Shite's pillar I am pressed against? his mind inquired.

He thought there might have been a sound out there in the pictures that might have been memories:

"Yoshi...come closer...."

"Master," came back Yazu's voice, instead.

"Takezo?" called out Gentile from below. *"E nomini rex coeli."*

Their voices were blurred and blotted by the background roar of wind and surf. He felt the push and sting of spray or rain – couldn't tell which. His eyes felt as if they were sealed in wax and there was no point trying to open them.

"That cur, Yoshi, is gone, master," called up Yazu, voice not changing position. "May 10 devils eat his heart in the third hell!"

The remarkable, dull, sickening pain in the *ronin* detective's hands focused his recovering attention. Tried to move his arms but they were stiff, dead wood. The pain would gather and slowly increase after each effort. He had an impression he was clutching hot coals that were being fanned and expected his flesh and bones were reducing to char.

He was pretty sure he said something more to his companions but everything went silent and he could see, again, though he knew they must be memories but how could you be sure something was a memory and not a dream? Then a gust of red flared into memory's focus out of the ship's hatch blasting him into slowed time and he had an impression the flames had a face, a gaping mouth fanged with fire and eyes full of smoke and emptiness....

Did that happen? His mind asked. *Or...*

And he was back to dark agony...hearing voices that might have been the sea's speech violently inflected on the wind....

"Where are we?" he called out, voice raw in his throat.

"Oh, *sensei*," called up Yazu from somewhere below in the gale-wrung darkness. "What horror!"

"I cannot move," Takezo mumbled. His lips hurt. "Why is that?"

"You hang crucified on a tree," called up Gentile, then, in Italian, to himself: "In the plight of our Lord."

"We are bound here below, master," Yazu explained above the noise.

Takezo sighed. His burns hurt; his bruises hurt and his pierced hands were an amazing torment. He had the natural warrior's ability to isolate pain as well as his meditative detachment but this was pushing his limits. He wanted to be unconscious.

"Had I eyes," he called out, light-headed and scornful, "I suppose I'd have good view of something."

"Not much to see," responded the Italian. "Fog and smoke and flames. The city burns like tinder and the waves grow."

"Suspended," he sort of laughed in a ghastly way, "with a view of my blindness." He didn't like the sound.

I am a ghost, he thought. *Yoshi is a ghost...what we were is long lost...once I walked the earth among men...there was love and other things....*He was, he considered, almost laughing again, the spirit come back in the *noh* play. *This must be Shite's pillar....*

He did laugh again and it was worse, this time....

Along the coast

As the sun set the flames expanded, the red reflection covering more and more and more of the bay, the reflected light moving with the water's massive rhythm, painting the beach, the trees and themselves in an almost regularly shifting latticework of bright and shadow as the mists thinned and thickened.

Taro was limping. He'd caught one foot behind a seat as the boat dug in and pitchpoled into the beach spilling them into the slapping, churning surf. He was leaning on a pretty straight, heavy piece of driftwood that served for cane.

They had a good view of the fire as it exploded and contorted in the bursts of gale, eating into the unresistant city.

Osan was looking for the shore road that looped towards her castle home. She knew this stretch of coastline very well, since childhood.

uMubaya had seen wildfires race across dry fields fast as most men could run; he'd never imagined anything like this.

Like 10,000 huts burning, he considered. *What thing next? Will this whole land sink into the sea?* Maybe 300 yards ahead masses of smoke and fog blowing across the bay hit shore and made an undulant wall. *So thick, amazing....like winter porridge....*

Osan had never been so weary. Unused to prolonged exercise, her legs wobbled, slightly, with each barefoot impact. She gathered her will and kept on, concentrating on getting home and saving the Scot. She believed her cowardice was to blame.

Taro was dazed, generally. He'd observed that the wind was blowing the flames away from his district so he could assume his family was safe. For now. He'd never heard of such a fire.

They didn't say much among themselves, at this point, and then the smoke- amplified fog billowed up to meet them in semi-solid sheets so that they had to stay very close in a choking world of dull-red, shifting light and groping shadows.

Osan felt like a bug being crushed under a random foot. uMubaya thought they might be among the half-forms and shadows of devils while Taro formed no ideas at all, just angling along, digging in his improvised staff and favoring the hurt foot....

And then something more solid showed. There were rhythmic, clopping, cracking sounds like hooves; devil's hooves uMubaya thought, and deep voices shouting what might be the stony accents of some demonic language. That might have been better because, as visibility fluctuated, amplified by the weird illumination, horsemen seemed to coalesce from the twisting fumes and fine ash and they made out, first, a round, flattish face, scarred nose and cheek and small eyes, features that seemed carved to emblemize anger.

"The one called Yoshi," the Zulu said to Taro.

"Hold up!" Yoshi yelled as his two men were passing, becoming less substantial again. These semi-shadows turned back and, more or less, hemmed them in with their backs to the beach.

"No reason to wait," sneered Taro. "Proceed on to Hell."

"Ah, Osan!" Yoshi yelled from his belly. "How fortunate to find you. Your father and mother grieve. We will protect you from these bad men."

"Thank you. I know you not," she responded. "These men are friends, sir."

They reined closer. Yoshi glared, sword drawn. His horse snorted and rocked sideways.

"Bad choice of friends, Lady Osan," he asserted. "I serve your mother and the clan!"

"What of my father, the Daimio? You do not mention his name?"

"He is a traitor! His power is done! Mount up behind me, Lady, please."

"Go away," she retorted. "What things you say!"

"Kill the men," Yoshi ordered.

"Brutal fools!" she cried. "You force violence everywhere!"

She stooped and picked up two good-sized stones as the horsemen closed in, swept by in the wild, blurring, stinging, shifting atmosphere that (she thought) could have been some dark, tormented underworld....

Hand washing

Now candles and lanterns brightly lit the chamber. The wind sucked and puffed at the unshuttered windows. Maybe a dozen or so retainers plus a few women stood around where Hideo's corpse was being wrapped in a sheet along with the head.

One of the women was working on the big blood splash and what suggested an attempt to scrawl some message in indecipherable calligraphy – in fact, where the head had rolled, erratically, after Reiko dropped it.

Reiko stood on the slightly raised platform facing the room.

"Men are searching the grounds," an average sized, lean, scarred captain was reporting. "The gates are sealed." He was pondering the bloodstains, too, where the woman with a bucket and rags was trying to clean up; not much progress. The stains seemed to have seeped into the polished boards. *"Ninjas,"* he whispered, harshly. "Who could bear this disgrace?"

Reiko winced and adjusted his bloodstained kimono which was slashed open across his chest. He kept a cloth pressed to the wound.

"We must bear it, Captain Katsu," he said. "We are about to attack the very enemies who sent their sneaking killers to do this terrible deed." He paced onto the raised level of the floor where Issa was slowly recovering consciousness. The two candles on tall metal stands sketched shadows over his long, wide-browed, arguably handsome face. He stood now just above where the bloodstain sprayed out. He gestured at the recumbent woman. "We must rally behind this, our lady, who has shown the courage of Keza Gozen!" He had everyone's attention as he shout-spoke. "Had I not arrived when I did she would have been slain too, no doubt. The villains fled out the window using their despicable arts." He drew his sword, face set as if carved, eyes slits of shadow. "The hand of Nobunaga and Izu is here seen! Their armies are on the march! Good men are gathering to resist them. We must fight to avenge our lord!" He pointed to the blood on the floor that the woman was still, ineffectually, scrubbing. "Every man must seek vengeance or live in shame!" The men in the room drew their swords and shook them overhead, glinting in the soft, uncertain light. "If we must die, then we die with our swords in their bellies, not ours in our own! No suicides! Vengeance! Vengeance! Only vengeance!"

As they cheered he just stood there, frowning at the dark shape on the floorboards that suddenly reminded him of a face...eyes maybe weeping or bleeding...except it was all bleeding...

He blinked hard; kept staring. Someone was talking to him. He frowned. Didn't follow the words because his attention was caught by the rills and dribbles left by the bounced and rolled head that tantalizingly suggested writing.

He knew he'd never left the room but, still, had an absurd idea that someone had tried to scrawl a message, in his lord's blood, revealing something....He was sure there were no spirits but kept wondering if the ghost had done it.

"Nonsense," he muttered, still staring, squinting.

"Why do you say that, Lord Chamberlain?" the Captain reacted, frowning, thinking Reiko meant what he'd just said about organizing their troops.

"It comes from seeing plays," Reiko murmured. "Ghosts always come back in plays." He turned away with an effort just as he was imagining he identified the characters for cursed and doomed, suggested by the soft brushing of flame-shadows on the gleaming, red-dyed boards.

"Chamberlain?"

"Plays should be forbidden," he said.

"Sir?"

The *samurai* still in the chamber were listening, puzzled, wondering if Reiko's mind was wandering from grief.

"Actors make lies seem real." His eyes rolled back to the splashes. His subject changed, somewhat, and his confidence increased. "He couldn't write anything."

"Write what, Lord Chamberlain?" the Captain asked, hopefully.

"Without a head, what can a man say?" With that he stormed forward, feeling giddy and nervous, and kicked the woman's bucket so that the water sprayed and it rolled erratically across the shadowy floor.

"Disgrace!" he shouted. "Why do you play with our lord's gore? Making pictures?"

"My Lord," she responded, backing away on her knees covering her face with both hands. "Please, what do you mean?"

Reiko turned away, looking at Issa, now, who was trying to sit up.

"Clean up!" he ordered.

The Captain was looking at the retainers who were pretty much trying to look at nothing. Reiko went closer to Issa, stepping back up on the platform. They didn't speak. Turning to the men, he said:

"Go, to your duties!" As they left he said to the Captain: "I thought something was written there."

"Where, Chamberlain?"

"On the floor. On the floor." Shook his head. "But there's nothing."

"No, Lord," the troubled retainer said, bowing himself away. "Just blood."

"That's right. That's right."

Issa was sitting upright, partly supported by a woman. She was taking it all in, her unreadable eyes remote and inward.

Forty-Six

Out of the fog

The first two horsemen crashed forward, striking down at the Zulu and the big policeman.

Taro flung a handful of pebbles and sand into his attacker's face, ducking alongside the animal's flank. The shrewd and tough streetfighter reached up and under, avoiding the rear hooves and driving his fist into the unprotected testicles. It got results: the mount bucked and the momentarily blinded rider tipped to the side and Taro caught him with his stick, knocking his arm loose from his sword, the sound of cracked bone like a shot.

Taro got the sword in hand in time to meet the next attacker who thrust his spear savagely. The policeman deflected, side-stepped and got in a cut at the back of the rider's leg above the stirrup, he tried to wheel around, bumping off the first horse which was bucking sideways and backwards in testicular agony, then blending into the shroud of whipping fog and smoke as uMubaya went for Yoshi, slashing with his *naginata*. The second man, recovering from the collision, tried a jab at the black

297

man's back but missed, stunned by one of Osan's rocks banging off his helmeted skull.

The Zulu ripped his stick-with-a-sword at Yoshi's nearest arm but the furious captain blocked and countered, just missing. The fumes and sea and mist suddenly thickened, again, and blotted them all to shadow and sound.

uMubaya took Osan's arm and the three of them stayed close and moved along the beach into the featureless, faintly red-glowing blurring.

"Good throw," the Zulu told her.

"A cruel man," she said. "Without even the pretense of *Bushido*."

Which is itself a pretense, she thought, leaning against the changing wind, balancing on the wet, uneven sand, as they struggled on through the flowing semi-solidity of night, fog and smoke....

Further On

uMubaya stopped and gestured them to a halt. Because there was something strange about the huge, twisted shape looming, half-melted in the mist, above their heads. Imagination made it a giant beast with long, clutching arms, swaying in the seething clouds, gathered into a monstrous, primal rage.

The Zulu felt, suddenly, puny.

"Ghost, hold back!" he cried in his own language.

The fireglow from across the bay brightened and dimmed as the clouds thinned and thickened in the twisting sucks of wind.

"Aiiiii," signed a voice from beneath what proved to be an enormously thick pine tree.

Moving closer they discovered two men tied by ropes running around the girth of the bole. The black man recognized Yazu and then Gentile.

"What is this?" he wondered, in Spanish,

Taro limped closer and looked up at where Takezo hung, tied and nailed through his palms to a cross limb.

Takezo was comfortable. He was missing many pieces of the puzzle of himself but was calmly contemplating a young girl playing, alone gathering tiny purple-red berries alongside a ditch full of water that fed the rice paddies, standing up to the knees, barefoot, the blindingly reflective surface enhaloing her in gold and blue sky-shatters; though he'd never seen her as a child, he knew it was Miou. No way to tell if it were

298

dream, imagination or some stray memory. He knew she was an image and he knew she was real. It lived in both their lost hopes and purity. There was her soul refracting the world in light without pain or dull shadows....

"*Dio mio*," cried Gentile, staring up at the crucified man on the massive tree as the red-tinted foggy smoke boiled around alternately making him ghostly, then drawing open the curtain on utter, bloody solidity. "*Lasciate ogni speranza,*" he whispered.

Taro was already working on the ropes that bound the Italian to a much smaller pine as uMubaya used his sword-bladed spear to free little Yazu.

"Poor man," sighed Osan, looking up at Takezo's bleeding palms, swollen around the short suicide daggers driven into the dark wood that, if the ropes fell away, would surely slice through his hands completely.

"Blades out first," observed Taro.

"*Si*," said Gentile, rubbing his stiff, sore limbs and staring at Osan, now. "Ah," he whispered. "You...."

uMubaya had Taro up on his massive shoulders, both leaning into the rough-barked trunk, so he could reach the knives. He tugged them out with one terrific, quick yank.

Osan and Gentile helped support the ruined *ronin* as they lowered him to the ground, Yazu holding the legs until they sat him with his back to the tree, Osan holding his arm and shoulder.

The wind had momentarily lulled and the smoke-clouded vapors had pulled back far enough to show the crashing surf in the filtered fireglow.

"What cruel masks we wear," she said with bitter contempt, "to hide our true faces."

She cut away a strip of her soaked kimono with her sash dagger and wiped and dabbed Takezo's face and hands.

"Ah," breathed the *ronin*, "is this the first paradise?"

"Poor master," sighed the kneeling Yazu.

"My darkness now comes and goes," Takezo said. "Better than before..." Winced and sucked in a pained breath when Osan touched one punctured palm. "...before it was always dark...."

"Your eyes improve?" asked Taro. "They don't look good."

"It was most dark when I could still see...are these my hands?"

"Yes, master, at the ends of your arms."

"A strange place for them…" He smiled and the effect made Gentile wince. "Are there still fingers? I used to touch her with my fingers even when I didn't see her at all…." the *ronin* said to no one not even himself.

"Whom, master?" Yazu wondered.

"We'd better get going," Taro pointed out anxiously, looking around for signs of Yoshi and his men. Nothing.

"Now, I see her…sometimes…She's dead, you know…."

"Yes, *sensi*."

"But she is clear to me, now."

"We must go," Taro reaffirmed. Listened: just the sound of the massive waves crumbling into the shore.

"He has fever," said Osan.

The pictures were back and this time there were several at once; none of them moved. He looked at the man in the steel mask and dark armor, sitting in dimness intercut by shafts of golden light that seemed to imprison him…saw Yoshi's face…just his head on the floor of the barn among scrawls and blots of blood, near the feet of the man in the mask trapped behind the sunbeams and Yoshi's was smiling as if at some secret….

He heard voices; wanted them to go away. The words weren't really words and Miou, standing there in motionless silence, said things that he only felt. She seemed to float, nude, in a garden of night among mist-melted moonstains, flowers gleaming on bushes of shadow like great pearls and he had trouble focusing on her exquisite outline because it shifted like smoke. He wanted to just follow her, into that mysterious, mapless world….

The second trial

Not long past dawn the court convened. There were fewer spectators, this time. Even in the shelter of the porch the wind was unpleasant. The sand covering the yard was being sucked up into mini-whirlwinds in the walled enclosure. The sunless sky was covered by low, churning clouds. The thick, wet, moving air took off some of the humid heat. Pennants flapped wildly; shutters broke loose here and there; and at peaking gusts, shingles lifted and some bounced and sailed loose.

Colin was sitting on the sand, again, roped to the ears, facing the judge. Izu and his bodyguards were there. Issa, sallow and tense, sat on the stool beside Reiko and various clansmen and witnesses.

Everyone was somewhat distracted by the arriving storm and the mounting masses of smoke on the other side of the city that were blending into the rapid, curving clouds overhead. It was hard to pay close attention to this rather flaccid trial.

"No reason to waste time here," declared the judge. "The end is clear."

"Agreed," said Reiko. "The fire may turn this way."

"Yes. Witnesses state that the accused and the black devil kidnapped, raped and murdered the young woman, Osan."

Colin strained to read expressions and was satisfied he was doomed. This time he wasn't going to duck and hide and finally escape and become a sailor. Well, he reflected, he hadn't really escaped at all. Men, a Druid priest had told him, have strings held by fate that move them, that they refuse to notice….

"Time is short," Reiko said, standing up, gesturing at the sky. "The city burns. War threatens. We bring one more witness."

Issa just looked at him and seemed about to speak as the vassal stepped forward to testify. She'd seen him around the castle. She thought she could see the lies in his eyes. She was still trying to compose herself. The drug hadn't entirely worn off. She was still too numb to really take in the image of Reiko chopping off her husband's head. She knew she was going to have to do something about it, one way or another.

I am in so deep, she thought. *Who am I to now quibble at details?*

Because she sensed, whatever happened, she'd have to give up her life.

Still, numbly, and in a strange reprise, watched a group coming through the red-lacquered gateposts led by a woman who seemed to have a gleaming face and a monk she instantly suspected was Takezo, the bony-bandy-legged little commoner flanking them, beside big, wide, tough-looking Taro who was limping a little. And the Italian. She sighed at herself for that one. She had no real explanation for her impulses. All that seemed so thin, tawdry and uninteresting, now. Like another time, another world….

"Madness approaches," she murmured to herself. She faintly liked the idea.

301

As they came closer the judge was already waving his hands in denial.

"No, no!" he expostulated, "no more witches and dead men's heads testifying!"

The woman, Issa now saw, was wearing a polished mask and might have been a man on stage playing a female part. She caught her breath, seeing Takezo's face at closer range: swollen; burnt much worse than the first time. And his eyes now totally shut, his hands like lumps of raw, bloody meat.

"Ah," hissed Reiko. "So, here he comes for the last time."

"Arrest them all," cried the judge, "if they brandish a single body part!"

View from the darkness

Madness may be a mad idea conceived by the sane who are merely dull, Takezo proposed to himself.

Everything had blended into a single pain. He felt like a lump of muck. Everything that mattered to him had been mist in his clumsy hands. The pictures came and went with the fluctuations of his fever. Otherwise there was just darkness.

The wind pushed and twisted at him and he judged it was increasing. His feet were alright. His arms hung at his sides, hands dead weight. No way to swing a sword, he noted and concluded that was appropriate. The specific pain seemed to have been absorbed into his overall numbness.

From the voices he knew the Italian was on his left, and Taro his right. Yazu was in front and the woman behind.

"While I hung up there," Takezo suddenly spoke as his fever billowed up and he had the impression he was talking to Issa. "I realized all things come to a single point. All things," he repeated, "come to a single point."

"Takezo-san?" Gentile wondered.

*Point...point...all of this comes to one point....*Nothing else was solid in the swirl and swirling of time. *The point where I cannot hold a sword...the point...else it was for nothing....*

"We are slaves, otherwise," he said.

The woman's voice said:

"Yes. Freedom is necessary."

302

"No...just a point is necessary...." He laughed and it hurt his face. "Or else you're a slave to pointlessness."

"Do you know where we are?" Taro asked, gently.

On level ground, the wind banging around what sounded like shutters and boards; leaves whooshing; close and distant voices, undulant, calling and shouting.

"On the main street of the city of the dead," he decided.

"Maybe a pretty good guess," said the policeman.

"Put on your headpiece," suggested Gentile to the Zulu who was back in his monkish robes. Osan had on the same simple kimono.

"Put on your head first," the blind *ronin* recommended. "Too many loose hats with nothing to sit on top of.

"We are coming near the magistrate's place," Yazu put in, uneasily. "Not a place I favor."

"How's the fire doing?" Takezo asked, remembering, wincing as the bright image of the explosion replayed in a huge, motionless flare of light and heat. "It's like my life. Burning bright with destruction."

"Ah. For now, fairly far south," said the Italian. "But the wind is blowing this way. Can't see much in this smoke and mist."

"*Sensei,* we will leave you at the witch's house to recuperate," his bony pupil said. "We take Lady Osan to the trial where her parents will be found."

"He's mad from fever," Taro murmured.

"No," said Osan. "Not mad at all. Just too truthful to be endured."

Takezo tried to flex his hands: the thickness and pain almost amused him. His bare feet felt good on the warm dirt of the street.

"I must go to the trial," he said. "Yoshi and other crawling things will be there."

"Sir," said Osan's voice, "you must rest and heal."

Takezo laughed through his sore, burned lips.

"Heal what?" he asked. "But it is all clear, before me."

"You can see, master?" Yazu wondered.

"All is dark and so it is plain." Snorted. "My eyes confused me. It's better, now. At the trial there will be darkness in human form." The wind filled his ears with damp, thick air. He was trying to sense what was around him. "What of the fire?"

"It burns, Takezo-san," said Taro. "Like your fever."

"There will be rain soon, I think," remarked uMubaya inside his headpiece.

"I am amazed you can walk, like this, Takezo-san," put in Osan.

"A three-wheeled cart can be driven," he told her. "One pain takes your mind off another."

"Rain better come soon," said Taro.

"Lady," Gentile said, "it may be dangerous for you at this trial."

"Thank you, sir," she said. "In a nest of snakes is one place safer than another?"

Ah, he thought. *Yes...why, we are really walking and talking, like this....*

"Is this a wonder, foreign Lord?" asked Yazu.

"Well...I thought, imagined such things while believing she was dead, so...."

If it stays like this, Takezo was thinking, *it will be good. Just darknes....*

PART II

One

Trial again

"Are you traveling players?" demanded the judge. "What is this disrespectful mask?"

The wind was stronger, still undulating and there was a smell of smoke, now.

Takezo cocked his head. He thought his right hand fingers had just moved, a little, in the deep thickness of their pain.

"Are not courts theaters," he inquired, "where the play is always bad?"

"I know you," the judge said. "Your face is even worse this time." Then, to Osan and uMubaya: "Uncover yourselves, priest or no. This is a court of law."

"As a *zato*," the *ronin* said, sniffing the air, "my sense of smell is already stronger. Reiko is here unless a dog has just passed wind."

Someone on the porch laughed. He was sure Issa was there, too, and pictured her smiling behind her fan. The fever was down; he was more himself.

"Blind man," said the chamberlain, "where is your begging bowl?"

"Why? Want to rob me?" To Taro: "Open my pouch and put the ring in my hand."

The judge was saying something with considerable ferocity that the wind blew, mainly, away. As Takezo held out his blood-crusted, agonizing paw, Taro dropped the ring on it. He heard Osan, voice muffled by her old-man-mask she'd picked up beside the road on the way. He remembered the conversation from between his semi-hallucinations.

"Treason and treachery," she said. "Where is *Daimio* Hideo?"

"Show yourselves!" repeated the judge

"Murdered by evil assassins!" yelled Reiko. "And the villain behind it is known!"

"I know one villain!" Osan's voice, just ahead of Takezo who felt the fever coming back – not so good because there were pictures, again.

The suit of armor stood there with dull fire inside the eyeslits.

305

If your eyes are flame, his mind commented, *do you have smoke for brains?*

"I will defeat you," he told it.

Two

Osan

She moved up close to the porch where they sat, wind tugging and whipping at their loose clothes. The chamberlain was still declaiming but she only partly followed his words because anger and disgust blotted everything out.

She pushed her palm out at him as if it were a weapon.

"You," she cried, behind her old-man mask, "you are false!" Then she pulled it off. Issa stood up, obviously as surprised as Reiko wasn't. "Where is my father?"

"Who is this?" the magistrate asked.

"The dead girl," the *ronin* said to the fire-eyed metal face. "We always bring the departed with us."

"My daughter," Issa said.

Takezo felt something...her voice showed feeling he didn't expect. There was a tremble there. The judge fidgeted; wind blew; big raindrops sailed wide and scattered, slanting nearly sideways in the veering gusts.

"What is the purpose of this trial?" the blind *ronin* addressed the mask-face, the only thing he could see.

"To reveal evil!" the metal face answered – except he knew Reiko's voice.

The chamberlain raised his gold and red fan over his head as a clump of horsemen came barreling through the gates, armored, led by Yoshi, his face set, it seemed to Osan, in anger so deep it had been carved into his flesh.

Habits set bars of steel around our souls, she thought.

"Where is my father, my mother?" she asked.

"Dead," Issa said, eyes looking like she might laugh or weep.

"Slain, while helpless, by Nobunaga's puppets!" declared Reiko, looking at Izu so that the *daimio* gripped his swordhilt and his men bristled.

306

Yoshi and his men arrived, sandy dust swirling as they reined-up, closing around the proceedings in a loose half ring. The judge was frowning.

"What does this mean?" he demanded.

Osan held the old-man-mask up at Reiko as if it were a talisman. He was glowering at her.

"Here is your true face, vile deceiver," she informed him.

Her mother's eyes seemed calm while her features tensed. Big raindrops spattered loudly on the wooden overhang.

"Quiet!" he responded. "I am your father now."

"Would my father put his hands on my body?" Osan demanded.

"What words are these?" cried Issa.

"Silence!" ordered the judge. "This is a trial, not a dispute in a tavern!"

"Your lover betrayed my father," Osan said, holding up the mask. He -"

"Quiet!" yelled the chamberlain, again, raising his fan. To his men: "Take her away and protect her! She has been given evil potions. Her mind is not her own but filled with Nobunaga's evil fumes!"

"Let us have order!" shouted the furious and confused magistrate, leaping to his feet – unusual. "Let the young lady speak!"

Two clan bodyguards moved in position behind the young woman, hesitating because Izu's men had moved with them, faces set for combat. The tension was peaking. Yoshi leaned down, studying *Zato Takezo* with one eye on Reiko.

"This man," Osan said, pointing at Reiko whose fan rapidly tap-tapped along his leg "came upon me alone in my bath. He declared his passion." She covered her face with the mask and spoke with a coarse, guttural voice. "You must be mine, you are so sweet that no heavenly spirit can match you. I wish your sweet feet to tread upon my helpless body as if I were a poor mat."

"The poison potion speaks!" cried ever resourceful Reiko as all eyes were on him, Yoshi curling a semi-smirk across his harsh lips.

"The chamberlain is not on trial here," observed the judge, nevertheless clearly interested in the irrelevant testimony.

"Take her away for her own good, as I commanded," Reiko repeated. Having to repeat was not good and everyone knew it. He looked at Yoshi who smirked wider but nodded.

307

Gentile was ready, hand on the dagger he'd acquired. uMubaya was looking back at the burning city, the wildly curling and scattering flames as if, indeed, somebody's hell had burst through the earth.

"He groped his hands all over me," Osan said, "all in a lecherous sweat."

Then dropped the cruel-faced old-man mask from her extended arm, sleeves fluttering, as you'd drop, Gentile thought, a rotten fish.

"Seize her" yelled Reiko, lashing out with his fan.

Issa was in front of him, now. Two of Yoshi's men dismounted and stood and added weight to those around the girl. The raindrops were hitting hard enough to sting.

"Who is next to die?" Issa asked. "Am I next?"

"Be still, woman," snapped Reiko.

Their retainers seemed undecided. The captain who'd witnessed Reiko's strange antics with the bloodstain, looked troubled and considered his superior with leveled eyes.

Issa moved closer to him. She seemed to be following the storm clouds or studying the billows from the great fire that (as the massive, oncoming sheets of rain poured down) threw up fresh gouts of steamy smoke. Distracted, Reiko didn't look at her.

"My daughter?" she asked, semi-shouting over the increasing windsound, shielding her eyes from the dust with her fan.

Three

Takezo Zato

Takezo was listening but the voices were filtered through the mouths of black-armored riders on steel-looking horses who were clambering up out of the blazing pit that had just opened there, wrung gusts clinging around them, buffeting the landscape, wilting trees as they passed, charring houses, setting peoples' clothes aflame. A man walked in front of them. He had armor but no head.

The leader was mounted and masked and Takezo knew him by his fire-eyes and palpable fury: fury like radiant heat from gouting lava. His own rage was cold but a match for it.

He wasn't sure the voices made any sense – why would they? The waking world or whatever it was that time chewed and swallowed was basically a meaningless jumble outside the clarity of fever. The darkness blended it into a soothing, motionless silence. Maybe that was all he ever wanted.

The flame-men were coming to him. Fine. He had questions and answers for them. The leader had to be there. Which? One more mystery…maybe the last….

"Come," he said. "I'll cut off your mask and see the true fire of your face!"

Four

uMubaya

The rain whipped past faster and faster. He glanced back over the south wall where the smoke from the city massed thick, he thought, as root soup. The rain seethed heavy down there and deeper billows of steamy smoke boiled up into the sweeping stormwind.

uMubaya felt ready. He was there and his history had no more substance than a dream. Gripped his *naginata* and nodded, a little amazed by the curse of his fate: he'd turned to the ship and the sea; headed up the gangplank keeping his back to the shore. He never looked behind at his diminishing country as they worked their way out of the South African bay less than two years ago. He faced what lay out before him, never measuring time or distance like the obsessively "civilized." He simply was where he was.

He wasn't bound to duty yet unlike his father the King or a married man. And he didn't even have to think about her; but he did. That was incurable….

The first day he could get to his feet he moved shakily out of the netting of thorns, vines and branches she'd built around him. He had a gnawing hunger and terrific thirst. He felt faded, dried-out and vague as a twist of dew mist.

It was a clear morning. Blue shocks of water left from last night's downpour showed on the plain as the sun topped the ragged, bare hills. He was near the line of twisted trees where the lioness had charged him.

He took a few steps and knelt to cup a drink from the nearest puddle. The earth-scented coolness was a miracle in his mouth. Nothing had ever been so good and complete.

She'd even left dried food in his bag and he chewed, slowly, squatting over the imperceptibly shrinking puddle as the sun tilted higher,

309

intent on the wet, green scent, blinking like a child at his own reflection cut up by bright sky and spiny grasses.

Then movement...a caterpillar was working its way around the splash as if it were a lake, steady, legs ceaseless, fat body struggling on, barely moving but maybe racing breathlessly from its own point-of-view.

He felt vague, tentative. After half a day of semi-tracking he believed more than saw; decided he was like the caterpillar: straining his entire being to move inches in a world of miles.

The landscape was a drowsy murmur under the hot, bright sky. The redbrown, ragged mountains hemmed in this long, rolling valley.

He finally stopped at a crease of stream that zigzagged across the fields, then waded into the middle (maybe 3 feet deep) and just stood there, watching his reflection emerge as the ripples settled, as if his dark shape coalesced, backtilted, from the soft flowing....

'Look there,' he said, 'see a fool.'

He went on, anyway...didn't count days...now and then believed he'd glimpsed her far ahead, a shadow a movement...on...sometimes thinking he was back in his fever sleep when he got weak and tired and the hills and clumps of trees reeled by in rocking blurs...after awhile he was sore but getting stronger and the forest he'd entered was getting denser. His scars were stiff but she'd done a good job and they were healing well.

Leaning against the shifting gale, it came back to him as he watched the now smoldering city above the wall.

I followed the shadow of a ghost then, he thought, turning back to the gathering violence in the yard. *Maybe I still do....*

Five

Takezo Zato

"Get me a sword!" he said to Yazu over the wind.

"Master?"

"Sword. Now. How it begins is how it ends."

He was listening as if his ears had eyes and that other strange sense was reaching out.

The fever seemed low. Felt clear: there was nothing to see but nothing. Felt his disciple press the swordhilt into his right palm.

He gradually closed the hand, listening to Issa, Reiko and others bickering, demanding and accusing in the wind's undulations. The smoke

310

in the air was thickening. Felt like he was gripping shattered glass: his fingerjoints were pure pain. As he clamped shut the blood started to flow and made a sticky paste of his scabs.

"The sword sticks to your hands," he quoted, too low to be heard.

It locked. The pain was now glue. Cocking his head, he started moving forward a few steps, Yazu beside him.

Please, he sort of prayed, *no more fever...no pictures....*

Heard Osan's wind-twisted voice shouting into a welter of counter-shouts and curses:

"This...man is...betrayer of...."

And the Italian:

"Release her, *schiavettzi!*"

"Cease! Cease! Cease!" cried the judge.

Cocking his head, the blinded *ronin* moved towards the voices, blade clamped to his hand. The weight felt good.

"No seeing," he muttered. "No more mad pictures."

Outcries and struggling sounds. A gust shoved him sideways and he felt Yazu stumble and then a sting of rain.

Voices for and against the chamberlain were being raised. Yoshi shouted something lost in a snapping gust. A clash of arms behind him and outside the walls.

"Where are you, enemy?" called out the blind *ronin.*

In a burningly vivid scene the blaze peeled back like a curtain and there was the masked and armored lord resembling a giant frog with his widespread feet and bulky armor.

Six

Gentile

Madness, he thought. *What next?*

As the smoky clouds blotted past, for a moment it was a picture with figures emerging into movement, robes flapping, swords waving, horseshapes looming and over the low wall a mass of foot soldiers and riders coming down the middle-distance slope formed and unformed into a two dimensional sketch....

For that moment he lost concentration as if the deadly reality around him was less intense and real than its design. At the same time he was already moving, reaching for the samurai holding Osan who was yelling at her mother:

311

"Your husband dead! Why is your hair so long?"

Loose, cape-like outer robe flapping like a flag, Issa looked wildly around and snatched the 3 foot long tail of silk-bound hair from behind herself and sliced it near the neck with her short dagger, then flung the length into Reiko's face where it looped and was held by the wind.

"Rapist and traitorous murderer!" she cried as he swung his fist, missed her and she got her blade somewhere into his side as his second blow caught her cheek and sent her spinning into the smoky clouds of wind.

Fighting broke out between his committed men and the other Hideo clansmen. Yoshi's fighters went after Izu and the others. Gentile got a hand on the massive man holding Osan who was struggling like a butterfly in a net as a gust of thickening, wind-blasted rain tipped him. He staggered past, ripping the floppy sleeve as the samurai's instant draw and cut just clipped his shoulder. The blade was so keen it barely hurt.

Seven

Yoshi

Yoshi was worried about the storm's effect on the armies advancing to the city. He was cursing the foreign weapons that had proved a disaster.

"Temptation," he muttered to himself. "See the result!"

Rain ripped into them. His always simmering anger and frustration bubbled up. Fear, too, because there was no space to fail in. He tried to decide what to do first.

And here was that Takezo, back like a ghost in a play; not singing or dancing, at least. Was he really blind? He'd been ordered not to kill him with weapons except in self-defense – which explained the technicality of the crucifixion.

"Time to strike," he said. "Too late to think."

One of his men leaned from the saddle close enough to talk.

"Orders, captain?"

"Take the girl. Kill Izu. Protect Reiko. I'll deal with the rest."

He was thinking what fools they all were to stand in line and bow to authority. One reason he resented Takezo was because he didn't have to pretend to bow. Yoshi dreamed of chaos where he could step over the lords and take their seats. He concieved that when the war was won, Tanba would choose to remain in the shadows he so loved and let Yoshi rule. The idea was less than real but more than fantasy.

Holding his mount in place, he watched Takezo shuffling forward against the wind.

"Blind fool," he hissed, "take your final steps to nowhere." He felt it like a cold well rising within: he could displace them. Anyone could be killed, just strike first. He had that from his father. Consider Iaysu, who put sandals on samurai's feet, now Nobunaga's chief general. "A man can rise."

Bending into the wind he chucked the horse close to Takezo and swept a cut at him. Either a gust or the *ronin's* sixth sense shifted him clear. A miss. Yoshi pulled his horse aside to avoid a possible counter. His ankle still hurt from the clipping cut the *ronin* had landed in the rain-blasted garden after the *Noh* drama.

Takezo was lost behind a screen of dust, smoke and sheets of erratic rain. Yoshi's horse shied and fell back from the terrific gust. Struggling figures were all around. Then Yoshi was close to Colin, the Scot, who was on his feet, tilted, still wrapped in rope like a roast beef.

Yoshi kicked his rearing horse, yanked the reins, as the animal plunged and threw him, already running with the gale, vanishing into the blinding atmosphere.

He was close to the Scot who could only move his legs a few inches at a time and was, painfully, trying to hobble towards the dimly visible porch, wobbling, crouching, falling forward, then back, then sideway, reminding the samurai of an ant in an empty sake bowl.

"Where are you going, foreigner?" Yoshi said, stepping close. He felt a cold rush of spite and anger. "You are helpless," he sneered. "I am not!"

The day before, in the same inner garden where Miou had sat with Tanba and pondered the bleak pebbles and gray walls around the circular, fishless pool 10 feet across, full of lily and lotus, Yoshi conferred with his master. His steps crunched as he paced around the rim, wrapped in a dark robe, looking at the slim leader who was sitting crosslegged on a low bench, staring into the water as if to read something in the broken reflection of the gray, fast-moving clouds.

'You protect him,' Yoshi said, 'though he's a threat.'

'I protect you, too, though you are a fool.'

Yoshi stopped, then started pacing again; Tanba didn't look up.

313

'I am your son,' the stocky Captain declared, stopping across the pool and glaring.

'But not the only one.' His father didn't look up, hands folded inside his dark kimono. 'I know what you want but you will take your place when our enemies are thrown down. Take pride in your training and not in yourself.'

His son stood still as stone and wasn't even not looking at him, now, as he said:

'I do my duty.'

'Do more. Do this: after you dispose of the obvious opponents, finish the one who thinks he is our friend.'

'Yes, father.'

'Reiko is weak and subject to women.'

'Yes.'

'Do not trouble yourself about your position.'

'No, father.'

'No reason for anger. Just duty.'

'Yes, father.'

'Your "yes" sounds like no.'

After that conversation Yoshi took a closed kaga to a big, gold-gated teahouse behind a harsh-looking garden of sharp dark rocks and a wide, sluggish stream that almost suggested a moat, reflecting dull gray clouds darkening as twilight seemed to seep from shadows. A few spatters of rain plinked down.

Passing serving women and one courtesan with a pile of hair she seemed to be actually balancing on her head, he went directly to a private second floor room. It was lavishly decorated with flowers almost to the point of bad taste. The air was thick with perfume and incense.

On a mat behind a floor table full of orchids and lotus, sat a very young beauty with lustrous hair held with combs and picks, full, pouty lips and big eyes that showed a kind of general, lewd contempt as if they'd been stained by what they'd had to see in so few years. Yoshi knelt-sat opposite and extended his thick, short-fingered hand for a sake.

The courtesan hesitated, just a beat, before pouring one and holding it out to the stocky Captain through a break in the floral excess. Yoshi didn't react to the subtle near discourtesy – which would have surprised those who knew him. He just kept looking at the exquisite *downtilted face across the flowers from him; the long, delicate fingers, knowing, mocking eyes.*

Sweating in the humidity, Yoshi knocked back the sake and said:
'Come close.'

Again the hesitation, pink tongue moistening the lower lip as if some sweet juice lingered there.

'Ah,' the soft voice said, 'as you wish, handsome Captain.'

Yoshi opened his robe, bare barrel chest gleaming in the fading, gray daylight.

'You want a present first, you greedy whore?' he wondered.

'Ah, you have a present, my handsome Captain?'

Yoshi sneered, as the beauty slowly unfolded and in a shimmer of pale silks and flowerscent knelt-walked, very slowly, around the table.

'Like to kill you,' Yoshi sighed, reaching with suppressed violence for that delicate, fluid breath of loveliness.

'Then must I die, Shi-san.' Placed one perfect, even-toed, golden foot on his knee. 'How sad.'

The sweaty, blocky samurai took it by the heel and pressed the soft toes to his lips, like a greedy gourmand with a delicacy. He growled in his throat with desire and frustration.

'This passion sickens me,' he said as the remote-eyed whore pressed the tasty rounded bits into his mouth.

'I have a cure,' was the reply.

Yoshi's blunt hands groped, almost violently over the completely naked, infinitely smooth, firm flesh under the kimono. Opened the long, slim legs holding both feet and looked down at the dark gleamings between the parted thighs. Inhaled the musk and perfume as he dipped his head down, heart pounding, body knotted, desire's flesh achingly hard, powerful, unstoppable and utterly weak because he was helpless before his desire, a slave of a slave, he had already contemptuously thought.

Bent there, as if to drink at a pool, he closed his hand on the hard, hot, agonizing shaft and rubbed as tenderly as a mother might caress a baby, gasping, holding himself back so close all the sleek, golden flesh was a blur in the blurring twilight.

'No other can have you,' he choked out, stroking up and down. 'No one!'

The boy sighed with pleasure.

'Mmm,' he voiced, both hands fluttering over the blocky,

315

obsessed lovers cheeks and shoulders. 'Difficult, Shi-san.'

'So beautiful,' Yoshi gasped, taking the tip with his tongue and lips, a hint of salt and sour-sweet crushed flowers. 'I...I will buy you a house...' Sucked, longingly and deep, pulled back. 'Ahhhh...gold...soon I will have gold and...no other can have you!' With a shudder of need he took the sugary stick as deep as he could until he choked, a little.

'Ahh, you are my joy, Shi-san.' Smiled as the dimness closed down. 'Turn me over, sweet slave, and kiss the place you love best.'

With a groan of helpless need, the samurai gripped the sleek, resilient buns and twisted the boy around without his tongue losing contact with the delicious flesh and buried his face and his being as he'd been commanded, there, in the reek of too-rich flowers and cloying clouds of thick incense.

'You...' he mouthed, as he helpless lapped and suckled. 'I will kill you, someday...I will kill you....'

'Yes, lord,' the boy sighed, facedown, now. 'Spear me to death, now...now...ah, now....'

"You are an insect," Yoshi told Colin who stopped struggling on and turned to face him.

"What say me?" Colin wondered.

"Stupid insect. So stupid. Unimportant."

"What?"

"Meaningless sack of guts. Die and nothing changes. Live and nothing matters. So I step on you."

Red hair, pale skin, blue eyes like bright chips of glass: a foreignness that sickened. Emblem of a curse. Powerless against Yoshi. Actions about to be stopped forever; brain about to be emptied of foreign thoughts...emptied.

Smoke and clouds swirled around as he struck at the alien paleness and jarring colors. Behind his battered face the Scot looked remote, uninterested.

"No more, I free you," said Yoshi. "Ha-Ha. Free myself, too." Saw the delicate neck of the boy whore in the almost sickening room of flowers and sweet smoke, the lips, the painted face, the sweet contemptuous passion. Saw his expression change as the blade parted the head from body, the perfect, infinitely sensual eyes showing a soul that could no more be truly possessed than smoke could be held in the hand.

"Die, homosexual!"

Eight

Colin

Thought about ducking and trying to roll away into the storm-blast's obscurities as the fighting erupted all around. Couldn't make himself. He was staring up at the hillslope where the two armies jarred together: now blurred...now solid...now gone....

He refused to actually look at his killer. Why give him the satisfaction? So he stared off into the blinding, swirling air where sudden clumps of men clashed, swords and spears sticking and ripping, blood and shouts and screams torn away by the wind.

Then looked up at the clouds, piling in thick and wild, rain slashing through harder so that the stocky armored killer was a shadow at the edge of his sight and that was alright because he'd accepted it all and was ready for the wind, to let it lift him and ride it, wondering why it was taking so long to happen...long enough for an unbidden memory:

A fast-flowing mountain stream cut by dense trees, sky like shattered crystal. Spiky red flowers lined the banks. He was a boy barefoot in a ragged kilt, stepping with infinite care through the raspy long grasses and brush to where he overlooked the water, saw himself in the shimmering brightness.

Looked through his reflection at the rippling fronds, quirks and swirls of current where a cluster of trout hung, swimming just enough to not move.

The seven hung there fragile as a breath. He'd never seen them feed or go any distance without coming back and taking the same positions again.

He'd tried tossing pebbles, larger stones, poking sticks to break up their formation. They came together, each time, as if drawn back, the way water itself could only be momentarily hollowed, splashed or blocked.

Now, one suddenly began moving upstream and he followed. His memory was an impression: as he followed, close to the bank, pushing through bushes, hopping rocks, gripping branches, slipping; keeping it in sight, the sliver glitter always just ahead of him, zipping and then lazing through light and shadow as if it meant to lead him. He chased on as if it were life or death, losing all sense of time, spatters of sun and shade

317

flicking past...then a sudden wall of overhanging rock, wet and too sheer to climb so the last thing he saw was the slim, steady, effortless fish flashing like an arrow around the bend and then, winking into the shadows beyond... gone....

So he wasn't surprised by the cold push through his neck, a pressure like a violent cough that tilted away his head. There was just the stream that wasn't just a memory anymore and he was following the fish, this time, up around that mysterious bend into the mystery he'd been blocked from solving so long ago, in childhood....

Nine

uMubaya

The big Zulu rushed to help the fallen Italian.

"Help her!" Gentile cried, staggering against the wind which was ratcheting up towards full typhoon level.

Horses were struggling with their riders and loose ones were bolting; the sound of clashing armies from the slope above. Gentile stagger-stepped after Osan and her captors as they made for the door of the court building where others were taking shelter.

Clutching a post as the smoke blotted past, uMubaya saw the cloudy, armless-looking outline he didn't realize was Colin, bound like a sausage, being struck by a squat machine-like shape he didn't know was Yoshi...cloud gust...then the bound shape was a head shorter.

Another vicious gust sent shingles flying...then the blot of Izu ducking under a spearthrust and then pirouetting in the vicious draft, vanishing...blotted...Colin's bound body still leaned on the air as the Zulu crouched closer, then went down in a slow spin.

In a blast of rage and recognition he charged the armored outline...

Ten

Colin

As the fish went up around the bend into the mysterious shadows of his childhood's highland hills, he was still seeing a blurred swarm of shapes, that might have been men and horses, going up on a wild tilt; then a silent, jarring but unfelt impact as the world soundlessly faded. The sandy ground spun, then half- spun...rocked...stopped at a tilt...a shrinking tunnel of vision as memory slacked away and he recognized a woman struggling to her knees, her cheek crunched flat into the sand, her eyes so close and big...nothing moved, just the shrinking circle of fading that melted her expression into mist...shadow...nothing....

Eleven

Osan

Having only partly slipped the grip of Yoshi's samurai, Osan was staring, inches away, eye-to-eye with the blue wide stare of the nearly upright head where (she wordlessly grasped) light was dying nothing like a sunset or shutting windows or a blown-out candle flame.

And her voice lost in the wind and his silence, her tears breaking up her sight into a burning blur:

"I apologize! So, so sorry! So...."

As she was jerked back upright, brutally, back up into roaring wind, shouts, screams and clash of arms...dragged away she glimpsed the blind Takezo crouching forward suddenly surrounded by samurai.

She saw him, through the boiling atmosphere, slash them away or maybe it was the wind because they twisted, flew and vanished in what might have been magic or illusion.

Twelve

Takezo Zato

He felt a close miss snap just short of his head. He didn't know it was Yoshi and didn't bother to counter. Let the wind move him because the fever-things were back; in fever-logic, with speed beyond even the air of imagination, he sliced and shredded the headless attacker who spurted flame from his open neck (as other demons in black armor) closed with him. His sword was finally the same as his mind and struck like a thought and they fell like bad ideas, and flopped and shrieked around him. He wondered, somewhere in the fever, if anything were actually happening. Then the vision faded, again.

I am supposed to get to the bottom of this wash of sewage and, I suppose, swim...so they pay me in gold and....

In the blinding atmosphere, jerked and pummeled by nature or things unnatural his blindness was no longer a true disadvantage. In the right circumstance, bad could be good.

319

As if they moved far and near he heard Reiko's shouts…Issa and others…the words became wind….

The fever moved far and near, too. It was moving away, just then, so he wanted to help Issa. He felt closer to her and it wasn't just because their bodies had beaten together.

He followed her voice, when he could track it, groping along the porch, crouched into the full, steady typhoon pressure. No visions now, just blankness. The rain slashed.

I am here because I get to the bottom of things…like empty holes…and careers….

Felt the fever pulsing back and didn't care. Liked the sudden glowing landscape where the atmosphere was slowly billowing coals and seemed to softly sustain him like water a fish so he didn't have to struggle along. Forms were visible in the lee of the glowing wind like shadows in the sun.

There was Issa, Reiko and others in what seemed a forest of sword-bladed rock-like trees where dwarfish, taloned, fanged creatures shifted and prowled.

Two of them were pulling a beautiful female who seemed an unearthly shape of soft, cloudy light, their harsh hands blotching her with blackness. He swam in pursuit.

He understood: a gout of darkness like a mouth formed a cavern in the fire and it seemed to be swallowing everything into that steel and stone landscape.

The fever heat seemed to clarify his mind; he saw with supernatural focus and concentration. There, *there* was the mystery's source and the one he sought, the last face behind the last mask of his life, down there in whatever incomprehensible fortress sitting on whatever razor-edged and steel-clawed throne.

So he swam into a charge, sword growing from his arm, sweeping up to strike….

Thirteen

uMubaya

The black man reached the porch ahead of Gentile. As he sprawled down again, a samurai bounced off him going the opposite way.

In a flap of blinding air he saw small Lord Izu clutching one of his men, spattered with blood, crouching, protecting his eyes.

320

The Zulu held a post in one hand, *naginata* in the other watching Issa, Osan and the samurai reeling along the porch to the doorway; the magistrate, oversized robes snapping like a flag, sailed out into the yard, was knocked over, then disappeared into the smoky dust. The clash of arms was all around now, formed then unformed by the wind.

This is worse than at sea. I think we may all die….

He was crawling into the semi-solid wall of air as boards pulled loose from walls and flip-flopped past. Things hummed in the air. A deep roar filled everything. He imagined the world being blown smooth, people sailing like helpless birds….

Pulled himself into the doorway. The room was full of friends and foes. Inside, the noise was worse; all hissings, whistlings, howlings and wavering shrieks. And then, there was Reiko, in the dim, secondary, streaky gray daylight, standing on a raised platform like an actor shouting, Osan under one arm, sword in the other hand, two bodyguards with glazed looks of blind loyalty beside him, his voice a raw rasp of furious authority.

"Our armies cannot be defeated!" he yelled. "I am lord of the clan! I marry Osan! Her mother is maddened by the murder of Lord Hideo by sworn enemies!"

He noted men in plain robes all through the room, armed like samurai.

When Issa and Gentile made a move towards Reiko they took them down, almost instantly. They had to be *ninjas*.

He threw off his robe and crouched, in his tunic, black skin gleaming, huge muscles reminding some there of the life-sized guardian statues of the gods of war come to life. Headed for Reiko, spear low and ready.

Everyone paused because he wasn't acting anymore Japanese than he looked: semi-dancing from foot-to-foot and chanting, deep and powerful from his slightly protuberant, muscular belly. The warriors felt the *chi* gathered in him.

Reiko's face was locked in insane rage. His left hand clutched the girl. The spots of blood from the slight wound Issa had inflicted stained his side. Dust streamed and puffed in through the shutters.

"Black foulness!" he cried. "Die!"

Thrust Osan into the arms of a bodyguard and came at the prince who snarled in Zulu:

"You are bad!"

Other warriors attacked at the same time. uMubaya was unmoved. He snatched up a thick wooden stool for a shield and blocked the first downcut from a *ninja* and countered with a thrust to the thigh, then parried the next cut as Reiko slashed and danced into the fight.

"You," cried out Osan from the platform, "you are...." But she was lost for words. Unheard of. "You are...."

And she twisted and whirled herself loose from the easy grip of her captor who was concentrating on the fight in the center of the room where the Chamberlain had just chipped the stool-shield and uMubaya creased the face of the second attacker with his *naginata* blade.

To her mother's amazement and admiration the daughter leapt onto Reiko's back and clawed his face, effectively saving the black man from the sidecut that would have split his side open.

"Her new intellectual ideas," Issa said.

Fourteen

Takezo Zato

Thousands of armored dwarves were swarming in waves over the black, harsh, razor-edged landscape. They dribbled flame like shaken braziers. He was pleased because he welcomed a chance to hit back at the shadows, even if he drowned in their darkness. He'd had enough lies and edges and blurs. Now he had eyes that saw only the nightmares sprung from burning sickness.

And then they were gone. The fever popped, again, like a bubble on a stream. They were gone and he was staggering to his knees as the stormwind dragged him backwards and across the yard he couldn't see towards the gate he didn't know was there.

Clash of arms, shouts, horses screaming. He brought up against what he didn't know was the gatepost; held on. A rider crashed past. Heard the *chukk* of a blade hitting flesh and armor, the sound sucked past on the intolerable wind. A following groan....

"It's dark," he said.

Voices suddenly close by, separating out from the general din and roar. He caught fragments.

"...Nobunaga men hold hills...we...impossible to...."

A voice he knew, the masked *ninja* master:

"Wait for the storm center...all must lie flat until...."

Have I found you? He asked himself. *In fate and wind?*

Held the thick post that made him think of being onstage, his right hand was dully throbbing, sword locked in his swollen fingers, ready to strike. Tried to hone in on the source of the voice. Then another, even worse:

"...so...refuse...." Yoshi yelled. "I...kill and...."

"Here I am!" cried Takezo. "Are you blind men too?"

Let's finish this, he thought.

"Who's that?" Yoshi wondered.

"Over there," another yelled.

"Where?"

"Here, you shit-squeezings!" the *ronin* yelled. "Let's finish!"

"I see the filth!" screamed Yoshi. "There!"

Takezo felt him coming through the mad wind. Was relaxed and ready.

"No!" commanded Tanba's voice through the mad wind.

Too late. Takezo felt Yoshi strike and countered like lightning; except a terrific gust spun him halfway around the post and he heard and felt the sword hit the wood as his own blade cut air. He tried a follow-up but was blown spinning away. The voices were drowned by the massive roar. Bits of detritus spatted into him. He rolled across the sandy ground, rolled back into the fever-world....

Fifteen

Issa

She whipped the deadly spike from her coiffure and jammed the needle through the ear and into the brain of the man holding her. Felt him spasm as she jerked herself away.

"Insect," she whispered, meaning Reiko, rushing at him where he struggled to spin her daughter from his back as uMubaya stood off his attackers. There was shame in her fury. She knew she'd not outlive this day, one way or another.

As he twisted around she glimpsed his face, streaked with blood from Osan's ripping nails as he rammed his elbow into her ribs and she dropped away but managed to clutch his knees.

"Crazy girl!" he cried, trying to kick free as Issa reached him.

There was no help or time. The various factions were still fighting. The Zulu had knocked one man down and stabbed the other and was

323

turning to the Chamberlain. He'd have to kill Issa to save his life. His sword went up....

Sixteen

Takezo Zato

He was at the foot of the jet black, shiny platform where the frog-like lord in darkly gleaming armor and red-eyed mask of a beautiful, softly smiling, somehow feminine face, moved in a very slow, stately dance. He was singing. His dwarfish minions were all around among the blade-edged rocks and steely trees.

Takezo understood the song. Understood the façade. Understood many things there were no words for. Like the beautiful female clothed in a cloudy exquisiteness. The frog was beckoning and singing to Takezo. Behind him the vague beauty seemed to have blended onto a giant screen painting of vast cliffs lifting up into a wild, heavenly skyscape of formally wild clouds and golden beings. Below were dark, multi-armed fiends. The black, gleaming frog was in his face, dancing, gesturing.

"You are one of us," he said in a croak and hiss. "Come."

Except Takezo was already up on the platform and running for the screen, aware if he got there fast enough he could blend into it, the space, sweet, soft, infinite colors, tender shades of edgeless love....

Gone.

Wind like a wall falling on him, rolling him and he heard the thunk of missed swordcuts and the clink as his blade met another, Yoshi's. He was flat on his belly, the erratic blasts ripping at his kimono.

"Still here," he grunted.

"Blind dog!" he thought he heard Yoshi snarl.

Another voice, just above his head, the one he wanted to hear, a hissing purr of command:

"Yoshi! Do nothing!"

A muffled response. Takezo groped around with his blade as if it were a cane. The numbing pain and exhaustion was starting to press him down flat like a vast stone.

"What else from him?" he responded. Touched something and twisted to snap a cut which hit nothing.

The voice was on the other side, now, and close.

"Wait!" he said.

Is he a snake? Takezo wondered.

"Why, killer of the innocent?" he returned. "More speeches to come?"

Takezo crawled back and to the left to maybe flank him.

This is the last man I mean to slaughter, he said to himself. *Assuming I can....*

"Just this," was the response, audible over the incredible roaring that blotted almost all other sound away. "Why did I hire you?"

"What?"

What? Good question....

Their heads were very close, now, so that the shouting was, strangely intimate and, still, barely heard.

"I already had the answers, Takezo. That was the point. So why did I hire you?"

The weight was pressing him down into darkness, again. His mind moved ponderously. He wanted the fever back where things were clearer.

"Why? Ah...."

"To find me. To find *me.*"

"Find...."

He was on the stage trying to reach the immense screen painting where the female shapes vied with giant flowers and undulant waterflows for sleek, curved and graceful perfection; the dwarfish, frog-looking leader blocked him, arms held out wide with fire-dripping ragged-edged swords in each. They were dancing and he was aware of music, this time, almost too deep to separate from the overall roar that sounded like mountains of fire and torrents of wild wind out in the surrounding darkness.

It might have been Miou, face and form blurred, veiled by sweet mists of perfume and the filmy translucence of those infinitely pale blossoms. The clash of fire and steel didn't matter. Nothing mattered but reaching her, slipping away, melting into that impossible forest where the only meaning was silence.

'Stand aside,' he demanded.

'Embrace me, my son,' was the response. *'Leave dreaming to sleepers. Awaken with me.'*

'No! There's only she. Shit on all the rest.'

Dozens of the tiny, machine-like creatures, spitting sparks and rasping, discordance swarmed around him. Metallic shrieks, rasps, clanks, bangings and long howls that might have been a storm-wind itself blowing through their empty skulls.

He tried to run and was tripped and held by the pack of them. He writhed and rolled and kicked. Got a hand on the master's leg and yanked him down. The ineffable picture loomed over them, and his sight flowed up and back into it, into the misty hints and partial forms and....

He was back in the howling darkness but his left hand agonizingly gripped what seemed a wristbone. That was good. Better to be holding something because they were rolling with other debris in some direction with, it seemed, nothing to check them....

Seventeen

Gentile

Felt the blood trickling behind his ear where he'd been hit by something. He realized he'd been unconscious. Came back... to a ripping-screaming, as the roof and walls tore apart under the incredible pressure of the storm. As he became aware of the blurred struggles of Issa, Reiko, Osan, the Zulu and others in the room that was suddenly open and roofless, he felt the strange fear (that children feel) of being bereft of protection, betrayed into an orphan's undefended world.

A flash and he was rolling to his feet and lunging, once more, to defend Osan. He felt like a boy because he actually shouted, in Italian:

"A, madre mia! Madre mia!"

And then, in an explosion of shattered wood, they were all scattered, tumbling, staggering, flopping the length of the vanishing building.

Is not the solid world a dreaming? his mind asked even as he flipped end over end with the rest.

So no blow landed and they all went out into the storm-blasted street. Reiko gripped Osan while two of his men looped and tied a rope around her neck and handed it to him. Issa was out of sight in the smoke and dirt blinded landscape and semi-solid rain. uMubaya was behind a mass of logs which left him in an eddy of relative calm. Gentile crawled closer, intent on Osan. He noted the wind was actually ripping clothes off people. He noted that Reiko was dragging her behind him as he clawed forward. It seemed mad. Where was he going? The world was blowing away.

Eighteen

Issa

Was going the wrong way because she hadn't seen her newly-exed lover dragging
her child towards the gate, the wind at his back. She groped along on her knees, eyes mainly shut as the wind clawed and rain slapped across her face.

Insect, she kept thinking. *I will stamp you to pulp....*

Yet, her mind was not entirely focused on that alone. Which peripherally surprised her. Her daughter yes, and the treachery of Reiko, yes; but she wanted to find Takezo. Desperately. Made no sense; desperately.

Free my child...help me, Takezo....

"But what can that blind fool do?" she retorted into the blotting howl. "What disturbs my mind?"

First help Osan...then find him? Why? He has no power, no prospects...I have no reason to persist...put an end to this...this life is stupid...what could that masterless samurai do for anyone? Are there not many lovers his equal? No power, no wealth...no....

Nothing but the ripping wind, sucking her breath away, stinging, blasting her down into the saturated earth.

"Osan!" she yelled, futilely. "Osan!"

In the end we are so simple, she saw. *Hunger...fear...and need for those we need...and what we need....*

The poison pin was back in her hair. It belonged in Reiko's heart. That was where she would sheathe it, in the end.

Reiko, she said in her mind, *I am hungry for you....*

Crawled, half-stood...fell...rolled...crawled on....

Nineteen

Takezo Zato

Their foreheads were touching where they clutched each other. Their shouts were audible as whispers. The storm pressed them flat like bugs under clear crystal. Isolated on little islands of blinding force and intolerable, ear-popping sounds, maybe moments from sudden death or wounding by wind-whipped objects. Driven glops of water and mud spattered.

"I have you," Takezo pointed out. "Explain."

327

"Simple," yelled the purring, voice. "You hid. You were found."

"So what? Why care? You, a great lord."

Something hit his back and Takezo grunted. Something soft. No damage.

"So are you," was the shouted whisper of an answer. "So are you. I test you. You fled the test when you were young. Could not flee this time, Takezo."

"You killed her," Takezo replied. "I now kill you. Is that the test?"

"It is good you are strong. Much stronger than your unruly brother."

"I am blind. Lost everything. No need to live. So, we both die."

"What about your brother? Want him to rule our clan?"

"I have no…."

"No?" The face was close. Takezo could feel the heat of his sourish breath. "Think another time. You took the name Jiro. What was your true name?"

"Who cares? What was yours?"

Are we really talking like this?

Because the storm was reaching a peak that seemed a notch away from blowing away the world. The earth bubbled; they were soaked; muddy pools seethed around them. They kept flopping into the air together, banging back and part-rolling. He wondered how far they'd been driven, already. Everything was catching up and his consciousness was slipping; he didn't want the fever, now. Wanted to finish this. He'd probably never get another chance, even if he survived to try again. Anyway, he didn't really want to survive.

So he twisted around between rolling bounces and ripped the blade, glued by blood to his swollen right hand, in an arc that would split the smaller man's spine…*except he was half in and half out of the strange painting in the coal-lit, harsh blackness of the underworld. The metallic little creatures had him by the legs and held him halfway dragged out of the lyric wonder of that magical landscape, an amazing world where the air, the plants, the sky, light, soft and soothing sounds all caressed him and the female was there, moving like a heatless flame among the rich, graceful fronds.*

The boss devil was standing at the border, the subtle barrier that blocked him from the picture-world except he stepped on the prostrate ronin and started walking up his body. He was suddenly a bridge for it to enter.

Already, the dark outline was staining the shimmeringly pure atmosphere. He struggled in nightmare. Cursed:

'You can't come here! You can't come here!'

'I am part of you. Where you go, I will be, my son.'

'Go back. You are a stench of darkness. When next I move my bowels you will be gone forever.'

The fever-dream broke as his sword stroke cut sand and the wiry ninja master shifted aside. Then a gust flipped them both end-over-end, still locked together.

"Fool," Tanba shouted in his ear. "I am your father."

Why not? he thought, gathering himself to strike again. *Why expect sense?*

"How do I test it?" he demanded. "Ask my mother?"

"You can she's not dead."

"Ha, ha. No one's ever dead. Miou is just in hiding."

"She betrayed our clan."

"You betray everyone!" Gritted his teeth. "You made me an orphan of lies!" *Dead mother...dead father....* "Why?"

The mouth, breath at his ear:

"Great ninjas should have no real history."

Takezo tried stabbing up along his own body this time and got a slice in.

"Idiot!" yelled his putative father. "Are you deaf as well as blind? You *are* my son." He gripped Takezo with steel fingers and shook him. "No one but me knows my history!"

'How wonderful you are."

The wind slammed at them. He let go his aching left hand grip and tried to break free. Tanba held him with hooked, steely fingers. The rain hurt, driven into his face.

"No more," he shouted, not even to the other; not even to himself. Just no more. "I can't even kill you."

He was trying to toss the sword loose, feeling it pull and tear at the raw flesh of his palms. His fingers stayed locked. His left hand shoved futilely at the wiry weight that clawed into his arm and body. A blast rolled them again, over and over.

He realized how weak he was getting. Fading. Why not?

329

Can't kill him...so...so...break away...why not? Can't...no place left...no place....

Because it wasn't really the picture either, not the fever, not...not...

"Let go!" he demanded, both skidding now, pelted by small objects that might have been pebbles; rolling and splashing, then hitting something big and soft that stopped them. A horse. Dead and bloody. The ripping downpour suddenly slackened.

"You found me," said Tanba.

"Have you no other children? Leave me in peace."

"You are the best one. I need you."

Orphan of lies....

He kicked and struggled, twisted, battering softly against the soft horse belly, blood thickly spatting.

"Let go! Great *ninja* my great ass!"

He wanted to sail out into the nowhere of the impossible storm. He wanted to let himself be cast like dice. He wanted to find Issa. It kept coming back to that. No reason, no logic, no sense: just that. As sensible as the raging, random air.

Twenty

uMubaya

Bleeding, he half-crawled out of the rubble, following Reiko who was dragging the girl behind him, covered by his loyal men, blurring, then going sharp as the streaming smoke and sandy soil whipped past.

Spotted Gentile crawling ahead of him with mad intensity.

He desires her, as I desire my other...this is as good a time to die as any...I will spear this dog and my name will never be known and that is fine, too....

Gentile stood up and dove forward into the wall of wind, digging in madly, getting close enough to grab the Chamberlain's leg and wrestle with him as his nearest henchmen closed in.

The Zulu's spear was in his right hand; his left touched the trussed, headless body of Colin.

"Aiiiii," he sobbed into the overwhelming fury; an idea was clear and was necessary.

330

While the Italian struggled with Reiko, the black man sliced the rope, freeing Osan and in almost the same motion he looped and tied the free end under the armpit of the dead Scot with a sailor's knot.

Gentile was dragged aside by one of the henchmen. Reiko, in a mad, intense, violent explosion of monomaniacal energy, dug in and plowed on.

"To the castle," he cried. "We wait out the storm. Then we destroy all enemies."

No one was close enough to actually hear him or wonder why he was dragging the dead body behind him into the typhoon's full fury.

Twenty-One

Gentile

Gentile kicked loose from the samurai, sailed several feet in the air, flopped and slammed into the thick wall at the end of the compound hard enough to jar a brief blackout.

As the blurring sheets of rain puffed away and were gone the wind thinned out the smoke so that he could see a lot more of the hillside where the armies were now clinging to the ground in lines and heaps, yet, incredibly, were still fighting in sporadic flurries, swords and spears whipping around as men were tossed and spun. He saw a mass of riderless horses galloping broadside to the wind in desperate panic, then they were suddenly blasted into a tumbling wave of flesh that broke over the struggling warriors in a crushing pile. A line of men were whipped together by a coil of wind.

It made a picture. He could see sprays of blood whipped into mist. Imagined the chaos of cries and agony.

"The painter is a madman," he said, meaning God, the words sucked away at his mouth,

And then a body hit him, soft and hard.

Ma, he thought. *Mano di divino....*

"Osan," he said.

He held her. There was no way he wasn't going to. The wind eddied and shifted but was softened by the backwash effect of the wall.

"You," she said.

"I keep trying," he told her, faces close, hair plastered flat.

"Yes," she responded.

"Maybe we're lost."

331

"Storms end."

"As do we."

"Yes. Are you afraid?"

"Yes."

"I am as well," she said, shouted. "I am afraid I have much less character than I believed."

This conversation, as the world was tearing itself to pieces, seemed perfectly reasonable. The feel of her, the scent, the clasp of her long fingers on his shoulder made him not want to move. There he was, bleeding, exhausted, trapped and probably doomed and was closer to being happy than he had any memory of.

"*Less*?" he wondered.

She looked at him from inches away. Her face was bruised, dirt-stained with a trickle of blood creasing down her forehead, eyebrows washed-away, soaked hair knotted and twisted by the wind. His breath caught in his throat, looking at her. He wanted to physically draw her into himself, press their lips together and melt flesh-to-flesh like blending sweet wines in a cup. His long, fine-featured face stayed close.

"What use are fine words?" she countered.

He put his lips to her ear, saying:

"Not words. The soul they express."

So she just looked at him in silence. Her other hand, violitionless, touched and caressed his cheek. The wind pulled and pushed. Smoke clouds opened and closed. Past her face he could see the warriors on the hill in the mad and absurd turmoil, knotted in confusion, blended by the varying air, chopping and stabbing without strategy or tactics, for no loss or gain, just fighting in a terrifying yet tawdry reflex.

"Ah," she murmured into his ear. "I am glad you are holding me. I think we may die."

"No, no," he said. "Storms end. They...."

She pressed her cheek against his.

"No need to talk," she said. "Just hold me. I understand, now."

"Yes?"

"What are words and ideas? I think, now, there is only this."

"Oh," he whispered. "I...."

"Just hold me, please, sir."

"Lorenzo," he told her. "Please, call me that."

"Ro-enzo," she whispered in his ear.

"Yes, Osan."

"Just hold me, please, Enzo-san."

"But...I want to tell you, I...so much to say, I...."

"Hush, please, Zo. No more words...no more...for what use were all my words?"

The blast coming off the wall swirled into mini-whirlwinds around them. On the hillside the soldiers struggled on in strange futility, their shouts and cries audible through the lulls and twists of the violent air....

Twenty-Two

Takezo Zato

"Son," cried Tanba, from inches away, "important! Hear me! We will rule this country. You will inherit my power! Do not be a fool."

Takezo twisted around and managed to press his father (he still hadn't really taken that idea in completely) up into the soft, bloody belly of the dead horse, at arms length. Except, as he tried to push away the wind kept shoving him back into the grip of the wiry man who was his superior in hand-to-hand techniques – and maybe everything else, too.

"Everybody's ruling this country," he yelled back. "I can't keep track. I want nothing from you. Return to the shadows, murderer of women." Rolled away but the wind just drove him back into the wiry embrace again. "I want...."

I'm getting weaker....

Fragments of buildings, even people blew by. The keening howl was almost no sound, now: a strange, terrible humming, high and far away. It was hard to breathe.

Broke off as the fever dropped down like a curtain and he was back, half in and half out of the picture that was a gateway to another world. He was still struggling, trying to push the massive demon chief down his stretched-out body and back into the black underworld outside the lucent landscape.

The female perfection was near him, her form soft, uncertain as a breeze shifting and showing its curves in masses of grass and flowers.

'The soul of a stone,' he thought she somehow said, wordlessly, 'is a cloud....'

The dark from the demon still standing on his abdomen was working its way into the lucid, sweet light of the picture-world leaking

333

from the distorted body and spreading like poison blood in a viscous black stain.

'You,' she was somehow telling him. 'You do not belong here. Go back and find me.'

'Everyone wants me to find them,' he responded.

The quality of his phrasing told him the fever was already lifting. He was between two worlds for what might have been a long, long moment; time, he was numbly pleased to observe, was as crippled as himself. It went upside down, sideways, backwards....

The blind dark was back, the dead horse and his supposed father clutching him with fingers like hooks.

Let me go, he thought, not meaning just him. The wind was a prison, narrow, locking and pressing them together. And there was no one to kill. Fine. *If I could open my hand I'd drop the sword....*

He lay there in the violent dark while Tanba went on saying one thing and another as if, in this mad circumstance, persuading Takezo had some tremendous meaning.

"I want her!" he suddenly yelled, really loud, surprised at the energy that still seemed to pulse within like a heart of flame. "I want to write poetry. I want to sleep for a year."

The wind slammed into them so hard, now, it was actually shifting the dead mass of the fallen horse.

"Son...so...I...want who...you can have...just join...all yours...."

I am mad or dead...these are earned Hell-world torments or the ghosts and shadows of the blasted mind....

Riding his strange, new energy he rolled and twisted and kicked and the almost solid-seeming air added leverage so that only one hand was left gripping his wrist as if he were falling into space instead of blowing roughly parallel to the ground. Tanba's other hand held the horse's foreleg so that, if anyone could have seen them through the mad storm's climax, they might have resembled puppets or toys. Their fluttering robes crackled and snapped.

And then he was free, sailing and rolling out into his contorted darkness and slamming earth. He imagined death was a bounce or two away. Anything, he felt, would be an improvement. He couldn't tell one world from another, anyway. He might not even notice the difference.

He seemed to be rolling uphill although he trusted nothing. Ideas rambled through his brain without apparent cause or effect or object. He liked that. It was like relaxing as you dozed off.

I've solved everything, he thought, laughing in his head. *Spied it all out....*

Then he went down, not very far and found himself in Hell....

Twenty-Three

uMubaya

He was alone in the middle of wherever he was. He'd locked his left arm around a solid post that had been part of the building's support system, spear in the other hand. He was patient. He'd hold on until he died or it ended. What could be simpler?

See what blows my way, he quipped.

Decided this would be a good time to think about Mer'ce but nothing came to mind. A couple of armored samurai rolled past. He had an impression they were cutting at one another, flailing, soundless, in the storm.

Determination, he reflected, *well misplaced....*

Considered asking the local gods for help but didn't know their names. Maybe Buddhists were meditating in the center of the violence. Someone else rolled by, almost nude in tattered robes.

Empty the mind, they say...but you better have something in it first.... Smiled, then chuckled. *Mer'ce would have something to say on that subject....*

"Hard to breath in this," he said.

Be good to live...so much blood to cleanse, so much killing....

Something tumbled past overhead that might have been a bird. He reflected on the idea that the air had become their enemy. There was a proverb he remembered: when there is nothing to do, do nothing.

Maybe I'll get to clean my spirit and tell this tale....

Twenty-Four

Reiko

He leaned on the wind, digging forward on all fours, partly sheltered by the walled, sunken road that curved downhill there. Dust ripped at him. Things sailed past but his concentration was unaffected. The battle was being blown away; if many survived the clan would never

335

unite under him. His mind was clear at the same time it knew it was quite mad. Easy to see that the tortured spirit of Hideo was behind these disasters. Yet, maybe Issa was a supernatural fox taking human form …made more sense….He'd kill her and see if she transformed to her animal shape…yes….Poor Reiko, cursed by this evil being…everything ruined…but words were just bubbles because his concentration now pushed all else aside: get to the castle and seal the gates.

"The blood can be washed," he declared to the wind, thinking about the stained floor where the *daimio* had died. "It signifies nothing…nothing…."

Get to the castle and unite the loyal. Hold to the end. He didn't need allies. Who could be trusted? An idea: Get a witch, call up the spirit of Masakado and thus destroy the vengeful fox-spirit. Masakado's name was used to frighten children. He'd tried to become emperor and was beheaded.

"Why not? Poison can heal poison. Yes. Wash the blood…kill all traitors…seal the gates…seal the gates….arm myself with friendly demons!"

Accept what you are; everyone died alone, everyone was bad – cowards, afraid of honest ruthlessness. If you could be a demon after death then you were the same demon alive. Cowards couldn't face such truths.

His mind circled the main point and enjoyed the anticipation of not quite focusing on the inexpressible pleasures to come. He felt the blood dripping and creasing down his body from Issa's blade. It didn't worry him. He just kept on, dragging the weight at the end of the rope that he believed was Osan, the storm too loud for her voice to reach him.

"Stop holding back," he said over his shoulder. "Useless to struggle."

"She" was just a blur at the edge of his glance. He seemed to see her, all the same, long bare limbs showing through the tatters of her silk robes, a flash of her softly sullen, exquisite face and warm hints of her breasts mixed in with what he'd seen that afternoon in the bath so that the picture was rich and complete and he allowed himself to relish it, shutting his eyes and seeing her in his bedroom on the mat, stretched out, painted, perfumed and perfect.

"Soon, soon," he said, nodding. "We'll be there soon, sweet girl."

Twenty-Five

Takezo Zato

Yes. Hell. Where was the fever-world when you needed it? Because he'd been blown into what he knew were the wind-wracked and torn armies that, clinging in clumps, were held down by their massed, united weight; many still, absurdly, hacking and smashing at each other.

The shouting and clashing got through the shrill, absorptive storm-shriek. The effect was soul-ripping.

Maybe I don't really want to die...a blind man can do many things... Being Takezo, he actually laughed, even as strange hands clutched at him as if he were the drowning man's straw and he understood that the situation had made the mass of men insane.

"A blind man," he shouted, feeling more than a little mad himself, "can rule this land!"

"Victory is near!" someone shouted in his ear. "Long live Lord...." The rest was lost as the mass shifted and heaved in a welter of screams and clashing weapons.

Victory, he thought, not even laughing this time.

The warriors immediately around him weren't fighting. Both sides, there, seemed united by the overwhelming storm. He heard fragments of jokes and obscene catcalls along with fragments of agony and pleadings from those wounded and buried under the mass that had to be three or four deep.

All storms have to end, he thought. *Then I'll....*

"Welcome," someone shouted into his ear.

His energy ebbed and flowed. He wanted to sleep. Someone was shrieking underneath him, a body or two down. He smelled vomit and feces and blood.

"Yes," he responded. "It's nice here."

There was a struggle beside him, upwind: suddenly someone broke loose from the mass, screaming, bounced and rolled over him and was gone. He wasn't sure how many hands were now holding him.

The head closest to his said:

"Fortunes ebb and flow. Poor fellow. This is a good place."

"Who would willingly leave it?" Takezo responded.

"Exactly. You are wise."

"Shut up!" scathed another voice, closer to the blind *ronin's* belly. "Or we'll kick you out!"

337

Those close enough to follow this over the insane drone of the storm shouted and laughed. Few of the words came through.

He'd about decided that the madness of this place was as good an end for him as anything else. At least his "father" couldn't find him and he could die fighting if he liked- except he didn't want to. Maybe he'd just compose haiku and wait for death....

The mass shifted, suddenly and he was lifted and spun with the others; felt the impact of heavy objects crashing mushily into them which sent bone-shattering waves through knotted soldiers. He kicked free for a moment...dropped...was covered and uncovered by the shifting heap...and then he was in a lee, a sudden drop into a shallow ravine. His face splashed into muddy liquid: the smell and taste was blood. As he scrambled and crawled away he sank to his wrists in it, going around and over dead bodies. He kept trying to spit the metallic taste out. The armies had clearly impacted there before the storm had peaked.

I can't tell one side from the other, he reflected.

Tried to imagine how blind men would battle if *no* one had eyes. Liked the idea. The weariness was pressing down on him again and he rested on top of a heap of the dead. The ravine was narrowing and the wind was just a low, humming shriek above, sucking away the air which made breathing even harder. It was now floored with bodies.

Tanba's men on one side, he considered. *Nobunaga over here...somebody else there...how do we know which is which? Maybe it doesn't matter...we all kill on a whim, anyway...or because somebody tells us to...How would we find the enemy?*

He started to laugh and this time he was afraid he really wouldn't be able to stop. He flopped on his back, half asleep on a couch of the dead. He saw thousands of blind men stumbling into battle, grabbing, clutching each other, groping with sword and spear for the other army....

Since we already have blind leaders it would produce greater harmony....

"No wonder my 'father' wants me to rule," he scoffed, shaking his head. "Ninja, in a world of lies truth is dishonest."

And suddenly he was back in the softly gleaming picture and this time he was moving through the landscape and could see what he believed were actual brushstrokes, saw soft, melting tones where the muted ink colors had pooled and seemed to have been subtly spread around dry-

edged rocks and cliffs and dense, watery mists gracefully stained with flowers....

There she was, moving like a soft breeze, perfect outline defined by the shifting leaves and flowers and flows of mist, blurred and floating just ahead of him.

'Wait,' he called, gently. 'Wait, please."

Because the blurring didn't matter, the exact face or form...no...she was what was behind the solid women, the essence, the mystery, the link to heaven.

'Go back,' she seemed to tell him. 'This world is dying. Cannot you see?'

'I try...I try....'

'Go back ind me.'

Sensing something he looked behind and there was the darkness, spreading like thick black ink, blotting away the lush rills and tones of this ineffable world and, wading forward, dripping and drooling the blackness from himself, came the humpbacked, toadlike shape that had entered through him, melting into shapelessness with each step....

He was in agony. He wanted to run back and attack it; wanted to rush ahead and enfold her in himself. Agony....

'Go back!' he cried at the spreading stain. 'There must exist a place without you!'

Twenty-Six

Gentile and Osan

They were still locked together in the shelter of the wall, faces close. He kept her soft, warm, sweet-scented cheek pressed to his. He wanted to tell her, so much.

"Osan, I...I want to...."

"Hush," she soothed. "No words. I was lost in words."

"But I think the wind is lifting."

"Yet, will it not come back, sir?"

"I love you, you understand?"

"No words, please, Lo-enzo-san."

"Yes," he said. "But I've wanted to talk to you for so long, you see...I...,"

"Yes. Say what pleases you, sir. Forgive me my silence."

339

"Angela mia," he whispered at her ear. "I thought always of painting and…what point if the world can simply blow away? I don't know…I don't know…."

The wind was falling off quickly. There were gusts and spurts. The air was changing from cool to a sweet warm, almost like a spring day. They could now hear the troops on the hill above. He looked past her shoulder: the smoke was mainly back in the heart of the city where they were still masses of smolder. The sky was a strange, powdery bluegreen in the center of frighteningly high, curved, swirling cloud-walls of the immense eye of the storm.

He'd never seen anything like it. It moved vastly and much faster than it appeared. He felt they were in an awesome, magical peace, surrounded by inconceivable violence.

He sat up, leaning on the low wall that surrounded the shattered court and jail buildings, holding her into his body. She made no resistance. Her head drooped almost formally on his shoulder. He was faintly reminded of the Noh play he'd watched. All around he heard cries, calls for help, anguish and a vast, wordless, deep roaring that he didn't realize was the renewing clash of the armies.

"Look," he told her, pointing at the sky. *"Dio mio!* Incredible, I…."

"Yes," she said. "We have a short time now."

"Should we go to your castle?"

She didn't move. Her eyes stayed shut.

"Why, Enzo-san? I am content to die here, in your embrace."

"Well…." he broke off because he was looking at the hillside now, at armored and unarmored men, climbing over and standing on bodies, falling over them, slashing, stabbing, thrusting, raging in a general din that almost approximated the overwhelming, total blast of the re-approaching storm. "Madmen," he muttered.

She didn't look – didn't have to.

"Yes," she said. "Can we stop them with words? Can we stop the storm with pictures?"

"What can we do, then, dear lady?"

"I told you."

He kissed her exquisite neck. Couldn't help it. Sighed like someone in some poem. Wanted to rave and reach into flowing, untapped

340

rivers of infinite force and elegance and express what she was to him. Didn't try. What would that stop either or make happen?

She is...a wonder...she is true...what does that mean? Words on words....

"You mean die?" he murmured, keeping his face lost in the scent and texture of her.

"Not so hard," she said. "What I ask is hard."

"Osan?"

"To be silent. And just hold one another, please. Just that. There's nothing left, I think."

"Ah. Yes. Easier for me as I love you."

Eh. Te amo...aiii...beyond all credence....Io t'amore....

"Still you ask words of me, Enzo-san?"

He forced himself to stop looking and listening to the senseless and insane conflict outside the walls. Kept his face close to her. Understood.

"This is enough," he told her.

"No. This is *all*."

Twenty-Seven

Little Yazu

He was sore and felt the dried blood cracking his wounds as he levered himself to his shaky feet and swayed there, half-crouched. He had two thoughts at once.

My family...ai...is all destroyed?

He was scanning the area, littered with shattered stuff and dead bodies, for any sign of his master. The sun blasted down again.

"The world is gone," he muttered.

What do I do? What do I do? Is all gone? My son...my woman...my master...my....

He'd been driven by fighting and forced by wind some distance away from the walled buildings down the same road that Reiko was now plodding along, bent into the weight of the corpse he was dragging through puddles and mud, all alone now, face set, eyes wide and not really seeing the ruins around him, the dead, the massively towering cyclonic eye seeing only what his mind screened over it....

Yazu's jaw dropped as the Chamberlain went by. He just stared.

Like a dog with a dead cat tied to his tail....

341

"What does this mean?" he asked himself. "Ai."

Home, he thought. *Yes...I must go home....*

He looked up at the oncoming other side of the eye and wondered if he'd have time. From what he could observe the whole city must be flattened or, at least, crushed badly. What chance had his frail house? And it was coming again.

Oh, my master, he thought. *I have no choice....*

Twenty-Eight

Takezo Zato

So he slashed the sword that seemed to grow from his arm and ripped through the center of the black shape that was melting into formless splashes and dribbles as it spread, blighting and blotting the environment. The slash went right through it and the sticky, cold stuff got on his hand and arm. He watched it start to spread into his substance, darkening him.

He shuddered and stumbled away Woke up.

He lay on his back, softly comfortable. He automatically opened his eyes, as much as the thick swelling allowed. A stir of wind like a cat playing with a crippled bird: a light buffet, an almost gentle, tentative touch. Clashing sounds of violent chaos further away, now. Down below him in what he immediately remembered was a heap of dead and dying men someone was whimpering and keening in dreadful pain.

"Still fighting," he murmured.

Fever's one thing, he considered, *but I haven't been drunk in years....*Smiled, partly to see how much his face hurt. All his memories were there in an almost unique continuity. Knew he'd slept just long enough to feel temporarily restored.

He was startled because there was light and color and, for a moment, he thought he was sinking back into the fever dreaming. Didn't want that. And then realized his left eye had just seen something, however blurred and senseless. Tried to focus but went blank, again.

He would have rested there except for the agony somewhere below, that, and the distinct smell of blood and shit. He partly sat up, struggling, sword still locked in his right hand, rocking on the uneven corpses.

"Sorry," he said, trying to open his hand and release the hilt. "What can I do?"

342

Rolled and stood up, feet slipping and skidding on slick armor, sinking into soft flesh, causing gurgles and blurps of flatulence from the cushion of dead. Knew there was blood on his feet. Well, there was blood on all of him. Nothing new. A puff of air scattered a little sandy dust, already dried in the terrific sun pressure, over the side of the corpse-choked ditch.

Climbed up the side of the ravine, a foot or two, and tried to see again: a hint of glow, nothing too specific. Felt the breeze tug a little harder at him. Realized it was the other side of the storm, hitting from the opposite direction.

I should stay in this ditch since I have no goal, he thought, kneeling on the soft earth in the strong, sudden, near noon sun. *Ah...wonderful...no one to kill. nothing to*
find....

Yet, there was something because the beautiful flow of perfect grace soundlessly said:

'Find me.'

How could I forget? he sighed to himself. *Even in mad dreams I get hired....*

As he started to stand a random gust tipped him back onto the mass of men. It was comfortable and disgusting. Sighed. Rolled to hands and knees and started creeping along on the uneven heap. Prepared to clamber up again and this time stay low. One arm sank down between bodies and dropped his face into a mess of blood and stink he knew were ripped intestines. Not a new smell.

Enough. He threw himself upright and jumped up over the edge on to solid earth. Rubbed his face on the grass, spitting and gagging.

Shut his eyes and they stuck....

He was running, this time, up a slope into the dense, blurred, wet mists of the rich, fragrant landscape of brushstrokes and washes of soft colors...so pure...so pure...the darkness spreading, widening at his heels, encircling now...she was just ahead, her being revealed by the gestures of the wet air, the soft fronds, the stirred mists...hints he tried to touch with his stiff, clumsy, groping hands....

'You must escape,' he cried in silence.

'I am not here,' replied the exquisite grace that just eluded him.

The darkness was a wave, gathering, rising, cresting, closing, crashing down....

Shuddered back to the world of stiff pain. Tried to open his right hand, prying the fingers with the left. It hurt. Then, on a fresh gathering of wind opposite the raging combat that was slowly spilling away south, he heard a woman cry out. It was not exactly fear or hurt, in that voice. A kind of righteous rage and immense disgust overriding pain. He flopped the sword around until it flew from his swollen hand, tearing open the scabs so that blood dripped, again.

The light he vaguely perceived was dimming. He knew what that meant even before the next, increasing shove of the reviving typhoon that staggered him.

Here we are, he thought. *Always a woman....*

He got up and angled towards the voice, trying to reactivate the left eye. He kept catching blurs...grass...scattered debris...broken trees....

Heard men laughing and mocking, arguing, too. Didn't like those voices. Caught a flash, a narrow strip of field and litter, some bodies, dead horses....turned his head and lost it. The voices were closer. The woman was scathing:

"Pigs! Go to your filth!"

Sounded familiar. Of course. There was never any chance he'd be able to walk past anything. All he wanted to do now was sleep until the end of the present age of the world and then go far, far away and sleep some more.

Then the world was slammed and went sideways...tripped...rolled and managed to get to his knees. The voices were close, blown into garble.

"Issa!" he yelled.

"What's this?" someone called back.

"A blind man," another said.

"Save him a taste of her," advised a third.

Laughter.

"He can lick her behind," recommended a third.

"He can lick mine too," declared another to stupid laughter.

"We better get to cover," was another opinion. "Looks bad."

"Bah," scoffed the first speaker, as Takezo homed in, creeping sideways on his knees. The wind had gone flat, for the moment, but that meant nothing.

He sighed. No storm or war, no holocaust could change the way men went about being cruel and stupid when they believed they were momentarily safe.

He almost tripped over a dead girl, glimpsing her in a fragment of sight. Her head was half cut off. Dark blood set it in a pool of mud. He saw where the men had Issa in a blot of shadows. He sighed again.

"How many are they?" he asked, closer. Counting to kill.

"Takezo," she said. "Too many." Her voice was controlled disgust and anger. "Ten pigs."

"Shut up!" one yelled, smacking her.

Takezo heard the impact but his sight was worse when he tried to see. He was among them now, though. Someone gripped his arm. He didn't resist. Not yet.

"Blind man," he said, reedy-voiced, "strip off your loincloth. Enjoy this Hideo clan whore."

"Only ten?" he said.

This is my life, he thought.

He blinked hard and got a twisted blur of vision for a moment. They were all around her. One was holding each limb so she was starfished on the ground.

"Go on, blind man," a guttural voice inveighed. "Stick it in the bitch."

"She's a lady," he told them.

"Go away, Takezo," she said. "These pigs are nothing. Have you seen my daughter?"

"Daughter?" reedy-voice said. "Let's find her for the 'lady.'"

General approbation. Laughter.

"Have you no fear of justice?" Takezo wanted to know.

"Ha, ha," said a deep voice. "All the fools are dead. The world is upside down. We do what we want."

Takezo knew where they all were, now. He could feel them, too. The man holding him and another who started pulling his loincloth off and forcing him down on her.

"I found you," he told her. "I'm a first-rate spy, after all. I find everything, in time." Laughed; that should have warned them. "Justice surprises one."

Laughter all around.

"A blind spy!"

345

"What does he see?"

"Put his face down there and he'll find her hole with his nose!"

Laughter and then a scream as Takezo disarmed the man clawing at his undergarment and stabbed the one holding him through the body; then a gurgling as he sliced the other's throat with a slow, long backcut.

"Eight left," he said, already whipping the sword in a kind of figure-eight back and forth between the ones holding her ankles and felt the satisfaction of chipping bone hits and awful screams of agony. "Six."

But he heard them already up and running and her voice:

"Is life so sweet, cowards?" To him: "Look out, your left!"

Because one had paused to hurl a dagger, point-blank, at the deadly swordsman.

A good throw, Takezo thought, sensing and partly seeing the glint as the blade flashed at him, deflecting it with his blade without even knowing how. That sped them all on. Then a massive wave of dirt-clotted air crashed into and over them like a tremendous surf. Everyone went down, including Takezo. He managed hands and knees.

"Come back," he called after them. "The world is yours."

She was holding him, her long, soft, perfect nakedness under his swollen left hand.

"Who is like you?" she asked, pressing her head softly under his chin. She smelled like blood, dirt, sweat and flowers. The wind rocked them.

"The world deserves to end, I think," he said.

"Not with men like you in it, sir. No. Not yet."

"Blind men? Fools? Slaves to lust and mad notions?"

"No, Takezo-san. Men like you."

"I saw you, for a moment."

"You'll recover, I think. I know a Korean master of healing. We can-"

"We. Are you alright? Did they….?"

She shrugged with her body.

"They disgusted me," she responded. "But what could they do that I have not done already? I am no hypocrite. When they were finished I would have killed some before they killed me." Shrugged, again. Kissed his neck, gently.

"We need to find your robes," he said.

346

"I like to be naked with you," she murmured. "No secret. Anyway, the storm is nearly come again."

"We need shelter." He worked the left eye some more. A blur...a blot...a flash of color. "Better head for Hideo stronghold. What else?"

Again, he realized how relaxed he always was with her, his former enemy. For all the passion of himself and Miou he'd always been unsure of what she was and wanted. With Issa secrets didn't matter. And she wasn't mean, afraid or especially selfish. She had drives and beliefs and could be ruthless. So could he. They had common ground.

She put her mouth near his ear.

"Anyplace else," she told him. "Impossible. If I return then I must cut my belly as a man would. Too much shame there."

"Yes," he said. "Anyway, I found you." Sighed a laugh. "I find everybody. Everything. Sooner or later. Makes it worse."

Too bad about the rest, he thought. *Too bad about my entire life....* Thought about his new-found father, Yoshi, Miou, Yazu, Osan, others, and all the dead lining the road behind. It *was* like waking from a dream. Good and bad. *If I go back I might as well kill myself, too....*

"You still can't really see," she said. "So I trust you to take us somewhere. It doesn't matter. Do you believe that, Takezo, my love?"

There it was. No sense of surprise. This was his life. The storm and darkness fell, tore, flatteningly, across the landscape, re-smashing the already crushed.

"Takezo, my love," he echoed. "So here you are."

"Like you," she told him, "I am an exile. Why not be honest, Ezo-san?"

Kneeling there, against the overwhelmingly gathering force, hammer of heaven that vibrated them together, he suddenly felt like a young man and crushed her into himself, laughing and almost crying too, running his dulled, clumsy ruined hands up her back, across her shoulders, cradling her long, sweet neck, kissing deeply as if he could inhale the magic from the fever dream that he understood was hidden in her flesh, too....

"You understand?" she asked with a slight sob, pressing into him.

"No," he said, cried. "No...no, no, no...."

"Ah," she responded.

"No...no...no...."

347

And then he effortlessly lifted her into his arms and started carrying her across the field he only saw in sudden, distorted glimpses, tilting, staggering, tacking, pushing as the wind was building into an explosion that would flatten almost any human construction or resistance.

"Ah," she repeated. "It was always you. Irritating man."

"We can't escape," he told her.

"Why try?" she wondered, in return.

"I mean the storm," he amended.

"I do not." She touched his face with her lips. "Carry me past memory. We will start there or die there."

The wind flung him forward and sideways in a semi-stagger. He had flashes, seeing grass, rubble, bodies and a bamboo grove ahead.

Be like bamboo, the great masters often said, he recalled. *No wind can flatten it...bend and come back....*

Twenty-Nine

uMubaya

When the wind died he'd walked away from the fighting and found himself drifting back towards the sea, passing the desolation and the dead, following descending lanes through the choked, flooded, corpse-strewn city's outskirts.

He could hear the sea for a long time before he got close enough to see the massed mist and enormous surf pounding the shore as if to grind it away. He had only vague ideas about what to do; he'd never seen a storm like this; could tell it wasn't over yet.

He sat on a bluff that overlooked the flat shoreline that stretched away from the city. The way they'd come after the boat broke up on the beach. Distant mountains were depthless gray, running out into the great bay. Studied the swirling, incredible circular wall of the eye. Estimated when the far side would hit. Decided where he was would be as good as anyplace else: he'd wedge himself up between the great rocks.

He lay back with his weapon beside him. He decided he'd survive and find a ship. Everything was possible. He rolled up to his feet in a single movement. Yes. Take the sea and fury of the sky into himself. After all, he was a king. Leave this fragile, precious, murderous land and find his home.

Inhaled the wind as it started to pound and press, gutter and twist, again. Began to find the pulse of it...held the spear in his hand and started

348

to move, feeling, listening...his flesh and bones were total flimsiness, shadows...yet, like sails the air, the force, the beat of time and the power of heaven and earth could fill them...the old magic...the true magic....

So he turned...stopped...bent...moved, first with the regular pulse of the huge waves...next the arrhythmic gusts and heaves of air...found the key to bind it to him...smiled, dark, remote eyes full of dimming sky, contorted clouds, sudden punctuations of slashing rain, last, lost, fading threads of sunlight....

Thought about nothing. He was part of it. Suddenly couldn't tell himself from the mounting tempest. Felt as if flesh was wind and bones were water.

And then, as the air began to scream and boom he found that sound, too, and shouted and sang with the storm's voice, indestructible as a cork on a wave or a feather in the wind....

And she was there, without words or a name...no more a memory than a dream growing out of itself; no more a dream that what's seen when eyes open in the morning.

It wasn't loss or love or hope or lack...or need...she was just there as his voice and body danced with the vast gathering of obliterating force....

She was there. He hummed and sang and drove his feet as if he were the weight of the world and the lightness of air. She was there. He understood. Didn't dare stop, now, as the gust and buffets slammed around and the waves were being churned and slapped into mist and foam...in a moment he might be ripped into the air or banged to mush on the rocks...but not while his flesh was wind and water.

After this he would be clean; if he died, he would be clean and if he came together with his love he would be clean....

Thirty

Osan and Gentile

The air streamed over them in the opposite direction, now, sealing them in strange isolation behind the wall. Things were flying overhead the opposite way. They were entwined, breathing one another's breaths.

"If we live," he started to say, but she hushed him again, lips by his.

"Please, Zo-san, no more words. Each one hurts my mind."

"Yes...yet, we...."

349

Pressed her soft fingers over his mouth. He sighed. The world was vibrating, the earth itself sounding a sonorous roar as the incredible typhoon gathered full power.

There was nothing now but the wall and the two of them, alone in the storm's lee.

Amazing just to be here... am I really holding Osan in my arms? How did this come about? The taste of her. The scent. The feel. *No words needed...how true...when the storm ends, what do we do? Where....*

"When this is over," he couldn't help saying into her warm hand, "where do we..."

She pressed his mouth shut with the palm and said nothing this time. Her wordless breath was warm in his ear.

It was enough. He understood better, now. He tried to think about the unfinished painting...tried to think about many things and found them slipping away.

Because this might be the end, now...or tomorrow...just words to those who think they are secure...nothing is secure...nothing...the words are obvious, everyone says them...poets love to speak of death...until it is upon them...Ah, my love, you are clarity, words cheapen it....

He wanted to say he loved her but feared her silence; he'd have to live without the familiar yes or no; whatever the truth.

She'd softly rolled herself under him and he was amazed by what her hands were doing and then, what his were doing in return. His breath thickened, it was far past words; far past even believing so there was just the wind, as good as silence, gripping the world, and the heat, scent, touch, incredible closeness as their bodies rode into rhythms that seemed as external as the storm, itself, blending them together as fluid as clouds or waves, sealing them from lips on down into an indistinguishable, indivisible movement....

No words. No pictures. Just what was....

Somewhere, in the swirling of himself and herself something still wanted to ask a question and do something about something...somewhere...far away... blown away as they melted together like a wax drowned candle...there was nothing to hold...no form, no line, no language....

It was brightness and honey and breath and bone...dissolution and solidity; need without names, fulfillment without intension....

350

He knew he said something that was only sound. He knew she answered. He knew her arms and breath were his and his front and back were hers. Inside-out, they had no history and no future; if they'd already died, neither had noticed....

He knew he cried out – or, maybe, just whispered or dreamed the sound:

"Osan."

Thirty-One

In the Bamboo Grove

Issa was light in his arms. Takezo tried to cover her with his blood and mud smeared, tattered rags. The wind had sucked the strips away immediately and left her naked, again, soft, sweet-scented and incongruously languorous.

He was going faster and faster as the wind kicked at his back. He went to his knees by the time they reached the slope of bamboo grove; fragments of sight blurred and blanked his glimpses of the thin and thick boles, tough, sharp leaves whipping and rattling in masses, the hissing swooshes audible over the background roar. Trees had gone down all around or been stripped of their branches but the bamboo still leaned and bent, lashed and bowed. Sudden blasts of rain semi-solidly slammed into the arched green canopy, blowing into spray. The ground was muddy, warm and pleasant as he tucked them into a rill above a fast, brownish, choked and swollen stream flooding from the hills above.

He cradled her as if she were the most precious thing left in the shattering, melting world. He was panting, drained. His heart labored. She was sleek, soft and quiet; kept her face on his chest as a child might. He'd never had a child. Interesting. All those women and no children.

"As good as any other place," he grunted near her ear. "Live or die."

He lay sideways, cradling her, head on the slope, the wet, long grasses flicking in waves of wind around them.

He knew it would happen if he shut his eyes and it did – except it was going to be brief (if immeasurable) this time:

He was back in the picture as the shapeless darkness was staining away the trees, flowers, hills and valleys and was running as that lifeless tide closed around him, his own flesh stained, too, and dissolving with each step....

There was a last stir and swirl in a gentle haze of tall flowers in dry and wet, meltingly graceful brushstrokes.

'Please,' he may have sobbed out.

'Sayonara,' he may have heard.

Blinked awake. She was still there, motionless in his embrace. The storm was pounding on, too big to comprehend. The bent bamboo arched over them making a kind of temple roof. He squinted that left eye and saw more, this time. A mixed blessing because there was a twisted, blurred outline that was worse than any vision in a fugue of fever: clinging to a tall, vibrating, six-inch thick stalk, digging in his feet, snarling and yelling, soundless at the distance, anchored by ripped, tattered-looking armor, was Yoshi. The head was bare and the furious face floated in semi-clarity, maybe 30 feet away.

Better to be mad and seeing devils, he said to himself. Blinked and there were only blurs. *Proves nothing....*

Her lips were moving over his face, their hair streaming together, lying just under the bulge of earth and long grass under the ripping rage of rain that whipped and hissed in the densely resistant bamboo leaves.

He was trying to locate what he hoped was just a spasm of his distorted sight. Her sweet mouth was at his ear, full of words:

"I never hated you," she said. "You made me think my life wasted."

"By all holy names," he said, stunned. "Why?"

"You were free and I was...what I was."

"A great lady."

"A sly whore and spy."

There, he thought. *But how could he find us?*

Slapped at his eye, twisted his face: Yoshi's was nearer, the face close to the ground, running rain and mud and blood, too, creeping closer.

"Go away," Takezo said, shouted.

"My love?" Issa asked, startled.

"Not you. Not you. The stupid follow us." He pushed her down the slope so that her bare feet were washed and vibrated by the rapid stream.

He hunched up into the blast that screamed bluntly through the lashing, whipping grove. Dirt and hot rain slashed into his swollen face. Pain had long since ceased to matter much. Sometimes kept him

352

conscious, he reflected. After being blown up and crucified, what was left? Thought he smelt a whiff of smoke; meant nothing to him.

He screamed:

"Ugly!!! Stupid!!! Go away!!!"

Had him in a blur, then lost the round, scarred face. Heard an inarticulate, raw, rasping raving from the maddened mouth of his brother. Then that unforgiving countenance was suddenly a few seething inches away, bent by rain, wind and abused eyes.

"Time is run out, drunkard," the mouth said, spitting, full of shadow. "I would crawl into Hell to cut out your heart."

He saw and sensed the movement as Yoshi struck at him with a short-sword, swinging down over the rim of the ditch-like ravine. He wasn't quite amused, but felt that if he were cut in any such way he would deserve it. Because the physical was the least of it and that strange energy filled him, instantly, like wind a sail, and the would-be assassin was disarmed.

"Go away!" he repeated. "Go to your father. I won't kill either of you."

He was aware that Issa had crouched up beside him. He pushed her down a little with his stiff right hand.

Yoshi was flat on his belly on the reverse slope, half his face showing where he was turned to one side. That should have told him something; except he was worrying about her getting accidentally slashed if another blade came into play. A distraction. Pale flowers and thin grass kicked in the gusts along the rim. Another scent of something burning that meant nothing to him.

So he was just reaching up to drag the monomaniacal killer over and down with the idea of dumping him in the water. Hold him in for awhile, short of death – maybe.

As he'd tried to teach Yazu, there was nothing more dangerous than a plan. As he reached up there was a barrel of a gun big enough to stuff an egg in, flat in his face. The burning matchlock fuse flared in the wind. What his almost randomly streaked sight picked up was just the twisted grin and bright mad eyes in a ballooned-out, melting face: he got one hand up on the lacquered wood and steel collar and yanked at the same moment (time had gone into that strange slowdown that no one ever got used to) he was aware Issa's nude body was going up past him, shouting something like:

353

"No, my love!"

As he was still pulling Yoshi, now suspended half out over the steep edge, he partly saw the flash and explosion that would have gone off in his face deflected by (he glimpsed in a shred of sight) her quick, strong, levering grip on the thick wrist. The blast was more of a whoosh that a bang. He felt the stinging heat, smoke instantly whipping away; felt and glimpsed in shadowy blur her body flung back and down by the impact, rolling into the muddy, swollen stream. His sight was now like a slatted blind so he caught slices of what was happening: the armored, stocky figure sailed out and down as Takezo uncoiled all his amazing force; her smooth body rolling in cuts and stops in the gray rainmist and green and white purity of flowers in their lyric sweep along both sides of the rapid stream. And the heart-stopping shudder at the bright blood flicking in the wild air and staining her honeypale, vulnerable being....

And he was already scrambling down, oblivious to everything, his mind pounding the same words, over and over and too fast for voicing:

Not again....not again...not again.....

Aware that Yoshi had landed on his face in the muddy water and was stuck, feet kicking the air, armor weight holding him under, Takezo scrambled to where the stream was starting to roll and carry her away.

He pulled her free and lifted her into his arms.

"Not again!" he cried, then screamed into the blotting, overwhelming wind that notched to a mad peak, sucking and shoving, blowing thick earth and flowerheads into the whirling, tortured air. "Not again!!!"

Thirty-Two

Osan and Gentile

They were wrapped and rolled together into what might have been an unconscious symbol of total union. Their eyes were shut. The wind slammed into and over the low wall. Rain scythed past. The world beyond their little island of breath, flesh and blood was a droning, violent emptiness seeming, he thought, to be rubbing the world away.

He been amazed that they'd made love, barely changing their positions, barely moving, just sheer intensity in the strange silence of the storm. The feeling that finally poured out of him was a distillation of passion he never knew existed. Emptied out of himself, poured his sense

354

and soul into her as if both were ecstatic air, melted into magical water where dreams floated like reflections in an unstirring lake....

He was glad she insisted on silence. He was afraid of words too. But he had to speak, anyway, before it was gone.

"Osan." Lips to her ear. "We are not to blame."

Her long, soft arms locked a little tighter. She didn't otherwise respond. Sighed and pressed her face deeper into his chest, like a child.

"Hmmm," she sounded.

"You are right. *T'a ragione, mi' amore.* This is all there is."

"Mn." Her lips bussed his chest, the surprising hairs her mother had once intimately likened to a bear's pelt.

Like the silent monks, he thought. *A vow of silence, words distract the spirit....*

He held her, tighter, closer, wishing he could really melt and meld into her.

We were air, starlight on water...transfigured flesh....

"More words," he said, into her sweet hair. "No better than pictures." Kissed her face as the wind howled and shook the foundations of the world. "*Ah, bellissima...la pella...corpa...sangue....*" Kissing until her somewhat bruised lips responded so there was the heat and scent of her mouth, too, now. "All there is," he said like a sob or a sigh. "*Silencio.*"

Thirty-Three

uMubaya

At some point the peaking storm was crashing onshore and he found himself dancing on the wind. He felt transparent to it; part of it, moving fluid, unbreakably flexible and impervious as a bending reed.

Maybe my mind is empty, was a passing thought.

He was dancing along the sheer bluff above the 4 and 5 story waves, in the air more than touching the ground, spear gesturing, mouth open sucking in and shouting out the mad, spray-filled air.

He felt he had wings and so leaped with no idea of any result; leaped like a prayer into the infinite immensity and felt himself float as if the immeasurable violence were a warm pool and he went up and out like a chip, a feather....

Carry me, his mind said, *to the beginning or the end....*

"Aiiiyaaaaa!!!" he cried – or the wind did through the enormous emptiness of himself....

Thirty-Four

Chamberlain Reiko

Reached the moat while the storm eye was still overhead. The water was clogged with debris. A half-naked body floated on its face in the mucky stuff. Shutters and most of an overhang had been ripped away from the upper stories of the castle. The sun was hot and bright and drove steam from puddles and the unshadowed half of the moat. His blood-soaked robes were stiffening. His wound was leaking less.

Behind him in the shattered, partly flooded street dozens of survivors were out, shocked, shaken, some kneeling before Buddhist statues; others pacing up and down beating prayer drums and chanting. They gradually fell silent and collected in a crowd, watching him as the second side of the vast cyclone inexorably closed in.

None of this was noted by the Chamberlain who stood in front of the first gate and kept pounding it with the hilt of his sword harder and harder, shouting in a rasping, flat, furious voice:

"Open! Open! Fools! I am Lord, now!" And on and on, for awhile. In one hand he held the rope to the Scot's bloody, muddy, headless body. He paused, turned and looked at it. Gestured with the sword. "Here is my lady. Show proper respect or you will all suffer!"

The crowd just stared, stunned-looking men and women under the incredible mass of a storm that might well kill almost everyone, watching a madman as if it were a play.

He saw what he saw. He went and knelt beside the exquisite, palely golden beauty, her angry eyes not fazing him because he knew he could win her over. Smiled with confidence, stroking her sweet bare flesh. Bending low, alive with lust, giddy from the relentless exertion of dragging the big, headless body all that distance and then pounding the door for five minutes, weakened by bleeding.

He was inside now, kneeling over the silken sleeping mat, soft candles hinting her lush outline and peach-sweet flesh. He inhaled deeply. There was incense like melting flowers, full sake bowls, screen paintings of lovers and courtesans dallying....

His hands moved lasciviously over her unresisting body, the tender elasticity of her goldenpale breasts, opening her sleek legs and running a hand over her loins, beneath, between, behind...

"What is power without love?" he cried, pulling aside his tattered, bloodstiff kimono.

356

He had no idea the astonished crowd had closed around him or that one of the guards from the castle had joined them, shoving a few aside, scowling, eyes wide as the nude Chamberlain prepared to mount the bloody, headless male corpse.

"He's mad," one fat-nosed commoner said.

"What obscenity!" a skinny woman cried. "Here with hell come to earth!"

"He's a demon!" another woman, fat and old with eyes lost in her fat. "Come from hell bringing destruction!"

The wind was starting to re-gather itself, gusts slapping the dust up, flicking across the oily moat.

"Ai," exclaimed the first man, "it comes again! It comes again!"

The wide-eyed samurai went closer, muttering to himself. He was short and wide and unbelieving.

"What shame," he muttered. "Beyond comprehension."

"Love is all," declared Reiko parting her fair legs, lifting them to insert himself in her. "All I have done was for love. For love."

With a sound, a *kiai* shout close to retching, the samurai parted the Chamberlain from his consummation with a two-handed downcut. Stood there, swaying in a windburst, sword at his side, blinking and still shocked. The blood had sprayed and spattered across the sandy ground in what could have been another message that no one was going to read....

Thirty-Five

Yazu

Found his street in the burnt and shattered neighborhood. The wind was almost playful, kicking up mini-whirlwinds in the dust of the flattened city. A swirl of ashes gently twisted past.

Found where his house had been. Found his son, sitting on a fallen roofbeam with some neighbors. The boy came to him and they held each other.

"Where is your mother?" he asked.

The boy just held him around the chest, saying nothing. A stunned-looking, tough-featured woman spoke up:

"Dead, Yazu-san. So many are. So many...ai...."

"Terrible, terrible," said the man beside her in a soft, shocked voice. "Ah, what terrors. What loss....Are we not cursed by heaven? All sins come home...."

357

"Dead," Yazu murmured. "You must take cover. The storm comes again."

Held the boy away from himself. "Be strong. Brace up."

"Yes, father."

"Good." To the neighbors. "Keep him safe. I must go find my sensei. Matter of honor." They just looked at him. "Stay with them, son." To them: "Where is she? She must be given good rites."

"In back," said the woman.

He looked at the flattened, shattered buildings.

"Back of what?" he wondered.

Thirty-Six
Takezo

Faint, final scatters of rain. The high, curving clouds were starting to pull apart like cotton wool. The wind was sinking into softness. The greenblue sky looked washed pure.

He was walking downstream with her in his arms. He was getting blurred flashes of sight in his right eye too, now, the left still showing narrow bands of clarity criss-crossed by dark, blotchy streaks.

He cradled her sleek, bare body into his torso, walking along the turgid, choked waterflow as it slopped and gathered in clumps of detritus, pushed around and over fallen branches, trickling, pooling spilling on....

He concentrated on working his way along the grass and mud without slipping. He wasn't going to drop her. He was desperate without panic to get her away from what had happened. The last memory he allowed himself was armored Yoshi upside down in the deep mud, legs kicking something like a frog's. He carefully fled as if, somehow, distance and time might actually cure her, as if the shock and thudding impact, spattered blood, her terrible, hollow gasp as the lead ball had smacked into her tender flesh would not have happened, time unwinding behind his desperate feet...a child's feeling and innocent hope....

So he went on, urgently quick-stepping as if nothing mattered but this, just her barely noticed soft weight and the problem of following the twists and drops of the stream through his bent and broken sight, as if the terrible moment only lived in the past and place behind him.

"I blew all those up," he suddenly said, carefully stepping up over a fallen tree, long blue and white flowers overhanging the steep rim of the

358

deepening ravine, flashes in slanting, late afternoon light. "Yet there was still one to shoot her."

If he could just get there soon she'd be alright. Enough had died, already.

Except feelings were suddenly starting to collect like thick, stifled breath in his chest and were pressing behind his eyes.

Takezo, my love, he remembered, with a choking feeling.

"I found you," he said, coming around a bend and half-skidding down a steep drop beside a sluggish waterfall, pooling into mud and soggy leaves. The sunlight speared through the still standing trees above and spattered here and there. "Wish I had not."

Fought so brilliantly, he thought, clear and bitter, *I saved her to die....*

"No, no, not die...not dying...no more dying...."

Tears were burning out now, melting the coagulations of face wounds so that he actually wept blood and water, wading through the shallow, warm pond, coming out into the flat land fronting the seacoast.

He could already hear the surf, dull and immensely deep on the soft onshore breeze, crunching as if the sea were eating the shore. He raised her face and pressed his lips on her cheek, staining her with his blood.

She's warm, he told himself. *She lives...yes...she will heal...it's certain....*

Thirty-Seven

Yazu

Found his wife where the porch had been: her head and shoulders were clear of the fallen building, face unmarked. He squatted there, by the edge of the goldfish pool that was now choked with mud and leaves.

"Wife," he said, "in my heart I always cared for you. Aii. All prayers will be said. Still, I was not a good man. I am sorry." He winced and looked away up over the rubble. The wind was picking up, hissing and whistling among the broken boards. "I must find my master. I must be a man of honor. This will be a gift to our son. Aiiii." He covered his eyes. He wanted to leave before the storm hit again. "We will be an honorable family."

He stood up, staring down, now, at the obliterated pool where a fish was half-buried, dead pale and glinting gold. Nodded. Looked at her face, eyes shut and strangely peaceful.

"I am not afraid to be honest, anymore," he said. Sighed. "All prayers will be said."

Thirty-Eight

Takezo and uMubaya

It had been as if he simply stepped onto the air and went down to the beach far below in a single step. Yellowish, feral eyes burned and a huge lion-like shape, all fangs and claws, reared-up and pounced, a silent shadow, a memory and vision... then blackness....

And, next, there was mellow, late daylight, soft warmth under him and the steady, soothing, massive sound of the sea crushing down nearby. He looked straight up at cloudless, pristine sky. Blinked hard and shifted his body to see what might be broken. Nothing, it seemed.

So the big Zulu sat up and looked at the bouncing, cresting mountain range of waves. The high line of the foamy, rippled, broken surf rolled up and backwashed close to him, edged by seaweed and driftwood.

He had no desire to go back to the city or where the war was or wasn't. Vaguely considered finding his way to the farming village near the sea. Maybe they'd let him work or hunt for them – despite the opinion of the farm woman who'd seen him miss the deer with a half-hearted spear toss.

He smiled, remembering her, the night in the barn....

As my father would say, a hunter needs a quarry, a warrior an enemy and a farmer, patience....

He stood up. He felt good.

Decided to follow the coastline, see if any boats had survived. Around a few bends, as the sun was going to orange back across the great bay, he came on Takezo and Issa lying, a sand dune behind them, in a litter of broken pine branches from the pretty much intact wall of trees behind.

Not over yet, he thought with some pleasure and misgivings. *This man has truly the heart and soul of a lion...nothing deters him....*

Takezo was practicing looking at everything except her. When he finally did she would have to be breathing. There was no question of that.

So, as the sun was setting and he was still forcing himself into a remote unrealism, he managed to keep both eyes open and get a kind of

360

almost coherent double image inasmuch as the approaching, dark figure resembled, more and more as he came closer, a man and not some bulged and bent morphic shadow staining the cleanly glowing western sky; not some horror or insensate, demented killer or relative.

"Father and brother," he muttered, in a raspy, dry chuckle, without amusement. "How nice to have a family, at last."

The big Zulu was now standing over them, his shadow stretching up along the soft undulations of dune and touching the secret, dark green mysterious network of the pines.

"Takezo-san," uMubaya said.

"Everything was lies," the *ronin* responded, looking past him at the reddening sun, no clouds at all to streak or alter the pure light. "More or less."

The big man knelt beside the woman. The deepening glow darkened her wound and the rills and creases of blood on her exquisite body.

"What a pity," he said, softly, setting down his long spear. "This land…so many women fallen like crushed flowers."

"She lives," said the other, looking at the doubled, overlapping sun above the hills under which Edo was lost in a gentle, violet haze, staining it with a blending, unbroken blur that might have been paradise, under the distant, perfectly, divinely drawn, melting outline of Mount Fujiama.

"Lives?"

uMubaya touched her hand, gently. Knew that coolness, that dull feeling. Began to chant a prayer, under his breath. A prayer of cleansing and freedom.

"I have been where she has gone, foreigner," Takezo said. "I will go and bring her back."

"Back, great warrior?" Sighed. "I wish I could bring back even the living to me."

The sun was just nicking the horizon. The cresting tops of the waves were red, a clean, clear soft red, a jewel-like tint. Takezo was seeing wide strips and rills of sweetly transparent fire.

"The doorway is a painting," he explained. "Like a screen. When I find it I will pass through it." Shrugged. "I find everything." He lay back on the sand and saw the first blurred star directly above. Closed one eye and the pale, bluish-white glow was single and clearer. Was each star a

361

heaven-world, as was said? All the blood and madness and pain behind him might dissolve away forever into that single, pure, perfect, quivering point of infinite light. He sighed and smiled and his face hurt, stiffly. "I will find the doorway," he said.

The Zulu touched his bare shoulder.

"Rest, now," he advised. "We will all sleep for a time. She is already sleeping." Shrugged. "In the new day we will do what we must do."

"Rest," said Takezo. "Yes, foreigner. I find everything. I have no wish to, but
I do." Puffed out his cheeks. "Like a drain all filth flows through."

The waves were just crumpling shadows now as the sun dropped away. The sand glowed soft and faint. The stars were showing sharp and clear. uMubaya covered him and her with his own tattered robe.

"I will go with you, lion-souled man," he said. He was thinking about the empty places on maps. "Maybe you will come with me, as well." Thinking about the empty place where his love was.

Takezo pulled the robe up, still looking straight with one eye where it parted across his face. The star gleamed in a purity he could never express.

"And, in the end," he whispered to heaven, "I lost every good thing I found."

New York
11:37 PM
2/26/04

362